RACING AGAINST THE CLIMATE CRISIS

THE CHANGE AGENTS

WHISPERS IN THE WIND

SARAH E. LEWIS

Paperback ISBN: 979-8-9850756-0-1
IS Paperback ISBN: 979-8-9850756-3-2
Hardcover ISBN: 979-8-9850756-1-8
Ebook ISBN: 979-8-9850756-2-5

Printed in USA Cover Design: Amelia K. Lewis
Editing: Tara Bailey (Bailey Publishing House)
Book Design: Amit Dey
Published by: Spotlight Publishing – https://spotlightpublishing.pro

Website: www.climatechangeagents.com

RACING AGAINST THE CLIMATE CRISIS

THE CHANGE AGENTS

WHISPERS IN THE WIND

SARAH E. LEWIS

Goodyear, AZ

TABLE OF CONTENTS

Dedication. ix

Endorsements xi

Acknowledgments xiii

Chapter 1: Contact 1

Chapter 2: The Meeting 11

Chapter 3: The Explanation 21

Chapter 4: On the Spot 29

Chapter 5: The Mission 35

Chapter 6: The Team 45

Chapter 7: Planning, and then Some. 53

Chapter 8: The Rescuer 69

Chapter 9: Philosophical Differences. 75

Chapter 10: White Lies. 87

Chapter 11: Encouragement 91

Chapter 12: First Dig, Take One 95

Chapter 13: First Dig, Take Two 99

Chapter 14: Media Beginnings. 105

Chapter 15: Postings and Plantlings 111

Chapter 16: Perspectives and Reactions 117

Chapter 17: Surprises 123

Chapter 18: Silver Linings 127

Chapter 19: Lights, Camera, Action 131

Chapter 20: Human Intervention 139

Chapter 21: Road Trip 147

Chapter 22: Cityscapes 155

Chapter 23: Assessments 161

Chapter 24: Storm Damage 165

Chapter 25: Tough Lessons 171

Chapter 26: Miracles 179

Chapter 27: Juggling 189

Chapter 28: A Visitor 193

Chapter 29: Apologies 199

Chapter 30: Next Steps 203

Chapter 31: Reminders 209

Chapter 32: Time Off 215

Chapter 33: In the Swim 223

Chapter 34: Logistics 229

Chapter 35: Sweets 233

Chapter 36: Flying 239

Chapter 37: Seabound 245

Chapter 38: Underwater Wonders 251

Chapter 39: The Farm 259

Chapter 40: Restoring and Storming 265

Chapter 41: Hoping 271

Chapter 42: Return Trip 275

Chapter 43: Back at the Office 279

Chapter 44: Pitching 283

Chapter 45: Red Alert 287

Chapter 46: Innovations 293

Chapter 47: Supply and Command 297

Chapter 48: Preparation 303

Chapter 49: Reconnaissance 309

Chapter 50: Skill Sets 315

Chapter 51: Introductions 317

Chapter 52: Respite 321

Chapter 53: Attention 325

Chapter 54: Firefight 327

Chapter 55: Observations 333

Chapter 56: Farewells 337

Chapter 57: Celebrations 343

Chapter 58: New Beginnings 349

About the Author 353

DEDICATION

This book is dedicated to Bebop, my faithful four-legged friend and companion, who left this world too soon and suddenly. Thank you for teaching me to make the most of each day, motivating and guiding me to write this book, and keeping me going as I penned it.

ENDORSEMENTS

Sarah Lewis has written more than a call to action to address the challenges of climate change. She has written a guide filled with moving exhortations. And while adults will enjoy reading *The Change Agents: Whispers in the Wind*, so too will young readers or both together, as we are all in this together, for that's part of the message: we all must act together as we are all in this together. This book has a dream-like quality as it unites all living creatures similarly at risk by climate change working in harmony for the good and preservation of nature upon which we all depend. Lose yourself in Sarah's world but take to heart her important message. Read, and act, now!

> **—Carl Howard,** Environmental Lawyer (US EPA), and author of the Climate Change Blog (NY State Bar Association's Environmental and Energy Law Section).

There may not be a more important topic than how we turn back the tide of climate change and the effects it has on us and all the creatures on our planet. *In The Change Agents: Whispers in The Wind*, Sarah E. Lewis brings us on a fun journey with a cast of unlikely characters who are doing just that. Most books on the topic focus on explaining climate change and what it means to us. Sarah's work goes far beyond this, engaging and inspiring us to become Change Agents ourselves.

If you love animals or the environment, enjoy reading great fiction, and want to help fight climate change, this book is for you.

—Dr. Don McGrath, Author of Best-sellers *50 Athletes Over 50, Vertical Mind,* and *The Climb.*

ACKNOWLEDGMENTS

There are many people to thank for supporting me in the writing and production of this book. First and foremost, I thank the creator for providing me with the skills, ideas, experiences, guidance, patience, and perseverance to present this story.

Thank you to my parents for instilling in me a love of and respect for nature and the environment from which this story emanates. I know you've been cheering me on through this writing and publishing journey and hope you would be proud to see this novel come to fruition.

Thank you to Jazzy for brightening my days after Bebop passed and sticking with me as I began writing, then motivating me to keep going even after you were called to join him.

Thank you to Earl Belcher, Jr. for believing in and encouraging me to undertake and complete this project of the heart.

Thank you to my coach, Don McGrath, for advising on the book and overall process to get it out there, as well as helping me navigate through it.

Thank you to my editor, Tara Bailey, for your endless patience in correcting similar errors over and over, and spot-on suggestions of how to strengthen the story and writing.

Thank you to my publisher, Becky Norwood of Spotlight Publishing, for your expertise and guidance on every step of the publishing process.

Thank you to my niece, Amelia Lewis, for your ingenuity and artistic talents to not only think of but create the front cover, and for your critiques and suggestions on the story and writing as it evolved.

Thank you to my family and friends who read drafts of the story and provided constructive comments and support.

CHAPTER 1

CONTACT

"Mayday, Mayday! I don't think I can hold this course. Too much in my way. I've lost control...," shouted Monty as he came in for a landing. His eyes widened and his body shook as he attempted to control his flight path during the descent.

"Stay the course!" came the reply. "You're almost there. Hold on!"

"Trying... Not... sure... Off... course..." Monty screamed in fright and desperation as he crashed.

"Monty. Monty, are you there? Monty, say something."

Monty lay limp with his eyewear twisted sideways on his head and the audio headset dangling from his neck. He came to slowly, sitting up and shaking his head to clear the stupor caused by the crash, then faintly heard mission control calling his name. He looked about, dazed, and noticed the dislodged headset. At least it still functioned.

"Monty, can you hear us?" queried mission control on the verge of panic.

Monty picked up the headset and spoke into it, "Yes, yes, I can hear you. Just had a bit of a bumpy landing." Monty surveyed his surroundings. Stuck in a nest of thick hair, he could see far and wide when he looked out since the vantage point sat atop a moving head exactly where Monty meant to land, but not in nearly as haphazard a manner.

Meanwhile, the human to whom the hair belonged, Eliza, continued on her walk through the woods, not bothering to stop after hearing a buzz in her unkempt locks. It wasn't unusual that an insect would get stuck in her thick hair, particularly as she walked tree-lined trails early in the morning. She often swatted them away before they became entangled but didn't bother on this sunny morning as she thought about the work she needed to do on her story for this evening's news. She heard and felt the commotion in her hair and halfheartedly attempted to wave the bug away, but otherwise paid little attention since they usually buzzed and made it out of the mess of her auburn mane by themselves. Despite the risk of insect intrusions, Eliza made sure she went for a walk every morning. She loved being outdoors. It relaxed her and set the tone for her busy days as a legal reporter.

Taking advantage of Eliza's nonchalance about his presence, Monty gathered himself after his turbulent landing in her bangs. He reached for his displaced goggles, and, to his relief, they were miraculously intact. He put them back on over his large, multifaceted fly eyes. Mission control broke in on the headset and instructed Monty to set up shop over Eliza's left ear. They knew she used her right ear to listen on the phone and didn't want any interference during their communications with her.

Eliza made it to the end of the trail and headed home for breakfast. When back in her kitchen, she poured granola and almond milk into a bowl, then stepped out onto the back porch to give herself more time to cool off. Not yet able to drag herself back indoors after eating, she instead walked around the yard and cleaned up the few leaves that had fallen around the shrubs during the early autumn morning. As she bent down, her face hit cobwebs, and she felt the strands from ear to ear over her mouth and nose. She jerked away and pawed the web from her face, spluttering to spit it out of her mouth. "Yuck, I hate that! I'll never remember to avoid those stupid webs before I dip my face into them." She chastised herself as she went back inside to change for work.

Eliza pulled one of her favorite dresses from the closet—navy, covered with flowers, professional but with a flair, and although cotton never needed ironing. She shed her walking wear and donned the dress, put on a minimal amount of makeup, and crimped her waves. In no danger of being disturbed because she hadn't used a comb or brush in years, Monty hunkered down in her hair to be on the safe side. Eliza donned her sneakers, threw her bag over her shoulder, rushed out the door, and ran to the bus stop, where she barely caught the bus before it pulled away from the curb.

"Cutting it close again," noted the bus driver while she hopped on board.

"Good morning, Leon," replied Eliza as she caught her breath, swiped her bus pass, and took a seat behind him. "Thanks, as always, for taking that extra look to see if I was running to catch you."

"One of these days you're going to have another driver who won't be as thoughtful and patient," he chided jokingly.

"You're right about that. It's actually happened a couple of times already and I've had to wait for the next bus. You'd think by now I'd have figured out how to leave a few minutes earlier to avoid having to run to catch you."

"You'll get it if you miss the bus more often."

"True, but please don't try to teach me a lesson and leave, as I'm just about at the door. I've seen drivers do that and feel bad for those they've left in their dust."

"That's the ultimate power trip for a bus driver. We sometimes practiced that in driving school." Leon grinned reminiscently.

"You're terrible! But seriously, I really don't like the stress of running to the stop each day and will work on being more timely instead of trying to do too much at home before heading into a long day at work."

"Believe it when I see it. Just keep wearing those running shoes."

Leon stopped to let more riders on. Eliza stood, allowing an elderly woman to have her seat near the door. "Thanks again, Leon, for lagging so I could join you this morning. I always know it's going to be a good day if I make this bus." She smiled and walked down the aisle where she found a seat, settled in, and pulled a nature magazine out of her bag. Thankful to be sitting rather than trying to read while standing and balancing as the bus started and stopped.

Eliza tore herself away from an article about the impact of climate change on biodiversity and stowed the magazine as the bus approached her stop. She disembarked, thanked Leon again, and walked briskly to the news station, always feeling pressed for time trying to keep up with her busy workload.

When she walked into her office she said softly, "Good morning, Bebop," to a picture of a wise-looking dog on the bookshelf near her desk. She'd already rung the rainbow bridge chimes hanging above his ashes at home as she did each morning and night. He passed away just over a year ago, and Eliza missed him terribly, her eyes brimming with tears as she thought about him.

Bebop was not only Eliza's best friend but also her faithful companion, the one who depended on her to take care of him, her biggest fan, and the dog who stole her heart. He was a regal Weimaraner with a point (or wisdom knot, as some said) on the top of his head, clumsy gait, and person-like facial expressions. The largest Weim Eliza had ever seen, some described him as ginormous. He made Eliza feel loved every day and his antics often left her laughing. She was absolutely devastated when he suddenly died at the young age of only three.

Try as she might to stop it, her mind kept bringing her back to that horrid day. Bebop woke her up around 3 a.m. as he lay at the foot of her bed, whimpering in pain. She checked him all over for what may be hurting him, then googled his behavior to figure out what it could be, and finally called the emergency vet clinic. On their advice, she rushed him to the clinic, and they immediately brought him back to the exam room. The vet massaged his chest and abdomen and instructed the vet tech to take him for X-rays. Not wanting to go with the tech, Bebop rushed over to Eliza and buried his head in her chest. She hugged him and assured him all would be OK, and the tech pulled him away.

After they left, the vet explained to Eliza that Bebop had bloat, and they needed to check whether his stomach turned as a result. Eliza dropped her head into her hands at this diagnosis, feeling as though someone blindsided her with a baseball bat. She knew bloat occurred when the stomach filled with air and was often fatal, especially if the stomach turned. The vet said they'd do everything they could, then escorted Eliza to the waiting room. Eliza slumped in a chair, crying, and praying Bebop would pull through.

The vet eventually came back out and knelt in front of Eliza, who looked at her intently, wishing for good news. "Bebop didn't make it. I'm so sorry." Eliza broke down and sobbed uncontrollably. They ushered her to the bereavement room and Eliza waited in a daze until they brought Bebop's body in so she could say goodbye. She cried and cried until her eyes were swollen and she filled the trash can with wet tissues. She couldn't bear seeing him there but didn't want to take her eyes off him because she would never see him again. Her hands caressed his soft head and ears in the hopes he would miraculously spring back to life. The tears ultimately waned, and Eliza gently gave Bebop's limp paw a last high five, a tradition whenever she left him.

Depressed for months, she didn't want to accept Bebop being gone. She often imagined seeing him in the places they spent time together, especially their favorite walking spots, and when alone, she talked to him aloud as she did when he was alive. Trying to mentally connect with his spirit, she stared at his picture on the shelf a little longer. Ultimately, she turned away, powered up the computer, and researched her story for the news later that day.

When she became a legal reporter after completing law school, she planned to cover environmental issues and 'save the world.' She never imagined she'd end up spending most of her time sitting behind a desk researching stories with legal elements, but usually, nothing to do with the environment. She made it on air once in a while if a reporter went on vacation. The salary allowed her to live comfortably, so she stuck with it. It paid the bills that kept accumulating. Writing a blog about environmental issues helped her feel she made some sort of positive difference. She squashed the feelings of being on the wrong path whenever they arose and instead tried to be thankful for what she had.

Her computer notification rang for the first item on today's calendar, a conference call with the local zoning and planning department to discuss a story concerning controversial proposed zoning changes. She dialed the number and asked questions while taking notes. As the participants discussed the proposal, she heard interference. It sounded like another conversation on the line at the same time. Eliza thought she heard "make contact", "stubborn", "patience" and "what if" from the other call but did her best to ignore the noise while finishing her discussion.

After hanging up the phone, Eliza checked the clock and made a mental note that she had three hours to meet the deadline for her editor's review. As with her continual lateness to catch the bus, she told herself she needed to manage her time better to avoid always scrambling to meet deadlines. While drafting, she again heard voices as she had on the conference call. She stopped typing, listened, and heard a little voice in her left ear say, "How am I supposed to do that? She never takes a break."

An authoritative male voice replied, "Like I said, just be patient and we'll let you know when to make contact."

The first voice then responded, "Aye, Captain, I'll keep waiting, but she's very focused and I don't know how I'm going to get her attention."

Shocked and scared to hear the voices, Eliza thought she must be imagining things and feared she could be going crazy from the stress of her demanding workload.

The authoritative voice, agreeing with the comment from the first voice, said, "Yes, she gets wrapped up in things, but we'll get through to her. Rumple and Tumple, are you in position and ready?"

Eliza shook her head in disbelief and fright. As she stared in shock into the air, a high-pitched, upbeat voice answered, "Tumple at the ready, sir!"

"Rumple's all set too, sir," added a low husky voice. "Looks like Monty's ready too, Captain."

Distressed to be hearing things, Eliza inquired under her breath in a shaky tone, while looking around the room surreptitiously, "Is someone there?"

Silence, then the authoritative voice commanded, "Go!" Almost immediately, two spiders appeared before Eliza's eyes, hanging from web strands rooted in her bangs. Tumple with the upbeat tone said, "Howdy do" and Rumple with the husky voice asked, "What's up?"

Eliza jumped up as soon as she saw the arachnids and frantically swatted them away from her face. Rumple and Tumple swung wildly from their web strands, hanging on for dear life as they tried to avoid Eliza's flying hands. "Whoa, easy there!" yelled Rumple with annoyance, while Tumple giggled and enjoyed the wild ride.

Rumple and Tumple rappelled out of Eliza's line of sight, and she ceased swinging at them, then sat down to calm herself. As she took a deep, soothing breath, Monty landed on her nose. Eliza jumped out of her seat in a frenzy, waving her hands instinctively at the fly, knocking Monty off her nose and again swinging Rumple and Tumple haphazardly back and forth. Her desk chair flew across the floor mat. Monty realized he was too close to Eliza's vision, flew off and landed atop a stack of files on her desk. Rumple and Tumple sprung away from Eliza's face and landed near Monty.

Eliza stared in shock as she stood behind the desk. "What the...?", she asked incredulously in a low, slow, and measured tone. She then hurried to her office door and shut it before anyone else witnessed what seemed to be a meltdown.

Monty said, "Very sorry, ma'am, didn't mean to frighten you. Hold please while I get the Captain on." Monty then took a tiny backpack off from between his wings and pulled out what looked like a minuscule speaker. Rumple and Tumple adjusted the device and Monty leaned toward the speaker, "Captain, can you hear me?"

"Yes, Monty, I can hear you clearly. Did you get her attention?"

"Yes, sir," affirmed Monty.

Eliza interrupted in a perturbed voice, "Did they get my attention? I nearly had a heart attack when these three showed up!" She then muttered to herself, "Seems I'm finally having that nervous breakdown I've feared would happen from the stress of this place. Can't believe I'm even acknowledging and talking to these apparitions." Looking at her visitors, she queried, "Who are you, and why are you here?"

Monty, Rumple, and Tumple peered at each other nervously but said nothing, then Monty inquired into the speaker, "Captain?"

The Captain explained, "We didn't want to scare you and we've been trying to come up with a plan to contact you causing no alarm, but we ultimately concluded there was no reasonable way to do that other than just showing up as we did. You're a tough one to get the attention of, Eliza."

Taken aback, Eliza asked. "How do you know my name? You wanted me specifically?"

"We've been watching you for a while and yes, you specifically. We don't need to get into all those details now. Our goal today was to make contact and set up a meeting where we could discuss why we're here. I will say this, we need your help. Please don't write this encounter off as a daydream. We'll fill you in at our next meeting. Are you in?"

"In for what?"

The Captain replied, "Meeting with us and letting us explain why we need your help."

Even though she couldn't afford time away from her busy schedule, her intrigue about these odd and unexpected visitors and why they needed her help prevailed, and she answered hesitantly, "OK?"

"Great!" exclaimed the Captain. "Meet us at noon Saturday at the cemetery, in front of the mausoleum on the right in the first gully."

Surprised at these instructions since she walked in the cemetery regularly, Eliza asked, "How do you know about the cemetery and that location?"

"We know [pause] because we know. We'll see you Saturday, rain or shine."

Rumple and Tumple turned the tiny speaker off, loaded it into the tiny backpack, and Monty hoisted it onto his back. "See you Saturday," declared Monty as he flew off.

"Toodle-oo 'til Saturday," said Tumple in a perky voice.

"Later," added Rumple, as he and Tumple jumped off the side of Eliza's desk and swung away on spider web strands.

Eliza fell into her chair with her mouth open and an astounded look on her face. "Did that just happen? What's going on with me? I must be losing my mind once and for all. Guess it was only a matter of time, what with all the demands on me, right Bebop?" She gazed at Bebop's picture, which she often talked to while asking for his advice as he stared back from the photo. 'What would Bebop do?' was a common refrain in her head.

Ultimately returning to drafting the story on her computer, her mind kept wandering to her visitors and the Captain's invitation.

CHAPTER 2

THE MEETING

Eliza found it difficult to concentrate on work the rest of the week as her mind drifted to the big meeting. She couldn't wait for the weekend, partly due to concern about losing her mind, but mainly from curiosity to find out more. *Why did they need her help? Who was the Captain? Was it safe for her to meet with them?* At times it seemed the week would never end, but Saturday finally arrived.

Eliza hadn't slept well since the surprise visit and instead either tossed and turned or sat up and read each night. Despite that, and her body being tired as a result, her mind woke her up early on the designated day—another abnormally warm, humid day for the time of year, but thankfully not as hot as others in the region recently endured. The northeastern United States rarely had many consecutive days with temperatures in the 90s, but the last few years each brought an increasing number of such days.

Eliza dressed in stylish yet practical khaki shorts, a bright blue short-sleeved shirt and a rather dirty pair of walking sneakers. Before leaving for the meeting, she cleaned up the backyard. When she bent down to pick up leaves, her face ran into cobwebs again. Brushing the webs away, she wondered if that's how Rumple and Tumple ended up in her bangs.

Eliza left for the cemetery early to give herself time for a relaxing walk before going to the designated meeting spot. She discovered the cemetery with Bebop after other dog people told her that dogs could be walked off-leash there. Some wouldn't dare venture through the gates for fear of walking among gravestones. That didn't faze Eliza, but she made sure to always leave the grounds before sunset. She spent many hours in all kinds of weather, walking there with Bebop. It was a place he could run, sniff, chase chipmunks and deer to his heart's content, and burn off some of his seemingly incessant Weimaraner energy. Even after his passing, she continued walking there on weekends, since it was a quiet place to think and decompress. Also, although bittersweet, it brought back fond memories of times in her favorite place, the outdoors, with Bebop.

A rural cemetery built in the mid-1800s, there were many walking paths and pavilions where folks traveling out from the city used to picnic and connect with nature on the weekends. Eliza preferred going to the older sections, in which the monuments were large and ornate. Those sections weren't kept up over the years in the way the descendants likely thought they'd be. It always struck her to see monuments, memorials, and family plots of well-to-do people—people who had towns, streets, and buildings named after them—overgrown with long grass, and the regal stairs and metal fences surrounding them having crumbled and fallen during the many decades since the deceased took up residency. Remnants of grand steel and stone bridges littered gullies where paths used to lead visitors across streams that divided portions of the cemetery. Seeing structures built of sturdy materials and old-world craftsmanship in ruins left Eliza wondering how the lower quality structures of recent vintage would survive a century or more from now.

Eliza reflected on the warm temperature and wondered what the upcoming winter would bring. The winter that just passed had its share of cold days, but every time precipitation fell it warmed enough that it rained instead of snowed. Snowmaking saved many ski mountains, but even that required below freezing temperatures. Eliza hoped the coming winter wouldn't be another one like last, and she could ski more often. Between low snow totals and her inability to take time off from work at the last minute if it did snow, she fretted she may lose her edge on the slopes. Winters in general didn't drop as much snow as Eliza remembered from her youth, and ski areas took a hit as a result. She feared when the temperature last Christmas hit a record warm that the winter would be abnormally mild. Unfortunately, that ended up being the case.

The odd weather trends continued into this year, with evidence throughout the cemetery. Uprooted trees and huge branches with jagged ends lay toppled after being flung through the air by severe wind and rainstorms. Others hung precariously on sturdy burial monuments, many of which were now broken from the collisions, the granite angels and obelisks that previously marked the burial places now overshadowed by signs of nature's destructive power. Grass and weeds shot up toward the sky between and around the perimeter of the prone wood, no longer kept in check by the mowers. A significant number of trees appeared to be well over a hundred years old and must have survived numerous storms unscathed, but now were being blown down or ripped apart. Symptoms of a warming climate.

Toward the end of her walk, Eliza looped to the stream she used to visit with Bebop. She often went there during her cemetery excursions. The stream formed a small swimming hole where it flowed out from under a bridge. On hot days especially, Bebop used to wade in until the water covered him and would swim around to cool off. Not a water dog, this was the one place he'd get entirely wet. She pictured him swimming in that hole every time she visited and could particularly feel his spirit when the sun hit a lower angle in the sky and brightened the water in soft bronze light through the trees.

Conveniently located near the designated meeting place, Eliza followed a path away from the swimming hole and along the stream. She entered a gully that felt like a primeval rainforest, with immense trees and uneven rock ledges overhanging the path and trickling stream. Ferns, ivy, and hostas covered the gully floor, more remnants of the care this place received in its heyday. Filtered sunlight provided the only light this beautiful and peaceful area ever saw, making it smell of dampness. The songs of birds filled the air, many of whom flitted about overhead while others hopped on tree branches. Every once in a while, the high-pitched squeak of a chipmunk interrupted the songs, and Eliza saw the furry striped creatures darting along toppled trunks throughout the gully or stones along the stream.

Eliza passed two mangled bridges, whose wrought ironwork and sturdy stone had succumbed to the ravages of nature and time. She crossed the stream at the top of a waterfall flowing off a huge flat rock. A crack ran across it and the deluges of water from recent storm surges gradually forced each side apart from each other. More fallout from global warming.

She headed back downstream on another path that dead-ended shortly after it started. Eliza continued through muck and over-growth until she arrived at the door of the mausoleum where the Captain instructed her to meet. Having visited this site a few times before, she wondered who rested inside since there were no mark-ings on the exterior, and it sat apart from other burials. Built into a hill on the side of the gully, the mausoleum reminded her of a hobbit home in the Shire of Middle Earth. Even though the door wasn't round, she half expected Bilbo Baggins to open it and come out to pick up his mail.

Early for the meeting, she waited in front of the door, watching a flurry of iridescent dragonflies flitting in and out of the sunlight. They appeared black at first but changed to green in one view and shim-mered to blue in another. Flying about randomly, they helped take Eliza's mind off the upcoming meeting. Nervous, she felt somewhat ludicrous to be here and tried to dismiss her doubts. She told her-self she might as well explore the surreal invitation—nothing ventured, nothing gained.

Monty abruptly interrupted Eliza's daydreaming by yelling "Hello!" in her right ear. She whipped her head around and saw him hovering at the side of her face with the tiny speaker strapped around him. He greeted Eliza with a smile as he bounced up and down in the air. "Glad you made it."

Eliza confided, "I have to say I considered not showing up but convinced myself I'm not crazy and didn't dream about meeting you in my office. Also, I had nothing to lose since I probably would have ended up walking here at some point today, anyway."

Monty stared at Eliza for a moment, as though sizing her up. Eliza felt self-conscious. Monty finally offered, "Yeah, Captain was right. You're almost too logical a person but have a good and inquisitive heart and would likely be here."

"Who is this Captain, and how does he know anything about me?"

"You'll find out soon enough."

Eliza then barely heard a small voice say, "Hey, are you ready?"

And another somewhat familiar voice added impatiently, "We don't want to wait here all day." She followed the sounds and saw Rumple and Tumple hanging in front of the mausoleum door.

Monty replied, "Yes, we're ready."

Eliza took a deep breath, thought twice about whether she should turn and run, and ultimately announced, "Ready as I'll ever be."

Rumple and Tumple swung the sixteen legs they had between them in circles. At this signal, the dragonflies simultaneously flew toward the large metal door and through a small square window partially obscured by cobwebs. Scuffling sounded from behind the door, and it slowly opened inward, creaking loudly and revealing a murky passageway ahead. Monty flew in front of Eliza as she crossed the door's threshold, pulling thick cobwebs off her face and body and trying to quell the fear rising in her. Once through the door, she noticed tiny flickering lights all around and realized thousands of fireflies were in the passage, lighting the way, making it somewhat less frightening. Clanking and grinding metal rang as the door slowly shut behind her. Eliza's eyes darted around looking for a way to escape if needed. She noticed at least twenty chipmunks running on wheels near the ground, which moved metal cables that closed the door. Quite an ingenious system, especially with the animal operators.

With the door fully shut, the chipmunks scurried in front of Eliza. She couldn't see them well with the firefly light, but Monty said, "Follow the chipmunks and fireflies down the path." Not knowing what to make of all this organized activity, she pinched herself to see if she may be asleep and dreaming. She moved ahead in small steps, being careful not to lift her feet too high for fear of stepping on one of her rodent guides.

Eliza no longer heard any sounds from the gully. Instead, an echoey quiet filled the air, punctuated by an occasional drip of water. The place smelled of mildew and wet dirt. Eliza didn't breathe too deeply. Although difficult to see in the low light, she focused her eyes on the chipmunks, thinking she'd surely lost her mind. She followed them through the crypt, past the walls with the deceased human occupants. Eliza wanted to scream from being closed in a dank burial with creatures guiding her to who knew where, but she choked it back. She reached what she thought would be the back of the mausoleum, but surprisingly, the path kept going. The walls glowed and Eliza's trepidation turned to fascination as she realized the light came from fungi of all sizes growing around the sides of the dirt tunnel.

Eliza followed the chipmunks well into the hill that held the mausoleum. The air smelled damper and mustier the further they walked, making Eliza thankful she could barely see what surrounded her. She suspected she wouldn't voluntarily venture into the tunnel if she could actually see it and wondered if and how she'd ever get out of there. Having second thoughts about agreeing to the meeting in the first place, she berated herself for jumping into this without fully thinking it through.

After what seemed an interminable amount of time, the tunnel brightened, the dimness dissipated, and the fireflies blended into the light. Grass suddenly appeared underfoot as the chipmunks reached the end of the trail. Eliza stepped out from the tunnel and her guides scattered away, having successfully completed their assignment. Eliza squinted as the sun hit her eyes. Once adjusted to the light, she peered in awe at a large field surrounded by old-growth trees and filled with green grass and wildflowers. The cheerful song of birds replaced the muffled silence of the tunnel, and the blue/green dragonflies continued their dances in the air. Eliza breathed deep to flush the dank tunnel smell out of her nostrils and replace it with the fresh scent of flowers and grass. A slight breeze blew her hair back from her face. Although much relieved to be on dry ground in sunlight again, Eliza remained on guard since she had absolutely no idea where she was, how to get out of there, or what was in store.

Monty hovered in front of her. "Welcome, Eliza. Please follow me." He flew away with Eliza in tow.

"Thanks, Monty, but where the heck are we?"

"You're in our part of the world now. The Captain will fill you in."

A myriad of questions swirled through Eliza's head. Before she could launch another inquiry, Monty stopped at a grassy circle surrounded by flowering bushes. They included every color of the rainbow and smelled like the best bouquet ever. Eliza closed her eyes, stopped her mind from racing, and breathed in deliberately, feeling immediately calm. She tried not to show her nervousness, but her mind kept questioning whether this could really be happening, and almost convinced her she must be asleep and dreaming about it.

As she stood with her eyes closed, taking deep breaths, she heard the Captain say, "Welcome, Eliza. I'm glad you came."

Eliza's eyes shot open, and she looked around but didn't see who spoke the words.

Monty asked, "Anything else for now, Captain?"

"No, thank you, Monty—good job."

Eliza turned to where the voice came from and saw only bushes. "Who are you, where are you, and what do you want to talk with me about?" she queried suspiciously.

Something moved behind the bushes. Based on who led her to this place, she assumed some sort of insect or small mammal would appear, but the noise seemed louder than what a small creature would produce. Eliza stared in the sound's direction, saw a faint shadow of something moving beyond the leaves a couple of feet up, and focused her attention there. Fear welled up and her heart raced, activating her fight or flight receptors. She again looked for an escape route if she needed to run from whatever creature lurked not far from her. What if it wanted to kill her? She scolded herself for not realizing her life could be in danger at this meeting.

The shadow and leaf rustling moved toward the end of the bushes. Eliza crouched slightly, poised to defend herself or run. The shape kept moving. Eliza's heart pumped faster, and she raised her hands, ready to fend off whatever approached, her mind fast-forwarding through the self-defense tactics she knew.

A figure came out from behind the foliage. Eliza's mouth dropped and her fighting pose relaxed. Flabbergasted, she couldn't believe her eyes.

"Bebop?" she exclaimed, bewildered.

The creature, now fully visible, stopped, looked Eliza intently in the eyes, and replied, "Yes, it's me."

Eliza almost fainted in shock, then stood speechless staring at him, thinking she'd definitely gone crazy, or her dreams had become quite realistic. She ran and hugged him. When she touched his fur, she knew it was really him. By some miracle, Bebop was alive! His cropped tail wagged a mile a minute as he jumped around playfully with her.

Eliza stopped and asked, "Wait, does this mean I died and am now at the Rainbow Bridge with you? The poem says we'll be reunited at the Rainbow Bridge when I pass away."

Bebop said reassuringly, "No, you're very much alive. We brought you here because we need your help with something extremely important."

Stunned, a million questions flew in Eliza's head, but she decided not to pursue any additional information at that point. Instead, she told Bebop, "I don't know how this is happening, but I'm thrilled to see you again, Bebop."

They ran and played, and Eliza hugged Bebop the way she missed doing since he passed away. As the initial shock wore off, though, she wondered why he left her and let her think he died if he was alive. She squashed the negative feeling and told herself to enjoy the moment and ask questions later.

CHAPTER 3

THE EXPLANATION

Eliza dropped the end of a stick after their friendly tug of war and told Bebop, "You win, you're too strong for me, as always." They fell into the soft, lush grass, tired from running and playing. Eliza instinctively reached for treats in her pocket but came up empty, remembering the day she tearfully removed all treats from her pockets after Bebop passed.

Eliza ruminated, "I keep thinking I'm in a dream. Is this real? Where am I? How can it be that you're here and talking with me, Bebop? How do flies and spiders summon me from my office? What's going on? I have tons of questions."

"I figured you would. It's a lot to take in all at once, but I can tell you it isn't a dream. You're in NoHoSap, which stands for No Homo Sapiens. This is a safe place for living creatures–animals, birds, insects, plants, and almost everything else–but human contact here is severely restricted. We can have human visitors with clearance under limited circumstances. We've seen what's happened in your world when humans are involved, and we want to protect this place from that." Eliza sadly acknowledged the truth of his statement.

Bebop continued, "NoHoSap is accessible from and a part of the earthen world, but it's hidden from human exploration. All living things other than humans can come and go from here. We use this as a haven to escape to and also as a place from which we monitor the humanly accessible part of the world, known as HuHabDom, short for Human Habited Domain. This part of NoHoSap also houses Mission Command."

"Command for what mission?"

"All in good time, Eliza. We'll explain that all in good time. To answer another of your questions, you can hear us because you're observant and are truly listening. Our voices sound like whispers in the wind. Many hear the wind. Those who really listen can hear our whispers, not knowing what they are. Only those who pay very close attention, and believe they hear more than wind, can learn to understand our whispers. We developed a sophisticated communication system that amplifies and translates our voices, allowing species other than our own to hear and understand us. You saw it in action when Monty, Rumple, and Tumple visited you in your office. This enables us to not only communicate with humans but almost more importantly, lets us communicate with each other, across species and locations."

"Wow." Eliza didn't know what else to say.

"Our scouts regularly visit HuHabDom and gather electronics and other equipment discarded by humans. We have a warehouse with all sorts of technology that we use as is or modify for speakers, amplifiers, cameras, monitors, computers, smart-phones, medical equipment, and more. You name it, we have it."

Once the shock wore off, Eliza said. "None of that explains why I'm here, though."

"True. It's time you knew that." Bebop paused before continuing. "You have been on a path since you were young to work with nature and help the environment and those who lived in it. Mission Command watched and guided you to follow those instincts. All was going well until you were presented with choices in your career and followed those that were more lucrative. Mission Command sent signals to pull you back, but your perseverance to stick with the path you chose was strong."

Eliza wanted to object but stopped herself before saying anything.

Bebop went on, "Mission Command sensed you were becoming disenchanted with your choices and sent signs to get your attention."

Eliza interrupted him, "You mean I was being set up on those odd encounters I'd have? Like the turtles on the road during my bike rides that I'd put in my saddlebag and bring to water?"

Bebop bobbed his head up and down.

"The squirrel falling out of the tree in the backyard that needed my help?"

Another yes.

"The cat with kittens in the toolshed?"

Yes.

"The stink bugs in my office that I brought downstairs to put outside?"

Bebop smiled slyly, indicating yes again and leaving Eliza astounded.

"Mission Command was checking to see if you had any of the compassion for nature you had when you were a kid. We've lost many along the way who we thought would be human ambassadors for our cause, but you passed each 'test' thrown at you. That's why Mission Command thought it was time for me to join you and bring you back to your destiny."

A look of faint suspicion came over Eliza's face. Bebop continued. "For the final test, they sent me to become your canine companion. My purpose was to remind you of your love for animals and nature and get you back outside and noticing things like you used to."

Incredulous, Eliza asked, "You mean it wasn't just coincidence that I found you as a stray?"

"No, Mission Command decided you needed an extra push, additional testing, to see if you were truly ready and willing to help us. They selected me when I was a pup to guide you back to your true path. After eight months of training in NoHoSap, Mission Command sent me to HuHabDom to become part of your life."

Eliza's jaw dropped in disbelief.

"You reacted positively right away, rescuing me from my 'life on the streets' and bringing me into your home. You took responsibility for me, gave me the best care, and took me for walks to be sure I burned off my energy."

Eliza remembered welcoming Bebop into her home, getting into a routine, and spending time outdoors with him.

"It seemed that when I came into your life something long-dormant within you awakened. When we were outside, I could see you opening up and letting the beauty of nature in. Your innate curiosity for the natural world was stirring. You sought out new places to explore with me, and I sensed our time together outside was helping you as much or more than it was me."

Eliza smiled reminiscently.

"But when I was your companion, your mind battled to reconcile what you were doing for long hours at the news station with what your spirit wanted to be doing. You kept stifling thoughts of following your heart in favor of keeping a job at which you excelled and that rewarded you monetarily, justifying it by telling yourself it enabled you to live comfortably and do what you wanted during your limited free time. When we went for walks, I could tell you still loved the outdoors and wanted to help those in the natural world."

Eliza looked down as if in shame. She had those discussions in her head repeatedly, giving herself pep talks that being a successful legal reporter should make her happy. She told Bebop, "I have to admit, I've been closer than ever to doing something different since you passed away. I see your picture in my office and hear you asking, 'Is this it—every day the same thing—pushing paper and reporting on incidental stories? Follow what you truly want to do, before more time passes and especially before it's too late.' I always thought I'd have more time with you, and when you left, I was lost, with a big hole in my heart. It reminded me that we can't count on there being a tomorrow. But I continue spending most of my time researching and reporting on stories that aren't the reason I got into this field. Sure, there have been successes and stories I've enjoyed, but if I had the courage, I'd make changes and do something more aligned with what I've always wanted–to directly help the environment."

Bebop looked away and replied nervously, "And that's why I had to leave you."

Eliza bolted to wide-eyed attention and inquired with anger, "What? You left on purpose? You chose to leave me with no warning?"

"I didn't want to go, but Mission Command ordered me to."

Eliza glared at him with tears in her eyes.

Bebop hurriedly continued to explain, "I argued with them not to take me from you, but they thought it was the best way to get you back. I'd been with you for over two years, and it was time to advance the mission further, but Mission Command didn't think that would happen if I stayed with you. They figured if I left it would be a wake-up call for you to finally follow your true purpose because you'd realize life is too short to do anything else."

Eliza's voice shook as she said, "I can't believe you did that, Bebop. My heart broke when you left. I wasn't prepared to deal with your passing and became severely depressed when you died, or at least when I thought you died."

"I didn't quite die. We have a team of insects and small rodents who have learned from the best and brightest humans by hiding in operating rooms, pharmacies, and medical labs, watching humans work, and bringing the expertise to NoHoSap. They made me drink water to bloat my stomach, then gave me medicine that slows the heart and brain functions to almost a standstill, making it appear death has ensued. After you said goodbye to me, they switched my body with a decoy for the crematorium, brought me back here, and reversed the medication. I've been working on the mission ever since."

Furious and perplexed at the same time, Eliza could barely speak, she was so upset. She finally said in a measured tone, "You have no idea how grief-stricken I was, how I struggled to deal with you being gone."

Bebop pled his case, "But I do know, and it killed me to see it. Mission Command monitored you to see if their plan was working; if my death would help you realize you should follow your heart to do what you truly wanted. They made me try to communicate with you somehow, to get you back on the path from your youth. It seemed you heard me because you'd talk to my picture and ask for my help to guide you in your loss."

Eliza cried as she re-lived the pain from Bebop's passing. "I just can't believe you put me through that. Why are you now contacting me?"

"Because I didn't think waiting any longer would increase the chances of bringing you back. I thought you were as close as you'd ever be to listening to us and making changes. So, I commanded the mission for Monty, Rumple, and Tumple to visit your office. I was ecstatic when you accepted my invitation to meet here. I've been waiting for this day since I had to leave you."

The revelation that the anguish she experienced after losing Bebop was planned and something in which he participated disturbed Eliza. She wanted to leave that feeling behind, though, and be happy he hadn't died, and they were together again. It was easier said than done, and she confessed to Bebop, "I'm very angry and hurt about your staged death."

"I apologize to you from the bottom of my heart. It was an awful thing to do, and I'm sorry Mission Command made me follow through on that plan. I hope with time you'll see why they did it."

"We'll see." Eliza seethed at the gravity of Bebop's betrayal. After calming down, she asked, "What's Mission Command, who runs it, and why did they want you to meet with me?"

"I hoped you'd ask. Mission Command is the control center for NoHoSap, charged with protecting NoHoSap and all living beings except humans. Since NoHoSap is on Earth, and humans also inhabit the Earth, it's a constant struggle to monitor the entrances and stay under cover to avoid being discovered by people. Mission Command keeps us secure in all parts of NoHoSap around the world and is otherwise responsible for keeping the natural beings on Earth safe. We summoned you here because we need your help on the penultimate mission—to save the world from the climate crisis. It's a mission we've been working on for decades, but that now consumes our time and energy. This mission will make the difference between life and death for all of us—the environment as we know it and all things, including humans, that live in it. If we fail, we die, all of us together. As a result, we must work together to change our destiny from an Earth with a climate that is unlivable for most."

"That's the biggest challenge of our time, of humankind's existence really. Not a day goes by without something on the news about climate change."

"It's the biggest threat to all on this Earth, but are humans really giving it their everything to address it?"

"Well, we're doing better and it's getting more attention."

"Exactly, but we don't have the kind of time it'll take if humans don't start working harder on it now."

"You're right, but who is the 'we' you keep talking about and how can I possibly help? What are you looking for from me?"

"'We' is an alliance of natural beings from NoHoSap working together to avert the disastrous consequences that will occur from climate change if we don't intervene. We're meeting within the hour, and you'll get all the information then."

Confused, Eliza said, "I have no idea what you want me to do on this mission, but I'm willing to hear more."

Bebop gave Eliza a high five the way he always used to when something good happened. He then retrieved the stick they'd been playing with, dropped it in front of Eliza, and waited for her to throw it. She obliged and Bebop ran after it.

Neither noticed Monty flying over to them, but when he saw Bebop retrieve the stick, he stopped in mid-air and watched in disbelief. "Captain, what are you doing?"

Bebop straightened up when he saw Monty staring at him. "At ease," said Bebop in a commanding voice, followed by "carry on."

Monty shook the surprised look off and told Bebop the meeting would start soon. Bebop thanked him and Monty flew off, bewildered.

Bebop told Eliza, "He's not used to seeing me having any fun. I'm the Captain and am always serious. Plus, there's no one to have fun with since you haven't been here. Now I can finally be myself again, at least around you. Anyway, Monty's right. We need to leave for the meeting. We don't dare to be late. Follow me."

Eliza's mind raced as she walked after him. Joyful about her reunion with Bebop, at the same time she felt angry and hurt by the truth of his fake passing. She also wondered whether this "mission" could be the path for which she'd been searching to replace her less than fulfilling current career. Time would tell.

CHAPTER 4

ON THE SPOT

Eliza fished for information while they trekked to the meeting. "Tell me more about this Alliance."

"The Alliance is the top of the ladder in NoHoSap. Mission Command runs our missions pursuant to orders from the Alliance. The Alliance decides the projects we undertake and leaves it to Mission Command to implement them."

"Wow, the Alliance is very important."

"That it is. I'm just happy you're here to have this meeting. It's been a long time coming."

They walked down a path and entered a pine forest. The trees were tall and slender, with pinkish bark. Breathing in, Eliza savored the fresh pine scent. The soothing, swishing sound of the wind through the evergreen branches differed from the sound of wind through the leaves of deciduous trees. Eliza likened the variation to brushes rather than sticks on drums.

"We call this the pink forest because the red pines have pink-hued bark and when that's the only kind of tree around, the pink stands out."

"It's beautiful." Eliza took in the sounds, smells, and sights of the moment. After walking a bit further in silence, she blurted out, "I feel totally unprepared for this meeting, especially with such an upper-level group. I don't like that feeling."

"You'll be fine. Just listen to them."

They reached the end of the path and walked into a clearing sur-rounded on three sides by rock faces overhung with pine branches, forming a stone amphitheater with an airy green roof. The rocks rose straight out of the ground to various heights of at least twenty feet, with small crags and shelves in random spots. A large boulder sat in the middle of the clearing, surrounded by six large stones of varying shapes, sizes, and colors. The circle of stones contained a gap that lined up with a path coming out of the woods.

Bebop moved toward some rocks around the perimeter of the amphitheater and Eliza followed. As she sat down, she noticed a vari-ety of animals, birds, reptiles, and insects gathered behind her. She looked up at the rock faces and noticed most of the crags were occu-pied by birds, mainly birds of prey. They surveyed the crowd from their lofty perches and emitted random piercing screeches that left the small mammals in the audience cowering in fear.

All in the clearing watched Bebop and Eliza. Eliza smiled at them, feeling uneasy. A wave of fear and doubt welled up in her mind. *Why did she agree to this meeting? Was she hallucinating? Was she in harm's way?* It dawned on her that she hadn't told anyone where she would be, and therefore no one would look for her if she didn't make it back to HuHabDom. Trying to remember exactly how she got here in case she needed to make a run for it, she looked at Bebop for reassurance but instead became angry at him for leaving her in such a cold way.

As Eliza calmed herself, a hush came over the clearing. She saw movement near the path, at the gap in the circle. Shadowed figures appeared among the trees. Bebop whispered that these were the mem-bers of the Alliance.

First to emerge from the path, an elephant ambled over to a boul-der and sat down with a thud. Its wrinkled face turned toward the crowd, scanning over everyone, then looked Eliza square in the eyes and smiled slightly. Perplexed, Eliza wondered how and why an ele-phant could be here, especially this far from its native habitat.

Next, a large white bird swooped out from the path and landed acrobatically yet gracefully on a tall stone. A seal came out next, maneuvering slowly but purposefully over the ground on its belly to a wide flat rock with a large depression filled with water, into which it settled comfortably.

On the heels of the seal came a sleek, spotted jaguar, which walked stealthily to the next stone, all the while moving its eyes back and forth across the clearing as though on the prowl for its next meal. Eliza looked for the exits as she worried for her safety amid these creatures. Shortly thereafter, a medium-sized bat darted out from the path, flitting high and low and landing on a tall, thin stone with a wide top.

The clearing grew silent, and a slow, methodical scraping sound filled the air, like sandpaper rubbing against wood. A long, low snout appeared at the end of the path, followed by the rest of the huge alligator to which it belonged. Eliza gasped and raised up from her seat to run away, but Bebop put his paw on her arm and motioned for her to relax. The alligator sauntered over to a wide rock platform and settled in like it owned the place.

A loud howl bolted everyone to attention. All eyes followed the direction of the sound, and a striking grey wolf ran out of the path and hopped onto the podium in the center of the circle. It howled again and then said, "I now call this meeting of the Alliance to order."

Struck by the assemblage of creatures and the meeting itself, Eliza's heart raced. If she had to escape, she likely would not be successful with a wolf, elephant, alligator, and jaguar after her. She couldn't remember if she should or shouldn't make eye contact with these creatures to avoid being killed and hesitated to break the silence to ask Bebop's advice.

The wolf looked calmly and authoritatively at the Alliance members and then scanned the attendees in the gallery, making all feel included. She said, "We called this special meeting of the Alliance to discuss a new development in our Climate Change Initiative. Mission Command has been working on a project for years now with the goal of partnering with humans to fight climate change."

The crowd released a collective exclamation while the members of the Alliance looked over the audience reassuringly.

The wolf continued, "The world is on a perilous path because of the warming climate. The more time that passes, the less time we have to avert disaster where our habitats are destroyed, and our species dwindle into extinction. We in the animal kingdom can only do so much in the climate fight. The sole way to have any chance of success is to enlist the assistance of humans to slow down and ideally reverse global warming. We are pursuing any involvement with humans cautiously, but after decades of working on our own, it's clear the beings who caused the conditions resulting in climate change must address it." The Alliance members shook their heads in agreement.

"We have information and capabilities that humans don't and working together is the only hope for saving ourselves and this planet as we know it."

The gallery members chattered among themselves, surprised to hear of the Alliance's decision to work with beings many viewed as enemies.

"Mission Command made contact with a human we believe can help us," informed the wolf.

The eyes of the Alliance and those in the audience all turned to Eliza. She immediately blushed and a 'who, me?' look came over her face. Bebop leaned into her for moral support.

The wolf went on, "The human who Mission Command has identified knew nothing of this mission, and we brought her here to fill her in on it now."

Discord erupted in the audience and a badger moved toward the front of the gallery. "May I ask a question?" he asked a number of times, each louder than the last in an effort to be heard over the attendees. Eventually the uproar settled and the wolf invited the badger to speak.

He cleared his throat and said, "We're concerned about a partnership with humans. They only care about their best interests and not ours. That's how we ended up in this mess in the first place. Why should we waste any effort working with them now?"

The wolf replied, "The Alliance had the same concerns and we've discussed it every which way for quite some time. We kept coming back to the reality that the actions needed to slow the warming can only be done effectively and most impactfully by humans."

A crow piped up from a rock above the gallery. "But what can we do to convince them to take action? They don't even listen to other humans, much less to us."

The elephant answered, "You're absolutely right, humans are a challenge, and we don't understand them. That's why we believe the only way to get our message to them is through another human. We've tried everything we can think of on our end and have nothing to lose by giving this a shot."

The gallery agreed and quieted down. Eliza wished she could crawl under a rock rather than be the center of attention and sole representative of the entire human race.

The wolf continued, "We feel this person can bring our message to humans directly and also help us connect with them to deliver the message ourselves. We need some time to brief her on this crucial mission and are hopeful she'll accept the challenge. In the meantime, please welcome Eliza to NoHoSap and help her feel at home. The Alliance will now go into Executive Session. Thanks to the gallery members for attending."

Dumbfounded upon hearing this information, Eliza struggled to process it, but the creatures in the gallery surrounded her, introducing themselves and wishing her well. Bebop ran interference with limited success. Although the announcement and reception overwhelmed Eliza, she kept her composure as best she could.

The hubbub subsided as the audience filed out of the clearing. The Alliance members conversed amongst themselves while waiting for the Executive Session. Bebop and Eliza stood alone at the edge of the group. An awkward silence fell, and Eliza tried to shake off the discomfort of being put on the spot without warning. Her ears rang from the gallery's reaction to working with humans, and she could still feel their stares after the wolf announced she was 'the human' they identified to help. Bebop hit Eliza's leg softly with his paw when he saw her withdrawing into herself in this unfamiliar setting.

She turned toward him, and her bewilderment changed to anger that he hadn't warned her she'd be the focus of the meeting. Her eyes narrowed as she pondered what to say without drawing too much attention. Before she could utter a word, Bebop asked, "What's wrong?"

The question bothered Eliza even more. She answered in a restrained voice, "How could you do this to me, Bebop?"

Bebop tilted his head in consternation.

"Why didn't you let me know what this meeting was about? You brought me here to spring this on me in front of an amphitheater full of animals? You could have given me a clue ahead of time. Instead, you didn't tell me anything, even though you knew full well what the plan was. I'm very disappointed you left me in the dark."

Disconcerted, Bebop considered what to say with the Alliance nearby, and offered matter-of-factly, "The Alliance instructed me to bring you to this open meeting and said they wanted to fill you in on the mission rather than me telling you, and that's what I did."

"So, you were following orders, just like you were following orders to fake your death and leave me," Eliza said hurtfully. "Good job, Bebop, you did exactly as you were told."

"I wanted to tell you something about the mission and the role we were hoping you'd play but didn't want to ruin the surprise. I actually thought it would come across better if the Alliance filled you in. I forgot that humans plan and divulge information differently than us."

Eliza reminded herself that Bebop, the Alliance members, and all in NoHoSap weren't people and she shouldn't expect them to act as though they were. She also realized being involved in this mission could be the life-changing event she'd been seeking. Softening, she said, "Alright, Bebop, I'll try to be more open-minded and less 'human-centric.' Please, though, give me some sort of heads up on what to expect here."

The wolf motioned for them to come over. Bebop said to Eliza, "OK, I'll remember that, but right now the Alliance wants us to join them."

CHAPTER 5

THE MISSION

After being summoned by the wolf, Bebop and Eliza walked toward the Alliance members. The wolf met them halfway and said, "Hello, Captain, good work." Turning to Eliza, she continued, "Welcome, Eliza. I'm Canlup [pronounced Cane-loop]. We're happy you're here."

Eliza responded, "Thank you, and very nice to meet you. I didn't know what to expect when I came here today, but never imagined anything like this."

Canlup smiled, "We didn't want Bebop to reveal much to you, only what he thought was needed to get you to this meeting. Thank you for agreeing to attend today. We'd like to talk with you about our mission, ask for your help and, if you agree, give you the details."

Eliza looked at Bebop to acknowledge Canlup's confirmation of his instructions from the Alliance, and replied diplomatically, "Bebop definitely gave me just enough information to make me want to hear more. I look forward to getting the details."

"Then follow me." Canlup turned and walked toward the center of the clearing. The Alliance members headed to their seats as Canlup and Eliza made their way to the podium. Canlup told Eliza to sit on a stump nearby. Bebop took a seat in the gallery, but Canlup motioned for him to come over to keep Eliza company. He sat next to Eliza and looked at her confidently, to calm her nerves.

Canlup instructed, "Let's first introduce ourselves and explain our individual interest in this mission. I'll start. My name is Canlup and my home is in Northern Iceland. Global warming is melting the polar ice caps in our region at alarming rates. This warms our water and habitats, melting the snow on which we depend." She became agitated and paused, then gathered herself and continued. "Our only options are to move, change our life habits, or die. Moving is a short-term fix, and not all in our ecosystem are mobile. That option, therefore, addresses the problem for relatively few. Changing our habits will take generations, and we don't have that kind of time because the climate is warming at such a fast pace. Many animals and plants in my home have died, and many more will follow unless we take action." A look of resolute determination replaced the sadness that shaded her eyes from the outset. She eyed the alligator to indicate it was his turn.

"Hello, Eliza. They call me Chompers and I'm from Indonesia." He had a surprisingly warm voice. "We've experienced weather events ranging from severe drought and fires to typhoons in recent years, all from the warming climate. Our homes and food are being destroyed time and time again." His voice swelled with anger and his huge tail swished back and forth. "As though that weren't enough, the lives we've lost are immeasurable. Many of our species exist nowhere else in the world, and climate change is pushing them to the brink of extinction. They often die before having offspring or leave youngsters behind that depend on them, which has a devastating impact on the survival of those lines." He looked directly at Eliza, "Just when we think we've adapted to the losses as best we can, the weather brings another surprise to challenge us yet again. We can't sit idly by and allow this to continue."

Next up was the bat, who spread his wings when all eyes turned to him. "I'm Sonar and am happy to meet you, Eliza. I'm from the forests of the three-country corner in Europe, where Germany, France, and Switzerland come together." He flitted into the air, upset. Upon landing he continued. "We've experienced very warm temperatures for extended periods, and it gets more unbearable every year. It's becoming harder to adjust to the changes, and more of our plants and animals die with each heatwave. To be honest, many of us are barely hanging on and it will only get worse." His voice trailed off as he turned to the next Alliance member, the big cat.

"Welcome, Eliza. My name is Mosa and I'm a jaguar from Peru." She paced back and forth, staring straight ahead as she talked. "We're suffering from severe hurricanes, rainstorms, and snowstorms, which cause mudslides, flooding, and wind damage. In between the storms, we have extended droughts and massive fires." Melancholy descended in her eyes. "Many have perished—animals, plants, birds, insects." Mosa shook her head, finding it hard to fathom. "It's difficult to go home now and see the wreckage that's occurring from the changing climate. My species is already on the decline, and if this weather and losses continue, we and many others in our habitat will be gone for good." She sat down, mentally tired from recounting the state of affairs in her home.

The seal maneuvered from the water portion of her seat onto the dry side and said, "I'm Jazzy. Thank you for being here, Eliza. My home is in the Atlantic Ocean, off the coast of Cape Cod." Eliza's face brightened, Cape Cod being one of her favorite places. "I watched you and Bebop walking on the beach on some of your trips there." Bebop smiled as he recalled the fun he had with Eliza on those outings. "Our waters are warming, leading to more red tides that impact our shellfish, violent storms that erode our coastlines and nesting habitats, and of particular impact to my species, longer periods when sharks are in our waters preying on seals. I've seen many changes during my relatively short life, and if they continue, the ocean will be a very different place in the not-too-distant future."

All then turned to the bird, who stood on the rock next to Jazzy's. "Nice to meet you, Eliza. I'm Schnee [pronounced Shnay]. I'm a snow goose and spend my summers in Canada, then migrate to Mexico each year for the winter." Schnee adjusted her wings. "The changes I've seen in my travels over the years are significant. The winters are getting shorter and milder, the summers are getting warmer, and I've seen the scars from wildfires and mudslides increasing on every trip I make." She stared into the distance as though picturing the sights she described. "The animals in my summer home in Canada complain they're barely surviving with the sparse snows and warmer weather. Those in my winter home in Mexico say they need to move north since the high temperatures are killing their food and water supplies. I feel for all of them and want to bring them some good news from what I see in my travels but am at a loss since I'm not seeing anything positive." Schnee looked down with a hint of a defeated look on her face.

The elephant rounded out the introductions. "Greetings, Eliza," boomed his deep voice. "My name is Tusko, from Africa, Botswana specifically. The stories I could tell. I'm the oldest here by far and have seen many changes in my lifetime. I want to shout in anger and cry in sorrow. We've seen horrible droughts, unbearable heat, wild wind, and torrential rains. The warming climate is ruining our home and killing the beings in it." He hung his head. "At first I thought it was just weather variations that come and go, but as it continued and worsened year after year, I became convinced that what humans call climate change is real. Many are suffering trying to keep themselves alive, trying to raise their young." Eliza saw tears in Tusko's eyes. "I can't bear to think how bad it will be in the future. The negative changes are accelerating and the living things in my home will continue to die grim deaths if the climate keeps warming at this pace." He looked around at the Alliance members and then at Bebop and Eliza, his gaze conveying both pleading and defiance.

All were quiet after hearing Tusko's somber analysis. Canlup broke the silence. "Thank you everyone for telling your stories. That's what brings us here today. As I mentioned earlier, we can't fight this by ourselves if we have any hope of saving the planet as we know it. We've watched humans become more aware of the changes occurring worldwide, but they're still largely apathetic about the dire effects of climate change. They've discovered ways to reverse the pace of the warming but are slow to implement them. We need to speed up the changes if we want to survive. We can't get the message across on our own, though. That's where you come in, Eliza."

Eliza didn't know what to say. She ultimately sputtered, "I'd love to help, but how do you expect me, just one person, to make any sort of difference."

Tusko commented, "We know it sounds ridiculous, and many in the Alliance had the same reaction when we first discussed the idea. We've implemented our own measures, but those things don't have the large-scale impact that's needed. We need humans engaged in the fight and we think you can help motivate them."

Jazzy added, "When I saw you with Bebop you were very observant and had a rare concern for the environment and for him. We also watched you on the videos from Mission Command showing you in action in your work as a reporter. You communicate calmly and effectively with humans and know the legal system in which many people and governments operate."

Chompers said, "We're not exactly in the position to approach humans ourselves and make them listen to us. I'd love to try but have been dissuaded by my fellow Alliance members. They seem to think humans may not view my communications too favorably." All Eliza could focus on were the huge, sharp teeth jutting out of his mouth. He smiled when he finished talking, but it showed his teeth all the more and made him look more menacing, even though he also batted his eyelids in an attempt to look sweet and innocent.

Eliza chuckled. "I'm sure you'd do a great job, Chompers, but agree that humans would likely be scared to death if you and your teeth approached them to have a conversation."

"My teeth, my teeth. Everyone has something to say about my teeth. They're a blessing and a curse, but the ladies do seem to love them." Chompers smiled widely.

"Alright, that's enough," Canlup interjected. "Let's get back to our important business and fill Eliza in on the plan." She turned to Eliza. "We have two approaches. First, we're already doing what we can to address climate change, like planting trees and restoring coral reefs. We're ready to let humans see this to inspire them to do their part. We need your help to get that word out. Second, humans with pets often have an appreciation of the environment that other humans don't because they have a bond with a being from the natural world. We feel these humans may be more likely to take action once they truly understand the impact they can have and realize the consequences if they don't."

Surprised at hearing this level of thought from animals, but not wanting to show it for fear she may insult them, Eliza said, "That all makes sense."

"We'll work together on the mission," advised Canlup. "You'll spread the word to humans about making changes. Emissaries from our ranks will continue on the projects we've been doing and will also let pets know how to guide their humans to make better choices in the climate fight."

"Wow," exclaimed Eliza, failing to contain her bewilderment, "you have this all planned out. I'm always up for a challenge, but what you're asking me to do seems near impossible."

Mosa offered, "We know it's a lot, but we don't expect you to do everything on your own. We're already working with some humans, and you can recruit others in addition. Also, we have many here in NoHoSap who've volunteered to assist. We have to start somewhere and will tackle it one step at a time. We can't afford to continue the way things are going now, with more frequent disasters ravaging our world and whittling us into extinction."

Canlup added, "If you bring the message to humans and we enlighten pets, we strongly believe our joined forces will drastically improve the chances we all will survive as our climate and world change. This is the dawn of a new era of cooperation between the human and animal worlds. We'll work together as we never have before, and you can be a driving force behind that. Will you take on this challenge with us, Eliza?"

Excited, intimidated, motivated, and scared all at once at the invitation to help on this monumental mission, Eliza's mind raced. She wondered whether they expected her to work with them full time, which would be a non-starter because she needed to pay her bills. Not generally one to take risks, it seemed fate called her in a new direction, leaving her conflicted about what to do. Bebop stared at her as though trying to influence her decision. Unable to answer without knowing more of the expectations for her, she asked, "Exactly what are you asking of me? Am I supposed to work solely with you and leave my job?"

The Alliance members seemed befuddled when she didn't answer yes or no. There never were any grey areas for those in the animal world. Bebop stood up and asked Canlup if he could speak and she agreed.

Trying to cut the tension, Bebop said, "Good question, Eliza. We forget humans have responsibilities besides keeping yourselves alive day to day. Mission Command rather than the Alliance handles the details of the project, and I'm leading the climate mission. We weren't planning you'd work full time on the mission. I know how important your job is to you. We'll be flexible around that, at least for starters."

Relieved, Eliza thanked Bebop for clarifying. She generally didn't make such big decisions without taking her time, wanting to explore every angle before committing to anything. All eyes were on her, though, pressuring her to answer. Bebop looked at Eliza intently and she imagined him telling her to join them. A tiny voice in her head reminded her, though, that he deceived her and maybe she shouldn't trust him. The anticipation in the air increased the longer Eliza remained silent.

Bebop ran interference again. "We really put you on the spot, Eliza, but we feel you're the right person for this mission and we'll work with you and your responsibilities at work to allow you to do both."

Eliza didn't know what to do. This could be the opportunity of a lifetime. Of all the humans in the world, they invited her to NoHoSap and were offering her this opportunity. If humans asked her to take a job like this, she'd jump at the chance. Concerned she may regret it if she passed this up, she pondered a little longer and eventually answered Canlup's question with a resounding, "Yes! I'll join you in this challenge!"

Canlup, the Alliance members, and Bebop immediately jumped up and cheered. They surrounded Eliza as everyone thanked and welcomed her to the mission. Bebop's tail wagged furiously, and he had the biggest smile Eliza had ever seen. Eliza crushed her doubts about what she may be getting herself into and instead enjoyed the moment.

Canlup called the meeting back to order after everyone welcomed Eliza to the mission. "We're ecstatic you've agreed to join us, Eliza. Now we must get down to business and move to action. We have much to do and no time to waste. Mission Command will be the boots on the ground working with you. The Alliance members are available to assist with anything needed in their homelands or areas of expertise."

Chompers chimed in, "Whatever we can do to help, don't hesitate to ask. We're in this together and want, actually need, to see results."

"Not to put too much pressure on, but this is our last shot to bring the change needed to divert the world from the path we're on," added Tusko. "We'll monitor the efforts and gladly help where we can."

Jazzy piped up, "Anything you need in the sea, I'm on it." The other Alliance members seconded that offer for their home habitats or knowledge areas.

Canlup instructed, "Bebop, you'll staff this from Mission Command and work closely with Eliza to devise an action plan for bringing the message to other humans and getting them to act. We must move the mission along and look forward to seeing you in action very soon."

"Eliza, you're welcome to stay here in NoHoSap as long and often as you want," Canlup offered. "We're happy to provide food and shelter to allow you to focus on the mission rather than also being worried about making a living in HuHabDom. Of course, the sustenance we provide would be solely vegetarian."

Eliza had no idea what it would be like staying in NoHoSap and wasn't ready to uproot her life at the drop of a hat, but politely advised, "I'm very grateful for the offer. I'll need some time to figure out how to balance my job with working on the mission, but it's comforting to know staying here is an option."

"Understood. It's been quite the day for all of us, especially you, Eliza," said Canlup.

Canlup adjourned the meeting, and all rose from their seats. Excited and scared, Eliza knew deep down she made the right decision. She looked cautiously forward to what the future had in store.

CHAPTER 6

THE TEAM

T he Alliance members filed past Eliza and Bebop on their way out of the clearing, thanking Eliza for agreeing to serve on the mission. Mosa and Schnee said they felt more optimistic about the future than they had in quite some time, and Chompers quipped about it being 'the dawn of a new era.'

When Bebop and Eliza were alone in the amphitheater. Bebop announced, "In the interest of starting the mission without delay, some members of the team are here, and I'd like to introduce them. All right team, show yourselves."

Figures of all shapes and sizes appeared from out of the trees around the clearing–they walked, flew, slithered, and jumped. A variety of wildlife soon surrounded Eliza and Bebop, including deer, lizards, birds, butterflies, snakes, rabbits, and bears. Eliza recognized some as well-wishers from earlier. A couple chimpanzees wheeled in a video monitor and, after some tuning, a multi-split screen appeared with each part of the display filled by aquatic species ranging from a whale, fish, octopus, snails, and eels.

Once all were settled, Bebop introduced them collectively. "Team, this is Eliza. Today she agreed to work with us on the climate change mission, by far our most important mission ever."

The team members all said 'hello' and 'welcome' to Eliza at once. Greetings even came from the water dwellers via speakers on the monitor.

When the crowd quieted, Bebop continued, "Eliza, meet the team."

Eliza smiled, waved, and looked around at the beings. "Very nice to meet you. I'm honored to be here and look forward to working with you on this mission."

Bebop proceeded, "We have a lot of work to do. Now, with Eliza's help, we can plug in the piece that's been missing—engaging humans to make the changes needed for real progress. Eliza, those here today are a small part of our forces. Each member of this team represents a group. Some groups are based on species, some on geography, and others on habitat. Each representative and group is uniquely qualified to undertake certain tasks. We've charted our ideas and will now add your skills to fill the gaps and hit the ground running."

A bell rang in the distance, catching the attention of those in the clearing. Bebop looked up and said, "The party's starting. Enjoy this time together before we embark on the next phase of the mission. I'll see you all back at work tomorrow. Dismissed."

The team members hurried out of the clearing, many telling Eliza as they moved by that they'd see her at the party and looked forward to working with her.

Trotting past Eliza, Bebop said, "Let's go—we can talk on the way." Eliza followed. "I know you have a very busy schedule at work and we're going to need you here or in the field. How are you going to give this mission the time it needs?"

"Geez, Bebop, you cut right to the chase."

"No need to beat around the bush or sugar coat anything. We don't have time for that."

"I understand why you're concerned and had the same thought myself, but you assured me we'd work it out. I don't yet know how I'm going to juggle this with my job at the station. Fortunately, things are relatively slow now and I have a fair amount of vacation saved up. I can scale back my hours to leave time to work with you and will also start using vacation."

"OK, I'll be a thorn in your side to keep you focused on the mission." Bebop turned to give Eliza a high five.

"Deal." Eliza slapped Bebop's paw.

They resumed their brisk walk, and a cacophony of voices and other sounds grew louder in the air. Bebop and Eliza reached the edge of a huge field teaming with creatures mulling around on and above the ground. Many of the beings were gathered in bunches talking amongst themselves, as humans would at a cocktail party. Piles of food were scattered on rocks and stumps, and animals either stood next to the vittles chowing down, or took a few pieces, walked away, and ate surreptitiously by themselves.

Eliza heard a drum and music, looked in the direction from which the melody came, and saw a band jamming away. She stood transfixed, while taking it all in. A chimpanzee held sticks and stones in its fingers and toes, hitting hollow tree stumps and rocks while laying down a nice backbeat and bobbing its head in time. A pair of crows carrying metal rods in their mouths strutted along, doing step moves while striking rows of metal plates with the rods like vibes. Birds sang in high and low tones, fast and slow, as they flitted above the chimpanzee and crows. The animals around the "band" were a sea of motion as they jumped, swayed, or otherwise moved to the sound. A goat sauntered out from behind the band and stood in front, looking cool with his soul patch goat beard.

The crowd went wild and yelled in unison, "Go BG, go BG!" Eliza stared in disbelief.

Bebop sidled up, amused at her reaction. "Didn't expect anything like this, did you?"

"Absolutely not. Why are they saying 'BG'?"

"Billy Goat, he's Billy Goat."

As if BG wasn't enough, a spotlight suddenly shone to the right of the crowd, revealing a pangolin on a turntable, leaving Eliza speechless.

Bebop yelled over the din, "Pango's a great MC but he doesn't get to do it often because the records are ruined from his long nails after he uses them only once, and records aren't easy to find anymore."

BG began rapping, met by more cheers from the crowd. Eliza couldn't believe the scene as BG swaggered to and fro, serving up serious rhymes, Pango mixed crazy tracks, and animals danced everywhere.

As the show wound down, Bebop broke into Eliza's reverie and instructed, "Let's go. Time to meet, greet, and eat."

Eliza took a deep breath, stepped into the field, and in no time a diverse array of all sorts of living beings other than humans surrounded her. Rather than being frightened as she had earlier, she felt fortunate to be there. It helped that all the creatures welcomed her and seemed genuinely happy she joined the team. Bebop introduced Eliza to countless new friends. She tried to catalog all the names and faces in her head. Never good at that, though, she knew she likely wouldn't remember names. Hopefully, the faces would ring a bell later.

The greetings continued while Eliza watched with incredulity. In the midst of it, she heard a male voice behind her say, "Hello Eliza, very glad to hear you'll be working with us."

Eliza turned to see a boy in his late teens and a younger girl. They appeared to be of Native American heritage. Surprised and somewhat relieved to see other humans, she held out her hand to greet them. "Mosa said they'd been working with some humans, but I haven't met any others yet. Very pleased to see you here."

Shaking her hand, the boy replied, "Hi, I'm Kanatase, but most call me Jacob. This is my little sister, Ojistah."

"I'm his sister, but I'm not little anymore, now that I'm twelve," remarked the girl defiantly as she shook Eliza's hand. "Nice to meet you, Eliza. Kanatase may not like to use his Indian name, but I do. You can call me Oji for short."

"OK," said Eliza, surprised yet impressed by Oji's feistiness. "Nice to meet both of you." She looked around, still astonished at the scene in the field.

Addressing her bewilderment, Jacob observed, "It must be a shock to see all this. Oji and I have been visiting NoHoSap with our parents since we were quite young. We've gotten used to all the things our animal kin can do."

"I never would have imagined anything like this," admitted Eliza. "Now that I see this place, I feel badly I've minimized the abilities of animals. I'm sure what I've experienced in a few hours here barely scratches the surface."

Jacob chuckled and said knowingly, "That's for sure."

"Are you both working on the climate change mission?"

Jacob replied, "I started working on the mission after I got my driver's license a couple years ago."

"They won't let me do much yet, even though I keep telling them I can help," lamented Oji.

"You have to be patient, Oji," explained Jacob with exasperation. "I'd tell them I could help all the time too, but you'll get to pitch in once you're truly ready and have learned the lesson of patience."

Eliza smiled at the exchange, remembering how her younger brother used to get on her nerves too. "I'm looking forward to hearing more of exactly what we'll be doing." She paused before asking, "If you don't mind, how did your parents know about this place to bring you here when you were young?"

Jacob answered, "As you may have assumed, we're Native American, Iroquois, mainly Mohawk to be exact. Our people have been connected with the NoHoSap world for our entire existence. As the human and animal worlds became more separated with the arrival of colonists, we appointed representatives of each generation to maintain close ties with NoHoSap, and that tradition continues to this day. Oji and I are the youngest in our tribe to have this honor. Our parents worked closely with Mission Command as they developed the mission. I enjoy being able to help implement it now."

"And I will too, once they let me," added Oji enthusiastically.

Eliza said, "I've always admired the connection of native peoples to the environment and wish other cultures would learn to be as in tune with the impacts and interactions among living beings and the natural world that keep everything in balance."

"I know," replied Jacob. "We're very far from that now, and it pains my people to see it. We feel we have much to offer in this fight but are largely ignored, as we have been for so long. I must say, though, we're very happy you accepted the offer to join the mission. We're here to help in any way we can."

"Yep, just let us know what we can do," Oji offered. The wheels already turned in her head of how she could convince Eliza to let her actually do something on the mission.

"I will, thank you both," said Eliza.

"OK, Oji, we need to get going. See you later, Eliza."

Oji begrudgingly followed Jacob and waved goodbye to Eliza as she walked away.

Bebop came over and said, "Glad you had a chance to meet Jacob and Oji."

"Me too. They seem very eager to get to work, especially Oji."

"That's an understatement—she never ceases to ask what she can do every time I see her. We put her to work as much as we can, but she's still young and there's only a limited amount she can do."

"Well, we don't want her to lose that enthusiasm."

"Jacob was the same way. He began visiting here when he was an infant and when he grew to a young boy he always wanted to help with everything. Once he had his driver's license, we recruited him to be our driver and delivery person."

"Must be nice to have a driver."

"Think about it, how are we supposed to get around in HuHab-Dom, especially when we're in groups, without drawing attention?" Eliza realized he had a point. "Jacob takes us places we need to visit but that are too far away or risky to get to on our own. Also, if we need any supplies, we can't find ourselves, he gets them. It's very handy to have him working with us."

Night deepened in the sky, and Eliza checked her watch for the first time since arriving at the mausoleum door. Surprised at the hour, she said "Bebop, I'd love to stay, but it's getting late, and I really should head out."

Bebop understood, motioned for Eliza to follow him, and called, "Need an escort to the gate."

Eliza and Bebop walked out of the field and suddenly the fireflies and chipmunks who guided Eliza into NoHoSap earlier that day appeared to show her back out.

Bebop asked, "Let's meet back here Monday at 5:30 p.m. The team will be working all day, but we'll give you a chance to scale back at work before you start putting in daylight time."

Eliza pulled out her phone to check her calendar. Bebop's eyes grew large with concern when he saw the phone. "Your phone–I forgot about your phone!"

"What about my phone? You know I carry it wherever I go."

"I totally forgot about that since we're not obsessed with having one with us at all times. Do you have location services turned on? You have to turn that off whenever you're in or near NoHoSap. We can't risk having humans find us by tracking a location on a phone."

"You're right, that would be awful if humans found this place. I don't like being tracked either and always have location services off unless I'm using the phone for directions. No worries, Bebop, it's been off the whole time I've been here." Bebop relaxed, relieved. Eliza continued, "And yes, 5:30 p.m. Monday works. I'll see you then. I'm looking forward to starting on the mission."

"We are too, Eliza. Get some rest tomorrow because it may be your last opportunity in a while."

CHAPTER 7

PLANNING, AND THEN SOME

The alarm jolted Eliza out of bed bright and early Monday morning. Generally, she'd dress in her walking clothes and go for a walk before getting ready for work. Since she had to leave the station early for NoHoSap, though, she planned to get to work before she generally did and make up the time.

"Monday, Monday," she muttered to herself while shuffling into the shower. As the water woke her up, she mentally planned her day at the station, knowing she had a lot to do, and the time would fly before she'd leave for NoHoSap.

Once washed up, she pulled a lightweight skirt suit from the closet to start the workweek on a conservative note. Thinking about wardrobe made her realize she should bring other clothes to change into before tromping through the cemetery and tunnel to NoHoSap. She threw some things in a bag and listened to the weather report. Although beginning as a beautiful clear and sunny morning, the forecast called for a cold front to move through in the late afternoon that would bring strong winds, heavy rain, and the chance for hail. Eliza stowed her rubber boots and rain jacket in the backpack to be on the safe side.

She took a banana from the fruit bowl on her way out the door and rushed to the car. Unfortunately, driving her gas-powered car would be a more frequent transportation choice than taking mass transit. With the bus, the trip from the station to the cemetery would take over an hour with one transfer, and the return buses stopped running before she'd be ready to leave. The car allowed her to arrive at the cemetery only fifteen minutes after leaving the station and drive directly home regardless of when she left NoHoSap.

On the way to work, Eliza contemplated her contributions to global warming and all the ways she could reduce her carbon footprint. Those thoughts often crossed her mind when she read an article or heard a news story about climate change, but she quashed them. She often procrastinated in implementing any changes, thinking there was more time. Her meetings the past weekend and her new mission made her realize she needed to be a better global citizen, especially if she expected it of others. They also made her wonder why the Alliance chose her rather than a human with a smaller carbon output.

Trying to reduce the guilt, she counted in her head what she did to help in the climate fight—riding the bus instead of driving (but now she wasn't even doing that), keeping the thermostat at home low in the winter and high in the summer, turning lights off when not needed, reducing and reusing plastics. Rather than helping her feel better, the short list made Eliza feel even worse. Talking to herself out loud, she planned. "OK, I need to get solar panels installed on the house and trade in this gas-guzzling car for an electric vehicle." The banana that comprised her breakfast caught her attention. "Enjoy the last of these exotic fruits that have flown thousands of miles to reach you. From here on out its local fruits and vegetables in season that don't require barrels of petroleum to travel to my table."

Her mind turned to all the takeout and microwaveable meal containers in her recyclable bin and garbage can from the fast meals on which she relied. She justified the single-use plastics by thinking 'at least I can recycle them,' even after seeing the stories that most of those plastics weren't actually recycled. Overwhelmed, wondering how she'd make all these changes, she arrived at work and parked, then switched her focus to the story she needed to write today. When she walked into her office, she greeted Bebop's picture with her usual "good morning" and smiled to herself since he was now back in the land of the living.

As Eliza predicted, the workday flew and before she knew it, she had to leave for NoHoSap. She put the finishing touches on her story for the night news, changed clothes in her office, and hurried off to the car, taking the back exit from the station so no one would see her leaving early.

The sky filled with rain clouds as Eliza reached the mausoleum door. Feeling somewhat less on edge since she'd already been through the entrance drill, Eliza entered the tunnel and made her way into NoHoSap. Bebop waited as she exited, his tail wagging feverishly, as it always used to when he saw her. They did their habitual high five greeting and Bebop moved left away from the tunnel. Eliza followed as they walked on a path through an overgrown field and modest forest.

They reached a rock outcropping where Bebop stopped and pushed down on a random rock with his front paw. A stone slab slowly moved to the right, revealing a small room with filtered light streaming from above through the rocks. Eliza stared in shock. Bebop stepped into the room and coaxed Eliza to join him. Hesitantly, she entered, looked around, and realized the only entrance or exit was the opening they just went through.

Bebop hit a lever on a wall, the rock slid closed, and the room dropped beneath their feet. Eliza grasped for the walls to steady herself, looking around in fear and wonder. Realizing where they were, she exclaimed, "It's an elevator!"

Delighted in Eliza's reaction, Bebop said nonchalantly, "You seem surprised."

"Of course, I am! You said you have gifted techies here, but I didn't realize the extent of their capabilities."

"You have no idea," replied Bebop knowingly, with a glint in his eye, as though hiding a secret. "You're not used to anyone other than humans inventing or using any sort of technology. Get ready to have your thinking rearranged."

The elevator stopped descending and the rock slid open, revealing a large area filled with creatures hurrying here and there. Teams of animals engaged in fervent discussions while pointing to video monitors clustered on the walls. Sole beings sat or stood on or next to rocks in scattered areas, working on tablets and computers.

"Welcome to Mission Command, Eliza," announced Bebop. Rather than look at the scene before them, he surveyed Eliza's awestruck face.

Eliza's mouth hung open; her eyes wide in amazement. They were in an underground cavern. Rock walls surrounded the open area, lit by glowing orbs either hanging from the ceiling or affixed to the walls.

"Oh… my… goodness." Eliza said in wonderment, gazing around, trying to take it all in. She couldn't believe the number and variety of creatures in action. Birds and insects darted through the air, some talking on mini headsets. A cow walked by with a squirrel on its back typing feverishly on a smartphone. A group composed of a hyena, anteater, Koala bear, toad, and ostrich argued over a map on a video screen and another group with a lizard, badger, python, hawk, and turtle were in serious discussion over a group of bar graphs.

"I hate to say I told you so," said Bebop as he enjoyed Eliza's surprise, "but I told you so."

"Woooowww," was the only thing Eliza could manage to say.

Eliza noticed that passersby immediately straightened up and came to attention when they saw Bebop. Many stared at Eliza as the odd human out.

"Hello, Captain. Greetings, Eliza," came Monty's voice. Eliza looked to her right and discovered him hovering between her and Bebop. He had the usual megaphone in front of him to amplify his voice, which Eliza now realized wasn't an unusual apparatus for the beings here. It actually seemed like an old-fashioned tech compared to what they used in Mission Command.

"Hi Monty." Eliza continued staring at all the new sights.

Bebop asked, "Is everyone assembled, Monty?"

"Sure are, sir. They're in the briefing area waiting for you, Captain."

"Thank you. Eliza, let's go." Bebop walked away.

Eliza lingered and eventually tore herself away from the wondrous sights around her, then rushed to follow Bebop as he sauntered through the hustle and bustle, with creatures scattering out of his way, often saying, "Pardon me, Captain" or similar acknowledgment. Bebop and Eliza entered an alcove on an outside wall of the cavern. It opened up into a medium-large space surrounded by rock walls and lit by the same orbs as the area off the elevator.

"Hello, Eliza," welcomed a number of voices, almost in unison. Eliza recognized a sparrow, rabbit, tarantula, and gazelle from yesterday's introductions.

With Eliza in tow, Bebop walked to a large rock in front of the gathering, then called the meeting to order and introduced Eliza.

He looked at her and whispered to her to say something. Flustered at being put on the spot without warning, she looked at the assemblage and said nervously, "Hello all. I'm happy to be starting on the mission today and working with you."

Many in the gathering smiled back, and some applauded or cheered.

Bebop took it from there. "OK, let's get straight to business. We have much to do and the sooner we get going, the faster we'll see results. Eliza, you're here to bridge between the gap with humans. We in the natural world agree we must all work together to try to combat climate change. Unfortunately, humans aren't pulling their weight. While there are many groups making progress, it seems the majority of individual humans are indifferent to the dire situation we face, don't understand it, or aren't motivated to make the changes needed to make a difference. Mission Command is doing all we can to combat global warming ourselves, but we must send the message to humans to join the fight en masse. You provide the missing link to get humans to notice and then make changes. We'll start by filling you in on what we've developed."

"Sounds good, Bebop." Bebop cringed and he subtly shook his head 'no' when Eliza called him Bebop. "I mean, Captain," corrected Eliza. Obviously important to Bebop that his authority not be undermined, Eliza reminded herself to treat him with the respect he deserved as a ranked authority in NoHoSap.

Bebop continued, "For starters today, the commanders of the two sub-missions we've developed will present the nuts and bolts of each." Bebop stepped away from the rock podium.

A small grey furry creature appeared, shuffling toward the front on webbed feet with long toes. It appeared to have trouble seeing because it kept bumping into the wall and attendees along the way.

Eliza asked Bebop under her breath, "What is that?"

"That's Cuthbert the mole."

"Oohh. I always wondered what they looked like," replied Eliza under her breath as Cuthbert climbed up onto the rock.

Standing near the center of the rock, Cuthbert faced the audience and cleared his throat. He appeared apprehensive, but eventually spoke softly and with a slight lisp. "The first sub-mission focuses on what we can do directly to help thwart global warming. Eliza will take pictures and post stories to show humans what we animals are doing on our own. We'll first focus on planting trees, which are important in the climate fight because they remove carbon dioxide from the air. Next, we'll restore coral reefs and repair the negative impacts of climate change on these critical ecosystems. We've already done this work in remote areas but would do the projects for human consumption in spots that are accessible and enable them to see our work."

"I like it," declared Eliza enthusiastically. After hearing details of her role in the mission, she became even more excited to be involved.

"Thanks, Cuthbert. Good work," added Bebop.

The team members clapped as Cuthbert sidled down and away from the rock podium.

Bebop introduced the next speaker. "Tabitha will fill us in on the second sub-mission."

A fluffy tan and white striped cat made her way to the podium, taking her time as cats do. While she sashayed along, a mouse with a headset ran up to Bebop, who leaned down to hear the small voice. Just as Tabitha spoke, Bebop exclaimed, "Very sorry to interrupt, but we have a situation that needs our attention right away. We'll reconvene tomorrow to hear from Tabitha. Tabitha, sorry to postpone, but please come with us. We can use your help."

Tabitha shot a perturbed stare Bebop's way, then shrugged it off and moseyed over to him.

"Eliza, Stets, Laurel, and Redeye, come with me and Tabitha," commanded Bebop as he hustled out of the room, through the main concourse, and toward the elevator.

Eliza grabbed her backpack and followed the others. They all hurried into the elevator. Once inside, Bebop said, "Don't be shy. Introductions to Eliza everybody."

He turned to Eliza and continued, "You already know who Tabitha is since I so rudely pre-empted her presentation."

Tabitha reacted with typical cat nonchalance, "Apology accepted." She then commenced grooming herself, ignoring the others in the elevator.

One of the other team members, a white-tailed deer, said, "Hello, Eliza, I'm Laurel. I've seen you walking in the cemetery and think you may have found an antler from my brother."

Embarrassed, Eliza offered, "Oh yes, that was a beautiful antler and I have it displayed at home—I can return it."

"Not a problem," replied Laurel. "Once they fall off, we have no further use for them."

"Phew, thanks. Nice to meet you, Laurel."

"My name is Stets," said the horse, who barely fit in the elevator.

"I'm Redeye," added a gray rat who fussed nervously in the corner of the confined space.

"Happy to meet you, Stets and Redeye," greeted Eliza.

The elevator stopped its ascent and the door opened. Bebop led the way out and all followed.

As he walked, Bebop explained, "We received an emergency call from one of our local team, a sparrow named Fidget. Seeking shelter from the storm that's currently raging outside, Fidget settled under the eaves of a house near the stream that flows alongside the cemetery. Fidget noticed a cat running frantically back and forth inside the sliding glass door, and he flew down to check it out."

Now at the tunnel, the group members rushed in and headed out toward the mausoleum door. The ground underfoot had turned to muck from the deluge of rain.

Bebop continued as they trudged on, "The cat yelled to Fidget through the glass, and Fidget eventually understood the cat's owner was sound asleep with her infant in a bedroom. The cat also desperately alerted Fidget to the rising stream behind the house. Both knew the home's inhabitants would be trapped in a flooding building unless they could get out. That's when Fidget radioed Mission Command."

Now out the mausoleum door, rain poured down on the team and the wind howled. Eliza donned the raincoat from her backpack, feeling awkward because none of the others had any protection from the elements.

Bebop told Tabitha and Redeye to jump into Eliza's backpack and instructed Eliza to hop onto Stets' back. Bebop then sprinted away, with Stets and Laurel following. Eliza hung on for dear life, jostled every which way as she gripped Stets' mane and hugged his neck. She'd ridden a horse only a few times before, but never without a saddle like this or at any pace close to the speed at which Stets ran. Redeye and Tabitha closed their eyes and buried their heads in Eliza's bag, also being thrown about since Eliza couldn't hold it steady while trying to survive atop Stets.

Raindrops blowing sideways pelted Eliza's face, stinging with each hit. The sounds of rain hitting the ground filled the air, along with trees creaking and billowing from the massive wind. Deafening claps of thunder at random intervals added to the discord, accompanied by brilliant lightning strikes making jagged patterns in the sky.

The team followed the gully through the forest, then turned onto a road, devoid of travelers due to the weather. Stets, Laurel, and Bebop ran faster on the solid footing. Knocked around even more with the increased speed, Eliza stifled the motion sickness in her belly. Distracting herself, she imagined what would have happened if she brought Bebop's raincoat and tried to put it on him. She used to make him wear it if they went out in the rain. She hadn't had the heart to dispose of any of his "stuff" after he passed away. It had been difficult enough to box it up and put it in the attic. She laughed, picturing him in a raincoat, and realized he would have been mortified if she pulled that out of her bag for him. Seeing him now, he obviously never needed protection from the rain.

They ran down a driveway to a house with a stream raging through the backyard, creeping closer to the structure. Eliza jumped off Stets and pulled her boots on while Tabitha and Redeye scrambled out of her backpack. A sparrow, who Eliza assumed to be Fidget, flew to Bebop as he ran toward the house, then excitedly motioned toward a glass door. Eliza saw a cat hysterically running and jumping on the other side of the glass. Behind the house, a pair of beavers cut down trees in the yard. Bebop shouted to Stets and Laurel, "Work with the beavers and build a dam to protect the house as much as possible."

Tabitha ran over to the sliding glass door. The cat inside the house became more frantic by the minute. Tabitha told him to calm him down and assist the team get into the house.

Eliza ran around the structure checking for a way in and advised Bebop all potential entry points were locked. He yelled for Laurel, then commanded, "Stay back everyone! Laurel, kick through the door to let us in there. Tabitha, tell the cat inside to take cover."

Laurel lined up with the sliding glass door behind her, raised up on her front legs, and kicked her hind legs with all her might into the door. It cracked but didn't break. "Again," ordered Bebop. On the third kick, the door shattered. Bebop shouted, "Eliza, get that mother and her baby out of there! Tabitha and Redeye, make sure the cat gets out and leaves with his family."

Eliza ran into the house and found the infant's room. Even with the raging storm and crashes of thunder, the mother sat in an armchair sound asleep. Wide awake, her baby daughter enjoyed the ruckus and giggled in her crib.

Eliza hollered to the mother, "Wake up!" No response other than a snore and the mother changed position. She shouted, "Hello, this is an emergency. You need to wake up!" She finally shook the woman since yelling didn't work.

The mother stirred and opened very sleepy eyes. She bolted awake when she saw Eliza, and immediately ran and swept her baby up in her arms.

"Who are you and what are you doing in my house?"

Eliza answered impatiently, "I'm Eliza. The stream outside is about to flood your house, and you and your baby need to leave right now!"

A loud thunderclap shook the house, emphasizing Eliza's warning. The woman ran to the back, looked out and saw the torrential storm and rising waters.

She screamed, "We need to get out of here. I had no idea. I was exhausted after getting Sophie to sleep and I passed out. Thank you for getting me up and rescuing us! I'm Maria."

"Hi, Maria. Let's get out of here! Get your car keys. The driveway is still above water and the roads should be clear going out of here."

They rushed out the front door.

"Do you have someplace you can go?" Eliza asked as they ran through the downpour to Maria's car.

"We'll go to my mom's house. She's not far away and lives on higher ground. Shoot, I need to get our overnight bag."

"There's no time for you to go back to the house. It's too dangerous."

"You're right, but where's Fisher, our cat? We can't leave him." As Maria said his name, Tabitha and Redeye dragged a terrified and soaking Fisher around the corner of the house and released him. He ran top speed to Maria.

Eliza heard guzzling water rushing and shouted, "Get in the car and go, here comes the stream!" Wind blew them from every direction, rain streamed down Eliza's face as Maria strapped Sophie into her carseat.

Standing up after hooking Sophie in, Maria asked, "Are you coming with us?" As she spoke, Eliza noticed her eyes moving past Eliza and widening with surprise and confusion. Eliza turned and saw what Maria did–the beavers, Stets and Laurel stacking downed trees in a makeshift levee.

"What in the sam-hill?" questioned Maria as she watched them.

Eliza interrupted and turned Maria back, toward the car. "Let's get you out of here."

Bebop ran out from the back of the house, ready to bark an order. He stopped upon seeing Maria and gave Eliza a look as if asking, 'Why are they still here?'

Maria motioned for Eliza to hop in the car. "Thanks, but I don't need a ride. My car's parked up the road."

The log dam tilted from the weight of the floodwaters. "Get going!" Eliza shouted.

Maria gave Eliza a big hug and thanked her profusely. "You saved us–I can't thank you enough. How can I get in touch to give you a proper thank you?"

"No worries. I'm happy to have helped." Although outwardly modest, Eliza patted herself on the back inwardly. Stoked this unexpected outing turned out well, she hoped it signaled good things ahead for the mission.

Maria hopped behind the wheel and sped up the driveway to safety. As soon as the car went out of view, the dam fell over with a loud crash, sending logs floating over the yard and down the stream. The beavers scurried to a hillock in front of the house, and Laurel and Stets ran over to Bebop. Tabitha and Redeye rushed to Eliza and hopped into her backpack. Stets sidled next to Eliza and she jumped on while Bebop ran past everyone, heading back the way they came.

The return trip to the mausoleum door seemed much shorter than the excursion out. Eliza shivered from the incessant wind, not to mention the breeze from the speed Stets ran. She didn't want to complain about being wet and cold since she was the only one on the team who had any protection from the elements. The others were totally exposed to the harsh weather, and they didn't seem to mind.

The mausoleum door opened, as Bebop arrived in front of it. Eliza disembarked from Stets, the rescuers entered, and sloshed through the tunnel, now housing a small stream underfoot.

Upon arriving in NoHoSap they hurried to the elevator and descended to Mission Command. When the elevator door opened, a crowd of creatures cheered in greeting. Eliza heard voices say, 'way to go,' 'you did it,' 'great job,' along with other forms of congratulations.

Bebop shook himself off before jumping onto a rock to happily acknowledge the throng, "Thank you. This was our first test, and we got the job done! It was a team effort and proves that if we work together, our new partnership will be successful. Many thanks to those in the field monitoring for danger and working to avert it, those at the controls relaying messages and tracking our progress, and those who provided all the support for this unexpected operation."

The crowd hollered.

"This trial shows we can do it! It's the perfect kickoff to our critical climate mission. Eliza, thanks for being the bridge to the humans. Without that we likely wouldn't have had such a positive result." Bebop gave Eliza an enthusiastic high five.

More cheers. Psyched up by Bebop's motivating words, the audience chanted, "We can do this! We can do this!"

"Yes, we can!" encouraged Bebop. "We can, no, we will, win this climate fight! Keep up the impressive work and stay confident all!" Eventually, the crowd quieted. "OK everyone, be safe tonight with this storm. Tomorrow we'll continue where we left off today and hear about the second sub-mission."

Bebop hopped off the rock, shook again, and walked over to his soaking wet comrades. Tabitha and Redeye hadn't yet left the cover of Eliza's backpack.

"Tremendous work, team! We did a good thing today," lauded Bebop.

He noticed Eliza shivering, her hair dripping with water, her lips blue. "Eliza, I forget humans are so vulnerable. You have no built-in protection from the elements. Let's get you warmed up." Bebop motioned to a raccoon, who ambled over.

"Jacee, take Eliza to the warming cave."

Tabitha and Redeye exited her backpack and Eliza followed the raccoon to the side of the main room, where the crowd congregated. They went along the wall, through a low door, and into a dark area. Trying to discern the environs, she heard a 'poof', smelled smoke, and the room brightened. She looked behind and discovered a fledgling fire in a depression in the middle of the floor. Jacee threw what looked like a burnt match into it.

"This should warm you up once it gets going," said Jacee in a comforting tone. He shuffled over to the side of the small cavern and took what appeared to be a blanket off a shelf in the wall, carried it back, and gave it to Eliza.

"Thanks! I really need this blanket right about now, Jacee."

"You're welcome." He headed to another part of the room. Eliza couldn't see him well but heard him dragging something over toward the fire. "Here's something for your wet clothes."

Jacee dropped an object near her, and Eliza realized it was a folded-up drying rack. She set it up near the fire.

"I'll be back." Jacee left the cave.

Eliza removed her wet clothes, wrapped herself in the blanket, then hung the clothes on the rack. Jacee reappeared, walking on his hind legs while carrying a covered wooden bowl with both front hands.

He handed it to Eliza and steam wafted out when she lifted the top. Closing her eyes while breathing it in, she smiled. "Mmmm, this smells delicious."

"That's Chef Cecil's special vegetable medley soup. Oops, I forgot a spoon. It wasn't even on my mind since we don't use them." Jacee ran toward the entrance but stopped and backed up as Bebop walked through the opening, holding a wooden spoon in his mouth.

"Heeere ya go," Bebop garbled as he tried to speak with the impeding spoon.

"Thanks, Bebop." Eliza took the utensil. "I can't wait to dig into this." She lifted a spoonful out of the bowl to engulf it but paused, realizing her impoliteness. "I'm sorry, would either of you like some?"

Both indicated no, and Eliza downed the spoon's contents. "Yum, Chef Cecil has skills!" The soup fell victim in no time to Eliza's hunger. Jacee scrambled away with the spoon and empty bowl.

Bebop planned for the next day, but Eliza interrupted him. "Sorry, Bebop, but before we start talking about tomorrow, I have a question about today."

"OK, what?"

"I've been wondering, why were you alerted to Maria's predicament and why did we help her and Sophie? I've never heard of animals rescuing humans in other dangerous situations."

"Fair question. You're right, we generally don't make it our business to help humans. We took this on today for two reasons. First, there's a longstanding beaver dam in the stream not far from Maria's house and she owns the land around the dam. That dam is critical for sustaining the ecosystem that has developed in the area and the life that depends on it. The people who owned the property before Maria made it their mission to preserve the habitats on the property, even under intense pressure from their neighbors and others to demolish the dam and kill the beavers. Maria and her husband bought the property about five years ago and had the same appreciation for the place, which is one of the reasons the prior owners sold to them. Second, a few years ago a gas pipeline was proposed under Maria's part of the stream, and Maria was one of the most vocal and involved opponents. She knew the project would forever alter a huge stretch of the stream, causing much of the life in and along it to be forced out or perish. She organized a group against the project and ultimately succeeded in blocking the line. We feel in her debt since she fought for us, and thought it appropriate to return the favor by our actions today."

"Wow, now I get it," said Eliza, surprised to hear of the animals' empathy, much less toward a human.

Bebop went back to planning. "Eliza, can you be here tomorrow at about the same time? We need to finish filling you in on the second sub-mission and start planning specifically how we're going to accomplish both."

"Yes, I'll be here then." She and Bebop hung out by the fire until Eliza's clothes dried. Bebop escorted her back to the tunnel, Eliza gave him a farewell high five, and went back out to HuHabDom, feeling enlightened and encouraged by all she'd seen today.

CHAPTER 8

THE RESCUER

As usual, the alarm rudely interrupted Eliza's deep sleep. Once awake, she wondered whether the previous day's events actually happened or were a dream. She turned the TV on to catch her station's news and realized she didn't imagine yesterday's adventures. The strong storms from the prior evening were the talk of the newscast, and footage documenting the damage streamed across the screen. Many had no power, trees were down everywhere, and the National Weather Service confirmed a microburst hit parts of the area. A flood watch remained in effect from the massive amount of rain.

Eliza shuffled into the bathroom to wash up, while listening to the news. Hearing a familiar voice she couldn't place; she went back into the bedroom to see the TV. To her surprise, Maria stood in front of her house being interviewed by Gary, a reporter from the station. The camera panned to the backyard, where the stream had receded after flooding the house. Holding Sophie, Maria told Gary about the good Samaritan who rescued them right before the water came into the house. Eliza hoped Maria hadn't recognized her. To her relief, Gary closed the story thanking the mystery person who averted tragedy for this mother and her infant, but with no further discussion about the rescuer.

Eliza realized she needed to prepare herself for the publicity the story would elicit. She knew people would want to identify the good

Samaritan, and it would likely be only a matter of time before her name would be revealed. Thinking about her rescuer quandary on the way to work, Eliza decided she'd tell Gary she rescued Maria and Sophie. It would come out anyway, and if she didn't mention it now, it would seem strange later when he found out. When she arrived at the station, she checked the reporter sign-out board, which showed Gary on location. She thought about going back to her car and driving to the scene, but had work to do, and decided to stay put.

Once settled at her desk, Eliza pulled up the company directory and found Gary's cell phone number. His voice mail answered immediately, and she asked him to call her back, saying she had some information related to this morning's story. She considered consulting with Bebop about it, and how coming forward as the rescuer may affect the mission. It wouldn't be a bad thing to have that conversation, but she had no way of reaching him and couldn't afford to take the time right then to go to NoHoSap. As a result, she stayed in the office and researched her next story—the pros and cons of banning styrofoam containers.

Eliza's cell phone rang, interrupting her deep concentration and identifying the caller as Gary.

"Hey Gary, thanks for returning my call."

"Hi Eliza, thanks for reaching out about this story. What information do you have?"

Thankful he didn't say Maria told him the name of the person who rescued her was Eliza, she replied, "I enjoyed seeing your coverage this morning." Pausing briefly, she continued, "Funny thing, I'm the person who got Maria and Sophie out of the house."

"What? Are you kidding me? This is great! We've been trying to figure out who did it, but Maria only mentioned a name and brief description. I never put together that it could be you. Can you come down here and be on air for the noon broadcast?"

Eliza hesitated. "I've got a lot to get done here today."

"Wait, you know better than anyone the importance of getting information out there fast. If you don't do it now, someone else may figure it out if they talk with Maria. We can't get scooped on this story. I know you're busy, but we really need you to do this. It's for the station anyway and I'm sure the higher-ups will understand if your work is delayed because you're involved in this breaking news. C'mon, Eliza," he pleaded.

Eliza knew he was right, and weighed the impacts of delaying her research and, therefore, her story, with the consequences if she didn't go on air today with Gary.

"You're right, Gary. OK, I'll be there for the noon news follow-up."

"Excellent, thank you!"

Eliza immediately hoped she didn't regret this, and Bebop wouldn't be angry. Realistically, though, it didn't make logical sense not to reveal herself and risk someone else blowing her cover.

Eliza made good headway on her story before heading to Maria's house. When she arrived, Maria and some other folks were in the backyard, surveying the damage. Logs from the beavers' makeshift dam were strewn haphazardly around the lawn, the grass covered in mud from being submerged under the floodwaters.

Maria spotted Eliza, ran over, and gave her a big hug. "Here she is," Maria announced excitedly. "Here's the woman who saved us."

A man Eliza didn't know came over and hugged her too. "Thank you, thank you for saving my wife and daughter," he gushed while Eliza blushed.

"This is my husband, Dante," informed Maria. "He was out of town for work but came home last night after I called and told him what happened."

"I couldn't believe it," said Dante. "I hate to think what might have happened if you hadn't gotten them out of here," he continued, with tears in his eyes.

Eliza downplayed her role, "I'm just happy I was here in the right place at the right time and could help." Dante excused himself when someone from the yard called for him.

Maria turned to Eliza and confided, "I called the station last night to let them know how you saved us. I thought others should know there's still kindness in the world."

"I saw you on the early news this morning and wondered how they found out about it."

"This is the station I always watch, and Gary said you're a reporter there too. I'm surprised I haven't seen you on air."

"I make it on air occasionally. Most of my time is spent researching and writing stories with legal aspects."

Gary came over with the cameraperson. "Hi Eliza, thanks again for coming. When we go live on the air, I'll announce that we have an update, have found the good Samaritan and it's our own Eliza Vernon. Maria, I'll then ask Eliza to tell us how she found you and got you out of the house. If you could stand here with Sophie and thank Eliza, that'll do it for this segment."

"That sounds good," Maria noted. Gary walked away while discussing technical aspects with the cameraperson. "Eliza, thank you again from the bottom of my heart for saving us yesterday. I want to let everyone know what you did for us."

"No need to do that. I'm very glad you and Sophie are safe. At least the waters have receded. Is the house badly damaged?"

Dante joined them and advised, "Well, our insurance agent said it doesn't look like a total loss, but the water did a job on the inside when it flooded everything. It's going to take a while to clean it out. The only thing that matters, though, is our family is all here and together." He put his arm around Maria and kissed the top of her head.

"Sophie's sound asleep in her carrier on the front porch table, with Fisher by her side, as always," said Maria, motioning for Eliza to follow her to the porch and take a look.

When Eliza peeked over the carrier, Fisher opened his eyes and lifted his head. He seemed to recognize her, and when he knew she meant no harm to him or Sophie, laid his head back on the table and fell asleep.

"If that isn't the picture of peacefulness, I don't know what is," observed Eliza.

Maria lifted Sophie out of the carrier and prepared for the shoot while Dante showed Eliza the house interior. Furnishings and personal belongings were scattered everywhere and the same mud that covered the grass in the lawn coated everything in the house. The water line on the walls rose over a foot above the floors. As if that weren't enough, the place reeked of stagnant water with a hint of mildew.

Surprised at the amount of damage from such a relatively short-lived flood, Eliza said, "Wow, I'm sorry this happened to your home."

"Who would have thought. The prior owners lived here for over thirty years. When we bought the place, they said the stream never came close to the house, but sometimes flooded the bank a little if there were days of rain on end. We didn't get flood insurance because the flood search didn't show it as being in a flood zone. Like I said before, though, we're lucky Maria and Sophie weren't hurt or worse. All this can be fixed or replaced."

"That's true; you have the right perspective."

Gary yelled, "Places everyone, we're going live in five."

Maria, Sophie, and Eliza gathered next to Gary and in front of the camera. The cameraperson held her arm up and counted down on her fingers to indicate when they were live.

Gary listened intently in his earpiece for the anchor to greet him, then looked directly into the camera and said, "Thanks, Don. Yes, we found the rescuer and it's none other than our own Eliza Vernon. Folks, you may recognize Eliza from our newscasts. She's our legal eagle. This time she's the good Samaritan who saved Maria and baby Sophie from their flooding house."

He turned to Eliza. "Eliza, how did you happen to find them?"

"Gary, I was walking my dog along the stream when the storm hit. I noticed the stream rising swiftly as we headed toward the car. We came upon Maria's house, and I saw a cat running frantically back and forth inside the sliding glass door. Since it seemed odd, I went up to the house, looked in the windows, and discovered Maria asleep in a chair next to Sophie's crib. She didn't wake up when I banged on the window and yelled. No doors or windows were open, and the water kept getting closer. I ended up breaking the door to get in because it was clear the stream would flood the house. Once in, I woke Maria up, and we hightailed it out to safety."

"Good thing you happened on it. Maria, what did you think when you woke up?"

"I didn't know what was going on. I'm a new mom and must have crashed after getting Sophie to sleep. I'm extremely thankful Eliza stopped in the pouring rain to check if anyone was in the house and then get us out of there. She's a lifesaver."

Gary broke in after receiving a signal to wrap up, "Tragedy averted thanks to our good Samaritan. This is one bright spot in yesterday's wild weather. Back to you in the studio, Don." He turned the microphone off. "That's a wrap. Maria, thank you for calling the station to let us know about your rescue yesterday. Eliza, thanks for identifying yourself and coming down here. I'll let you know if we do a follow-up."

Gary and the cameraperson headed back to the station van to find the next breaking news.

Dante came over. "We can't thank you enough, Eliza."

"We owe you everything and are forever grateful to you," added Maria, before giving Eliza another hug.

Eliza wished she could give credit to Bebop, Stets, Laurel, Tabitha, and Redeye because without them there wouldn't have been a rescue. Since that wasn't an option, she graciously said, "I'm honored to have been able to help. Good luck with the cleanup and hopefully you'll be back in the house in no time."

She walked back to her car thinking she did the right thing to appear in the story after all.

CHAPTER 9

PHILOSOPHICAL DIFFERENCES

Only her second day on the mission and the new routine seemed normal for Eliza by the time she arrived at the NoHoSap door at the end of her station workday. Even though it hadn't rained at all the entire day, the ground remained wet from yesterday's storm. Light filtered through the leaves of the gully's trees as the sun slowly began its descent. Monty met Eliza inside the mausoleum door and greeted, "Hello, stranger. Seems like you had another busy day."

"Hi Monty. No busier than usual." Thinking it strange he'd mention her day, she asked suspiciously, "Monty, why did you say that? How did you know what I did today?"

"Oh, no reason," he replied nervously as he flitted around more than he generally did, dodging Eliza's glance.

"Did you have eyes on me today, Monty?"

"I don't know what you mean. I've been here all day. Never made it outside our sanctuary."

"OK, just wondering." Eliza paused. "What did you think of Sophie and Fisher?"

"Oh, they're just precious. That cat takes such good care… of… her." Monty slowed as he realized Eliza set him up, and he fell for it hook, line, and sinker. "That's not fair, Eliza. I don't want to get into trouble."

"What do you mean, how are you going to get into trouble? I would have told you what I did today and don't mind you following me if you have to, but I do mind you lying to me."

"Drats, now you're mad at me, and soon the Captain will be too."

"What does Bebop, I mean the Captain, have to do with any of this? Did he tell you to watch me?"

"I already said too much. Please forget you heard anything from me."

They arrived at the end of the tunnel, where Bebop waited. Monty flew off when he saw the Captain.

Bebop sternly told Eliza to follow him. He led her to a secluded spot at the edge of the forest. Eliza didn't see or hear any other animals around.

"What's up, Bebop?"

Bebop gave her a chilling look and stayed silent for what seemed like an eternity. He took a deep breath to collect and calm himself before speaking. "You went to the media without a plan and without consulting us. Now you're out there for all to see."

"Wait a second. You never mentioned anything about keeping this a secret. Cuthbert even said yesterday that his sub-mission involved me getting the word out on what we're doing. I felt I had no choice after Maria told the station about the rescue. I had no way to contact you to discuss what to do after seeing the story on the news and decided it would be better to come clean than putting everyone on a hunt to find the good Samaritan. It would have been much worse if I didn't say anything and was later discovered to have been the rescuer. Plus, I didn't mention you or anyone else on the team." Starkly aware of how the tables had turned from her calling the shots with Bebop when he was her pet to now having to answer to him, Eliza stifled the urge to put Bebop in his place.

"It would have been much worse for you if you said nothing, but now it's much worse for us that you did."

"How do you figure that? I don't see how this impacts you at all or is any different from what Cuthbert said yesterday I'm supposed to be doing."

"That's the problem. You don't see how it impacts us. Now that you're out there you may be watched, and we can't have humans following you here to the NoHoSap door or beyond, or otherwise investigating you and happening upon our activities. Also, Cuthbert's plan is different in a critical way from what you did, since we'd control the content of the posts showing our activities."

"Oh." Eliza now understood Bebop's anger.

"We planned to embark on a plan for getting the word out to humans on our own terms and with our own message."

"I see." Eliza peered down, embarrassed to have made a mistake, especially this early in the mission.

"We'll talk about that more with the team today. In the meantime, and to avoid you not being able to communicate with us at any time when you're not here, we've assigned someone to be your detail. That way we can always be in touch."

"OK," acknowledged Eliza sheepishly.

"Noli, we're ready for you."

An angular stink bug flew by Eliza's face and landed on Bebop's head. Insects like this used to appear in Eliza's office fairly frequently and she always brought them outside, wondering how they ended up indoors in the first place. After the third one appeared, she did some research and discovered they were stink bugs.

"Here I am, Captain," advised the bug.

"Noli, this is Eliza," introduced Bebop. "Eliza, meet Magnolia, or Noli for short."

"Nice to meet you, Noli." Eliza looked at her, puzzled, and asked, "Did I rescue you from my office and bring you outside?"

"Actually, you did that more than once," joked Noli.

"What? You mean it was you each time—you kept showing up in my office even after I let you out?"

"That I did. Just following the Captain's orders to keep tabs on you."

"I see." Eliza turned to Bebop and said in an accusatory tone, "You've already been following me. Why make it sound like this is a new thing because I talked to the press without your approval?"

Bebop explained, "We asked Noli to check in on you before we approached you for the mission. We needed to see where your head was and whether you were at the point where you'd consider helping us. Now we need to be sure we can be in touch with you and vice versa. Noli will be our contact point."

He looked up even though he couldn't see Noli on his head. "Noli, you're all set, take a break and Eliza will see you tomorrow."

"OK, thanks, Captain. See you in the morning, Eliza."

"See you later, Noli." Noli flew away.

Back to business, Bebop advised, "We have a lot to do since we weren't able to finish yesterday's briefing." He turned and loped away.

In the elevator to Mission Command, they said little to each other as they cooled down from the heated discussion about publicity. After exiting the elevator, they walked through the bustle of animals going about their work to save the planet. Many looked up and greeted Bebop and Eliza, while others said "good job" and "nice work" from yesterday's success.

They entered the large space where Cuthbert gave his presentation. Tabitha sat near the podium, looking perturbed, because she had to wait to give her presentation until everyone filed in. Bebop called the group to order and said, "After our unexpected interruption yesterday, Tabitha will now fill us in on the second sub-mission."

Tabitha jumped onto the rock podium and explained that this sub-mission focused on domestic animals and how they could influence humans to make changes to help thwart global warming. She said Eliza's part in this sub-mission would be to convince humans they weren't crazy or imagining things if it seemed their pets were trying to get them to use more climate-friendly practices. At the same time, NoHoSap agents would train pets and other domestic animals on what their owners should be doing and how to communicate those messages to humans.

"Very interesting," noted Eliza. "What's the plan for implementing this and Cuthbert's sub-mission?"

"Funny you should ask. That's the next item to discuss. Flutter, you're up."

A large monarch butterfly flew to and fro and alighted on the rock. "They selected me for scheduling because they figured a creature like me may be better at organizing time, what with our metamorphosis and migration schedules and all. We've analyzed the various ways to set up projects for the sub-missions and feel we'll maximize the impact if we schedule for each sub-mission in bunches rather than alternating. We'll start by scheduling a few days of tree planting in the general area around NoHoSap. That way we won't have travel time to delay actions and Eliza will be posting things from the region where she lives. We'll then have a day in New York City where we hope to meet many people and pets in a short amount of time. Next will be a few days of reef restoration and then a few more days on the pet sub-mission in another urban area. As we add more projects, we'll schedule accordingly, but this is the general idea."

"Thanks, Flutter," said Bebop. "We'll select the team members, locations and times today for the first round of tree planting. Thanks all for attending." The listeners disbursed while discussing the projects amongst themselves. "Eliza, let's head to mission planning."

Bebop led Eliza to a smaller room off the edge of the large space. Luminescent rods hanging from the ceiling at random heights lit the room, which had a video screen affixed to the wall at the far end and an oversize touchscreen board laying horizontally below. Bebop went over to the board and hit it a few times with his paw. Eliza watched in amazement. The screen filled with an assortment of small pictures of different animals. Bebop continued hitting the board, selecting traits to sort the pictures, and they were reduced to a more manageable number, which also increased the picture size to better see each creature.

"That's better. Now to further narrow it down, let's see who's in the neighborhood."

His paw touched the screen a few more times, resulting in 12 pictures displayed–four rows with three columns each. Shaking off her disbelief at the process and particularly the equipment, Eliza focused on the screen and noticed many of those pictured were diggers, including a woodchuck, gopher, armadillo, and even a couple of dogs. The selections also included an ox and a mule. "All of them are near here now?" Eliza asked.

"Not yet, but they're on the way. Cuthbert will lead this part of the mission. He's quite the digger himself."

"That's an understatement, Captain." Cuthbert said as he entered the room.

"Cuthbert, what locations have you identified for our first round of tree planting?" asked Bebop.

"I have a few, Captain, and would like your and Eliza's help narrowing them down. We want places where our work will be noticeable, but where having a crew won't draw attention. No humans should see us while planting, enabling Eliza to take and post pictures in a controlled and deliberate manner," explained Cuthbert.

"Exactly," agreed Bebop while giving Eliza an 'I told you so' look.

Cuthbert shuffled over to the touch board and, not seeing very well, asked Bebop to open the mapping application. Bebop maneuvered his paw on the board and a local map appeared. Cuthbert instructed him to add a specific overlay, which highlighted ten locations.

"OK, here's a mix of potential project spots, ranging from parks, streets, hillsides, and even in the cemetery where trees have toppled," informed Cuthbert.

"I have a question," said Eliza. "How will we not be noticed while we plant trees in a park or on a street?"

Cuthbert replied, "Thought you may ask that. These spots are in remote areas with few visitors and the street locations are not busy thoroughfares. Also, we'll be there during times that are documented to be the slowest, and we've prepared signs to reroute humans while we're there. I must say I'm impressed by the work of our sign team."

"That is until a light shines on them and you see where fluorescent paint hit the team members and not the signs," added Bebop in jest.

"Wish I could see that level of detail," mused Cuthbert.

"I'm sorry, Cuthbert, you're so observant about everything that I forget moles don't see well."

"That's OK, Captain, I'm used to it. We couldn't accomplish nearly as much or as successfully if we all had the same abilities. Thank goodness we're all differently abled in some way–I call it diffabled. Back to the matter at hand. For this project, it would be best to work either early in the morning or later in the day. Since we don't know how long we'll need, I think later would be better and we can work longer without incident. We should be able to simultaneously cover two locations each day, assuming the team you selected is large enough for that."

"I chose twelve for this team, which is enough to work at two locations. Let's start with the two that are closest together." Bebop tapped two spots on the map and more information about each popped up. He then split the screen with the screen of selected animals and dragged their photos to the location to which he assigned them."

Cuthbert turned toward Eliza and instructed, "Eliza, you'll cover both locations, take pictures at each, and bring them back here where we'll discuss what, when, and where to post."

"You want me to publicize these organized events on my blog, Facebook, Instagram, Twitter, and other social media feeds?"

"Yes," answered Cuthbert. "We could take pictures and make posts ourselves, but we're not as hung up on the details that result in good pictures as humans are and figure the quality will be much better if you do it. Also, you can add comments that are more relevant to people than what we may say."

"I'm not the best photographer, but I have an appreciation of angles, vantage points, lighting, and a few other things that will probably help."

Bebop observed, "We have some here in NoHoSap with photography experience, mainly for surveillance purposes, but we're not obsessed with taking and posting pictures like humans are. It seems to be second nature for people. Honestly, we have more productive things to do with our time."

"Well," replied Eliza, "please exclude me from that generalization about humans being obsessed with taking pictures of themselves. That's a pet peeve of mine too–I just don't get it."

"What's a peeve?" asked a flummoxed Cuthbert. "I've never heard of that type of animal, although I thought I had a good knowledge of what things humans made pets of."

Bebop looked at Eliza and shook his head, indicating Eliza shouldn't make a big deal of Cuthbert's lack of understanding.

"Sorry, Cuthbert, a peeve isn't a pet, but a pet peeve is a human saying about something that annoys you," Bebop explained.

"Oh, that's good to know. Much to learn about humans."

"You're not concerned that once people see these posts, they'll discover your elaborate world here and your capabilities?" inquired Eliza.

Cuthbert acknowledged, "That's a risk, but we feel it's a very slight one. We actually thought the larger risk would be to you and your reputation, because folks may think you changed the photos or are crazy."

Eliza thought about Cuthbert's observation. "You're right, Cuthbert, the risk is really mine. I'll have to be especially careful with the pictures and content of those posts."

"What's the timing for the first project, Cuthbert?" asked Bebop.

"Tomorrow, Sir, 5:30 p.m. We'll mobilize from here before then and will be on location with trees and tools by 5:30. We'll follow the same plan for three days, which will cover six locations."

"Sounds good. I'll let the team members know. Eliza, you're welcome to meet us here and go out to the sites with the team or meet us there. You can let Noli know on each day depending on your workload."

"Will do. Thanks, Cuthbert, for scheduling at a time that fits my work calendar."

"It's convenient the lower traffic times happen to be when you're available. Good night, all."

As Cuthbert exited, a bat flitted in. "Sonar, to what do we owe the honor?" asked Bebop.

"I heard about the rescue yesterday and wanted to congratulate you on a job well done," commended Sonar as he alighted on top of the video monitor. "Have to admit, I had my doubts about combining forces with humans, but for the sake of the world, I hope you continue to prove me wrong. The Alliance members like what they're seeing." Sonar swooped out of the room as quickly as he entered, leaving no time for Bebop or Eliza to react.

"Typical Sonar—to the point and out," observed Bebop.

"Nice to hear a vote of confidence," Eliza said. "We start with the tree project tomorrow. Do you have a schedule for the remaining tree plantings and other upcoming projects? Also, what should I do to prepare for everything?"

"Noli will give you the schedule tomorrow for the next week to enable you to calendar the project times and let the station know when you'll be absent. Be thinking of ideas for posting information on the sub-missions and talking with pet people about how they can help the planet."

"Got it. Anything else for today?"

"Actually, yes, Chef Cecil appreciated the good things you said about his cooking yesterday and invited you to the kitchen for dinner tonight."

"Really? I'd love to. I'm getting hungry thinking about it."

"You mean you weren't hungry already? You always had an appetite when I was with you."

"Alright, you know me too well. Yes, I was hungry before you said anything, but now even more. I hope Chef Cecil is making enough. You had quite the appetite yourself, Bebop."

"No worries, he knows how I eat, and I warned him about you."

As they made their way to the kitchen, the air filled with delicious smells. Bebop held his nose up and sniffed.

"We must be getting close."

"Uh huh," said Bebop, breathing deep through his nose.

Eliza heard pots clanging and other sounds of cooking activity. She and Bebop turned around a rock outcropping and found themselves at the edge of a bright, busy kitchen. Pots steamed and pans sizzled. Birds and insects flew through the air, carrying sprigs of herbs and spices, and rodents bustled across the floor with food in tow. A myriad of small monkeys busily chopped and grated vegetables, all while talk-ing up a storm that Eliza couldn't understand. She wondered which creature was Chef Cecil.

They walked further into the kitchen and Eliza noticed a high shelf that looked over the entire place. A large lop-eared rabbit jumped onto the shelf from the counter below, pointing and yelling. "Chopped car-rots and celery in the sauté pan. Pinch of salt onto the grilled veg-etables. A strong dose of hot pepper in the sauce. Check the potatoes in the roaster." As he shouted, various members of the kitchen crew jumped to follow each instruction.

"I assume that's Chef Cecil?"

"Sure is —the one and only." Cecil looked in Bebop and Eliza's direc-tion and Bebop waved his front paw. Cecil yelled, "Our guests are here–start plating!" Pairs of rats rolled plates and bowls over to the various spots where food was cooked. Jacee and a couple of monkeys dished out the delicacies and walked them over to a table in a far corner of the kitchen.

Eliza stood dumbfounded. She tried to hide her gut reaction of disgust at seeing rats anywhere close to the food she was supposed to eat and confirmed as she watched that they didn't touch the food or parts of the dishes where food was placed.

Bebop said excitedly, "Let's eat!" and headed toward the table. A step behind, Eliza noticed long strings of drool hanging from his mouth.

"Bebop, you're drooling."

"Can't help it. It's ingrained and thought you were used to that."

"I thought since you're a big Captain now you would have gotten that under control."

"No one cares about drooling or other bodily functions around here —that's a human thing, You humans get all caught up in appear-ances and what you feel is proper or not. You seem to like spending time on all that stuff, including making people feel bad if they don't conform with some subjective standard, and that takes you away from focusing on what really matters."

"Whoa, where'd all that come from? I thought we were just going to have a nice meal and was only joking about the drool."

"Are you done now?" asked a voice Eliza didn't recognize. She and Bebop arrived at the table where Chef Cecil waited, Eliza not having noticed him while she and Bebop were caught up in conversation.

"Yes, Cecil, sorry for being distracted," apologized Bebop. He turned to Eliza. "Eliza, it's my pleasure to introduce you to Chef extraordinaire Cecil."

"I'm honored." Eliza bowed toward Cecil to pay tribute to his cooking prowess.

Cecil feigned being surprised. "Thank you, but you shouldn't say that until you taste the meal we've prepared for you today." He motioned for them to take their seats. Bebop and Eliza sat, closed their eyes, and breathed in the aromas drifting from the food on the table.

"Today, we've prepared cabbage salad, roasted red potatoes, grilled mushrooms, peppers, and tomatoes with spicy sauce, and sautéed summer squash with tofu and parmesan topping," advised Cecil. "We hope you enjoy."

"Yum," said Eliza as she picked up a fork and dug in. Bebop didn't waste time saying anything and instead buried his mouth in the food, gobbling it up.

Cecil shook his head. "I'll never learn that presentation doesn't last long with this guy. So much for keeping things separate on the plate."

"Well, I enjoy my dishes separately and very much appreciate the presentation," said Eliza with her mouth half full. "Everything's totally delicious and I don't know what to eat first or last."

Cecil beamed, enjoying the enthusiasm with which Bebop and Eliza relished his creations. "The best compliment is seeing the joy on your faces as you eat."

Eliza finished the beverage in her glass with a satisfied, "Aaaaw-www. What is this stuff? It's delectable, as is everything else."

Jacee appeared at her left elbow with a pitcher full of the beverage and offered more. "Hey, Jacee. Oh yes, please fill 'er up."

"That's lavender lemonade," Cecil answered. "Made from lavender and lemons grown right here in NoHoSap, just like everything else we create."

"It makes a huge difference being locally grown," complimented Eliza. "I can't stop eating or drinking any of this."

Cecil smiled as he watched Bebop and Eliza partake in all the delicacies from his kitchen. Satisfied eaters were the best reward of all for him.

Eventually, Bebop and Eliza each sat back in a food stupor. They'd often found themselves in that state when they overindulged while Bebop lived with Eliza, who loved comfort food and sweets.

"Our pastry chef didn't have time to pull together dessert but wanted to be sure we'd save room for a sweets smorgasbord another time," Bebop apologized.

"Thank goodness we don't have dessert to follow. I couldn't eat another bite."

Eliza asked Cecil how he came to be a chef. He explained that nibbling plants with his fellow rabbits never satisfied him. As a young hare, he instead collected vegetation and other edibles from fields and forests and experimented with various flavor combinations for himself and any other animal who would eat them. His friends encouraged him to expand from raw foods into cooking. He followed his passion and became a chef.

The conversation fascinated Eliza, but she eventually said goodbye and headed back to HuHabDom, looking forward to the next time she'd be with her new friends.

CHAPTER 10

WHITE LIES

The next morning, Eliza walked into her office at the station and immediately heard a knock on the door. She looked up to see Ezekiel, a tall, athletic, handsome man with perfect waves in his hair, and a straight, clean line around the edges. He was Eliza's closest friend at work, roughly Eliza's age, and a reporter, covering sports and some lifestyle/entertainment news. A musician on the side, he played saxophone in a jazz trio on random nights at various restaurants around town. Music was really what he'd love to do full time, but being a journalist paid the bills.

"Mornin,' Zeke," greeted Eliza absentmindedly as she traded the sneakers on her feet for dress shoes.

"Mornin'? That's all you have to say after your big rescue and news coverage?" chided Zeke, a wry, hurt look on his face. "I take a couple days off and return to you being a hero and also having a dog you never even mentioned to me? I thought you were still in mourning over Bebop."

It suddenly dawned on Eliza that she hadn't talked with Zeke since before the encounters with her new mission mates. She also realized she hadn't prepared herself for this conversation and the questions Zeke would inevitably ask. Thinking on her feet, she smiled self-consciously and replied, "That's right, a lot has happened over the last few days, and we haven't had a chance to catch up. I feel like I've been caught up in a whirlwind."

"What gives? You got a dog out of the blue and, while walking it in a rainstorm, you happened upon a house where somebody needed rescuing?"

"Pretty much, crazy as it sounds." Eliza knew it seemed outlandish that her sensible self would do such a thing and contemplated how much to tell Zeke but could hear Bebop's voice warning her not to divulge too much. Something moved behind Zeke's head and Eliza saw Noli crawling atop a picture frame on the wall. Noli saw Eliza looking at her and waved. Eliza tried not to laugh and looked immediately back at Zeke. She didn't want him to turn around to see what her eyes followed on the wall. Noli's presence confirmed to Eliza that she was being watched and better be careful with what she said, or she'd be in for another heated conversation with Bebop.

Zeke had a 'C'mon' look as he gestured 'give me something.' Eliza wanted to blurt everything out to him, which was her general nature with Zeke, but instead measured her words as she tried to concoct a plausible story about getting a dog.

"You know I've been checking rescue sites for Weimaraners even though I haven't felt ready yet to adopt another dog," She wove her yarn.

"Right."

"Well, I found one Saturday who looked exactly like Bebop. When I saw he was within driving distance, I contacted the rescue group on a whim." Eliza felt a pang of guilt for making up the story but didn't know how else to explain why she'd been walking a dog, since she mentioned that on the news. She now keenly realized how telling one lie could easily snowball into having to tell more and more untruths to fit with the first one.

She continued spinning the tale. "They said they received other calls about him and asked if I wanted to meet him. I wasn't planning to adopt yet but looked at Bebop's picture and asked if he thought I should meet this lookalike dog. He seemed to say I should, so I went, we clicked, and I brought him home with me." She took a deep breath, visibly relaxed and relieved to be done telling what she told herself was just a little white lie.

"Good, I'm happy for you—congratulations!" To Eliza's relief, he appeared to believe her. "You were heartbroken about Bebop's passing and hopefully this dog will bring happiness into your life. What's his name?"

Not anticipating this question, Eliza gulped, knowing she had to come up with something fast. She answered slowly as her mind worked, "His name was Buck, but I'm changing it to Bop."

"Nice. Looking forward to meeting him. Not to change the subject from this good news, but how'd it feel to be the subject of the rescuer story yesterday instead of the person asking all the questions?"

"Weird. Gary did a super job with the story. I never thought anything would end up on the news. I happened to be in the right place at the right time to be able to help." Eliza stopped herself from saying any more about the rescue, since she couldn't divulge how she ended up there and who helped with it.

"The coverage came across very well. Are you getting much follow up from your heroism?"

"Not really. Folks have posted comments on the station's feeds, but I didn't link to my personal accounts because I didn't want to toot my own horn."

"And that's where you and I differ. I would have been linking and posting to all my accounts for publicity and exposure. You never know where it may lead."

"True," Eliza agreed as she looked over at Noli, who watched Eliza intently. "I didn't want to make a big deal about it." She figured she better leave it at that, knowing full well that her instincts to link and post were the same as Zeke's, but Bebop would be livid if she did anything like that without sign-off from the NoHoSap team.

Changing the subject, Eliza asked, "Hey, how was your time off?"

"Great—made for a nice long weekend. I played here with the trio Friday and Saturday nights and went down to the Big Apple to see some live jazz Sunday night." His face always relaxed and his gestures were more animated whenever he talked jazz. "You'll have to come out and see us play again. We've added some new tunes, including one I wrote."

"Congratulations–that's very cool! Keep me posted on your upcoming gigs. I'll be working on some projects in the evenings and weekends over the next few weeks but would love to see you play."

"Will do. It would be nice to see you at another gig. Working on anything interesting?"

Caught off guard again, Eliza blurted out the first thing that came to mind. "Training Bop and getting him acclimated to the routine. Then there's a bunch of stuff I've been putting off but really need to get to." She felt uncomfortable making things up and thought for sure he'd catch on since she was uncharacteristically cagey.

To Eliza's surprise, he didn't seem to notice anything unusual and simply replied, "OK, I'll let you know the next time we're playing. Guess we both better hit the grindstone now."

"Yeah, time to get to it." Zeke left while Eliza turned to her computer and the day's work.

CHAPTER 11

ENCOURAGEMENT

Tree planting time arrived in what seemed like the blink of an eye. Eliza had ambitious plans to make progress on projects at work and change clothes for NoHoSap, but as generally happened, found herself scrambling to get out the station door by day's end. With no time to meet the crew at NoHoSap, she headed straight to one of the two project spots, an open field near the back of a local park preserve, telling Noli to let Bebop know they'd meet the team there.

Eliza knew the site from walking there with Bebop. She found it on the map when looking for open spaces to let him run off-leash, and liked that it was within walking distance, albeit a long walk, from their house. She and Bebop first ventured there on a warm spring day. As usually happened on their walks, people along the way gravitated toward Bebop, with kids wanting to pet him and asking lots of questions. Bebop seemed to enjoy the attention.

While wandering around on her many walks in the preserve with Bebop, Eliza discovered an overgrown trail system, along with a lake choked by weeds. Parts of the water were so overgrown with plants that it appeared you could walk over the top. The first time Bebop went near it he thought it was green land and fell in. Eliza laughed until he came over to her after climbing out of the water, shook, and splattered her with the bright green algae that already covered him.

That led to one of the many baths in the backyard, hosing off whatever grossness he'd gotten into on the walk.

Eliza snapped her mind back to the present as she parked the car near the more secluded entrance to the preserve. She hoped there wouldn't be anyone riding the trails on motorbikes or ATVs, which she used to see and hear there frequently, fearing the threatening roar of the vehicles.

To Eliza's surprise, no vegetation hid the trail and instead mulch covered the path, keeping it clear of weeds. Someone obviously spent a lot of time cleaning it up and making it more accessible than it used to be. On her way to the lake, she came upon two middle-aged men carrying a rowboat overflowing with a tangled mass of wet weeds. The men strained to carry the boat and all its contents. Eliza lauded, "You've been busy."

One of the men replied, "Sure have. This has been our project since summer, but we're making progress."

They placed the boat down and took a much-needed rest. The second man explained, "We played here as kids, learned to fish, and loved exploring this neighborhood spot when we were young. There were three lakes then, but one's now filled in and another's almost gone. The fishing club we formed back then continues to this day. We get together and fish even now, and it all began here."

The first man added, "A few of us came back last summer for old time's sake. None of us had been here for a while and we were disappointed to see how the place had been neglected. It appeared the only things people used it for were motorbiking and beer parties. We thought it was such a loss and wanted the neighborhood kids to have a place where they could learn to love the outdoors like we did."

"We decided to do what we could to bring it back," said the second man, "We've been cleaning up the trails and pulling the weeds from the main lake ever since. Folks from the neighborhood are starting to help and we even had a fishing clinic for the kids, which went really well."

"That's great," Eliza said enthusiastically. "There's no better way to get an appreciation for nature than being out in it as a kid. It's been a little over a year since I last visited. You've done an awesome job clearing things out from the way it looked then. That's a lot of hard work."

"You got that right. You ain't kidding," said the men almost in unison.

The first man observed, "Seeing the wonder and joy in the kids' faces as they catch their first fish, play with the dragonflies, and watch tadpoles turn into frogs makes it all worth it. We hope this place will once again be a sanctuary, adventure park, and learning lab for the local folks like it was for us."

Tears welled in Eliza's eyes, hearing these efforts to connect people with nature. "I love seeing people giving back and wanting to help kids appreciate the environment. Thank you and your club for making such a difference."

"It's the least we can do since this place gave us so much," said the second man. "OK, Bud, pick 'er up and let's get this load outta here, then it's chow time."

The men hoisted the boat and resumed trudging down the path. Inspired, Eliza thought that with more people like them maybe there was hope the world could make a difference to curb climate change. Her mind then turned to why she was there in the first place, to join the NoHoSap team on the first planting project.

CHAPTER 12

FIRST DIG, TAKE ONE

Eliza continued down the hill toward the lake. The last time she visited, a huge fallen tree blocked the trail, but it now had no obstructions. She took the path through the lake and headed back up the other side to the project site. Hearing signs of activity, she became more vigilant, looking for other people in the preserve. Hopefully, no humans would be there and they could do their work on this first project without onlookers.

When she entered the field, she saw the crew on the far side and walked over to them. Cuthbert greeted her, then introduced her to the workers, including a gopher, woodchuck, dog, and mule. The mule pulled a trailer carrying potted trees ranging in height from six to ten feet. Cuthbert marked where the holes should be dug and directed one animal to each of the first few spots. As they lined up at their locations, Cuthbert motioned for Eliza to come closer and then told her to take pictures of the complete process, from digging to placing the trees to filling in the holes. Eliza asked whether she should shoot any videos and Cuthbert advised that short videos without sound would be fine.

"How are you going to move those big trees off the trailer and plant them?" inquired Eliza.

Cuthbert smiled and said, "We have a special guest for that."

"Are you talking about me?" Eliza turned and saw Tusko emerging from the trees at the edge of the field. Her heart jumped since she never expected to see an elephant here.

"Tusko, we're honored you're joining us," lauded Cuthbert. "It's not often we have an Alliance member doing the dirty work with us."

Eliza immediately worried about his presence. As an Alliance member, he was important to the mission and NoHoSap, and it seemed extremely risky for him to be out and about in this area. He couldn't easily hide from being discovered.

Tusko seemed unfazed and told Cuthbert, "We want to show our support for this all-important mission by participating directly where we can. Plus, you don't have many options for creatures to lift these trees and hold them while the holes are filled."

"We very much appreciate your support, sir," Cuthbert acknowledged. "Let's get going before we draw attention."

Tusko turned to the perplexed Eliza. "Good to see you again, Eliza, and happy you're starting with this project."

"Glad to be here and see you again too, Tusko." She paused and thought about whether she should say what was on her mind since she hadn't planned this work party but decided to go for it. "I hope I'm not being out of line, but is it safe for you to be here? If anyone sees you, we could have a tough time keeping you protected. You're part of the Alliance and I'd hate for something to happen."

Taken aback by Eliza questioning his project and Tusko's decision to help, Cuthbert jumped in on the defensive. Tusko intervened and waved his trunk between them, as though officiating a boxing match, then said calmly, "I appreciate the concern, Eliza. You're not the only one who thinks it's a risk for me to be here. When I told Canlup I planned to assist, she tried to convince me to stay in NoHoSap. I've lived with this large body my entire life and know very well that I'm noticed wherever I go. Because of that, there aren't many ways I'll be able to help on the ground with your work, but I wanted to be part of at least this first outing. We have sentries set up around the perimeter to warn us if any humans approach."

"That's a relief," replied Eliza. "Sorry to question anything, but I'm a worrier and am not good about keeping things to myself."

Cuthbert interjected, knowing they needed to move along with their work. "Thanks, Eliza, for your concern and Tusko for confirming you're safe. Now let's get going and keep it that way."

Each animal lined up at its assigned hole and started digging. Eliza took pictures with her phone, circling the workers, shooting from high, low, near, and far, surprised how rapidly the holes deepened. Soon the woodchuck and gopher were barely visible as they disappeared into the holes they were digging, with flumes of dirt flying out. The dogs' forequarters were well below their rear ends and dirt continued spewing out of the holes between their hind legs.

"Team, you've dug deep enough," yelled Cuthbert. "Now widen out to allow us to get the full roots of these trees in the holes."

Like clockwork, the diggers dug horizontally, with Eliza snapping pictures all the way. She had to be careful to avoid the flying dirt, but it became difficult as the animals turned randomly to widen out the holes. Eliza felt like a target for clods of soil zooming every which way around her.

"Stop!" commanded Cuthbert. "Great job, team! Move over to the next few holes and do it again."

The digging process commenced again on more holes and repeated itself a few times until there were as many holes as trees.

"That's it—you're done on the holes," shouted Cuthbert. "Time to get these trees planted. Tusko, you're up."

The diggers stopped and sat or lay down after working hard to move the Earth. Tusko sauntered over to the trailer, wrapped his trunk around a tree, and lifted it effortlessly. Team members tapped on the pot and pulled until it fell off. Tusko then placed the tree in the first hole and held it there.

"OK, dig team, back to you to fill in the hole," instructed Cuthbert.

The diggers all gathered around the one hole and filled it with dirt in no time. "Pack in that dirt. We need to support this tree to enable it to thrive well into the future. Stubbs, do your thing while we plant the next tree."

The mule meandered over to the planted tree and stomped on the fresh dirt around it. Eliza watched in amazement through her camera lens as the animals planted the trees in assembly line fashion. Soon the trailer stood empty, and a stand of new trees graced the field.

"Tusko, would you mind doing the honors to add the finishing touch?" asked Cuthbert.

"My pleasure," replied Tusko, as he sidled away toward the lake. When he returned, he used his trunk once again, this time to spray water at the bases of the newly planted trees. Eliza backed up to pan a picture of all the trees together. She could barely believe how her new friends accomplished this. Who would have thought animals could pull this off. Invigorated, she thought perhaps this partnership between animals and humans may have a shot at success.

"That's a wrap," Cuthbert exclaimed. "Nice teamwork! Travel safely back to NoHoSap and keep under the radar. Eliza and I are headed over to check on the other dig."

Tusko acknowledged, "Cuthbert, thank you for planning and coordinating this, and for including me. I'm encouraged by the progress on this first sub-mission. Keep up the good work. Eliza, I'm looking forward to hearing the human response once you post the photos and videos from today. Good to be working with you."

"The honor is mine, Tusko. Thank you for bringing me on to the team."

"You're welcome. Let me know if you need my help on any other plantings or projects." With that, Tusko lumbered away and disappeared into the forest.

Cuthbert turned to Eliza and said, "Let's go. Probably best if you carry me to your car since we'll get there faster.

CHAPTER 13

FIRST DIG, TAKE TWO

Cuthbert climbed onto Eliza's hand, she carried him to her car, and they took off to the next dig site. "Hopefully they're not already done with the second project. I want to get some more pictures."

"They shouldn't be. I asked them to start a bit later than we did, to give us time to get there before they finished. We still need to move along, though."

Eliza took the shortest route she knew to the next location, not far away, in another park. Cuthbert explained the new trees at the second site were being planted to replace old trees that died or fell. After parking in a remote area, Eliza picked up Cuthbert and they trekked to find the second dig team.

They arrived at the venue, with work underway. Bebop oversaw this project team, which included a prairie and a domestic dog, skunk, and fox. Eliza chuckled when she saw him working with the skunk, remembering a very unpleasant run-in he had with a skunk when he lived with her. It happened at the outset of a short vacation by the ocean. After a long drive cooped up in the car, Eliza thought Bebop needed some exercise. Although night-time, they walked to a large open field they'd visited on prior trips. Eliza let Bebop off the leash, and he sprinted away, chasing something.

He doubled back toward her, and Eliza saw the white stripe on the back of the animal Bebop trailed. She screamed at him to leave it alone, but the skunk sprayed him in the face and ran away. Bebop pawed at his eyes and rubbed his head in the grass while the fresh skunk odor permeated the air. Eliza could barely breathe, the stench burning her nostrils. Livid, she put Bebop on the leash, walked back to the motel, secured the leash around a tree near their room, and went to a nearby supermarket for tomato juice to cut the smell. Upon her return, she dragged him to the motel's outdoor "car wash"—a hose—and gave him multiple juice baths with cold rinses. Despite her best efforts, he still stunk. Knowing the motel room would reek if they stayed, Eliza begrudgingly loaded the car and made the long drive back home with the windows open. Tempted to remind Bebop of that foiled trip, she restrained herself from embarrassing him in front of the team.

Eliza put Cuthbert down on the ground as the group finished putting soil around the third tree they'd planted. Cuthbert instructed her to get to work taking pictures, which Eliza promptly did from all angles.

A bunch of trees remained on a trailer, pulled by an ox named Bruno. Without Tusko there to assist, this team used a pulley system to lift the trees. A Rhesus macaque monkey, who Bebop introduced as Makita, handled the system. She maneuvered the fourth tree from the trailer into the hole. The dig team filled it with soil to stabilize and keep the tree standing straight, then Bruno packed the dirt down.

"Looking good, team!" complimented Eliza.

Cuthbert instructed them to dig two holes at a time, enabling them to move along faster since he sensed the sun setting. Bebop helped with the digging to speed up the process. Once the next two trees were in, Bebop directed Bruno to move the trailer to the next location and the double tree planting process repeated itself.

Makita improved her skills at maneuvering the rope around each tree and swinging them into the holes. Eliza snapped pictures and videos until all the trees were in the ground.

Makita jumped away from the pulley system and ran over to the trailer, filled with now-empty tree pots as well as a large plastic drum. She wedged stones in the drain holes of one of the pots and filled it with water from the drum. As she struggled to carry the heavy vessel, Eliza came to her aid, lifted one side, and together they watered the trees, refilling the pot as needed.

While they worked Eliza asked how the trees would continue to be watered, a critical element until they established root systems in the soil of their new home. Bebop mentioned that some of the male dogs on the sub-mission volunteered to visit the trees each day and pee on them. Upon hearing this suggestion, the dog on this project, a female, rolled her eyes and shook her head in disgust. Bebop acknowledged the trees wouldn't benefit from that type of liquid and said Cuthbert came up with an ingenious system to keep them watered.

Cuthbert explained, "We knew we couldn't have someone out here regularly with pots or otherwise pouring water on the trees, because that would increase the risk a human may see them. As a result, I designed a subterranean watering system and called on my friends who dig underground. They fashioned tunnels leading from the trees' root systems to either a water source or out-of-the-way place we could water without being noticed. We lined the tunnels with plastic bags humans have discarded to minimize water being absorbed before it can reach the trees."

Eliza listened in awe. "That's incredible. There's a watering system underneath us?"

"Yes, my teams have been hard at work since we identified the sites yesterday and have dug tunnels far enough underground that they shouldn't collapse from activity on the surface. Tonight, they'll finish the ends of the tunnels to connect to the trees. Starting tomorrow and continuing on days when it doesn't rain, our watering team will come out. For those tunnels connected to a water source, we installed gates made of plastic coffee lids to block water from going into the tunnel. The team members will lift those dams, allowing water to pass to the trees. The other tunnels have an above-ground entrance into which the watering team will pour water. Once the trees are well established, we remove the coffee lid dams and plastic bag liners and send them to the recycling bin."

"Wow," said Eliza, in astonishment.

"Excellent work, everyone," complimented Bebop.

Cuthbert added, "That's a wrap, team. Good job."

The team members looked at their work proudly and Cuthbert instructed them to head back to NoHoSap, telling them to be safe along the way.

Dusk settled in and Bebop asked Eliza if she wanted to go back to NoHoSap for dinner. She politely declined the invitation, since she wanted to get a good night's sleep after all the recent excitement and late nights.

"Totally understandable," acknowledged Bebop. "Let's meet at NoHoSap tomorrow around 5:30 p.m. to review the photos and videos from today."

Cuthbert added, "No posting in the meantime."

"I know, I know," Eliza said in exasperation. "I learned my lesson on that after the first time and the stern talking to from Bebop. You don't have to tell me twice."

Cuthbert climbed into a small sack Bebop took from the trailer and now held in his mouth. "Nice ride, Cuthbert."

"It'll do, but I have to be careful not to fall out when he jumps over things."

Bebop gave Eliza his usual high five before going their separate ways. Eliza found it hard to fathom how much her life had changed since the weekend. Her new work on the mission energized her, but she worried nonetheless because it involved some risk. *What if the station fired her or she had to give up her job to focus on the mission? How would she pay her student and car loans, rent, and other expenses if she didn't have a steady paycheck? Would people think she'd gone crazy once she posted the unbelievable pictures and videos from events like today?* She told herself to stop thinking negative thoughts. Until now, she always took the safe route and it landed her unhappy with her day-to-day life and dreaming of what she could do to make a difference. Everything unfolding for her now seemed to be exactly what she hoped for, albeit coming from an unexpected source. She knew she had to quell the doubts and instead roll with it. Turning her thinking around to focus on the positive, she became excited about what tomorrow would hold rather than being worried about what the longer-term future may be.

CHAPTER 14

MEDIA BEGINNINGS

The next morning, Noli landed on Eliza's dashboard during her drive to work, startling Eliza. "Noli! Good thing I'm stopped at a light, or I might havedriven off the road with you showing up like that," chided Eliza. "It's nice to see you but give me some warning next time."

Noli smiled back and did a half-hearted salute with her tiny front leg. "Good morning to you too, Eliza."

"Yes, it is a good morning. I didn't see you at the digs yesterday. Did you get a break from following me?"

"I went with you when you rushed out of the office and watched the first dig, but then settled into your bag for a nap when you headed to the second location. What a beautiful bright morning! Let me take advantage and soak up this sun." Noli slipped into a sunbathing trance on the dashboard. When they arrived at the parking lot she hadn't budged. "Noli, we're here. Want a ride in my bag?"

Noli jerked up and looked around, appearing dazed until she saw Eliza and realized where she was. "No, I'll ride on your shoulder. That way I can see more."

"Uh, that's a good idea, but I don't want folks in my office to think I have bugs if they see you on me. If you hide in a pocket in my bag, you should still be able to see but be less conspicuous."

"Gotcha, will do." Eliza tried not to show her relief.

Arriving in her office, Eliza changed from sneakers to dress shoes. She had social media training that morning–quite the coincidence, what with the work she'd be doing on the climate mission that evening. As she headed down the hall toward the conference room, she ran into Zeke leaving his office.

"Fancy meeting you here, Eliza. Pay close attention to this training today. That way next time you get into hero mode, you can post on social media and spread the news far and wide. You'll be a big celebrity before you know it."

"Good morning, Zeke. I'll be sure to take a lot of notes today. Maybe you could also teach me some lessons since you seem to be a social media expert."

"I wouldn't say that by any stretch, there's always more to learn, especially since the field changes so fast."

Eliza typed copious notes during the presentation. The station gave regular training to be sure the journalists were up to date and distributing news in the most ways possible. She couldn't believe how much had changed since the last social media seminar. Zeke had been right on point in that regard.

After the presentation, she hurried back to her office to finish up the story for the evening news, and then left for NoHoSap. Monty met Eliza when she emerged from the tunnel.

"Welcome, Eliza. The first digs went well from what I hear."

"Hello, Monty. Yes, I thought the digs were successful. I enjoyed meeting and working with the team members. I'm looking forward to reviewing the shots I took and getting the word out."

"Speaking of that, Bebop and Cuthbert are in the media room-follow me."

Eliza assumed they'd be in the same room where Bebop selected the dig team members, but the elevator to Mission Command stopped at a floor that Eliza hadn't been to before. They exited the elevator into a cavernous room. Eliza heard voices and saw a hint of light to her left toward the far side of the cavern. Monty flew off in that direction.

They reached a recessed area shielded from the rest of the room by an almost solid rock wall with openings that allowed some sound and luminescence to escape.

Monty and Eliza entered to find Bebop and Cuthbert discussing how much to post for their first project in HuHabDom. Monty left them to their planning. Eliza looked around the room, stunned, as usual for her in NoHoSap. Video monitors of various sizes covered the walls, many of which streamed news from different parts of the world, including China, London, Delhi, Moscow, Columbia, and the United States. Rock seats filled the center of the room, each equipped with a remote control and headphones.

After taking it all in, Eliza waited for a lull in the conversation between Bebop and Cuthbert. "Hey you two. Sorry to interrupt, but how about we first take a look at what I shot yesterday? I haven't reviewed anything yet and if there's a ton of crappy pictures with only a few good ones, it'll impact what and where we're able to post."

"OK, that's a good idea," acknowledged Cuthbert.

Bebop pointed with his paw. "There's a hookup for your phone in the panel over there. Plug it into the system and let's see what we have."

Four monitors activated when Eliza plugged in her phone. She pulled up the photos on the first monitor. An array of pictures appeared, and Eliza spread them out, using two monitors of pictures for each dig.

Cuthbert said, "Let's go through and weed out any that don't look good. That'll narrow down what we need to consider."

Eliza blew up one picture or video at a time and Bebop and Cuthbert said yes or no to each. They agreed for the most part on the deletions, not difficult since some were blurry or cut off and clearly weren't worthy of further consideration. That weeded the choices down by about one-quarter.

"OK, now let's choose those we like most," suggested Bebop.

Eliza went through the shots again. A slower process. She pulled similar items up, side by side to enable them to select those that best showed the action. That process narrowed them down to about one-third.

"That's plenty for now and we can put those we didn't pick in this round in a 'maybe' folder for safe-keeping," said Cuthbert.

"Good idea," agreed Bebop.

Eliza moved the 'maybe' photos out, leaving a multitude of images on the screens. Pleased with how they captured the work and attentiveness of the teams, Eliza asked Bebop and Cuthbert if they were concerned about posting pictures of Tusko.

Cuthbert answered, "I'd like to include him if we can since he's quite impressive."

"How do you want me to go about posting—what, where, and when? Actually, before you answer that, today we had a seminar at work about the latest in social media and there are some more sites and methods I didn't know of before that I can use. They said one of the most important things is naming the post, site, hashtag, etc."

"Good to know," replied Cuthbert. "I thought we'd post on various climate change sites. Maybe our handle could be something like 'animals joining with humans to fight climate change'."

"We could do that, but they said the name should be short and sweet, boiling down to the essence of the message. Also, I sense that anything with climate change in the name could turn people off from the get-go since it can be a controversial or too-sciencey subject for some. We want to grab their attention, not turn them away."

"How about 'an unlikely alliance' or 'agents of change'?" suggested Bebop.

"I get the idea. We need something catchy. What about 'the climate brigade'? 'The change forces'?"

"Wow, good ideas, you guys. Nothing's jumping out at me yet, though. Seems like these are close, but not quite there. How about 'the anti-warmers' or 'change alliance'? I like the names that imply some action. We're close with these but..., what else could the name be to capture our mission in a couple words?" pondered Eliza.

All stood deep in thought until Bebop shouted, "The change agents! We're the Change Agents!"

Cuthbert's and Eliza's faces lit up.

"That's it, Captain!" exclaimed Cuthbert.

"You got it, Bebop!" congratulated Eliza excitedly. She typed on her phone. "I'm making sure that the moniker is available." More typing while Cuthbert and Bebop waited impatiently. More typing. "It's available on social media!" More typing. "Done, we got it!"

More typing. "Shoot, the name isn't available for a website," she announced with disappointment. All looked dismayed. "What's similar that may be open? We don't need a website now, but likely will eventually." More typing as Eliza tried the name with 'the', a dash, different domains. "Climatechangeagents.com is available. What do you think? We'll still be The Change Agents to keep it short, but the website and anything else where change agents isn't available will be climatechangeagents."

Bebop and Cuthbert looked at each other, not understanding the nuances of naming for social media purposes. Bebop shrugged and said, "OK(?)"

More typing by Eliza. "Done! The Change Agents will use climatechangeagents.com! I'll set up accounts accordingly."

CHAPTER 15

POSTINGS AND PLANTLINGS

With the media outlets designated, Bebop, Cuthbert, and Eliza discussed which photos and videos to post where and what captions should accompany them. Eliza cautioned that people would be suspicious if the footage looked doctored, and the publicity would start off on the wrong foot, which they definitely didn't want. Since these pictures showed animals doing unusual things on their own, without guidance from humans, Eliza suggested they spin the posts with a comedic twist. They had to use discretion to build a following and, as with the name, the serious matter of climate change may not be the best approach.

Cuthbert said, "OK, so instead of saying animals are taking things into their own hands to address climate change, we should say something like 'check out these digging skills', 'who knew they were digging holes for trees' and 'amazing—animals planting trees!"

"That's the idea," praised Eliza. "Eventually we'll have to answer the inevitable questions about what the heck is going on, but we don't have to address that now. We should just be aware we need to figure out our reply soon and then when it does come up we'll be ready."

Eliza went to work setting things up on her phone. Bebop summoned the supervisor of NoHoSap's IT team, a colorful parrot named Cheshire, to pull up the internet on a few monitors, making the setup easier and allowing them all to see the posts. Bebop explained

Cheshire used to live with a person who happened to be a technological wiz. The human met an untimely death and Cheshire fled the person's apartment when humans came to clear it out. While living on the street, Cheshire met a cat who frequented NoHoSap. The cat brought Cheshire to Mission Command and introduced her to Bebop. He added her to the IT team after hearing of her expertise in that realm, gleaned from years of watching her human work on the computer. In addition to her IT knowledge, Cheshire also had experience with social and other media.

After Cheshire made the internet connection, she helped with posting pictures and videos, to which Eliza added comments and hashtags. Their growling stomachs alerted them to the hour, much later than they all realized. Bebop called on his headpiece and ordered dinner. Soon Jacee appeared, along with another raccoon and two squirrels, all carrying containers from which wonderful smells wafted. Cuthbert, Bebop, Cheshire, and Eliza dug in and gulped down the food and beverage from Chef Cecil's kitchen, very grateful for his cooking prowess and the speedy delivery by Jacee and friends.

After dinner, they posted a few more items and wrapped up. All watched with pleasure as the number of likes on the various sites kept coming. Bebop asked Cheshire to set up a system to track reaction to the posts and make that system available to the Alliance, Mission Command, and all others in NoHoSap as well as Eliza. Cheshire told the team to let her know how else the IT team could assist.

Before they disbanded for a well-deserved night of sleep, Bebop commended the group. "Thank you for the work tonight to start sending our message to humans. This is an exciting time for all of us as Change Agents and we look forward to seeing our mission move forward in new ways. Eliza, our next planting sub-mission will be tomorrow, and Saturday will be our last planting project this round. We'll use the same dig teams since the members know the process. Cuthbert and I will pick the locations tomorrow and let you know through Noli. Rest well."

"OK, sounds good. Hey, Bebop, where do you get the trees we've been planting?"

Bebop smiled. "I wondered when you'd ask that. I'll show you on the way out."

They took the elevator up to the surface. A crystal-clear sky greeted them, with an almost full moon and stars as far as the eye could see. A light breeze blew the crisp air across their faces and Eliza heard a multitude of peepers. Eliza loved nights like this and kept looking up at the sky's dazzling brilliance while breathing in the cool air. The moon highlighted the path as she followed Bebop through a field where Eliza believed the outdoor party had been not long ago, and then to an open area near the tree line of the neighboring forest. She noticed trees and bushes of all types and sizes—both in pots and planted—everywhere around the area.

"Welcome to the NoHoSap tree and plant nursery," said Bebop proudly.

"What? You have it all here?"

"That we do. We grow trees and other vegetation here, then plant it in NoHoSap and HuHabDom. Our nursery team collects seedlings from various areas and plants them either in the ground here or in pots that we get from HuHabDom. We supplement the soil with compost produced here, which makes everything grow very well."

"Captain Bebop, what can we do for you?" inquired a voice behind Eliza, who jumped in fear, then turned but didn't see the source of the greeting.

"Bea, sorry for the late visit, but Eliza asked where the trees that we've been planting come from." Eliza strained to see to whom Bebop spoke.

"Oh, this is Eliza," mused the voice. "Eliza, very nice to meet you." Eliza heard the voice closer to her ear, but she didn't see anything there."

"Nice to meet you too, but where are you?"

"That's right, there's minimal light and you can't see me. Captain, may I use your head?"

"That's fine. I almost suggested you use Eliza's hand but didn't want you to startle her more than you already did."

Eliza stared at the top of Bebop's head and something landed on top of it. She leaned closer and saw a large honeybee.

"Hello, I'm Bea. I lead our arborist team. We're very proud of our program here. We grow a variety of trees and other plants that are instrumental in our planting program in HuHabDom and in keeping NoHoSap as green as it can be."

Mystified, Eliza said, "You do great work. The trees for our first tree planting projects were very healthy. I had no idea you grew them here."

"Yes, we do a lot here. Visit us during the day sometime and I'll show you even more," invited Bea.

"I'd love to."

"Bea is everything OK?" said a voice from afar.

"Yes, Chat. Captain Bebop stopped by for a visit with a special guest," advised Bea.

"At this hour?" came the voice from a closer spot.

"Sorry for the off-hours disturbance, Chat, but Eliza asked where we get the trees we've been planting and figured I'd show her," explained Bebop. As he talked, a red squirrel hobbled into view.

"You're always welcome to stop by, Captain. Pleased to make your acquaintance, Eliza." The squirrel stood on his hind legs and held a front paw out to Eliza. "I'm Chat."

"Nice to meet you, Chat," said Eliza as she shook the outstretched paw. Eliza's curiosity got the best of her and she blurted out, "I don't mean to be rude, but Bea is the least imaginative name I've heard in NoHoSap, since you're a bee."

"You're not the first to mention that, believe me," replied Bea. "My full name is Beatrice, and my nickname is Bea, spelled B-e-a and not B-e-e. It doesn't actually have anything to do with the fact that I'm a bee. I'm named after my great, great, great, etc. grandmother, a queen bee named Beatrice. Her hives supplied honey to the British monarchy and the royal family's beekeepers maintained them for decades."

"My goodness. That's very impressive."

"Yes, we're honored to have such royalty here in NoHoSap helping to maintain our nursery, making sure everything is pollinated and productive," observed Bebop.

"And I'm lucky she agreed to work with a mere commoner like me," said Chat. "I grew up in the forest and, to my family's dismay, I found it much more interesting to run around in the trees exploring how they grew than to collect nuts. Unfortunately, my adventurousness got the best of me and one day I jumped on a branch that turned out to be rotten. It gave way from my weight. I fell to the ground, and the branch landed on my lower back. My friends carried me to NoHoSap since I couldn't move my hind legs, and Red in the medical unit miraculously kept me alive and nursed me back to health. With therapy, I learned to walk again, but my rear legs aren't nearly what they were before and I'm no longer jumping around in the trees. Instead, I instruct a team of enthusiastic acrobatic arborists how to prune and maintain our trees here."

"That's awesome," Eliza acknowledged.

Bebop knew they could talk all night and didn't want to hold Eliza up anymore from getting home. "Thanks, Bea and Chat. It's time for me to get Eliza back. Enjoy the night." Bea flew over to Chat and landed on his back as he ambled out of view, while Bebop and Eliza headed back in the direction from which they came.

"Thanks for showing me the nursery, Bebop. I'm realizing I've had quite the egocentric view, thinking humans are the only beings who can do a lot of the things I now see are being done here in NoHoSap."

"As you humans say, you never know what you don't know. I learned an awful lot from living in both HuHabDom and NoHoSap. There's nothing like experiencing things from another vantage point to put it all in perspective and broaden your view."

"Very true." They made it to the tunnel entrance. "See you tomorrow, Bebop." They exchanged the usual high five and went their separate ways.

CHAPTER 16

PERSPECTIVES AND REACTIONS

Eliza couldn't believe Friday arrived already. The week went faster than ever, what with being busy at work and with the mission. She watched traffic on the NoHoSap posts from the first dig, heartened to see them picking up traction. None of the initial posts went viral right away, but they did fairly well from the start and the interest increased steadily. Eliza liked and commented on all the posts to expand coverage to her friends and viewers, knowing it would be a slow process unless and until the right contact with the right audience picked it up. She told herself to be patient—not her strong suit, because she always wanted immediate results.

After Eliza arrived in the office, Noli landed on her phone and advised, "Cheshire will send you a text with the locations for today's digs. Cuthbert thought that'd make it easier for you to find them."

"He's right. With a text I'll be able to map my way to the exact places. Who knew animals are in tune with all this technology?"

Zeke popped his head into the door unexpectedly and asked, "Who are you talking to?"

Eliza jumped and answered self-consciously, "Just talking out loud to myself. What's going on, Zeke?"

"Same old, same old. I noticed the posts you shared. Where'd you find those? Seems odd that animals were willy-nilly planting trees on their own. Humans must have set that up and trained the animals to dig and plant."

"Just happened to find them, probably because I'm plugged into so many animal and environmental sites." Her guilt at telling untruths lessened as she continued, "I don't know where they originated but am going to try to find out more about them."

"Let me know what you learn."

"Will do."

"Back to work."

Eliza checked her phone after Zeke left and saw Cheshire's text with the dig locations. Luckily, they weren't far away, which meant Eliza could work a full day before heading out to the first site. The day flew, as usual, and before Eliza knew it, Noli let her know she had to wrap things up and leave.

"Thanks, Noli. I better do as you say, or I'm going to have to answer to Bebop." Eliza never dreamed her former pet would call the shots for her and found herself somewhat resentful of the situation.

A beautiful evening, the second day of digs went off without incident, using the same procedures as the first projects. When they finished the work, Eliza asked Bebop and Cuthbert, "Should we meet tomorrow to go through the pictures and videos from today like we did last time?"

Bebop replied, "Actually, since these digs moved right along and it isn't that late, let's do that tonight. I don't think it'll take nearly as long as last time since we now know the process. Are you up for that?"

"Sure, might as well do it while it's fresh in our minds. I'll give you both a ride to the cemetery."

As she drove, Eliza mused, "This still all seems unreal. If it's not, I'm overjoyed to have you back, Bebop, because most people don't get that when they lose their best friend."

"You're right. We all need to make the most of each and every moment. I now have a better idea of what it means to live in the present."

"That's for sure. It makes a lot of sense but is easier said than done, at least for me," admitted Eliza.

Cuthbert added, "You're not the only one, Eliza, it also applies to climate change. The world is changing swiftly. Each day could be the last for many plant and animal species that are living on the edge due to warmer temperatures. Humans feel the impacts when their homes are flooded or burnt down from events caused by a warming climate, but most don't seem to think the environment as they know it now could come to an end."

"Sad, but true," admitted Eliza. "Many people appear to believe climate change won't impact them much and therefore go about their business as usual. Also, a lot of the messaging about climate change is doom and gloom, which is depressing and can lead people to not pay attention or give up. We need to spin this differently to drive positive changes on the human front."

Bebop offered, "That gives you food for thought not only on the posts we're doing now but also for our upcoming first project in the next sub-mission, bringing the message to humans who are pet parents."

The trio disembarked from Eliza's car and headed to NoHoSap, ruminating on their impromptu discussion. They found Cheshire hard at work when they entered the NoHoSap media room.

"This is a nice surprise," Cheshire commented as she looked away from her computer screen and toward the visitors. "I've been working on a media summary with links to the various places we've posted. All's progressing nicely and I planned to roll it out to you tomorrow, but tonight will do."

"Sounds good," replied Bebop. "We have more posts to make from our work today. Let's do that first and then see how the human public is reacting."

"OK, I'll keep monitoring and summarizing in the meantime."

Eliza connected her phone to the computer and pulled up the day's work. The pictures turned out much better than those from the first outing. Bebop and Cuthbert went to town marking photos for deletion–less than last time–and choosing what they wanted to post. Eliza took care of the postings in short order, pleased it went much faster than before.

"The Change Agents postings are all updated," she announced.

Bebop thanked her and called to Cheshire. "Ready for the status update, Cheshire."

Cheshire reported, "Our posts have been well-received by humans, for the most part, and interest is increasing slowly."

'Why do you say, 'for the most part'?" inquired Cuthbert.

"Our general research shows that for every post there are always smart alecs who make negative comments," explained Cheshire. "Our posts are no exception, and the comments range from people saying there's no way the pictures can be real, to criticisms of the photo quality, to comments on why the pictures are being posted in the first place, to insults against whoever is posting. On the plus side, the 'likes' are significant in number and most of the comments are very encouraging, such as being amazed at the footage, thinking it's very cool, and wanting to know how animals can be trained to do such things."

"That's good news," said Bebop.

"Eliza, have any of your followers mentioned the posts to you?" asked Cuthbert.

"Just one so far, a friend at work. He questioned the authenticity of the photos and wondered why animals would do anything like that unless trained and prompted by humans."

"Obviously someone who doesn't understand or appreciate the abilities of animals," commented Cuthbert.

Eliza stifled her initial inclination to defend Zeke, particularly because she'd also been troubled by his opinions on the posts. A question had been on her mind since her conversation with him, though, leading her to ask. "When, if at all, should I let anybody know I took the shots and the posts are mine?"

Bebop replied, "We haven't figured that out exactly but don't feel it's time yet, especially this soon after the news story about your good

Samaritan efforts. People will put it all together but may make less of a deal about it if there's some time between. Plus, with our upcoming efforts where you talk with pet people, it's too much to connect right away. We don't want to increase your, and therefore our, profile quite that soon."

"Fine with me," Eliza said with relief. She didn't know how being connected with this effort would impact her at work or her job in general and felt no rush to find out.

Cuthbert advised, "Our last digs for this series will be tomorrow morning. Eliza, here's a map of the locations, the second of which is on the other side of the cemetery, after which we can meet back here in NoHoSap."

"OK, sounds good."

"Chef Cecil's team made sandwiches and salad that are waiting for us in the kitchen if we're hungry," said Bebop. "Jacee has the night off and he didn't have a crew to deliver them."

Never one to turn down food, Eliza acknowledged, "You don't have to tell me twice. Lead the way."

Cuthbert and Cheshire declined the invitation, but Eliza convinced them to take a break and accompany them for a delicious meal shared among friends. Chef Cecil saved some cookies made in the NoHoSap bakery, which Eliza particularly enjoyed.

As Eliza prepared to head home, Bebop reminded her, "You know, as Canlup mentioned when you joined the mission, you're always welcome to stay in NoHoSap rather than going home and coming right back in the morning."

"Thanks, Bebop. Staying over would make sense at times like this. I'll throw a bag with a change of clothes in my car and be prepared for the next time. See you in the morning."

"Good night, Eliza," said Bebop with a high five before Eliza left.

Upon arriving home, Eliza packed a bag for staying in NoHoSap overnight. If only she'd thought of that earlier, it would have saved her time the next morning and allowed her to sleep a little later.

CHAPTER 17

SURPRISES

The alarm woke Eliza the following morning before she wanted to rouse. "Stupid alarm," she muttered while stumbling to her dresser to turn it off. "So much for sleeping in on the weekend. Looks like those days are over for a while."

She put the overnight bag in the car on her way out and stopped at a nearby bakery for an apple fritter, as she often did on weekends. Eating the sweet treat helped wake her up fully. Generally, by this time of year she'd have cocoa too, but not in this warm weather. *Could climate change be causing this uncharacteristically mild autumn?*

Eliza arrived at the first dig site to find Cuthbert's team assembled. The planting went smoothly. When all the trees were in, Eliza invited the team members who could fit in her car to ride with her to the cemetery. Not wanting to draw attention to the second dig team by driving to the planting location, she parked near the swimming hole and walked to the dig site. Cuthbert rode in her backpack while the other members of the first team went back to NoHoSap.

Eliza and Cuthbert were almost to the second dig site when Bebop catapulted toward them, running at full speed. He stopped and ordered, "Don't go any further!" as he panted for breath, shaken.

"Bebop, what's wrong?" asked Eliza, worried.

Looking distressed, Bebop caught his breath enough to talk. "All went well, but when we moved the fourth tree off the trailer, a group of people surprised us. I barked commands to disburse immediately. All the team members ran in different directions, but the people are still there inspecting everything."

Attempting to calm him, Eliza said, "Bebop, you made sure the dig team members got away safely. Who knows how much the people actually saw."

Bebop remained agitated. "Other than when Tusko participated I never thought to set up lookouts around the dig spots. Of all places for this to happen, it had to be here. The last thing we need is to have curious humans traipsing around the cemetery and the NoHoSap entrance. How could I not have realized this? What a huge mistake."

Cuthbert offered, "You're being too hard on yourself, Captain. Humans are everywhere and are very curious. We're lucky no people discovered one of our prior digs. If they choose to spread the word about what they saw, which I'm sure they will since that's what humans love to do, it could add legitimacy to our posts and work. Cheshire said some people questioned whether the pictures were real. Now we have human witnesses to confirm they are."

"Good point, Cuthbert," Eliza complimented. Bebop still looked dejected.

"Hey, I have an idea!" exclaimed Cuthbert. "We can capitalize on this if Eliza goes over there now, talks with the humans, gets their take on what they saw, and finds out if they're going to post anything about it. She can let them know she recently saw posts of animals doing similar things and wondered if they were fabricated pictures. Also, she can get their contact information to allow us to find them again and use them to corroborate our work."

"I like it, Cuthbert!" said Eliza excitedly. Bebop perked up after hearing this idea. "I just had a thought of how we can make even more lemonade out of these lemons."

Cuthbert looked at her, puzzled. "What are you talking about? We have a serious situation here and you're changing the subject to talk about beverages?"

Bebop chuckled, less distraught after hearing Cuthbert's idea. "Cuthbert, it's a human saying about turning what could have been a bad situation into a good one. I didn't understand a lot of these things either but caught on while living with Eliza in HuHabDom. What's your idea, Eliza?"

"I could do a story on the news about what these humans saw and tie them to our posts on social media. This could be the link we need to bring everything together and get more publicity, assuming the station would want to run the story, but I think they will."

Bebop and Cuthbert were quiet as they considered the idea. Neither had anticipated much human attention to their cause at this early stage.

Eliza cautioned, "Not to rush you, but if we're going to do this, I should get over there soon, before the people leave the area. I'll act like I'm out for a walk and happen to discover them."

Cuthbert broke the silence. "I think it's a great idea. What do you think, Captain?"

"I'm on board. Get going, Eliza, we'll wait for you to report back here."

"Alright!" said Eliza as she gave Bebop a high five. "Be back soon." She left for the dig site at a brisk walk.

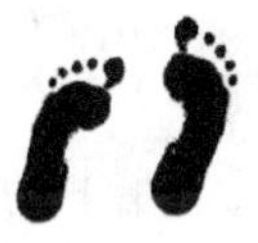

CHAPTER 18

SILVER LININGS

It didn't take long for Eliza to hear human voices ahead. She rounded a bend and saw four people–young to middle-aged, two men and two women–milling around the trailer and the three trees that had been planted. "Good morning," she greeted.

All the people looked over, since none had noticed her approaching. "Good morning," they replied, almost in unison. One of them, a short young-ish man with brown curly hair, went back to taking pictures and the younger woman, with long light brown hair, said to Eliza, "You wouldn't believe what we saw here this morning."

"What happened?"

The second woman, a bit older than the first, with short blonde hair, advised, "We were looking for gravestones to use for rubbings and came upon this area where there were a bunch of animals with this trailer full of trees." She pointed to the trailer. "They had one of the trees in the air, but when they saw us, they dropped the tree and took off running."

"Wow," said Eliza. "That's odd. What were they doing?"

"Near as we can tell, they were planting trees," commented the man taking pictures. "See, here are three freshly planted trees, a bunch of holes, and more trees on the trailer with a rope and pulley they must have been using to lift them off the trailer into the holes."

"Geez." Eliza acted surprised. "What kind of animals were they? Were there any humans? How could they have been doing this on their own?"

The second man, tall, slim, with thinning hair and about the same age as the woman with the blonde hair, noted, "We have the same questions. They ran out of here so fast we didn't get a good look, but I thought I saw a couple dogs, ox in front of the cart and skunk near one of the holes."

"I could have sworn I saw a monkey," said the blonde woman, "along with the ox and what could have been a fox. I didn't see any people and wondered how the animals happened to be out here. They had to have been trained by someone to do this."

The man taking pictures added, "If it weren't for the evidence they left, I might have thought I imagined it, but here's proof of what they were doing. Wish I'd gotten my phone out right away to get pictures of the animals."

"This is striking. I'm a journalist and think this would be a perfect story for our station, maybe for tonight's broadcast if you're willing."

"Really?" asked the younger woman. "That'd be cool and I'm game, as long as you don't portray us as crazies for seeing these things."

"Not at all," assured Eliza. "We'd report on what you saw and show the evidence that supports it. Just the facts, as some would say."

The people talked amongst themselves and the tall man said they agreed to be on the news.

"Great! I'll notify my manager and ask him to approve the story, then we'll get a camera crew here. If you'd like to continue finding gravestones for your rubbings, that's fine and I'll let you know when we're ready for the taping. Please give me your contact info and I'll be in touch."

Eliza gave each of them her card and they provided their information before leaving in search of gravestones. Eliza headed back toward where she left Bebop and Cuthbert. Before getting too far, she called her manager, Ira, and explained the breaking news she discovered. Ira agreed to run it on that evening's news, told Eliza to go with it, and congratulated her on the good work to find the story and bring it to the station.

She arrived back to Cuthbert and Bebop, who were waiting in anticipation. "How'd it go?" asked Bebop nervously.

"It went well. They told me what they saw, I got their contact information, and I'm doing a story for tonight's news about it."

"Perfect," said Cuthbert. "Seems the plan is coming together nicely."

Bebop inquired anxiously, "What did they see? Should we be concerned about anything?"

"No, they said you all ran away before they could see much. They think they saw an ox, monkey, skunk, fox, and a couple of dogs. They noticed the tree in the air and surmised from the rooted trees, trailer, and holes that you were planting trees. They didn't see any people nearby to direct what you were doing."

"OK, I guess that's not too bad, and we're making the most of it. I'm interested to see the reaction after you run the story on the news," said Bebop.

Cuthbert offered, "There's another benefit to the story. Now Eliza will be associated with our cause. Ideally, that'll start making her the go-to person for animals, and soon people, on our climate change mission."

"That's true," admitted Bebop. "Guess there's a silver lining after all to what seemed a dire situation."

"What are you talking about, Bebop?" asked Cuthbert. "There's no silver, jewelry, or anything with linings involved here."

Eliza and Bebop laughed. "Sorry, Cuthbert, another human expression," advised Eliza. "Guys, I'm going home to change, and will be back with a camera crew to film the story. There are woods nearby where you can watch if you'd like. I think Noli's at the house and will bring her back with me. She can then keep you posted on the story."

"OK, that sounds good," said Bebop.

"We'll head back to NoHoSap and wait to hear from you," added Cuthbert.

CHAPTER 19

Lights, Camera, Action

Eliza rushed home to get ready for the story. Since she didn't go on-air often, she wanted to make the most of this opportunity. Every other time she'd been on had been during the workday and the station's wardrobe people helped with her clothes while make-up artists took care of her hair and makeup. This time she had to figure it out on her own. "What to wear, what to wear," she asked herself while trying on different outfits and checking them in the mirror. "I want to look down to earth, but not earthy, professional, but not stuffy." I'll never take the wardrobe folks for granted again. She finally settled on a comfortable but savvy blouse and pants. Makeup was another source of delay while she experimented with different levels of foundation and eye shadow colors.

Excited to combine her new mission with her current job, she practiced the interview out loud, wording the questions to lead the interviewees to the answer she sought. Her trial practice classes in law school trained her to think that way—very helpful in the journalism world.

"Eliza," said Noli, near Eliza's ear.

Deep in thought about the story, Eliza jumped and looked over to see Noli on her shoulder. "Noli, you startled me."

"Sorry, but I wanted to ask if you needed me to go somewhere with you? Bebop sent a cryptic message that you were on your way back here and I should talk with you when you arrived."

"Yes, that's right." Eliza almost forgot about bringing Noli to the cemetery with her. "I'm going to the cemetery to do a story for the news tonight. I'd like you to go with me and let Bebop and Cuthbert know when we're going to start filming. That way they can come out and watch from the woods."

"OK, I'll take care of that."

Eliza finished putting on her makeup and calmed her hair while talking through the interview. "All set, Noli, let's go." Noli braced herself on Eliza's shoulder and they headed out the door.

The news van with the camera crew arrived at the cemetery entrance just before Eliza. She pulled up next to the driver and shouted out the window, "Follow me."

They drove through the main gate and continued to the far side of the cemetery. The "witnesses" waited for the crew as Eliza and the van pulled up, having been alerted by Eliza of the meeting time. "Noli, please let Bebop and Cuthbert know we'll be filming in about 20 minutes."

"I'm on it." Taking advantage of cool air remnants left from the air conditioning, Noli settled in one of the car's air vents, adjusted her mini headset, and talked into it as Eliza left.

Eliza walked toward her interviewees. "Hey everyone, how did the gravestone rubbing go?"

"Fine," said the blonde woman, "but we had trouble focusing because we kept thinking about the animals with the trees, what we were going to say, and how we'd look on the news."

"No worries. It'll go well and you'll come across great. Let me introduce you to the camera crew."

Eliza walked over to the man and woman who disembarked from the van shortly after Eliza left her car. They pulled camera equipment from the back of the vehicle.

Interrupting their unpacking, Eliza said, "Thank you both for coming out right away on a weekend. I'm Eliza Vernon and don't believe I've worked with you previously."

"Not that I remember," replied the man as he gathered a wound-up cord. "I'm Rodrigo, camera operator."

"I'm Alice, technical coordinator."

"Nice to meet you. Can I help?"

"Nope, we got it." Rodrigo lifted a large camera onto his shoulder.

Alice inquired, "What did you have in mind for shooting the story, Eliza?"

She motioned for Rodrigo and Alice to follow her toward the planting area. "I thought you could start by showing the trailer. I'll begin talking but will stand on the other side of the trees over there. The camera pans toward me while I continue talking, and when the camera hits me, I'll walk back to stand between the trailer and trees, where I'll interview our guests. I'd like to splice some close-up shots of the trees, empty holes, and trailer into the story while I'm talking with the witnesses."

"OK, got it," affirmed Alice. "We'll take shots of those things now while you're telling the interviewees how this will work."

"Sounds good." Eliza walked back to the foursome, explained where the camera would pan, when they should walk into the scene, and where they should stand. "Remember, we'll be taping audio too, so please do not talk until I ask a question. Also, only one person should answer each question. As a result, indicate to me by a subtle gesture who wants to field it, and I'll move the microphone over to you."

The group listened intently and when Eliza asked whether they had any questions, indicated no.

"OK, great. Rodrigo, Alice, we're all set."

The crew finished taking pictures of the scene and joined Eliza and the witnesses. Alice instructed, "Eliza, take your place over on the far side of the trees. Folks, please stand right here for now. I'll let you know when you can go into the scene. Please enter quietly and discreetly. The camera will follow Eliza as she walks back toward you for the interview."

Eliza went to her starting spot. Alice said, "On my signal, Rodrigo will roll film and start panning toward Eliza and Eliza will start talking."

Rodrigo and Eliza waited. Alice put her open hand in the air, then closed and lowered it to signal 'Go'. Rodrigo recorded, Eliza talked into the mic and told the story as she walked toward the trailer.

"Hello, everyone, Eliza Vernon here at the Rural Cemetery. We're bringing you a remarkable story. As you can see, there are a few newly planted trees behind me and a trailer with more trees on it." She stopped next to the interviewees. "These folks were here to do some grave rubbings and happened upon something unexpected. What did you see?"

The tall man leaned toward the microphone and said, "We came around the bend in the road and saw a bunch of animals near the trailer with a tree in the air. They scattered when they saw us."

"What animals did you see?"

The younger brown-haired woman answered, "There was an ox, dog or two, and a skunk."

"Don't forget the monkey," added the younger, picture-taking man.

"That's quite a combination. What were the animals doing?"

The older blonde woman said, "We couldn't tell at first, but it looks like they were planting trees. A few trees were just planted, and the number of trees left on the trailer match the number of empty holes."

"Did you see any other humans around?"

The younger man answered, "No, we looked for someone but didn't see or hear anybody. It appears the animals were acting on their own. By the way, I have a message for the viewers."

Perplexed, since they hadn't discussed any additional messages, Eliza paused. As she did, the man ripped open his jacket to reveal a bright green T-shirt with a globe on it captioned with "Love your Mother." Eliza gawked in horror at the display that could sabotage the story. She jumped in front of the man while Alice frantically signaled to wrap up.

Struggling to keep her composure, Eliza calmly said, "Thank you all for talking with us," then turned toward the camera and continued, "There you have it. Looks like animals are taking their own initiative to make this a greener place. We'll keep you updated with any more developments on this story. I'm Eliza Vernon and thanks for watching."

Alice yelled, "Cut! That's a wrap."

Eliza turned the microphone off and Rodrigo lowered the camera from his shoulder and rolled up the power cord. The three behaving interviewees berated the younger man, asking how he could ruin the story by putting all the focus on himself. Eliza squared off with the shirt flasher and scolded him for pulling a fast one. "What were you thinking? That shirt incident could mean the story won't air. You may have ruined getting this information out by taking a stand that was entirely inappropriate."

The man smiled sheepishly and explained he never planned to show his Earth shirt but got caught up in the moment being on TV. "I don't know why that seemed like a good idea at the time. I'm sorry and hope you can edit that out so the story may air."

"We'll see. If you see it on the news tonight, you'll know we succeeded. If not, it didn't make it out of the cutting room."

"We'll cross our fingers, it's the former," observed the older woman as she glared at the younger man.

"Thank you all for your time and willingness to share this story. If you see any more activity here or otherwise, please give me a call."

"Will do," "OK" and "thank you," along with another "sorry," came the replies as the group left to continue their day.

Eliza handed the microphone to Alice. "Can you believe that? I hope you can edit that display out. With the station's policy of not airing stories involving people or topics 'on the fringe,' we can't air it unless you can delete that part."

"We'll go back to the studio and work up the story. We should be able to splice that out and it will still flow nicely. I'll text you when it's ready to review in the share box."

"Excellent! I'll be on the lookout and will clear it to air ASAP. Enjoy the rest of the weekend and thank you again!"

Eliza walked toward her car while checking the phone for messages. Once the news van drove out of sight, she headed to the neighboring woods. As soon as she entered the cover of the trees, Bebop and Cuthbert appeared.

"What did you think of the coverage?" Eliza waited for feedback but heard only silence. Bebop and Cuthbert both looked as though they didn't want to let Eliza know they weren't pleased with her work. Disappointed, Eliza didn't know what to say.

"Gotcha!" exclaimed Bebop after what seemed like an eternity. He smiled and his whole body wiggled as it tried to follow his tail. "Great job on the story!"

"I thought so too!" agreed Cuthbert. "Although I wanted to tell you right away and not play Bebop's prank."

"Very funny, Bebop. You had me going there, but I'm pleased you liked it."

"Yes, it came across very well. I even liked the flasher's stunt."

"That's going to be edited out. He had some nerve to pull that on-air."

"Now the question is, what do we do with these trees?"

Cuthbert pointed out, "We can't come back to finish the job since people may be watching the site, but the trees won't last long with their roots exposed."

"Good point, Cuthbert."

Bebop offered, "We can call Jacob and ask him to put a small team together to plant the trees later today."

"I'd like to help and will ask Zeke if he can, too. That way we can do a follow-up on the station's website and social media about planting the trees to save them from dying. I'm sure Zeke would appreciate the exposure. I'll check with him and be back once I change into outdoor clothes." Eliza walked away while texting Zeke.

"Hey, wait. Don't leave yet." Bebop said impatiently. "We won't be here when you come back and plant the rest of the trees, and we didn't talk about the schedule for tomorrow yet."

Eliza turned back, mildly annoyed. "You didn't mention anything for tomorrow, and I planned to catch up on things at work since I had to leave early a few nights last week for the digs."

"Sorry for your luck, but we planned to visit Central Park in New York City tomorrow. We lined up a couple other humans and animals for this project." Bebop had no sympathy for Eliza's workload. "We're leaving bright and early in the morning and are doing a briefing on the way there. We're not meeting tonight, though, and you can work then."

"OK, I'll deal with it. When and where are we meeting, and do you want me to bring anything?" Eliza realized the time would soon come, that she'd have to scale back at the station to enable her to focus on the mission.

"6:00 a.m. at the parking area across from the cemetery's chapel. Bring some donuts if you can. Chef Cecil is packing lunch for us."

"Alright, see you then." Bebop gave her a high five, then trotted away with Cuthbert waving from the bag hanging out of Bebop's mouth.

CHAPTER 20

HUMAN INTERVENTION

Eliza finished texting Zeke on the way to her car. He agreed to assist, and Eliza told him she'd pick him up at the station, where she planned to check the story since she had trouble viewing the share box on her phone. Upon arriving home, she changed back to her walking clothes, loaded a couple shovels and work gloves into the car, then headed to the office.

As she hoped, Eliza arrived before Zeke, which gave her time to sign into the share box from her office computer. Fortunately, Alice had been able to cut out the earth shirt stunt. Eliza made a few edits to the story, then released it for airing on the news later that day.

Zeke stepped out of his car as she made it back to the parking lot.

"Thanks for helping with this."

"Sure thing, especially since I had nothing else going on today other than a trip to the gym."

"Looks like you go to the gym frequently." Eliza never saw him in anything other than work clothes and was surprised to see his toned physique in the shorts and T-shirt he wore today.

"It's part of my regular routine," he replied, seemingly oblivious to Eliza's subtle compliment.

"I figured you'd appreciate the publicity because it's a follow-up to a story that'll air tonight."

"Really? What'd you stumble upon for a story on a Saturday?"

Before answering, she settled into her car, giving herself time to figure out how to answer Zeke's question. "I took a walk in the cemetery and came upon some people who'd just seen something newsworthy."

"What was it?"

"They said they saw a bunch of animals planting trees."

"And since when do we do stories about what crazy people see?"

Acutely aware of the station's rule about not covering events that aren't verifiable or that sound outlandish, especially after the T-shirt flashing incident, Eliza said, "We don't, but there were remnants of the work being done, these folks didn't seem to have any screws loose, and they were very genuine telling me what they saw. I called Ira, and he said to run with it."

"Wow, seems like you happened on a good one." Zeke had a touch of envy in his voice.

"Don't sound so surprised. I can find worthy stories too. They're not all boring legal analyses."

"Not quite all of them. But you have it tough being the legal reporter because those stories can be very dry–no offense."

"Gee, thanks for letting me know." Eliza pretended to be hurt. She and Zeke often joked about how the topics he covered were generally more interesting than those Eliza handled.

"By the way, where are we going?"

"The Rural Cemetery. Have you been there before?"

"No, and why should I have been? I don't have a dog to walk and even if I did, I wouldn't want to hang out in a cemetery–it's creepy."

"It's not as bad as you think. It's actually a cool place, especially the older parts, with sculptured monuments and walking trails through the woods."

"To each his own. We just better be out of there long before the sun sets."

"That shouldn't be a problem. There are about 6-8 trees to plant and the holes are already dug. I also wanted to take some pictures and post them on the station's website to follow up on the story that'll air tonight. That way you'll get some nice exposure for your work today."

"I'll take it. Every bit helps."

They drove through the main cemetery gate and Eliza noticed Zeke tense up. She pointed and shouted, "There's a ghost!"

Zeke bolted to attention and looked wide-eyed to where she pointed. Eliza cracked up. Realizing he'd been had, he scolded sarcastically, "Not even funny."

"I couldn't resist—you seemed uptight as soon as we got here. You should have seen the look on your face." Eliza giggled. "The trees are on the other side of the cemetery. We'll be there soon."

"Isn't this private property, should we even be planting trees here without permission?"

"I never thought of that. Many people walk here, making it seem like a public place. I don't think there's time to get permission before these trees dry out, but I'll follow up with the cemetery superintendent Monday."

"OK, I figured you of all people would be thinking about the legalities of this, but if you're not worried about it, I'm not either. If anyone says anything, I'll let them know my attorney said it wasn't a problem."

"Fair enough."

Eliza parked next to the trailer with the trees. They exited the car and Eliza took the shovels from the trunk. Zeke checked the planted trees, then surveyed the holes and trailer. "This looks like the work of humans. Maybe the animals were here looking at it when the people found them."

"No, the people said the animals were doing the work, that they had a tree in the air but ran as soon as they saw the humans."

"Hmmm, it just seems hard to believe."

Eliza thought, '*If only he knew everything the animals could do with absolutely no human involvement.*' They discussed how they were going to get the trees from the trailer into the holes and hold the trees up while filling the holes with dirt.

A young girl's voice sounded, "Hi, Eliza, we're here to help plant trees."

Eliza and Zeke both looked up to see Oji and Jacob walking toward them.

Jacob said, "Hi, Eliza."

"Hey, you guys. Yes, we could use some assistance. Jacob and Oji, this is Zeke. Zeke, meet Jacob and his sister, Oji. We met out here walking dogs."

Oji looked at Eliza oddly, knowing they didn't meet that way. Jacob preempted Oji, "Yes, we see each other out here quite a bit, but left our dog at home when Eliza called to say she needed help."

Not suspecting they were making up stories, Zeke didn't bat an eye. The three shook hands and exchanged pleasantries.

"What can we do?" asked Jacob.

Eliza instructed, "Well, there's a rope already attached to this tree. Let's lift that and swing it over to the next hole, then plant it. Zeke and Jacob, if you two take care of that Oji and I will fill the hole with dirt once the tree's in."

Oji's face lit up when she heard she had a job. She picked up a shovel and stood at the ready. Zeke tested the rope and pulley system, then lifted the tree. Once fully upright, Jacob guided the tree toward the next hole and Zeke lowered it.

"Good work, Jacob, hold the tree steady once it's lowered and we'll dump dirt in the hole." As Eliza and Oji finished filling the hole and stomping the dirt down, Jacob tied the rope around the next tree, Zeke lifted it up, and they did the process again.

Eliza laughed at Zeke's speed. "Looks like you're not taking any chances of moving this along. You really don't want to be here when the sun sets, do you?"

"You got that right. This isn't a place I want to be after dusk. Plus, I saw the sign when we came in that the gates lock at 6 p.m., and I need to be out of here well before then in case they lock early."

"We'll be done before you know it with that attitude,"

To Eliza's surprise, Zeke seemed to be enjoying himself. He always made fun of her outdoor activities, saying he wasn't into nature and all that. She remembered she needed to take pictures to post on the station's website, and snapped away, including some of Zeke manning the pulley and moving the trees.

The remaining trees were planted in short order. The four admired the freshly planted row, Jacob found a hose and faucet nearby, and Oji watered the somewhat wilted foliage as Eliza took pictures.

"What should we do with the trailer, rope, and pulley?" inquired Zeke.

"Good question. I don't know where they came from."

Jacob offered, "We could put them at the edge of the woods to get them out of the way for now. Maybe the cemetery maintenance people will pick them up."

Eliza wondered if those were actually Bebop's instructions. "That'll work. Thanks, Jacob."

Hard at work trying to wheel the trailer to the woods, Zeke said, "Geez, this thing is heavy. They must have had a truck to get this here."

"Something like that," acknowledged Jacob as he reached for the trailer to help pull.

Oji took ahold too, looked at the front of the trailer and said, "But there's no…."

Eliza interrupted, "There's no way to know unless the cemetery has hidden cameras, which I don't think they do." Eliza also noticed the trailer had an ox yoke rather than a trailer hitch. She assumed that's what Oji wanted to point out and thought it best that Zeke not be alerted. Looking at Oji and Jacob, Eliza shook her head 'no' to indicate they shouldn't make comments like that around Zeke.

"Nice work everyone–thank you!"

"Glad to assist," Jacob acknowledged before turning toward one of the walking paths leading away from the worksite.

"Good to see you again, Eliza, and thanks for letting me help," Oji said with a smile, before following Jacob.

As Eliza drove back to the station, she told Zeke she'd post the pictures in the morning, as follow-ups to the story airing tonight. The story showed the extra holes and trees, and Eliza thought it important to plant the rest of the trees because she didn't want viewers thinking they were left to die.

Zeke agreed and thanked her for including him. "I'm generally not much into outdoorsy, nature stuff, but have to admit I enjoyed being out there today." He almost said he enjoyed the time with Eliza too but didn't want to sound awkward or too forward.

"Nothing like getting your hands in the soil. It brings us back to being connected with the Earth, which is easy to forget in the world we live in today. We can be isolated from anything natural, living in concrete cities, getting food already made from takeout places, maybe seeing a tree or hearing a bird every once in a while."

"You know, I never thought about it like that, but you're right. I'm never out for a walk just to be outside. I'm always going somewhere or playing some sport outdoors, but not noticing anything around me while I'm there. And I definitely never think about the food I eat being grown in some natural place. I know I like sunny days better than rainy ones and don't like it to be too warm or cold, but I don't realize how that impacts things that live or grow outdoors."

Seeing an opportunity, Eliza jumped at it. "And there you go, people forget those things and we end up with a warming planet and all the things that result from it–melting glaciers, rising oceans, cold weather species struggling to survive, unpredictable weather with more severe storms and long, dry heat waves, people losing homes to fires and wind and rain events–I could go on and on."

"I always rolled my eyes and tuned you out when you'd start talking about all that. Maybe I should pay more attention."

"Hopefully you will, but that's the challenge, to get more people engaged and noticing the connectivity of everything, then maybe we can better address and implement solutions to the issues."

"Yeah, I see. For me, I plan to spend more time outside and pay attention to what's going on around me while I'm there."

"Sounds good, and I'll hold you to it. If you got a dog, you'd spend more time outside because you'd have to walk it."

"Don't push it. It's a big step for me to do stuff outdoors. I'm nowhere close to wanting to get a dog. That's your thing."

"I know that, but thought it was worth a try. You're always welcome to walk Bop."

"Speaking of that, when am I going to meet him?"

"Good question. I'll have to bring him to the station."

"Or maybe I could walk with you after work or on the weekend some time."

Eliza blushed. "That would be nice. We'll have to figure out when we're both free."

They arrived at the station. Eliza pulled into the parking lot and Zeke said goodbye, got out, then headed to his car. Eliza watched him walking away, caught herself, waved as he arrived at his car, and headed out.

She hurried home to catch up on work and weekend chores since tomorrow would be a long day in the City. She also hoped to get a good night's sleep before getting up early the next morning. Although pulled in many directions and worried about keeping up at work, she felt more energized than she had in a while and thought what a difference it made doing something she enjoyed and that would have a positive impact on the larger world.

CHAPTER 21

ROAD TRIP

Eliza and Noli arrived at the appointed time and place the following morning, bringing donuts, as Bebop requested. The rising sun revealed few clouds in the sky, but the forecast for later in the day called for scattered thunderstorms that could be powerful, particularly to the south where they were headed. Eliza toyed with bringing Bebop's raincoat as a joke, but decided against it because she didn't want to undermine his authority.

Shortly after they arrived, a van pulled up and Jacob jumped out, with Oji not far behind.

"Hi, Eliza. I get to go with you today," Oji announced.

"Good morning, Eliza," said Jacob. "Oji begged to go and wore me down until I agreed to bring her. I almost mentioned yesterday that I'd see you today but figured I better not since I didn't know if Zeke was wise to it."

"Morning. Good to see you again. That was the right decision because Zeke isn't working on this mission and doesn't know about my involvement in it, but I thought he'd be helpful yesterday."

"That he was. We got the job done in no time with his help." Jacob motioned toward the middle of the van. "I'd like to introduce you to Lee."

Eliza realized someone was sitting behind the passenger seat, and waved to the figure. A hand waved back through the window.

"Wait a second, I should put the window down," Jacob turned the ignition on and lowered the window. "Sorry, Lee," he said over his shoulder to the person in the back seat.

"No problem. Must be a childproof lock because I couldn't open it."

"Hi Lee, I'm Eliza." Eliza looked through the window and saw a woman with short, almost black hair on a shiny red scooter. Her left arm hung in her lap.

"Very nice to meet you, Eliza," replied Lee. "That's Midnight." She motioned toward the back of the van. When she said the name, a black Labrador Retriever stood up, walked over to the window, and smelled then licked Eliza's hand.

"He's sweet."

"He's my service dog–don't know what I'd do without him. He's helped me in countless ways since I had the stroke that took my left side."

"Oh no! I can't even imagine." Eliza didn't know what to say.

"No need to feel uncomfortable." Lee tried to put Eliza at ease. "I don't mind talking about it. It's obvious and I'm not trying to hide that I have some physical challenges."

Bebop's voice came authoritatively from in front of the van, "Here are the rest of us. Alright, team, into the van, and let's get moving."

Bebop approached with two smaller dogs.

"Morning, Bebop," greeted the humans almost simultaneously.

"Good morning, all. This is Curly. He's a cockapoo, a cocker spaniel and poodle mix. And this is Boo. She's a Bugg, a Boston terrier and pug mix." Curly and Boo lifted their paws in greeting. "They're rounding out our team today. Jacob, take this bag off my back. Cecil loaded it up with lunch, but it's weighing me down."

Jacob undid the latch around Bebop's waist and put the bag under the passenger seat. "That bag is heavy. Seems Chef Cecil hooked us up."

"Would you expect anything less? Let's go, time's a wasting." Bebop hopped into the backseat next to Lee's scooter, and Oji squeezed in between.

Jacob opened the rear door of the van. Curly and Boo took a running start and landed in the back with Midnight. Eliza took the passenger seat in front.

"We're off," announced Jacob as he drove away.

Eliza offered donuts to everyone, and Bebop lunged at one. Following his lead, everyone else ate up and polished off the first dozen and then some in short order.

"Thanks, Eliza, that hit the spot. Now we can focus on the details of this project without being hungry. Today is an experiment. We'll see how it goes and then decide if we replicate it in other locations."

The human and canine travelers listened to Bebop intently.

"We're going to Central Park and will pretend we're humans with their pets out for a walk. We'll arrive during the off-leash time to allow us dogs more latitude to make contact with other off-leash dogs while they're not near their humans. Midnight, Curly, Boo, and I will engage dogs and bend their ears about getting their humans to make climate-friendly changes. At the same time, Eliza, Lee, and Jacob will talk with the dogs' humans. They'll discuss the odd weather, changing climate, and things they can do to help, like eating locally-produced foods, cutting back on plastic use, being more energy-efficient, planting trees, etc."

"Sounds good in theory, but how are we supposed to bring those topics up out of the blue with people we just met?" asked Lee.

"I had the same thought," Eliza agreed.

"I know it's a challenge and don't have a specific answer for you. We thought about devising some suggested scripts you could use, but then decided you as humans would be better able to figure that out."

Jacob offered, "We could start just like Bebop said, by talking about the weather. Say something about how warm it's been or how the rainstorms have been stronger, or how you heard it's supposed to be a seriously cold winter."

"Yeah, I guess that'll work," said Lee. "It may be more difficult to talk about what should be done to reduce the warming, but I'm more optimistic I'll be able to get there once the conversation turns to climate."

"That helps, Jacob, thanks" Eliza chimed in.

Bebop continued with the plan. "I'll go with Eliza, Midnight will be with Lee, and Curly and Boo will accompany Jacob. We'll start at the sandlot near the ball fields. We should stay where we can see each other but keep enough distance that our conversations—either human to human or dog to dog—can't be overheard. Pay attention to who the others are talking with because we don't want to waste resources by talking to the same person or dog twice. Once the off-leash time is up, we'll walk a bit on-leash, but if that doesn't appear to be productive, we'll cut it short."

All human and dog members of the team confirmed they were up to speed and ready.

Eliza mused again at how the tables turned and she now followed instructions from Bebop. It wasn't long ago that she'd get perturbed at him for not doing what she told him. She knew he was a smart dog, but never imagined he'd be leading a mission like this. Then again, why would she in her wildest dreams think there was a place like NoHoSap and she'd be teaming up with its inhabitants and Bebop to save the world?

"What do I do?" inquired Oji.

Bebop looked at Jacob as though asking why he brought Oji anyway, since he didn't have a job for her, then became pensive, trying to come up with something for her to do.

Lee suggested, "Oji, why don't you hang out with Midnight and me? You can introduce Midnight to some other dogs."

"I like that. Thanks, Lee!"

"Now that the instructions are out of the way, I'll take a maple donut, please," said Bebop. Boo and Curly split one and everyone else other than Lee helped themselves to another donut. Lee mentioned she had to be careful not to eat too much since she didn't burn as many calories, what with using the scooter instead of walking to get around.

"Lee, if you don't mind, when did you have the stroke?" Eliza asked.

"About ten years ago. I was in my mid-thirties when it happened. They still don't know why. It hit me without warning and the next thing I knew, my left side didn't work. At least I survived and the left side of my face eventually came back. It could have been worse, although I didn't think so at the time."

"Geez."

"I didn't adjust well to no longer being able to do many things I enjoyed–no more skiing, cycling, gardening, walking without great difficulty, or doing anything that required me to use both hands and arms at once. I became very dejected and angry, didn't feel like going to physical therapy even though they said it could help, didn't feel like doing much of anything. I took time off from work and went back after a few months. The accommodations they provided didn't really help, though, and I resigned without having a backup plan. My fiancé was my biggest supporter, encouraging me to do the work to get my strength back, and taking care of me with my many limitations. I was extremely bitter with my situation, though, and took it out on him, the one closest to me. He stuck it out for about a year, during which I was constantly depressed. I kept postponing our wedding because I wouldn't be able to walk down the aisle or dance. I could see him turning into a negative person, and to resent me for holding him back. Hard as it was, I eventually told him I thought we should go our separate ways. He resisted at first and ultimately realized that may be best. He said he only wanted the best for me and prayed I would want the best for myself."

Lee paused and sighed, then visibly gathered herself and continued. "To make a long story short, I finally contacted a group my fiancé previously suggested I call, a group that worked with people in my predicament to get them back in action. They taught me how to deal with my condition, physically and mentally, and brought me Midnight. Midnight improved my life in many ways. He kept me company and comforted me when I felt down, didn't get upset with me during my foul moods, was always eager to see me no matter what, and helped me see I had many things for which I should be thankful. I still get angry and sad about what happened but would be in really rough shape if it weren't for Midnight and the group that brought him into my life."

All in the van were quiet after hearing Lee's story. Eliza broke the silence. "Thank you for sharing, Lee. It must be painful to talk about it, but you're very brave to do so. I'm crying just thinking about it and am so sorry for what you experienced."

"It's gotten much better, which is part of the process. There will always be good days and bad days, but at least now I have many more good than bad days, which wasn't always the case."

"Tell them how you got involved with the Mission," suggested Midnight.

"He loves it when I tell that story. You see, Midnight here isn't your 'ordinary' service dog. He, like Bebop, trained in NoHoSap before being sent to HuHabDom to work with me. He moved through the service dog training in no time. After he'd been with me for a while, NoHoSap emissaries visited me since I can't get into NoHoSap. They asked if I'd be interested in being a human contact working on their cause. I'd always been a vocal advocate for climate change awareness, especially before my stroke, and they felt I could be helpful. I've managed a blog and written articles since then to try to get the broader word out, but it seems to be falling on deaf ears."

"Stick with it, Lee, we've seen positive comments from folks who are engaged with your blog or have read your articles," advised Bebop. "Maybe not what you'd hoped for quite yet, but it's well worth your efforts."

"I know, that's what you keep saying and that's why I keep writing."

"Hey, wait, is your blog 'Stay Cool'?" asked Eliza.

"That's the one," Lee answered proudly.

"I've followed that for years and always appreciate the balanced approach. Who knew we'd have a chance to meet one day. You have a lot of great information on your blog, Lee."

"Thanks. I try to keep it simple and focus on what regular folks can easily do to help reduce the pace of warming. It's not hard to recycle, reuse bottles and containers, change light bulbs to LED, walk, bike or take public transportation, be more efficient about when and where you drive, or turn lights and computers off when you're not using them."

"True but breaking habits and doing new things instead is the tough part."

"That and getting the word out to motivate a critical mass of people to change and demand changes from others," added Lee. "Once that happens, we should see a real difference. I need to increase my following but have found it hard to do, especially since I don't have many contacts. Also, I feel like a broken record with many of my posts but am hoping the more they hear what they can do the more likely they'll start doing it."

"Hopefully it'll turn around once the NoHoSap posts on which we're working take off. We link to you already and are trying to increase our following too. I'll also link to you on my site for work."

"Thanks, I appreciate that. It's hard for me to be patient, but I know everything takes time."

"Bebop, you sure do have very capable humans working on this mission."

"We've been able to recruit well-qualified people and you're all in good company as Change Agents."

"We're the Change Agents?" asked Lee. "I noticed some hits on my blog from the Change Agents and wondered who it was.

"Am I a Change Agent too?" asked Oji.

Eliza confirmed, "Of course you are, Oji, we're all Change Agents."

"I like the name, Change Agents," opined Lee.

"Me too," agreed Jacob. "I feel almost like we're super-heroes now that we have a name."

Eliza and Lee laughed. "Hey Bebop, when do we get our Change Agents suits?" joked Eliza, which was met by more laughter from the other humans.

"We should come up with a theme song," suggested Jacob through the chuckles. Oji sang a ditty off the top of her head about the Change Agents, and everyone cracked up.

Bebop shot them a look, showing he didn't appreciate the joking. "This is serious business. We don't have superpowers and, although we are trying to save the world, we're going to do it without fanfare. We need to focus on the mission and that's it."

The humans quieted down, although each now imagined themselves as special agents in a battle against the formidable enemy of climate change. Not necessarily a bad way to think of things for extra motivation.

CHAPTER 22

CITYSCAPES

Sun brightened the trek to the City. When they arrived, Jacob found a spot near the park and the team disembarked into hot, humid air. Eliza, Jacob, and Lee put collars and leashes on their canine companions, and they all headed toward the western edge of the grounds. Waves of putrid smells hit them, especially when they walked past vents and drains. Curly and Boo gagged and said, "pee yew" each time they breathed the odors, and Bebop softly scolded them to be quiet, not wanting humans to hear them talking.

When they reached the park entrance, Bebop motioned for them to take separate routes to the sandlot. The park sidewalks and roads teemed with people in all modes of moving—walking and talking nonchalantly, running, walking dogs, cycling, and even roller-blading. Most people with dogs let them off leash once they were inside the park, and the dogs tore away running as soon as the leash hooks clicked open. Eliza, Jacob, and Lee did the same, but the NoHoSap dogs stayed with their humans, especially Midnight with his service dog duties.

The team spaced themselves out on the edges of the sandlot, abuzz with activity. Dogs chased each other in circles, ran after balls, sniffed each other's butts, and sidled up to humans to see if they had any treats.

An energetic pit-bull mix ran over to Bebop, crouched down and jumped to entice him to play. Bebop ignored her. He hadn't played for quite a while; it wasn't appropriate for a Captain to act like that. Eliza pressed him to let go since he used to love to jump and wrestle with other dogs.

"Go, Bebop, play!" Bebop looked at her as if to say, 'Please, I'm not interested and am not doing that.' She continued and he finally threw a paw at the other dog, who jumped around even more after getting a reaction. Eliza kept on him and Bebop threw another paw, then crouched down, remembering how to play. Soon they were running around the sandlot and wrestling. Laughing, Eliza enjoyed watching Bebop have fun.

"I didn't think she'd get him going," said a voice next to Eliza. A woman with a leash around her shoulders walked over. The woman continued, "She's very persistent and it's rare that other dogs don't end up playing with her. Your dog held back for a while but is giving her a good run now."

"I'm glad he gave in. He'll be tired after this."

The women discussed their dogs–their ages, where they got them, where they liked to walk, etc. Eliza struggled to get to the topic of climate. As she thought about how to bring up the weather, the sun disappeared behind a thick cloud. Eliza took advantage of the natural segue.

"This weather's been odd lately. Looks like we may get some of the storms they predicted. Hopefully, they won't be too damaging."

"I know, we had some fierce ones this summer," agreed the pit bull's human. "I've never seen as many trees and limbs down in the park and on the streets before."

"Those trees can't be easily replaced. It took decades for them to grow, and they're wiped out in the blink of an eye with these winds. Are they planting new trees in their place?"

"Not that I've seen. You're right, it's definitely a loss."

Going out on a limb, Eliza said, "I'm involved in a group upstate that plants trees in our parks to fight climate change. There must be some organizations here that do the same thing—the park conservancy or neighborhood associations?"

"Good question, you'd think there would be. I'll have to look into that. I prefer landscapes with trees."

"I do too. Hope you find something. It makes you feel good seeing areas improved with new foliage you planted."

Bebop and the pit-bull mix were back, panting like they needed a break. The pit's human said, "Thanks for the workout, she'll sleep well this afternoon. Hopefully we'll see you here again."

"Likewise." Eliza turned to Bebop, "Looks like you could use some water." She spotted a water fountain at the far end of the sandlot, and they headed toward it. On the way there she noticed Midnight, Curly, and Boo playing with other dogs and Jacob and Lee talking with other humans—good signs.

Designed for both dogs and humans, the fountain had a drinking spigot for humans and a bowl at the bottom with a faucet for dogs. Eliza freshened the water in the dog bowl. While Bebop lapped up the water, a German Shepherd tried to push him out of the way. Bebop gave him a dirty look but, not wanting to start a fight, let the other dog in.

"Sorry, he's a bully and a water hog," said a man as he pushed the German Shepherd away to make room for Bebop.

"That's OK, it's not good for him to guzzle too much at once," replied Eliza.

A conversation similar to the discussion with the pit bull's human ensued, although Eliza found it easier than before to make the connection about how the human could help curb global warming. As they talked, the sky filled with rain clouds and thunder rumbled in the distance. Bebop paced in front of Eliza to break up the conversation. She said they had to go and the German Shepherd and his human left. Eliza bent down to see what Bebop wanted and he asked her quietly to let Jacob and Lee know they should go back to the van before the rain began. He and Eliza would stay a bit longer to make a few more contacts.

They walked over to Lee, waited for her to finish talking to another human with a Labrador Retriever, and Eliza let Lee know the new plan. Oji ran over, heard they had to leave, and said the news bummed her out. Looking at the clouds, Lee agreed they needed to go since the scooter shouldn't get wet. She called Midnight, they went over to Jacob, broke the news, and left for the van.

In the meantime, a young Weimaraner discovered Bebop and wanted to play. Very interested to talk with Eliza about having such a high-energy dog in the city, the pup's human bent Eliza's ear discussing the ins and outs of Weimaraners. Eliza heard the thunder getting closer as the sky grew more ominous. She mentioned the weather and tree planting to the Weim owner before they went their separate ways. Then she and Bebop hightailed it toward the park exit.

They didn't get far before rain pounded down and thunder roared loudly. Eliza suggested taking cover under a nearby bridge. The sky opened up just as they made it underneath. One person slept along the walls, oblivious to the storm. The wide, sturdy stone bridge appeared to be a perfect refuge. It offered an unobstructed view out toward the sandlot. The rain poured incessantly while thunder rang out and lightning flashed.

Bebop and Eliza stood under the bridge, watching the downpour, hoping the rest of the team made it to the van before the sky opened up. Soon water puddled under the edge of the bridge. They thought nothing of it until it grew and crept inward, closing in on the person sleeping. Eliza woke him and pointed at the encroaching water. He stood up groggily, collected his belongings as the puddle expanded toward him, and alerted Bebop and Eliza to another large puddle encroaching from the other end of the bridge. The dry area shrunk as the three stepped closer and closer together. The man who'd been sleeping made a run for it up the hill, away from the bridge to a small stone building, whooping as he jumped through puddles. Eliza and Bebop huddled together in the vanishing dry spot. When it became obvious the area would flood momentarily, they ran as fast as they could from under the bridge. The rain barreled down in big, cold drops, reminding Eliza of the weather during Maria and Sophie's rescue.

The pair made a beeline to the stone building up the hill. It had a porch in front, where the man who'd been sleeping under the bridge huddled with five others beneath blankets. They appeared to live in the park, knew each other, and chatted as the storm continued. Eliza wondered how they survived living outdoors with all the uncertain weather events.

The rain continued falling heavily, even though the thunder subsided. Suddenly, simultaneous phone alerts sounded, and all the humans pulled out their devices. The man from under the bridge chuckled and said, "It's a flood alert. Like we can't see there's a flooding problem. Duh." Everyone laughed.

Bebop paced, impatient to leave. After what seemed like forever but likely lasted only about ten minutes, the sky brightened, and the rain let up. Eliza said she and Bebop had to go and wished them well. They left the building and walked in the light rain to the van, hoping the rest of the team would be there safe and dry.

Jacob jumped out of the van when he saw Eliza and Bebop and opened the doors for them. "Glad to see you guys! We didn't know where you were or what may have happened. Looks like you got a little wet."

"Yes, but not nearly as much as we would have been if we hadn't found a dry spot to wait it out." Bebop shook himself off.

They all hopped into the van and took their seats.

Bebop inquired, "You all made it back before the rain hit?"

"Just barely," answered Lee. "I put the scooter into overdrive to get back here and these guys had all they could do to keep up. Good thing I charged it fully last night."

Jacob pulled the van away and the group left the City, pleased to be going back to NoHoSap.

CHAPTER 23

ASSESSMENTS

Midnight splayed out on his side in the back of the van, worn out. "I'm not in shape for that kind of running," he admitted, as Oji massaged his shoulders.

Half asleep, Boo and Curly didn't bother to add their two cents.

"Our project was cut short today, but at least we made some connections," Bebop summarized. "What's your assessment of the effectiveness of this process? Is it worth doing again?"

Since no one spoke up, Bebop asked Lee and Midnight what they thought. "To be honest, even with Jacob's coaching, I still had problems getting to the topic of climate change," admitted Lee. "It took a while to bring that up and by the time I did the conversation waned. I may have struck some nerves but don't think it'll make a big impact."

"I had fun playing with other dogs," advised Midnight, "but these city dogs seemed self-absorbed and clueless about nature or trying to communicate with their humans about anything other than food for themselves or walks."

"I noticed the same thing," agreed Boo.

Curly added, "I had a nice conversation with a beagle about messaging his human to eat more local foods. He'd been rescued after living in the woods, though, and was more in tune with the environment."

"I talked with one person who brought up climate change before I did and that was a productive conversation," said Jacob. "I gave some tips on how to make a difference to the others with whom I spoke. One person didn't seem interested, and I'd say the others were split fifty-fifty on whether they'd do anything.

"That was my experience, too," Eliza agreed. "The people I talked with may take some action, and hopefully they do, but for the most part they didn't seem to care much."

"I've never been to New York City before, but everybody seemed uptight," remarked Oji. "I talked with some kids who were there with their parents and dogs and felt badly for them because they don't spend much time outside."

Jacob said, "You don't know how lucky you have it until you see what others do and don't have. We take a lot for granted."

"I don't know what I'd do if I couldn't be out with grass and trees every day," confessed Oji.

Bebop reported, "The dogs I talked with wanted nothing other than to play. One even told me he only had this short time each day to run and he wasn't going to waste it standing around talking."

"That's harsh," Eliza said.

"I thought so too, but to each his own. I think we can use our resources more effectively by doing other things. This trip was worth it, though, because we may have made an impact and know we don't need to plan any more of these outings right now."

Jacob reminded everyone of the lunch Chef Cecil packed. They opened the bag, and all enjoyed the sustenance. After eating, the group grew quiet, and some fell asleep while others looked out the window. They were almost back to NoHoSap when clouds overtook the sun, the wind increased, and rain began. Soon all heard an urgent beeping.

Bebop jumped. "My headset—it was in the bag with lunch. I didn't want to have it on during the project and raise any eyebrows. That's the signal there's a problem. Lee or Curly, you're near the bag, hand me the earpiece."

"Wait, Behop, I set up the van to run the feed through the speaker system like a phone," advised Jacob. "I'll switch it over to your headset."

The beeping rang through the car speakers and Jacob hit the answer button on the dashboard screen. "Hello?"

"Hello, this is Mission Command. Is Captain Bebop there?"

"Yes, I'm here. What's going on?"

"Captain, we need you to get here as soon as you can."

"What's the problem?"

After a slight pause, the response came. "Severe storms moved through, and we need your help."

"We're on our way, but you have all the resources at your disposal until we arrive. What do you need?"

Another pause. "Captain, the winds were very strong and blew many limbs and trees down. The tree that holds Jacee's home is uprooted and hanging over the stream. We're trying to get his family out, but the waters are raging right under it."

"Geez." Bebop closed his eyes and shook his head, not wanting to believe it. The top of his head furrowed deeply. He gathered himself. "OK, assemble the eagles, beavers, and squirrels right away and tell them I commanded their most able and adept members to get out to that tree ASAP and rescue Jacee's family. His kits are very young, and the eagles will have to lift them out. The squirrels must maneuver to the den and lead his mate to safety with the beavers' help, as long as the water isn't running too strong for the beavers. Tell Jacee we have this covered. We'll be there soon. Keep me informed in the meantime."

"Roger that, Captain."

"Step on it, Jacob!"

CHAPTER 24

STORM DAMAGE

The crew in the van sat silently as Jacob navigated the highway, thinking about Jacee and his family. Bebop muttered, "Please let his family be saved. Ringloo and those babies are Jacee's life." He referred to Jacee's mate, Ringloo, and his relatively newborn son and daughter.

"I remember when he met Ringloo," recalled Boo. "He told me he knew male raccoons were supposed to have more than one mate but didn't think he'd ever be able to take his eyes off her. When she became pregnant, he was overjoyed and couldn't stop talking about the two kits when they were born, often saying he had it all with a loving mate and a baby girl and boy on top of that."

"He couldn't wait to get back to them once his shifts were over. He always looked out for leftovers to bring home to the den," mused Curly.

"We'll be back to them as fast as we can," advised Jacob.

The van approached a curtain of rain. Cars coming toward them had their lights on and windshield wipers going full steam. When the van crossed the rain line it poured. Water covered the road and Jacob reduced his speed to better navigate the conditions.

"This isn't what we need right now. We have to get back for Jacee." Bebop struggled to think how he could help when he was in the van rather than on-scene.

"I know, but I'm going as fast as I can in these conditions."

"I know you are, Jacob. I'm not mad at you, I'm mad at the situation and that I'm not there to direct the mission for Jacee."

"You're directing it from here, Bebop." Eliza tried to calm him. "You have the same team on it you'd have if you were there, right?"

"Yes, but I'd be in the field. I could help them get Ringloo and the kits to safety myself. I just hope they can get to them, or we arrive in time to help."

"We're not far away," informed Jacob. "If this rain lessens, I'll pick up the pace." Cars stopped on the shoulder to wait it out, and those on the road crept along as the rain pummeled down. The windshield wipers whipped back and forth, and the glass still wasn't clear. Wind blew the rain sideways into the van.

"It's getting brighter," declared Lee optimistically. "Looks like some breaks in the clouds ahead."

"Hopefully we'll be out of this rain soon," agreed Eliza.

As rapidly as the rain started when they drove into it, it stopped drastically when they drove out of it, and blue sky peeked through the clouds, although the wind remained.

"Floor it," commanded Bebop and Jacob obliged.

Not having heard any updates from Mission Command, Bebop tried contacting them. "Pick up, pick up. Why aren't they picking up?"

"Hold on, Bebop, we're almost there," comforted Jacob. "The tree with Jacee's den is in the North Woods, right?"

"Right."

"I'll go straight there, at least as close as we can with the van."

They arrived at the woods and Bebop waited impatiently inside the van while Jacob parked. He jumped out as soon as the door opened and took off toward the heavier woods. Lee wished them luck and said she and Midnight would wait in the van.

Jacob, Oji, Eliza, Curly, and Boo went running after Bebop. Fortunately, Boo knew the way, since Bebop soon disappeared from view.

As the woods thickened, the sound of rushing water grew louder. They arrived at the stream to see a group of animals intently watching the rescue operation. Jacee stood on the bank yelling directions toward a tree hanging precariously over the torrent. Trees and branches underneath held the larger tree out of the water, breaking randomly but consistently, unable to support the weight of the big tree that held Jacee's den. Ringloo and the kits looked in terror out of the den in the trunk. Ringloo couldn't carry both kits out by herself and wouldn't leave one alone to carry the other out. A few squirrels ran out the trunk, but it kept dropping as the support's broke underneath, thwarting their efforts to make it to the den. Beavers braced themselves in the rushing creek underneath, but Ringloo wouldn't drop the kits toward the water. An eagle landed on a branch next to the den and Ringloo lifted her little girl, Looloo, up by the scruff of her neck and handed her to the bird. All breathed a sigh of relief as the eagle flew Looloo to safety. A second eagle alighted on the branch, ready to take the boy, Junior. Ringloo picked Junior up and moved him toward the eagle, but the tree jerked and dropped, throwing Ringloo off balance. Trying to recover as the branch fell, her mouth opened reflexively, and Junior dropped out. The eagle reached for the kit but missed. Ringloo screamed and lunged after her young son as he descended toward the stream. Her horrific cry of "Junior!" rang out before they both disappeared into the surging water.

Jaycee wailed, "Nooooo!" and the crowd watched aghast as the beavers rushed to find the victims. Bebop jumped into the stream and flailed around, desperately searching for Ringloo and her kit. He didn't have experience swimming, much less in a strong current, and the water swept him downstream. Eliza sprinted along the bank to get ahead of where he was in the stream, jumped in, and waded out as far as she could without getting caught in the flow herself. Leaning out over the churning water, she snagged Bebop's hind leg as he sailed by, and heaved him ashore.

Bebop lay motionless on the bank, disheveled and soaking wet. Eliza kneeled over him and cried, "No, Bebop, I can't lose you again. Bebop, wake up, you have to be OK." As she put her hands on the side of his chest to feel for breathing, he coughed, moved his legs and sat up. She cried harder, elated to see him alive, and hugged him tight. "I thought I lost you again!"

Bebop stood up gingerly, visibly shaken after seeing his life flash before him. "I blacked out. I remember looking for Ringloo and Junior, then the water swept me away. I think my head hit a rock and next thing I know I'm here on the bank."

"I thought I really lost you this time, Bebop. You were lifeless when I pulled you from the water."

"You saved me? How'd you do that with the water rushing so strongly?"

"It doesn't matter. You're safe now."

Bebop buried his head against Eliza's chest while she hugged him. "Thank you, Eliza. I'm forever in your debt for saving my life."

The sound of sobbing snapped them back to the catastrophe with Ringloo and Junior. "Jacee! We're wasting precious time with my rescue when we need to find Ringloo and Junior."

Bebop ran over to comfort Jacee. Not wanting to intrude, Eliza joined the other members of the project team, who stood together away from the animals, heartbroken by the tragedy they just witnessed. Oji cried openly while Jacob stalwartly tried to hide his tears. Dumbfounded, Curly and Boo denied that Ringloo and Junior could actually be gone.

Jacee huddled in the middle of the group of animals, bawling uncontrollably. Bebop shook off the fear of himself almost having been a victim of the storm surge and moved forward to console Jacee. Looloo sat next to Jacee, having been deposited there by the eagle. She whimpered and tried to snuggle with her father, but he was much too upset to comfort his baby girl. Two squirrels came to her aid and brought her to a warm dry spot, then took turns feeding her nuts and berries from nearby trees and bushes, which she nibbled, oblivious to the losses she and her father just suffered.

Bebop suggested they get Jacee back to Mission Command, but Jacee refused, saying he wanted to stay near the tree in case Ringloo and Junior made it out of the stream and came back. Bebop didn't argue but asked the other animals to go and leave him and Jacee alone.

Feeling awkward after the animals left and unwilling to accept that Ringloo and Junior were gone, Eliza announced to the rest of the project team, "I'm going to check downstream to see if they were able to get to shore."

"I'll go with you," said Jacob.

"Me too," announced Oji.

"We're on it with you," advised Curly and Boo as they followed.

Jacee continued sobbing, with fits of calm in between as he tired himself out from crying constantly. Bebop said softly, "I'm very sorry, Jacee. I'm sorry for your losses and sorry I wasn't here to help with the full rescue."

Jacee wailed after being reminded of the tragedy, but eventually calmed somewhat. As he looked at Bebop, a shadow of disdain settled on his face, and he cried hysterically again. He gulped for air between sobs. "You should have been here from the start! You're supposed to be here taking care of us, but you were off with the humans, on the mission to help humans."

Seeing Jacee in such a state, along with his guilt about not being there from the beginning and falling victim to the stream himself instead of finding Ringloo and Junior, shook Bebop to the core. "Jacee, I'm always here for you. I commanded the rescue through Mission Command and rushed to be here as soon as I could. It kills me that I wasn't here to personally help the entire time, but I did everything I could."

"Funny choice of words, 'kills,' because you're here, and Ringloo and Junior aren't." Jacee shook as he spit the words out between gut-wrenching cries.

Bebop hung his head, not knowing what to say. He felt the same as Jacee—he should have been there for everything—but didn't want to admit that to Jacee. It never dawned on him that commanding the climate mission would make him feel as awful and conflicted as he did in that moment. The pair sat silently, with Bebop providing what support he could.

TOUGH LESSONS

Eliza, Jacob, Oji, Boo, and Curly, checked the downed tree with Jacee's den and inspected it thoroughly underneath, but found nothing. They continued downstream, examining every nook and cranny of branches and stone overhangs that Ringloo or her kit may have held onto, including those hanging into the stream. A difficult task already, the swollen stream moving at a feverish clip from the storm made it even tougher.

They traveled at least a mile downstream but found no sign of Ringloo or Junior. Each tried not to let negative thoughts in, but feared Ringloo and Junior may not have survived the strong current. The water could have easily swept one or both of them underneath and held them there long enough to perish. They found a rickety bridge, crossed the stream, and scoured the other side.

Meanwhile, the squirrels tending to Looloo became anxious. They had their own families to take care of and knew the baby should be with her father to have someone familiar by her side. They brought her to Jacee and said she'd need a nap soon. Bebop thanked them and suggested to Jacee that he and Looloo stay in Mission Command for a while. "You've taken such good care of us for so long, Jacee, let us take care of you."

Jacee slumped over in defeat and agreed to leave. The three of them got up and headed away from the tragic scene. Jacee kept looking back, hoping to see Ringloo and Junior running after them, but to no avail.

They arrived at Mission Command and a bevy of animals rushed to Jacee's and Looloo's aid, ready to set them up with food and shelter. They were rushed away, leaving Bebop alone with his self-doubting thoughts. He knew who he needed to see. He stopped in the Mission Command control center and asked if Harold the Wise was in NoHoSap. The control center attendant affirmed Harold was in Lone Bay. Bebop thanked them and trotted off. He took the elevator up to the outside areas of NoHoSap and headed left once the doors opened, a direction much less taken than straight or right, as evidenced by the minimal amount of wear on the grass trail.

The path began on short grass that became a narrow line of dirt winding between tall plants. Fall blooms of purple and gold, dainty white Queen Anne's lace, and milkweed pods in various stages of opening surrounded the trail. Breathing in the smells of early autumn, Bebop tried to calm his nerves from the tragic events of the day and Jacee's harsh words. The storm clouds and strong winds had given way to a beautiful sunny late afternoon. Bebop left the field and entered a forest mainly of hardwoods with a few scattered evergreens. The edges of the maple leaves had changed color and acorns dropped to the ground sporadically, announcing cooler weather on the way. Running in all directions, squirrels and chipmunks found and stashed nuts for winter. Bebop remembered a time when he would have instinctively chased them, but his training in NoHoSap after leaving Eliza eventually broke him of that habit.

After a jaunt through the woods, Bebop arrived at a wide rock outcropping overlooking a large lake. He barked loudly twice, sat in the middle of the rock, and waited. Soon a high-pitched call sounded from over the lake. Bebop stood. A huge white and grey bird glided gracefully above, heading toward the outcropping. The albatross landed clumsily near Bebop.

"Harold, I'm glad you're back with us in NoHoSap and not on the open sea," greeted Bebop. "Thanks for answering my call."

"Of course. Anything for you, Bebop," Harold said in a deep, grandfatherly voice. "I always enjoy catching up with you and hearing about your adventures. I don't get out there like I used to, and instead try to live vicariously through you." Bebop smiled. "I hear you're up to great things. You brought the human, Eliza, in on the mission."

"Yes, we moved into the human phase of the mission. I enjoy working with Eliza again. She managed to forgive me for dying on her and agreed to help us." Bebop hesitated, "Actually, I wanted to talk with you about this part of the mission. You know I've always treasured your insight and advice. "

"What's on your mind?"

"Well, you were the head of the Alliance when the human phase was first discussed and were involved in the conversations about it. You also have more history than almost any other being here, not only with the mission but with climate change."

"Yes, I've been around quite a while, Bebop. My species is graced with longevity, although lately, I wonder if that's a good thing. I've seen many of my friends pass away, and the environment has been altered in ways that no longer support life as it used to. I often wish I didn't know how things used to be, or how much harder it is to survive on this planet now. There have been many, many changes during my decades on this earth, most of them for the worse. Enough of my melancholy perspective, though. What's troubling you, Bebop?"

The pain of losing Ringloo and Junior on his watch weighed heavily on Bebop's mind and in his heart. Eventually, he answered, "I'm questioning whether we should be working with the humans; whether it would instead be better if we stuck to ourselves and did what we could to keep us safe as the climate changes."

"I see you're in anguish, Bebop, leading you to wonder whether we're doing the right thing. Your concern sounds familiar, as the Alliance has talked through all aspects of it more than once. Why are you questioning it now?"

The guilt overtook Bebop's face. "Today we had a team in the City making connections with humans and their pet dogs. While we were gone, the tree with Jacee's den blew down during the terrible storm that came through here. I directed a rescue effort while we were on our way back from the city and made it here to help, but Jacee's mate and young son fell into the water during the rescue attempt, and we lost them. If I'd been here from the start, they might be alive with Jacee now."

"Oh, Bebop. You don't know if the result would have been any different if you were here. You did the best you could with the information you had and the situation you were in at the time. You had the same team following your instructions as you would if you were here in person."

"I don't know if I'm doubting involving humans in the mission or doubting my own abilities to carry it out."

"Bebop, the Alliance and Mission Command asked me who should lead this mission. I chose you for many reasons and trained you with care. I have no doubts whatsoever you're the best creature for this role." Bebop sighed with embarrassment while Harold continued. "You were young and didn't have much time to develop before being thrown into the human world to establish a bond with Eliza. When you returned, you rose in the ranks seamlessly, possessing a drive and compassion that are rarely seen together. You achieved big wins in short order as you accomplished mission after mission without negative incident. That's great training, but the downside is you didn't experience failure. I remember thinking after all the successfully completed projects, it was going to hit you hard when something didn't go according to plan. You continued on the upward trajectory and now, unfortunately, something went wrong."

Bebop said softly, "Boy, did it ever go wrong."

"It's an extremely tough lesson, but we can't control everything, and things go awry, relatively frequently on average. The best thing we can do when bad things happen is to learn from them, thus minimizing the chances they'll happen again."

"I guess."

"The worst thing we can do is to give up." Harold lowered his head and looked up with encouragement into Bebop's downturned face.

"I know you're right, which is why we call you Harold the Wise. I feel terribly for Jacee and his family, though, like I let them down. If I was the only one impacted, I could deal with that, but they're the ones who have to pay the price. It's just not right that I make a mistake and they pay. The guilt is almost too much to bear."

"It often is someone else who must pay the price. That's a burden of being a leader. We do our best to lead people to accomplish goals, but there are countless outside variables that can help or hinder the team and leader along the way. One of the critical attributes of an exceptional leader is being able to bounce back in the face of adversity and keep going, no matter what obstacles are thrown in the way. I know you can do that, Bebop. I believe in you–always have, always will. This is your first test on recovering from negative results. There's nothing wrong with showing your compassionate side and mourning the awful result here, but you also need to let Jacee and everyone else know you're going to keep going even though this happened, and you'll try even harder to never let it happen again. Jacee needs to see that in you to give him an example to follow since he'll have to pick himself up and take care of his daughter."

"You're right, I've been very lucky to not have had any failed missions. Here I thought that was the norm but it's not realistic at all. If only this result had been less catastrophic. I'm really having trouble handling it."

"Wish I could tell you it gets easier, but it doesn't. The losses will never leave you and will invariably pull at your conscience. With time you'll realize that in the end it always works out, in ways you never would have seen until you've been through it and look back."

"Thank you for your wisdom. I appreciate you, Harold. Thank you for always being there for me."

"My pleasure. You've been like a son to me and I treasure the opportunity to pass along some of my knowledge to you. Are you prepared for me to fill you in on why the human part of the mission is so critical?"

"Yes, it would be good to know the history behind that to keep me from questioning it as I did today."

"OK, I'll explain. There's been tension about interfacing with humans for all our existence. As you know, we've communicated with indigenous people around the world for many, many years because they understand our interconnectedness and honor the role we and the natural environment play in each other's lives. For the most part, we lived our lives separate from humans but mutually respected the other. That changed as humans developed the world around them, taking our habitats for themselves and killing beings of the natural world faster than we could propagate. They killed us for sport, our feathers, our coats, and our meat. They destroyed our homes and food supplies. We retreated to more and more remote areas, but humans infringed on even those spots—building houses, malls, roads, and dams, clearcutting forests, and polluting the air and water. We knew much of the construction and other developments the human's called progress wasn't sustainable in the long term and noticed the impacts of those activities on the environment immediately, but it took humans much longer to see and acknowledge it. They understand better now how their activities impact the complete ecosystem and cause warming, among other issues. As you know, Bebop, since animals haven't caused climate change, there's not much we can do to reverse it. Humans must act and they're obviously reluctant to make real progress in that regard."

Bebop agreed and Harold continued, "The thing to remember about the human part of the mission you're questioning is that our decision to work with humans wasn't driven by any sort of desire to help them. Quite the contrary, embarking on the human phase was done solely to protect ourselves and our world. That's it, plain and simple. It's for the self-preservation of the natural world and our planet—nothing else. A collateral result may be that humans are saved too, but that's not our goal. We need to stop the climate crisis in its tracks and humans are the only ones who can do that. They can think we're trying to help them if they want, but that's not our motivation in any way at all."

Bebop's eyes widened at Harold's bluntness.

"You have a bond with humans that most of us here have never experienced. Consequently, it may be hard for you to hear the bottom-line goal of this mission. You, Jacee, and everyone else here in NoHoSap must remember you're helping our world with everything you do for the climate mission, even though it may take you out of NoHoSap and into HuHabDom. Hard as it is, we've all lost loved ones, seen our habitats ravaged, and suffered other dreadful losses from the impacts of climate change and will continue to do so. Storms, flooding, fires, winds, and droughts exacerbated by the climate crisis have taken the family, friends, and homes of countless species across the globe. Humans are now being affected in this way and that will hopefully push them to realize the threats from a warming climate are real, are happening now, and they need to do something about it. The losses are terrible ways to have to learn a lesson, but that's where we are. This is a very real and present danger and no one, human or animal, will be unscathed in this climate emergency."

"I know it's scary and sobering to hear this, Bebop, but that's the reality we face. Believe me, the stories Tusko and I can tell of what we've seen over time as this climate enemy has been wreaking havoc upon us and our world would break your heart. Now you've experienced firsthand with Jacee what climate change does. Use it to fuel your desire to fight back and get humans to make changes so this doesn't continue."

Bebop jumped up with enthusiasm, motivated by Harold's inspiring words of hope. "Thank you for opening my eyes and putting it in perspective, Harold. I'm ready to do what needs to be done to make our mission a success."

"You're just the one to do it, kid," praised Harold as he patted Bebop on the head with his huge wing. "I'll be watching you and cheering you on," he continued with a smile and a wink. Harold turned and flew off gracefully into the distance toward the sun, flapping his wings and gliding peacefully out of sight.

Bebop felt confident, energized, and extremely grateful for Harold's guidance. He remembered the day, while still a puppy, he met Harold at a training through Mission Command. Bebop and other animals ran through exercises while Harold, the other Alliance members, and higher-ups in Mission Command watched. When the exercises ended, the participants rested while the onlookers consulted one another. As Bebop left the area, Harold came over and stopped him. Intimidated by the big bird, Bebop sat immediately and didn't move. Harold laughed, told him to relax and said he wanted to offer Bebop a big opportunity. He then explained the plan that ultimately led Bebop to HuHabDom and Eliza, then back to NoHoSap to lead the climate mission. Extremely patient and understanding, Harold helped Bebop through every step of his development, telling countless captivating stories along the way that always had a relevant message for Bebop.

With his new perspective from Harold's latest tutelage, Bebop turned and headed back through the woods and field toward Mission Command. A nagging sense of conflict remained, though, due to the reality that Harold described. Bebop's connection with humans made him concerned about their condition. At the same time, being part of and charged with the protection of the non-human part of the world and its inhabitants, he had a responsibility to them. Until now he thought the mission would protect both, but hearing Harold's words he now felt traitorous getting Eliza involved since the climate mission wasn't designed to protect her or any humans. Bebop buried those feelings in the recesses of his mind, instead focusing on being inspired by what Harold shared with him.

CHAPTER 26

MIRACLES

While Bebop talked with Harold, Eliza and the others continued their search for Ringloo and Junior on the other side of the stream. About halfway back to where they started, Curly heard cries, leading the team to investigate. The sound seemed to be coming from a fallen, partly submerged, evergreen tree. Thick boughs made it difficult to see much in the branches, but the noises came from somewhere in the tree. It could only be accessed by wading into the stream. Before anyone could stop her, Oji ventured into the calmer water behind the tree. Jacob scolded her and told her to be careful while she waded into the downed branches and scoured them for the source of the sounds. She kept going into the tree until she disappeared. Eliza told her to keep talking, to let them know she was alright.

"OK, I'm fine," came Oji's voice. "The branches are scrunched together and it's hard to get through."

"Be careful!" yelled Jacob, concerned not only for his sister but also for the trouble he'd be in if he went home either without her or with an injury.

"The sounds are getting louder. I'm getting closer!" Oji stopped and listened intently, then heard the cry again. "That seemed like it was next to me. Let me look in these pine branches right here." Another noise. "So close, where are you?" asked Oji aloud, carefully moving packed branches away in search of the source of the sounds. The team waited.

"I see something–looks like wet fur!" Oji continued moving pine boughs away with both hands and gently pulled a large ball of fur out of the branches. As she did so, the cry sounded again. "This is where the noise is coming from!"

"Is it Ringloo or Junior?" yelled Eliza in anticipation.

"I can't tell. I can't see much in here. I have it and am coming back." Oji carefully navigated out of the tree, clutching the find against her chest. Whimpers came from it.

Oji gave the furball to Jacob as she climbed ashore. All gathered around and looked at the bedraggled fur, clearly a raccoon. There was no sign of life in it. Then the noise sounded again from the fur. They looked at each other in consternation. Oji carefully felt the object and realized the creature had curled itself into a ball. She found the head tucked way in and massaged it out.

"It's Ringloo!" she exclaimed. "But she's not moving." Another cry came. Oji caressed the body and it gradually unfurled. As it did, small paws appeared from inside. The whimper came again, and Junior's head popped out from the curve of Ringloo's belly. Everyone whooped in happiness to have found the youngster alive. Ringloo's paws moved almost imperceptibly as the group celebrated. Oji massaged the body more and Ringloo's head moved ever so slightly.

"Oji, you found them, and it looks like Ringloo is alive!" praised Eliza.

"Yay! I knew they didn't die." Oji beamed.

Jacob alerted, "We need to get them, especially Ringloo, to the med unit in NoHoSap right away."

"Right, let's cross back over the bridge and head to the van, then rush to Mission Command," directed Eliza. Ringloo curled back up, keeping Junior safe inside.

They made it to the van and showed Lee their rescues. Ecstatic, she took Ringloo while the crew tumbled into the van. Lee then wrapped

Ringloo in a blanket, held and comforted her, and unrolled her a bit to allow Junior some fresh air.

They arrived at the parking lot near NoHoSap and exited the van to hurry Ringloo in. Lee said she'd wait since her scooter couldn't maneuver into NoHoSap. The team forgot she had those limitations and looked dejected that she couldn't accompany them. Lee assured them she'd be fine and looked forward to hearing Ringloo's condition once they got her to the med unit.

Oji carried the blanket wrapped Ringloo and they rushed to the NoHoSap entrance. Monty greeted them and asked what the blanket covered. They explained they found Ringloo and Junior and Oji lifted a corner of the blanket to reveal its contents. Seeing Ringloo's rough condition, Monty rushed off to get help, leaving the chipmunks and fireflies to guide the rescuers through the tunnel.

Monty found Bebop as he stepped into the elevator to descend to Mission Command. Barreling up to him, Monty tried to talk but couldn't catch his breath after the frantic flight. He finally managed to speak and blurted out between deep breaths, "Captain, [breath] come quick [breath]."

Monty didn't often get worked up in this manner, concerning Bebop. "Monty, what is it?"

"You're not going to believe it, Sir. Hurry, follow me." He turned to fly away but still couldn't catch his breath and instead paused in mid-air.

"Here, I'll give you a ride. Where are we going?"

"To the tunnel," directed Monty as he landed behind Bebop's ear. Bebop took off running, with Monty holding onto his short fur for dear life.

Bebop and Monty made it to the NoHoSap end of the tunnel as Eliza and Jacob emerged, with Curly, Boo, and Oji close behind. The chipmunks and fireflies who escorted them stuck around rather than dissipating as they usually did when their guiding duties were done. Oji delicately cuddled the blanket.

"Bebop, it's a miracle!" Jacob exclaimed.

"What are you talking about? We could use some good news on this awful day, but miracles are hard to come by."

"I know, but that's about the only way to describe this," asserted Jacob as he motioned to Oji.

Oji gingerly lifted the edge of the blanket to reveal wet, disheveled raccoon fur.

"Geez, is that Ringloo's dead body?" asked Bebop in disgust. "Maybe Jacee will be relieved you found her, but it feels more like a slap in the face to see her dead. I wouldn't call that a miracle at all."

"Wait, we thought she was dead too, but she's alive, just barely, but she's alive!" said Eliza as Oji lifted more of the blanket to reveal Ringloo's curled-up body. "And that's not all..., look." As Oji held Ringloo, Jacob carefully uncurled her front legs. revealing a frightened Junior cuddled up tight against Ringloo's belly.

Bebop's mouth dropped open. "Oh my," was the only thing he could manage to say. Everyone stared at the mother and her kit.

Bebop snapped out of his reverie. "I thought you were playing a cruel joke, but this definitely is a miracle. How did you find them?" He doubted himself again since he didn't send a search crew out.

"We were all in shock after seeing the failed rescue, but Eliza jumped into action and said we should look for Ringloo and Junior downstream," advised Jacob. "Neither she nor Oji would accept that they were gone without seeing proof and pushed us to inspect every nook and cranny in and around the stream. Curly heard a noise and we, actually Oji, finally found them."

"Excellent work–thank you, team! We need to get Ringloo to medical care right away. Let's go!" Bebop turned and led the others to the Mission Command elevator. On the descent, Bebop instructed, "Monty, go get Jacee and Looloo and bring them to the med station. Don't let them know about Ringloo and Junior, but tell them we want them to be checked after all they've been through today."

"On it, Captain." Monty flew off when the elevator door opened. The other elevator occupants hurried to the medical station, in a quiet area removed from the hustle and bustle of the Mission Command control center. Bebop and the rest of the project team hurried through the door to the med unit, a large bright area with lights on the ceilings and walls. The medical station's occupants bolted to attention upon Bebop's arrival. "Hello, Captain," greeted a wizened orangutan.

"Hello, Red. We have an urgent case for you." Bebop looked at the blanket and bobbed his head to indicate Oji should uncover Ringloo and Junior. They obliged as Red came closer and peered into the blanket.

Initially taken aback when they uncovered Ringloo, Red reached out to touch the raccoon and felt for a pulse. As Red examined the patient more carefully, Junior cried. Red exclaimed, "What?" She drew her hand back initially and then explored to find the young kit clenched tightly to Ringloo's belly.

"Is this Jacee's mate and baby? They survived?" asked Red in disbelief.

"Yes, the team found them downstream from where they fell in the water." Bebop wished he could take some credit for the find but knew that wouldn't be right. "Ringloo's in rough shape. Is she going to be alright?"

Other medical staff watched from a distance and heard the conversation about Jacee and his family, leading to a small gathering around Red, her new patients, and their rescuers.

Red answered Bebop's question carefully, trying not to give anyone false hope. "She's badly hurt and is barely holding on to life right now. We'll run tests to see if she has any broken bones or internal damage, then hook her up to an IV, dry her off, and keep her warm. With enough rest and TLC, hopefully, she'll pull through. She obviously has a strong will to live since she survived after her heroism saving her son."

Jacee's voice sounded from behind the gathering, "What's going on? Why did you need us here right now? We really just want to be alone. We've already been through too much today."

All looked back to see Jacee standing with Looloo. They both looked exhausted and bedraggled, and Jacee seemed annoyed.

Bebop quietly told Red, "Take them back and get them comfortable. I'll be in with Jacee and Looloo soon." Red put the blanket back over her charges and whisked them away. Looking at the animals who'd gathered, Bebop visually indicated they needed to go about their business. He then went over to Jacee and escorted him and Looloo to a cavity in the wall, designed for private conversations. The humans hung back.

"Jacee, I have fantastic news." Jacee looked at Bebop with tired eyes. "The project team searched downstream and found Ringloo and Junior!"

"What? Are they alive? Where are they? I need to see them!"

"They're alive, but Ringloo is in rough shape. She needs medical attention and is getting that now. Red's going to run some tests to see exactly what's going on, but you and Looloo can go back and see them."

"They're alive, they're alive, hear that Looloo, they're alive!" shouted Jacee as he danced in circles, his demeanor immediately changing from grief to hope. He ran over to Jacob, Oji, Eliza, Curly, and Boo, thanked them profusely and hugged them, then hustled back to where he'd seen Red go. Bebop guided Jacee and Looloo past beds of all shapes and sizes where other creatures recuperated.

As the group wandered through the medical station, a chickadee flew over, stopped them, and told them to follow him. He led them to a secluded area where Red tended to Ringloo, Junior by her side, whimpering now and again. When Jacee saw them he ran over and Looloo followed. "Ringloo, Junior, we thought we lost you," he said through tears.

Ringloo struggled to turn her head toward Jacee and tried to open her eyes while Junior climbed right over her to nuzzle his sister and Jacee. Ecstatic to see the heartwarming site, but knowing the family should be alone together, Bebop backed out of the area, and left.

Eliza, Jacob, and Oji were waiting in the arrival area of the medical station when Bebop made it back. "It was wonderful to see Jacee and Looloo reunited with Ringloo and Junior, with them all alive. I never expected the day would end like this, but thanks to you it did. Thank you," praised Bebop.

"Thank Eliza and Oji, they wouldn't give up and insisted we keep searching for them," Jacob observed.

"We had to do everything we could to find them," said Oji. "Jacee looked so sad I really wanted to help, and Eliza said we needed to check downstream."

"She always was a persistent one," observed Bebop. "Today I'm extremely grateful she is."

"Alright, that's enough," chided Eliza. "Curly heard sounds and Oji scoured the submerged tree. They deserve the credit for finding Ringloo and Junior. We got lucky today and I'm ecstatic for Jacee and his family that we did."

"For sure," agreed Jacob.

"Hey, did Lee and Midnight make it back safely?" asked Bebop, realizing they'd been in the van with Jacob and Eliza, but Lee wouldn't have been able to participate in the search or venture into NoHoSap.

"Yes, they're waiting for good news about Ringloo's condition," informed Jacob. "Lee comforted Ringloo and Junior on the way here. They really wanted to come with us to NoHoSap, but Lee can't get here with the scooter. We need to figure out how to fix that."

"You're right. It would be nice for her to see what we're doing here," agreed Bebop. "Hey, this good news has made me hungry. Anyone want to accompany me to Chef Cecil's kitchen to see what we can scrounge up?"

Eliza, Oji, and Jacob answered enthusiastically, "Yes!" and "We're in."

When they barged into the kitchen, they were met with applause from the full staff. Cecil jumped down from his post and hopped over to the trio. "Well done, all! We're honored you stopped by. I hope you're not too full from the lunch I packed to have dinner."

"Lunch was delicious," applauded Jacob, "but it seems like a while ago that we ate it because a lot has happened in the meantime."

"That's for sure," agreed Eliza. "I thought we ate that lunch yesterday. Hard to believe it was earlier today."

"I'm always ready to eat, and love everything you cook, Chef," said Oji.

"Enough talking, let's eat," admonished Bebop jokingly as he trotted toward the table in the far corner. Animals and birds milled around the table while placing all sorts of dishes and accompaniments on it. Bebop asked Cecil to wrap up meals for Lee and Midnight since they waited in the van.

The group didn't waste any time or wait for invitations before making themselves comfortable and helping themselves to the delicacies. Bebop finished first, not surprisingly, with Oji not far behind, and they sat back to watch Eliza and Jacob partake. Bebop announced, "Eliza, take tomorrow off from your mission responsibilities. Tuesday we'll focus on social media postings and replies once you get here after work. Next weekend we'll execute our first reef restoring sub-mission. We'll prepare for that Wednesday and Thursday, then leave Friday to get a head start on the trip."

"Busy week," noted Jacob. "Let me know what I can help with and keep me posted on how Ringloo and Junior are doing."

"Don't forget me, I always want to help," Oji added.

Cecil hopped over, as if on cue, and handed her a basket. "Here you go, bring this to Lee and Midnight. They can't go hungry tonight." Oji gladly took the delivery, thrilled to be entrusted with a job.

Bebop smiled at the youngster's exuberance. "Jacob, we'll let you know what we need and appreciate you being available on short notice. We'll likely need medical supplies since they'll be going through a fair amount for Ringloo. If our medical emissaries can't get anything, I'll be in touch."

Eliza savored the last bite on her plate and thanked Chef Cecil for preparing such a mouthwatering meal again. She then looked at her watch, which she hadn't done all day. "I'm sorry to eat and run, but lost track of the time with everything today. Bebop, please update Noli on Ringloo's condition and she can let me know."

"OK, I'll make sure Noli has access to that information. Rest up, guys, it's been a long day. Thank you again for going the extra mile for Ringloo and Junior."

"Just thankful Oji found them alive," reflected Jacob.

"You've been through a lot today, Bebop," said Eliza, seeing the exhaustion creeping across his eyes. "Hope you're able to get a good night's sleep and recharge."

"I will after I visit our medical patients again. Good night, all."

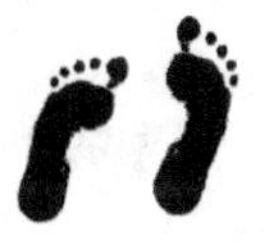

CHAPTER 27

JUGGLING

Arriving home after the long, emotional day in the City and NoHoSap, Eliza checked her phone, which she hadn't done since early morning. A text from Zeke greeted her, congratulating her on the news story Saturday night and letting her know he enjoyed it. He said he didn't see the follow-up pictures on the station's website or media pages showing they planted the trees left on the trailer and asked when she planned to post those.

Eliza hit herself on the head, having totally forgotten to post the photos, what with the early morning start and events of the day. She texted Zeke, thanked him for the reminder, and apologized for not taking care of it earlier. Mentioning she ended up going to New York City, she said the postings slipped her mind.

Without further delay, Eliza reviewed the pictures of the work party with Zeke, Jacob, and Oji. She posted the best ones and notified Zeke. He replied within a few minutes, said they looked good, and were a nice update to the story. Zeke also thanked her for involving him in the tree planting and said he looked forward to hearing about her trip to the City. Eliza countered with a thumbs up and said she'd see him tomorrow. After completing her Sunday tasks, she set the alarm for bright and early the following morning to allow her a productive Monday at the station before resuming her duties with the climate mission on Tuesday.

Immediately after the alarm rang the next morning, Noli's voice surprised Eliza. "I have an update on Ringloo."

Turning on a light to see Noli, Eliza blinked the sleep from her eyes. "Noli, morning. I hope all went well overnight. How's Ringloo?"

"She has broken ribs, a concussion, bruised kidneys, and water in her lungs, along with bumps, scrapes, and bruises all over. Red said she's hanging in there, is stable now, and will be on painkillers and an IV for at least today. Still too weak to talk or move much, she became a little more aware overnight. Jacee's been by her side constantly and they set up an enclosed area for Junior and Looloo to play and keep the family together. Ringloo manages a tiny smile when she hears her kits nearby."

"Excellent! Thanks for letting me know and getting me up before I hit the snooze. I have a lot to do today. Please keep me posted on Ringloo's condition."

Eliza took the bus to work since she had a day off from NoHoSap. Without driving, she felt better that she was doing her small part to combat the climate crisis. If she expected other humans to do something, she should too. Leon said he hadn't seen her in a while, and she reluctantly admitted she'd been driving. One of the regulars on the bus overheard her and commented he'd never take the bus if he had a car. Eliza chuckled, noted it was way better for the planet that he took the bus, and said that was why she preferred public transit. The man looked at her like she was crazy, leading Eliza to reflect to herself that this was the problem—many people didn't think about the bigger picture. Some either didn't know or care how their actions contribute to climate change, and others who did know weren't taking the steps that would collectively make a difference. Acknowledging there was much more she could do, she vowed to implement the action items Lee presented in her climate blog and to otherwise become a better global citizen.

Eliza arrived at work much more relaxed from walking to the bus stop and reading on her commute than the days she drove through traffic to get to the station. As she walked to her office, she heard congratulations all around on Saturday night's story about the trees at the cemetery.

Ira stopped in her office after she settled in. "Congratulations on the story, Eliza. Glad you took advantage of being in the right place at the right time. The follow-up posts about finishing the tree planting were a perfect idea and show the station is environmentally responsible."

"Thank you, and thanks for approving it."

"Sure thing. When you described it to me, I had doubts about whether it would come across the right way, but the witnesses were very believable and appeared to be rational."

Eliza always wondered about the station's 'no fringe' stance and wanted to know the reasoning behind it. "We won't air a story if people don't seem believable or rational?"

"Generally, no. We can't be a platform for people who appear crazy or are too over the top. Viewers want to see news that's real, not sensationalized or communicated by folks on the fringe."

"Interesting." Ira left as Eliza ruminated on what he said and made a mental note to remember this sobering confirmation for her media and outreach efforts going forward. She needed to stay even-keeled while getting the word out, and to make things interesting but realistic and credible, particularly for the climate mission, a topic already plagued by naysayers.

Zeke knocked on the door frame and came into Eliza's office shortly after Ira left. "Nice work on the story and update. Thanks again for including me and taking care of the posts yesterday."

"My pleasure. How have your fans reacted to seeing you do manual labor?"

"A lot of likes. Some people asked if I'd do their landscaping, but that's about it."

"Its nice folks saw another side of you. It's good to be well-rounded in this business."

"What was up in the City? I heard they had bad flooding from storms that moved through similar to here. Hopefully, you were undercover when they hit."

"Not quite." She should have remembered Zeke wanted to hear about her trip to the City but had many other things on her mind and it didn't dawn on her, leaving her with no ready-made story to tell him.

She didn't like thinking on her feet and telling falsehoods, but here she was stuck between that rock and a hard place again. This time she didn't have to stray too far from the truth. "I decided to go at the last minute to socialize Bop. The storm hit while we were in Central Park." She told him about the bridge flooding underneath and meeting new friends while waiting for the rain to stop, then walking around, and coming home.

It felt good to not lie about everything. Eliza considered telling Zeke about Bebop and the Change Agents' mission but ultimately decided against it. She really wanted to tell someone, though and didn't know how much longer she could hold off mentioning it to Zeke. It seemed safe to mention her upcoming absences to him. "Zeke, I want to dig deeper into what the people said they saw in the cemetery, along with those posts I showed you about animals planting trees. I plan to leave early when I can and take time off to do some research."

"Cool. I'm interested to see what you find. Time to put your investigative reporting hat on and get out of the law library." He grinned jokingly.

"Very funny, but it will be nice to get out in the field more." Surprised by and impressed with herself for weaving her absences into something work-related, Eliza hadn't thought to make such a connection until that moment but realized it made total sense and decided to tell Ira about it that afternoon. Maybe it'd be easier than she first feared to juggle what she thought would be competing demands and responsibilities for work and the mission. What Bebop saw as a botched tree planting project appeared to be creating nice opportunities for Eliza. Cautiously optimistic, she tried not to feel everything would work out for her. It seemed every time she became overconfident in that regard, something slapped her back to reality.

CHAPTER 28

A Visitor

Tuesday arrived in a flash and the day flew by, while Eliza focused on her next project for the station. She lost track of time to such an extent that Noli broke her concentration as the afternoon wound down, and diplomatically reminded Eliza they were expected in NoHoSap.

"Just let me finish this thought." Eliza continued typing and Noli gently mentioned again that they needed to get going. "Yes, I know, almost there." She typed feverishly, ending with a few strong strokes, then lifting her hands in tandem as though completing a piano concerto. "Done, let's go!"

Noli flew into an outside pocket on Eliza's bag and Eliza ran out the door. She drove somewhat recklessly to the cemetery and jogged from the car to the NoHoSap door, where Monty waited impatiently. They hurried through the tunnel, down to Mission Command and to the media center. Upon arriving, they found Bebop, Cheshire, and Cuthbert engrossed in conversation while looking at computer monitors. Cheshire, the consummate organizer, used a separate monitor for each posting site. She noted that some folks said they saw Eliza's story about the cemetery trees as well as the prior postings of animals planting trees and opined that the cemetery incident must have been a similar project the humans interrupted. Other people found the location after watching the news story, inspected it for themselves, and posted their pictures from the site. As usual, a few comments mused that humans and trained animals must be behind the incidents.

Cheshire pulled up the station's website and Eliza's posts about planting the rest of the trees at the cemetery location. Bebop interjected that he didn't see any replies from Eliza to the comments and questions posted by others. Embarrassed, Eliza defended herself, saying she'd been too busy to keep up with those postings and planned to react but hadn't gotten to it yet. She received no sympathy from a perturbed Bebop. "There's no time like the present, which is why we're here today. Let's get it done."

Ashamed about her lack of diligence checking the posts, but also upset at Bebop for calling her failure out in front of Cuthbert and Cheshire, Eliza shot a daggered stare toward him to let him know she didn't appreciate his comments.

Wanting to cut the tension, Cuthbert offered, "This works well because now we can provide our input."

Eliza calmed herself before saying anything. "OK, do you want to work on the station's website first?"

"Sure," agreed Cheshire.

"The comments to the post can be divided into those about the news story and those about our follow-up tree planting. I usually thank everyone for reviewing and commenting and would like to do that first." Eliza avoided looking toward Bebop.

"No problem there." Bebop's annoyance faded.

"Should we mention the pictures we posted elsewhere that show animals planting trees in other places? I could say I researched it and found them. I'm concerned that at some point commenters will press to know who took and posted those other pictures. I'm surprised people haven't focused on it already. If they discover it was me, I'll lose my credibility for not mentioning that from the start."

Something whirred from the back of the room, and all turned to see the source. "Surprise!" announced an elated Lee as she zoomed out from the shadows and into the room on her scooter. Midnight strutted by her side and Jacob brought up the rear.

"Omigosh, you made it to NoHoSap!" Eliza smiled broadly; psyched Lee could finally see the place.

"Sure did, with Jacob's help."

Jacob beamed and added, "I didn't do it by myself. The main issue has always been getting Lee over the relatively rugged paths in. I talked with Bebop about how we could make NoHoSap accessible for her. He said Eliza rode Stets for the rescue mission a couple of weeks ago. We both then realized we should try it with Lee."

"Concerned I wouldn't be able to hold on well enough with only my right side, I didn't like the idea at first, but Stets convinced me I wouldn't be in danger with a custom saddle and tie-downs."

"We enlisted the skills of our Australian friends, Oali and Hopper, who learned the ins and outs of saddles from horses traveling the Outback," Jacob informed.

"Let me guess, Oali is a koala bear and Hopper is a kangaroo?"

"You got it, Eliza." Jacob continued. "They designed a saddle with rails around the edge and shock absorbers to make Lee stable in the seat. It has an intricate system of ropes and cords to hold her in the saddle and the saddle on Stets. Good thing Oali is nocturnal because he worked all last night to build the thing. We brought Lee to the NoHoSap entrance near the parking lot this afternoon, and the saddle worked well to transport her into NoHoSap. Stets then came back and helped carry her scooter through."

"I'm excited to be in this miraculous place," Lee declared gleefully. "I heard about all the beings and technology here, but you can't imagine or fully appreciate it without seeing it in person. Wow!"

"Welcome, Lee! It's about time you're finally able to join us here."

"Thanks, Captain, for making it happen."

Eliza walked over to the scooter and hugged Lee. "This place is magnificent, isn't it? As the relative newcomers, you and I can learn about it together. Since you're here we could use your input on these postings."

"It would be my pleasure to help, especially since my blog is already linked to everything. Thanks for that, by the way."

"Thanks to Cheshire. Maybe Lee can help with the issue we just discussed. She could comment on her blog about the similarities between the postings with the animals planting trees and the news story."

"Good idea. We need to preserve our reputations as much as possible throughout this campaign." Bebop's comment reminded Eliza of Ira's recent observation.

Lee advised, "I don't know if that means you intend to throw my reputation under the bus, but I don't mind posting comments alerting people to similar posts. You want me to comment not only on the station's site but also on my blog and the other places you've posted, right?"

"Yes, that would be perfect. Hopefully, it'll draw in more traffic all the way around." Cheshire lent her optimism.

"Be sure to mention how animals appear to be taking things into their own hands to tackle climate change. I want to take every opportunity to make humans feel they're not doing what they should to address this themselves."

"OK, Captain, but I don't want to be too critical of people since we want them to keep viewing the site, and I also don't want to foster negative discourse that can result when folks are on the defensive."

"After following your blog for many years and seeing how you've diplomatically handled all that's come up over that time, I'm confident you'll spin it the right way, Lee."

"Thanks, Eliza. I'll figure out how to make the point without turning people off."

Cuthbert interposed, "I have no idea what you're saying when you talk about spinning and turning people off. We're not dealing with any spider webs or machines here, but I assume it's more human language stuff that I just don't get." He then asked nervously, "What I'd really like to know is whether you'd characterize these first tree planting projects and the associated publicity a success?"

Everyone looked at Bebop rather than answering themselves. Bebop waited for someone else to say something and broke the silence after realizing they wanted him to speak first. "Great job on these projects, everyone! Thank you, Cuthbert, for getting our overall climate change mission off to an excellent start and giving us momentum to keep moving forward." All agreed with Bebop's assessment. "I was upset when the humans discovered us on the last tree planting project, but we capitalized on what could have been a bad situation. To sum it up, yes, I'd characterize these initial tree plantings and the outreach a success."

Visibly relieved, Cuthbert acknowledged, "Thank you, Sir."

"Alright, Lee will post comments and link our efforts and postings on the tree projects. With that addressed, tomorrow we'll focus on the next projects—restoring reefs."

"Sounds good, looking forward to it." Eliza tried to hide her trepidation about what the reef projects would entail since she hadn't spent much time in the ocean.

"Not to change the subject, but how's Ringloo?" asked Lee. "I'd like to visit her while I'm here."

"Absolutely. She and Jacee would appreciate that. Ringloo's holding her own. It'll be a long road ahead, but we're very fortunate she and Junior are alive."

The group eventually headed off to the medical station, leaving Cheshire and the media team to continue monitoring not only the NoHoSap postings but world news for events related to the climate crisis.

CHAPTER 29

APOLOGIES

The group arrived at the medical station and turned down a hall leading to the back of the unit. A large toad hopped in front of them, blocked their way, and politely said, "Hello all. Visitors are limited to no more than three at a time."

"Yes, Bumpy, we know. Red's been very tolerant when we've had more than three visiting Ringloo. Could we all go back but have no more than three next to her bed at a time?"

"Very well, Captain, follow me." The group trailed Bumpy as he hopped down the hallway.

They turned around a rock outcropping to find Ringloo laying on a bed, hooked to an IV, with Jacee next to her holding her paw.

Bebop said, "Sorry to disturb you, Jacee, but we have a special guest who wanted to check on Ringloo. "Jacee, meet Lee. Lee, meet Jacee."

"I'm thrilled to meet you on my first trip to NoHoSap," Lee said joyfully.

Jacee jumped down, scrambled over to Lee, and hugged her legs. "Thank you for comforting Ringloo on the way to NoHoSap. She's starting to remember a few things and muttered that you held her while Jacob drove back here."

"I'm glad to have helped. I wasn't sure if she was alive at first or whether she'd make it but talked to her and stroked her fur for the short trip. She held Junior tight against her the entire way, even though he became restless. We were ecstatic that Oji found them."

Jacob and Eliza stood by Ringloo's side, and she tried to look toward Lee when she heard her voice. Lee went over and gently touched her on the head. "Keep up the good work, Ringloo, you're a fighter."

Ringloo blinked her eyes knowingly and managed a wee smile.

The kits became rambunctious in their makeshift playpen as Midnight frolicked with them through the playpen wall. Jacee put the kibosh on their play, not wanting to disturb Ringloo, and then motioned to Bebop that he wanted a sidebar. They gathered at a place along the wall, out of earshot of the others.

Jacee said, "I'm sorry for coming down on you so hard the other day, Captain. I was overcome with grief and took it out on you. The mission is much bigger than any of us and I know there's going to be some damage. I just never expected it would hit this close to home and my family would be impacted. We're more fortunate than most since they didn't perish."

"Thank you, Jacee. That means a lot to me. The recent events hit home for many of us. NoHoSap has been relatively sheltered from the catastrophes driven by climate change. We've seen the stories on the news and heard our friends' accounts from around the world of the deaths and destruction caused by rains, winds, mudslides, fires, and more, but most of us haven't experienced those effects first-hand. This made me realize we're all at risk. No one is safe." Jacee agreed. "The experience re-energized my dedication to the mission, and the need to pick up the pace. We don't have the luxury of time to get this done. Humans must mobilize now to lessen the ultimate impacts of a changing climate. I'm very sorry for what you and your family are going through, Jacee, but am also extremely grateful both Ringloo and Junior are still alive. We dodged a bullet. But they're going to keep coming. We need to do what we can to at least slow them down."

"You're right, Captain. You're the best being to lead the charge. We're behind you all the way."

"Thank you for the support, Jacee. I truly appreciate it."

Midnight came over and said, "Sorry to interrupt, but we want to let Ringloo get her rest and Lee asked if we could visit Chef Cecil's kitchen for dinner."

"Yes, we should go. Jacee, would you like to come with us or have something delivered?"

"Thanks. I'll stay here with Ringloo and the kits. Cecil sends food and drink over to keep us well-nourished and hydrated. He's so kind to help in that way."

Bebop went over to Ringloo's bed. "We're pulling for you, Ringloo. Goodnight, Jacee, Looloo, and Junior. Let us know if you need anything."

Eliza, Lee, and Jacob were at the back of the group as they headed to the kitchen. After leaving the medical unit, Lee motioned for Eliza and Jacob to stop. She reached into her bag, pulled out her closed hand, held it up for Jacob and Eliza to see, and then opened her fingers. Her face lit up as Eliza and Jacob leaned in to see what she held. "There's one for each of you. Go ahead and take them."

Jacob and Eliza obliged and looked closer at the round, shiny objects they retrieved from Lee's hand. "They're pins!" announced Jacob.

"They say, 'Change Agent'. "They're Change Agent pins. Cool!"

"Nice! Thanks, Lee. What a great idea," said Jacob as he put the pin on his shirt.

"You're welcome. I thought we could all use a little something to show we're Change Agents–like a badge of honor. Jacob, here's another for you to give to Oji."

"She'll be delighted."

"I love it. Thank you, Lee."

They heard Bebop's voice. "What's so interesting?" He'd circled back after they stopped, but they hadn't noticed him standing nearby while they admired the Change Agent pins.

"I made some Change Agent pins." Lee pointed to the pin she just affixed to her lapel and Eliza and Jacob showed off their pins too.

Bebop looked at them in amused consternation, not knowing what to say. He finally shook his head, smiled slightly, and muttered "humans," then turned and continued on. "Let's get moving. I'm hungry."

"Right behind you, Bebop, I can't wait to meet Chef Cecil and see his kitchen, not to mention get something to eat." Lee raced after Bebop on her scooter, with Eliza and Jacob jogging behind.

CHAPTER 30

NEXT STEPS

Eliza refused to give in to the urge to hit the snooze button on the alarm when it rang the following morning and instead got up to begin what promised to be an exciting day. She looked forward to visiting NoHoSap and hearing plans for the reef restoration. As usual, the workday at the station flew by. Before she knew it, she found herself driving to the cemetery, questions swirling in her head. *Where would they go to restore reefs? How would they get there? Who would help with the reef projects? How would she take pictures underwater?*

Monty greeted Eliza as she emerged from the tunnel. "Hello, Eliza, lots of new planning today, right?"

"Yes, Monty, I'm very curious to hear more about our next projects. The areas around here where we planted trees were much more accessible than reefs."

"I know what you mean, but you'd be surprised how well we get around this world. We're the original travelers, from huge migrations to ever-expanding distances we must cover to find food and shelter and also to avoid humans."

"I hadn't thought of it like that. Animals, birds, and insects have many modes of travel, not to mention reasons for traveling."

They made it to the elevator without Monty leading. "You're really getting to know your way around. Maybe next time I'll meet you at the elevator instead of the outer door or end of the tunnel."

"I know this one way to get to the elevator, but if I miss a turn or the light is low, I don't know where I'll end up. It's best you keep meeting me at the tunnel, Monty. Plus, I always like catching up while we go to Mission Command." Eliza smiled.

When they stepped out of the elevator, Monty led Eliza in a new direction through the hubbub of activity on the main floor. Many greeted Eliza, and more faces looked familiar with each visit. They rounded a corner at the edge of the main space and entered an area that looked like an aquarium. There were two large tanks, one on either end of the room, and each filled with aquatic plants, fish, and other underwater life. Monty explained one tank contained freshwater and the other saltwater. "We strive to keep all our water friends happy." He told Eliza to look up toward the tops of the tanks and she noticed more life, many that needed to be near but not necessarily always in water, including frogs, turtles, water skimmers, snails, starfish, and crabs.

"Fabulous! It's a whole underwater world. I never dreamed you had anything like this here. Where did you get the tanks?"

"Well, as with many things you see in NoHoSap, we took advantage of materials humans discarded. These tanks became available when humans upgraded an aquarium not far from here.

They couldn't find a use for these tanks, I think partly because they didn't want to move them, and they left them in vacant buildings behind the aquarium center. We had quite the challenge but managed to get them out at night without being noticed. Tusko was a huge help himself and also recruited other strong animal workers. Some of our human friends with big trucks moved the tanks and we set them up here."

As Monty and Eliza talked, animals, reptiles, and birds filed and flew into the room, finding spots to stand and hear the upcoming briefing. Bebop came over and said hello to Eliza and Monty.

"Things here in NoHoSap never cease to surprise me, Bebop. And here's even more with these tanks. I'm blown away yet again."

"On your first visit to Mission Command, I warned you that you had no idea."

"That you did. It's an extraordinary place."

Bebop trotted to the area between the tanks and called the gathering to order. "Welcome, all. As you know, we've completed a number of tree planting projects for our sub-mission highlighting what animals are doing to help thwart climate change. We're now embarking on the reef restoration part of that sub-mission and are honored to have a member of the Alliance here to talk with us about the next projects."

Jazzy undulated out from behind one of the tanks and climbed up onto a big flat rock next to Bebop that had a large depression filled with water. Eliza recalled Jazzy's seat at the Alliance meeting in the clearing had a similar setup.

"Thank you all for being here," Jazzy addressed the gathering. "We've been hard at work growing coral fragments and testing different methods here in NoHoSap's tank as well as in the ocean to see what does and doesn't work. Humans are also undertaking reef restoration and we've watched and learned from their successes and failures, although they haven't had the luxury of learning from us."

The audience chuckled, making Eliza keenly aware of her humanness.

"We've used our fragments with success on remote reefs and have identified more accessible locations in the Florida Keys where we plan to affix fragments for our upcoming projects, which are intended for humans to see. Here's a video to familiarize you with the process and players since these projects aren't as visible as the tree plantings."

A screen lowered above the podium and a film began. Jazzy narrated. "This footage is from our NoHoSap tank. We do the same thing here, although on a much smaller scale, that we do in the ocean. Our main reef workers are octopuses and crabs. They have the dexterity to affix the fragments to the frames, and then to the reefs, once the coral has grown sufficiently. The whole ecosystem is recreated here to enable us to keep everything in balance, meaning our reef is also home to fish, anemones, crustaceans, sea urchins, seahorses, eels, and turtles, to name a few."

Eliza and the others in the room watched the screen, riveted by the nimbleness of the crabs and octopuses handling the coral, as well as by the vibrant colors and activity of the reef.

"Our restoration for these projects will be done in the vicinity of where humans are restoring reefs in the Florida Keys. We plan to keep our sites protected during the work by sharks, who we hope will discourage humans from entering the area for enough time to enable us to affix the fragments and Eliza to take pictures. We'll leave Friday and return Sunday afternoon."

"Thank you, Jazzy. We really appreciate your involvement and assistance with this project."

"My pleasure, Captain. It wasn't long ago that I worked on these projects as a member of Mission Command. I'm honored to continue those efforts while on the Alliance."

"Thank you, everyone, for attending. We'll keep you posted on our progress and will let you know how each of you can help."

The crowd dispersed and Bebop motioned for Eliza to come over and join him and Jazzy.

"Hello, Eliza. Hope your snorkel skills aren't too rusty," greeted Jazzy.

"I can't say I ever had any snorkel skills, but the little I know will hopefully come back when I get in the water. How should I take pictures since my phone isn't waterproof?"

"We have a waterproof camera. I'll get it to you today so you can get a clean memory card for it."

"That'd be great. I'll also check out the features to make sure I know how to use it. How will we get to Florida from here?"

"We went back and forth about that. We have our own mechanisms for getting there, but it takes a fair amount of time."

"I'm picturing a boat pulled by porpoises or something." Eliza half-joked.

Jazzy and Bebop looked at each other as though asking what they should say.

"Well, that's not completely correct, but it's sort of in the ballpark," admitted Bebop. "In any event, it not only takes a while to get there that way, but it's also not the best for humans because there's not much protection from the elements. We planned to have another of our human friends fly us in his plane. That'll be better all the way around for this project."

"Wow, that's a nice connection to have."

"You may want to wait to see the plane before saying things like that," said Jazzy. "All this planning has made me hungry. When do we eat?"

"It's almost time, but before dinner, we have a special visit to make. We're headed to the med station first." Bebop walked away from the aquariums.

"The med station? Is Ringloo alright?" Eliza worried.

"Yes, she's improving every day. She's able to talk now and asked to see us while Jazzy's here. Jazzy, you know Jacee."

"Of course. I know him from my time in Mission Command. He was one of the hardest workers here. And nice too—never had a negative thing to say about anyone or anything. I heard what happened to his mate and son."

"We're fortunate they didn't perish as we initially feared, but Ringloo came close."

"I'd love to see her and give her and Jacee my well wishes."

CHAPTER 31

REMINDERS

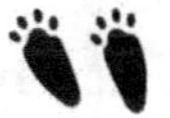

Jazzy, Eliza, and Bebop arrived at the medical unit and were greeted by Bumpy, the toad. He let them go right through. They passed Red on the way, who said, "Jazzy, welcome back. How's that flipper doing?"

"No issues, thanks to you, Red."

"That's why I do this, to hear successes like that. I'm glad I could help. Now, remember not to overdo it and watch where you walk. No more going over sharp rocks."

"I know. I always hear you telling me that when I'm near something with jagged edges. It's not worth the risk. I learned my lesson."

"Good, then I've done my job," noted Red. "Ringloo will be pleased to see you but remember, she's still very weak so don't talk with her long."

"OK, we'll be mindful of that," Bebop assured her.

Looloo and Junior played with each other as the trio entered Ringloo's room. Jacee sat near Ringloo and both were sound asleep. The kits scampered to the edge of the play area when the visitors arrived, waking Jacee. Initially startled to see others in the room, he gathered himself when he realized who it was. "Captain, Jazzy, Eliza, thank you for stopping by. Jazzy, I'm honored you're here.

"My pleasure. I'm sorry about what happened to Ringloo and Junior."

"We're making it through and getting better each day. Ringloo will be glad you're all here. She wanted to tell you something."

Jacee touched Ringloo's shoulder gently and squeezed it. She woke gradually. Upon seeing the visitors, she smiled and tried to sit up.

Bebop raised his paw to stop her. "Ringloo, please stay where you are. We don't want to disturb you, but we know you wanted to see us."

Ringloo said in a faint voice, "Thank you for coming. I wanted to thank Eliza for finding me and Junior." Eliza smiled. "When the tree fell, and I snatched Junior all I could think was that I had to protect him and hoped he'd somehow be OK. I remember hitting the water and being swept away but held on tight to Junior. The water rushed as I've never seen it and I kept hitting rocks while branches ran into me. I don't remember you finding us or much of anything until waking up here and seeing Red standing over me."

"It's OK, Ringloo, it's not important what happened in between," comforted Eliza. "The only thing that matters is that you and Junior are here now and you're alright."

"I know, we're extremely lucky to be alive. I can't stop thinking, though, that we could just as easily have died, and that many others have passed away as a result of these violent weather events. That storm was like no other. It just kept getting worse and worse, and we couldn't do anything with all the rain falling and wind blowing." Ringloo grew agitated.

"Ringloo, it's fine," reassured Jazzy. "You're safe now and don't need to relive that ordeal."

"It made me realize that what happened to us could happen anywhere to anyone. The impacts of the changing climate are here now. I'm scared for what the future may hold for Junior and Looloo. Please do everything you can to fight this."

"That's what we're doing, Ringloo," consoled Bebop.

"I know. Keep going and don't let anything or anyone discourage you from pressing on. Once I get better, I want to be out there fighting with you and will teach our kits what they can do too. I feel like we cheated death by surviving that storm, and maybe it's to allow us to do our part in the climate mission. Time isn't on our side."

"We know," agreed Jazzy. "We're fast-tracking the mission, which will enable us to make an impact sooner rather than later. We want to minimize the families that go through what you're dealing with now or, even worse, that lose someone."

Eliza thanked Ringloo for bringing this message to them and acknowledged, "There's nothing like a death or near-death experience for a wake-up call. I know most of what needs to be done has to be done by humans, and I'll do my very best to get the message out and drive change. I promise you that, Ringloo."

Ringloo whispered, "Thank you. I'm looking forward to joining you in the fight." She closed her eyes, drained from the conversation.

Jacee saw the trio out. "Thank you again for coming. She really feels she survived because she's supposed to make a difference in the climate crisis. You know we're all behind you. Let us know what we can do, especially once Ringloo is fully recovered."

"Your support means everything to us, Jacee," said Bebop. "I agree that the more we and humans realize what's at stake, the more likely the changes necessary to save ourselves will be made. We can't spread that message too often or broadly."

"Hang in there, Jacee," supported Jazzy. "We're pulling for Ringloo, you, and your family. The Alliance is behind you all the way."

Jacee hugged them before they left.

The trio walked to the kitchen in silence. Eliza eventually spoke up, "That was a somber message, but it sure did motivate me."

"Agreed," said Jazzy.

Bebop offered, "Part of the challenge is that many don't seem to realize how serious this is. The changing climate has sparked a myriad of other impacts that gravely threaten our ways of life. The frequency and severity of storms and fires are increasing. Glaciers are melting, raising water levels, and decreasing saline levels in the ocean. Ice sheets are disappearing, and water bodies are melting, preventing polar bears and reindeer from the annual treks on which they depend. Heatwaves are killing insects and plants worldwide. It goes on and on."

"You're right, Bebop, but there's a fine line between giving doom and gloom messages that can make the situation appear hopeless and motivating people to take action by letting them know they can make a positive difference."

Jazzy reacted, "Good point. If the situation seems too dire, then what's the use of making any changes? We must show that if we work to address the climate crisis, there's hope for the future."

"Exactly! We have to know the changes we're being pressed to make can result in a better outcome."

"I see. Our message has to be one of urgency, but hope. That's a challenging one."

"But we're the Change Agents and we're just the ones to send that message in the right way."

"I've heard the Change Agents moniker around here and like it. It's very fitting," said Jazzy.

"Bebop and Cuthbert came up with that one—clever and catchy."

They arrived at the kitchen, hungry and ready to eat. As usual, it hummed with activity. Chef Cecil hopped down from his station as birds and insects flew overhead and dropped sprigs of herbs on dishes of food covering the prep area. Eliza tried not to think what else could be dropping in the edibles from the helpers above.

"Jazzy, welcome!" greeted Cecil. "We haven't had the pleasure of your company since you joined the Alliance. Thank you for gracing us with your presence while you're here. I've prepared a number of your favorites."

"Chef Cecil, very good to see you again. I've been looking forward to your fine food since I arrived back in NoHoSap and hope you planned for some large appetites."

"Of course. I remember you didn't hold back when you worked with Mission Command, and I know how much these two love to eat." Cecil pointed toward Bebop and Eliza, proud to be known as hearty eaters.

The trio went to work when the food was served, grateful for the feast after a busy day. Chef Cecil noted while they dug in that nothing compared to good food and good company for unwinding at the end of the day.

As they finished and left the kitchen, a coyote scampered over to Bebop and dropped a bag on the ground in front of him. Bebop motioned for Eliza to pick it up. She did and pulled out an underwater camera.

"You can practice using it during the snorkeling session tomorrow."

Jazzy offered, "We'll have you try it out in one or both of the tanks to get you used to the equipment before you're out in the ocean with it."

"Sounds good. Thank you!"

Jazzy said goodbye and ambled back toward the tanks while Bebop and Eliza walked to the NoHoSap end of the tunnel.

"Eliza, I almost forgot. Since we're leaving for Florida Friday, it looks like you'll have to take that day off."

"I know. Hard to believe tomorrow's Thursday already. I'll let Ira know in the morning, which gives him only one day to pile the work on before I head out. I'll test the camera tonight. Have to remember to bring my snorkeling gear and bathing suit."

"See you back here tomorrow." They exchanged the usual high five and Eliza hurried off for another too-short night of sleep, energized for the next phase of the mission.

CHAPTER 32

TIME OFF

Eliza jumped into action the following morning when the alarm rang. Too tired the night before to pack for the training in NoHoSap, she threw swimming gear into her backpack. She then hunted for the snorkel mask and tube used only a few times many years ago at a local lake. Every place she thought it may be turned up empty, but she finally located it in a box in the back of her closet. Since the plane would leave for the Keys tomorrow, she packed not only for the weekend but also overnight in NoHoSap ahead of the trip.

Running late by the time she headed out the door, Eliza rushed to her car. Noli tried to calm her down, "I've noticed there's usually only a swing of 5 or 10 minutes in arriving at the station if you leave later than you usually do. Even though you feel like you're extra late, it doesn't make that much of a difference."

Not in the mood for Noli's comments, but appreciating her effort to help, Eliza softened her reply from what she felt like saying. "Thanks, Noli. I'm frazzled trying to put in the time I need to at work and hate to get a late start, even if only a few minutes, especially since I won't be there tomorrow."

"Seems you put a lot of pressure on yourself, Eliza. I don't understand. It must be a human thing, but I wanted to try to put it in perspective."

"Thank you. Don't take my snippiness personally. It isn't you, it's the situation."

Eliza ran into the station after parking her car and noticed when she sat at her desk and changed her shoes that she was only 5 minutes later than her usual time. She sure thought it would be later than that. Chuckling to herself, she admitted Noli had been absolutely right.

Eliza went to work on her latest story. When she hit a breakpoint, she stopped by Ira's office and told him she'd be out the next day. To her surprise, he said he was pleased to hear that. He remarked she didn't take many vacation days and should take more time off to avoid burning out. She thanked him for the concern and told him she'd try to do a better job in that regard.

She stopped to see Zeke on the way back to her office. "Good morning, Zeke. I just told Ira I'm taking tomorrow off."

"You're taking tomorrow off? Good for you, you never take time off."

"Does everyone think I'm a workaholic? Ira said basically the same thing and encouraged me to continue to take time."

"I can't speak for everyone, but I've noticed you rarely take time away. Even when you do, it's only a day here or there. I don't know about you, but I need a chunk of time off every once in a while, to relax and reboot."

"You're right. I don't know how long it's been since I took an extended vacation. I'll have to give it a try, especially if management thinks it's a good idea."

"Go for it. Doing anything fun with the long weekend?"

Eliza pondered how much to tell Zeke but decided not to fill him in on her Change Agents role quite yet. "Not really, probably just sleeping in and going for walks with Bop. Maybe I'll do some baking-haven't had a chance to do that in a while."

"Sounds good." Zeke hesitated before adding, "Let me know if you want company on any walks."

"Wow, thanks for the offer. I usually end up going at the last minute but if I plan ahead, I'll let you know. Back to researching the legalities of backyard chickens for my next story."

"OK, have fun with that," he said sarcastically, looking somewhat hurt Eliza rebuffed his attempt at an advance.

On the way back to her office Eliza wondered whether the tree planting helped Zeke turn over a new leaf or might he actually be interested in spending time with her. In either case, she felt disappointed she couldn't take him up on his walking offer. Even if she could, she'd dug a hole since she didn't really have a dog to walk and doubted Bebop would agree to go with her. He had more important things to do with the mission.

By the time early afternoon rolled around, Eliza needed something to eat. She'd been in such a rush that morning she hadn't brought anything. A salad from the café next door would have to do. She didn't go there often and as she checked out, noticed a picture of a dog on the cash register. Asking the cashier about it, the woman smiled, looked at the picture and said, "Yes, that's my Sir Puddles."

"Uh oh, hopefully, he's not named Puddles because he makes puddles in your house."

"Not anymore, but when he was a puppy he'd pee everywhere except the pee pads and that's where he got his name. He's precious and I love him though."

"They're hard to resist. I could have sworn there was a person in my dog when I first got him, his face was expressive like a human's." She showed the woman a picture of Bebop.

"He's very handsome. I can see why you'd say that."

Eliza had an idea and gave it a try. "Sometimes I swear he's trying to tell me something. I watch a lot of shows about the environment, and I feel like he picks up on what they say and tells me to turn the lights off or the air conditioner down."

The cashier laughed. "I know what you mean, Puddles tells me to give him treats after he sees commercials for dog food or biscuits on TV."

"Seems our dogs have trained us pretty well."

"That they have. You have a good day, now."

"Thanks, you too."

Eliza left the café, optimistic there may be a future after all for the sub-mission of using people and their pets. After the experiment in Central Park, they put it on the backburner because they failed to get the results they wanted, but it may work with a different approach. She'd have to let Bebop know about her conversation with the cashier and revisit that project with him.

Eliza ate lunch at her desk and before she knew it Zeke appeared in her doorway wishing her a nice long weekend. Deep in thought finishing the chicken story, she looked up somewhat dazed. Zeke understood her reaction after having been interrupted, and repeated, "Enjoy the long weekend. Eliza."

"Oh, thanks, Zeke. You too. I'll give you a call about a walk if I can give you advance notice. If not, I'll definitely take a rain check on that."

His face lit up, but he promptly toned the smile down, trying to instead look calm, cool, and collected. "It's a deal. I don't have much on the agenda this weekend. Have to practice since I'm working on new tunes for the group, but that's about it."

"OK, good luck and see you Monday if not before." Zeke left and Eliza finalized the story then packed up too. She'd have to change to her bathing suit in NoHoSap since she left the bag with the change of clothes in her car.

"Did you put your away message on?" Noli asked before Eliza logged off her computer.

"Oops, no I hadn't, Noli. Thanks for reminding me."

Eliza couldn't remember how to add an automatic reply that she wasn't in the office, signaling it definitely had been too long since she last took time off. Asking herself why she refrained from taking time, she concluded it was from fear there'd be adverse consequences. Hearing Ira's recommendation today about vacation made her realize her fear had no basis, and she kicked herself for leaving unused vacation days on the table every year. She thought about all the extra days she could have enjoyed being off from work. Rather than chastise herself for the past, she said aloud, "I've learned my lesson and won't let it happen again. At l least I realized it now."

"Very true, Eliza," piped in Noli. "Now all you have to do is stick to it. I'll remind you."

"Thanks, Noli. I appreciate it because I have a feeling it'll be hard to change my old ways. Off to NoHoSap." Noli flew onto Eliza's shoulder and the two were off.

When they arrived at the NoHoSap entrance, Monty said, "Looks like you're here to stay awhile, Eliza, what with the bag."

"No, I'm not running away from home, Monty. I figured I'll stay tonight after training since we're leaving for Florida in the morning."

"Good idea, although we wouldn't mind if you were here for an extended stay."

"Maybe one of these days."

They exited the tunnel and Monty moved to escort her to the room with the tanks. Eliza mentioned she had to change clothes first, leading Monty to change course. They entered a narrower part of the cavern than the main areas of Mission Command, and Eliza noticed large openings in the rock walls that led to smaller rooms. Monty turned into one and instructed Eliza to feel the inside wall to the right about one foot up and when she felt a protrusion, to push it. She felt around and eventually found a small round knob. Nothing happened initially when she pressed it, but luminescent spheres on the walls gradually faded on. Eliza looked around in wonder at a small room. A large, low rock shelf jutted out from one wall, covered with a huge pillow. In the middle of the room sat a fire pit surrounded by rocks, with a pile of wood against another wall.

"Welcome to your quarters." Monty grinned at Eliza's surprise.

"Very nice!" Eliza continued, taking it all in. "What are the lights made of?"

"Those luminescent orbs are rocks covered with fluid from departed jellyfish and fireflies. We collect their bodies after they die, use them for light fixtures as well as paint, and it's very effective. The living creatures are used where we can, but sometimes it's just not convenient since they have their own lives and don't want to wait around in the dark until someone needs a light."

"How creative. That must be the paint Cuthbert mentioned being used for signs to reroute traffic during the tree plantings."

"One and the same. It has many uses. Drop your bag since you'll stay here tonight. I'll leave you to change. When you're done, turn right out the door and I'll meet you in the open area.

After Monty left, Eliza explored the room and found it similar to the area where Jacee brought her to dry off and warm up after Maria and Sophie's rescue. She changed into her bathing suit then put a sweatsuit on since it was cold and damp underground. Picking up her bag with the snorkel gear, camera, and beach towel, she headed out to meet Monty.

Monty talked on his headset as Eliza came up behind him. "We'll be there soon. I took Eliza to her room because she needed to change. She should be out any minute now." Eliza scooted in front of Monty. "Sir, she's here and we're on our way." Monty lifted the headset from in front of his mouth and said in a perturbed voice, "He can be so impatient. I don't know what the big rush is."

"Bebop, I mean the Captain?"

"Yes."

"I know what you mean. He used to hate waiting for me as I readied for walks, what with changing my clothes and putting my shoes, coat, and other gear on."

"Yeah, I think he forgets you humans have a bunch of things you need to do to go anywhere and that makes you really slow."

"Well, no offense taken." Eliza feigned insult. "You're right, though. You'd think the extra time to put his winter and rain coats on would have given him some perspective on what it took to get ready to go out."

"Wait, the Captain wore coats?"

Eliza knew she shouldn't have let that cat out of the bag. "Uh, only because I made him. He never was a fan and probably didn't need them to stay warm or dry."

"Ha, ha, ha, wait until this gets out."

"Monty, please, you can't tell anyone else about that. Bebop would kill me. I never should have let that slip."

"But it's such a juicy piece of information, the Captain wearing a coat. I can't even picture that."

"Please, he needs to keep his authoritative reputation here and I don't want anything to ruin that. Like I said, he only did it because I made him. Remember, he was undercover then and didn't talk with me or anything. He really had no choice other than to do what I said."

"I hadn't looked at it like that. You're right, he couldn't do anything about it and had to obey you. Alright, I won't say anything."

"Thank you! That can be our secret."

"Deal."

Eliza remembered Noli likely heard the revelation while listening from somewhere on Eliza or her bag. "That goes for you too, Noli, don't say anything to anyone about Bebop wearing a coat."

"What?" asked Noli in a sleepy voice.

"Sorry Noli, I thought you may have been listening to our conversation."

"Conversation? Didn't hear…." Noli's voice trailed off as she fell back asleep.

"Off to the tank room. Follow me, Eliza," instructed Monty.

CHAPTER 33

In the Swim

Bebop paced as Eliza and Monty approached the tank room.

"Hey, Bebop."

"Hello, Eliza. Are you ready for today's training?"

"Yes, I'm all geared up to dive in."

Monty said goodbye and flew off as Bebop led Eliza behind the tanks. Each had a ramp going up to a platform at the top, for easy entry into the water. Bebop said, "Let's start with the freshwater and then move to the saltwater. Get up there and hop in."

"Before I do that, I have a memory card for the camera but need to put that in."

Bebop waited impatiently while Eliza put the card in the camera, took her sweats off, and donned the snorkel gear. She then fiddled with the camera to try to figure out how it worked.

"Whenever you're ready."

"What's your rush? I want to be sure I know how to take a picture before I get in the water."

"I know, I just forgot how long it can take humans to do anything-no offense."

"None taken, I guess. I'm going as fast as I can." Eliza walked up the ramp with the snorkel mask over her eyes, snorkel tube hanging off the side of the mask, and camera strapped around her neck. When she reached the top, she dipped her toe in the water to check the temperature, then looked for a way to gradually immerse herself and allow her body to adjust to the cool temperature.

"Just jump in." Bebop pleaded impatiently.

"I can't do that. I need to ease myself in—don't want to shock my system. Are there any steps or something to stand on and walk-in?"

"Not that I know of. All the beings here just go in the water, they don't prolong their entry."

"Alright, guess I have no choice. Here goes." Eliza put the snorkel tube in her mouth, closed her eyes, and jumped. When she surfaced, she spit the snorkel tube out of her mouth and yelled. "That's colder than I thought."

Bebop laughed. "Everybody else has complained the water's too warm for this time of year. Guess it works well for you because it was a hot summer and the water hasn't cooled off."

"Very funny. At least I'm in. Let me try out this snorkel stuff and then the camera." Eliza put the snorkel tube back in her mouth, lay on her belly at the top of the water, and dipped her face in. She rarely opened her eyes underwater but with the mask keeping her eyes dry didn't mind doing it now. A brand-new world revealed itself under her. Plants swayed back and forth in the current at the bottom of the tank, and fish swam everywhere. A turtle cavorted near the surface, not far from Eliza, its legs kicking and rocking its shell. Seeing the movement from below rather than above gave her a fresh new perspective. She heard a kerplunk and saw a frog shoot by like an underwater missile after jumping off a lily pad on top of the water.

Eliza reached for the camera and took a few shots while floating on the surface, then dove underwater, beyond the length of the snorkel tube. When she made it back to the surface, she focused on blowing the water out of the snorkel instead of breathing it in. After doing this a few times, she took pictures while well below the surface. Success! As the diving and picture taking became second nature, Eliza heard knocking and saw Bebop hitting the side of the tank. He looked up to signal it was time for her to go back to the surface, which she did without hesitation, but not until taking a picture of him through the water.

Bebop stood on the platform next to the tank when Eliza's head popped out of the water. "Looked like you were a natural down there."

"Once I remembered how to snorkel and dive, it was a lot easier, but it took a little to get to that point. Good thing you started me in the freshwater tank because I had more tastes of water than I'd like to admit when trying to remember how to clear the snorkel after being underwater."

"I thought that may be the case. Time for saltwater now."

"I'm ready. Best to get in there before I dry off." Eliza marched down the ramp from the freshwater tank, up the ramp to the saltwater tank, put the snorkel tube in her mouth, and jumped in like a pro. "Woo, feels a little colder in here," she said as she surfaced. "Aacckk! Something just brushed my feet! Are there sharks in here?" Eliza looked around and underwater in fright.

"Just me," announced Jazzy, after her head popped above the surface behind Eliza. Eliza whipped around with wide eyes–scared for her life. Seeing Jazzy, she immediately relaxed and breathed a huge sigh of relief.

"You nearly scared me to death! I thought you were a shark!"

Bebop cracked up laughing.

"Sorry to scare you, but I couldn't resist. Also, I wanted to teach a lesson that you always need to be alert in the water. Even though we have a pact here in NoHoSap about not eating each other, that's not how it works outside here. We all have to be continually vigilant, especially since most of us can be prey to something even if we're predators ourselves."

"Lesson learned. I won't forget that any time soon. Hopefully, I won't be too scared to get in the water in the Keys after that fright."

"I didn't mean to scare you that much. We'll have extra lookouts around our project areas there, but you'll still need to be on guard."

"That's kind of terrifying." Eliza tried to calm down. "Let's give this a try in saltwater."

"Where are your fins?"

"Oh, I never actually had any. Do I need a pair?"

"I've always found them helpful, although I've never tried it without them." Jazzy raised her flippers out of the water.

"Good point. I guess I would swim better if I had some."

"We should be able to find a pair for you. I'll put the word out. Now on to business-I'll show you our reef made from coral fragments we've grown here in NoHoSap. That'll get you familiar with what we'll be doing in the Keys and how to best capture it with the camera."

"Perfect. Lead the way."

Jazzy swam by Eliza and then past a rock wall to the part of the tank that couldn't be seen from the viewing room. Eliza fell behind and Jazzy circled back to her, then continued again and stopped at their destination, where she waited for Eliza to catch up. Out of breath upon arriving, Eliza admitted, "I think fins would be a good idea."

"I agree, those human feet just aren't big enough to propel you like fins would. Look below the surface."

Eliza dipped her mask in the water to be greeted by a wondrous world of color and movement. She stared in awe at the brilliance of the scene spread out beneath her, with life and vibrancy everywhere. Seagrass, fish, sponges, seahorses, starfish, anemones, jellyfish, to name a few, moved in harmony, dancing to an orchestra of waves. Jazzy waited expectantly for Eliza's reaction when she lifted her head out of the water.

"I don't think I've ever seen anything more beautiful in my life!"

"It takes your breath away, doesn't it?"

"Wow, it sure does. I had no idea it would be as fantastic."

"I have something else to show you. Follow me, and I'll go at your speed."

Jazzy didn't swim too far before stopping again. Once Eliza caught up, Jazzy instructed her to look below. Eliza obliged and stared in shock at what she saw—white coral with hardly any sea life on or around it. A few pieces of coral with some color hung in random places. Eliza had a feeling what Jazzy would say.

"And that's a bleached reef we're working to restore."

"It looks awful. Such a strikingly sad difference from the healthy reef. That's what we have to look forward to with climate change? How depressing."

"Yes, but not if we can help it. The part of the reef you saw first looked similar to this not long ago. It gives us hope we can reverse this trend, but restoration won't help if the water continues to warm and more coral dies than can be restored."

"Geez, seeing it firsthand is distressing."

"That it is, but we need to focus on the positive, on what we can do to make a difference, and to show it's working. That's what our story needs to be and hopefully, that'll motivate more humans to do what they can to change the direction we're headed."

"Agreed. I need to practice taking pictures to tell this story." Eliza dove underwater, swam along the reef, and snapped photos of the live fragments. As she checked pictures, she noticed movement beyond the camera, looked at the reef, and saw a large octopus crawling along. Her initial fear subsided after she remembered the video from the NoHoSap training yesterday showing crabs and octopuses working on reef restoration. Looking closer, she saw the octopus carrying reef fragments in its tentacles. It stopped, affixed three fragments to the reef, looked over at Eliza, and lifted one tentacle in a long undulating wave. She waved back and took a picture.

Eliza continued surfacing, diving, and taking pictures, until Jazzy stopped her. "Looks like you have the hang of it. We don't want you to get too tired before our Florida excursion. That'll do it for today."

Jazzy invited Eliza to hold on to a flipper and whisked them back to the tank entrance, where Bebop waited.

"How'd it go?"

"Eliza did quite well. We need to get her some fins, though, since those human feet are holding her back."

Eliza brushed off the comment about her human failings. "The restored reef is absolutely beautiful, and the bleached reef is grim. It's encouraging we can do something to bring them back, but it all takes time. I saw one of the octopuses."

"Cephalo is obsessed with his work," Jazzy said. "Seems like he's out there whenever I am. If he's not there, he's watching over the fragments as they grow to be sure they get to the point where they can be tied to the reef. He draws immense pride in bringing our reefs back."

"As he should."

"Eliza, let's get you back to your room and you can change into dry clothes."

"Good idea." She knew she'd get cold if she didn't dry off soon.

"I'll show you back and we'll then head to the media room to take a look at your pictures from today. Jazzy, will you join us there?"

"Sorry, not tonight. I have to update my log for the Alliance. See you in the morning, though. Good work today, Eliza. You're ready for the ocean tomorrow. At least the water will be warmer for you there."

"Really? That'll be nice. See you tomorrow and thanks for your help today, Jazzy."

"My pleasure. The warmer water isn't my favorite. I much prefer it in the northern climes, but at least it'll be more comfortable for you. Good night."

CHAPTER 34

LOGISTICS

After wishing Jazzy a good night, Bebop and Eliza walked back to Eliza's room. To Eliza's relief in the cool, damp air, a fire burned in the fire pit. While Bebop waited outside, she changed to dry clothes, hung her bathing suit, sweatsuit, and towel on rocks that protruded from the walls, and hoped they'd dry before morning. As she exited the room, she complimented the accommodations and asked Bebop to thank whoever lit the fire.

"Since you'll be here in the morning, you can see the bakery and try some fresh-baked treats."

"Yum, I'm looking forward to it already. I better not eat too much for dinner tonight and instead leave room for breakfast."

Eliza followed Bebop to the media room. Cheshire stood by a keyboard in front of a monitor, hard at work as always. Cuthbert sat next to her while she read him recent posts from the tree plantings.

"Cuthbert, glad you're here," greeted Eliza.

"Eliza? I thought you'd moved on to the reef restoration. What brings you here?"

"Reef restoration is up next. Today I trained on snorkeling and taking pictures in the water. We're going to look at the photos now to see what I did and didn't do right."

"Oh, very brave of you to get into the water. I'm afraid of it."

"Understandably, moles aren't water creatures. Nothing wrong with that."

Cheshire connected the camera to the computer, then pulled the pictures up on the monitor. The first ten or more were unrecognizable. The group discussed the rest—what was good and bad, and suggestions for improving them. Eliza hadn't appreciated the differences between taking pictures underwater versus on land. Cheshire said she'd done some research and suggested Eliza be closer to the subject, use the flash, and shoot from under or at the same level as the target instead of above. Although no one said it out loud, they all hoped she'd be able to take better shots at the project sites. "I'll do better for the project shots. Thank goodness Bebop suggested I get my feet wet and practice ahead of time, no pun intended."

Bebop and Cheshire snickered, while Cuthbert looked baffled. "Bad joke, Cuthbert. Not worth explaining."

Cheshire shrugged and moved on. "Lee's doing a superb job making connections, linking our posts, and commenting that animals appear to be taking things into their own hands by doing things to combat climate change. Responses are coming gradually and are picking up."

"Nice, that's just what we want. Cheshire, keep up the good work tracking and tallying our progress." Bebop appeared pleased.

"I've been thinking, for our work this weekend I could send the pictures to Lee, and she could post them."

"That'd work, Eliza," Cheshire agreed.

Bebop pondered the proposal. "If we do it that way there will be posts before we're done with the projects. Could people figure out our location and find us while we're still working?"

"Good question, Captain," Cuthbert said. "We found a way to handle it when that happened at the cemetery, but I wouldn't think it's easy to escape and hide if you're discovered in the ocean."

Cheshire replied, "We don't have any location links in our posts and, unless there are markers in the pictures that could reveal the location, no one should be able to find where you are before you're done."

"I always have location services off and will be careful not to include any location identifiers in the pictures," assured Eliza.

Bebop considered it. "OK, let's give it a try."

"Sounds good. I'll contact Lee and see if she's able to help this weekend," Cheshire offered.

"Alright, we're set with the media plan. Time to eat and get some rest before an early morning and busy day tomorrow. Follow me to Chef Cecil's if you're hungry."

Cheshire stayed to continue working while Cuthbert and Eliza left with Bebop. They had a wonderful meal with Chef Cecil, as usual. As they sat letting the meal digest, Bebop told Eliza he'd meet her outside her room at 7 a.m. and they'd go to the bakery.

Cuthbert added, "You'll love the bakery, Eliza. They make delicious sweets, but you have to get them early or they'll all be eaten."

Bebop laughed. "Sad but true, unless you're able to grab extra and hide them during the day, there aren't any baked goods left by the afternoon."

"I'll have to take advantage and get what I can while we're there tomorrow."

"Don't be shy in sampling whatever you want. Everybody else here does, including the bakers, so you might as well too. Good night." Bebop gave Eliza a high five.

"Good luck on the reef restoration. I look forward to seeing the pictures," Cuthbert said wistfully.

Bebop asked one of the birds who assisted in the kitchen to show Eliza back to her room, where she set the alarm then fell onto the bed exhausted.

CHAPTER 35

SWEETS

"Eliza, are you ready? It's 7 o'clock." Bebop waited outside Eliza's room.

"Yes, Bebop, I'm finishing my exercises. Be right there." Eliza finished stomach crunches, picked up her bag and headed out the door.

"How'd you sleep?"

"Very well. I didn't wake up until the alarm rang. The training yesterday really tired me out."

"I'm sure it did, but the other thing that may have helped is we don't have any background noise here. There are no cars, planes, ambulances, people walking by, or any of the other things I used to hear when I lived with you."

Eliza focused on listening while they walked. "You're right. I hadn't noticed or thought about that. It's totally quiet here. We're used to noise around us all the time in HuHabDom and don't even realize it's there. What a difference not having that to disturb our minds."

"Sure is."

"Bebop, I've been meaning to tell you, I think there may be a different approach with humans that'll work for the second sub-mission of pets trying to get humans to change habits and lessen their impact on climate change."

"I'm listening."

"I talked with someone in the café at the station yesterday and we had a nice conversation about our pets and how her dog communicates with her. The discussion made me feel better about being able to do something with that sub-mission than I did after our attempt in Central Park. I think if our approach isn't as forced as it seemed in the City, we could make progress."

"That's good news. I knew we'd figure out how best to approach that one. Now we'll have a head start."

Eliza smelled a hint of all the scrumptious things associated with bakeries, and her train of thought immediately moved to breakfast. "Bebop, my mouth is watering. I smell fresh baking and am picturing breads, cakes, cookies, pies, and all the things I love." Strands of drool hung from Bebop's mouth. "Guess you smell it and feel the same way." Fixated on food, he ignored the comment.

Sounds of whirring mixers, and clanking pots, pans, and dishes filled the air. Bebop and Eliza rounded a large opening in the rock hallway and were hit with a wave of sweet smells. They stood at the top of a short stairway leading down to a well-lit room full of activity. Similar to Chef Cecil's kitchen, birds and insects flew purposefully through the air, carrying sprigs of ingredients for the treats being made. Wooden kitchen-islands stood scattered around the room, which had ovens around the walls and racks full of baked delicacies at the back. Animals milled around the racks, selecting sweets to eat.

Eliza's eyes were drawn to a wooden block toward the center of the room at which a huge brown bear stood. It appeared to be rolling out dough. Bebop barked. The bear looked up, smiled, and waved. Bebop descended the stairs and walked toward the bear, telling Eliza to follow. As they grew closer, the bear seemed even bigger than it appeared from the entrance. Eliza held back in fear while the bear lay the rolling pin on the block. It hopped down to all fours and faced Bebop and Eliza. Eliza hung behind Bebop.

"Eliza, meet Brownie. Brownie, this is Eliza." The bear lifted a massive front paw toward Eliza. Bebop reassured her. "Nothing to be afraid of, Eliza, Brownie's one of the kindest beings you'll ever meet."

"Nice to meet you, Eliza," said Brownie in a soft mellow voice while holding her paw up.

Eliza reached out gingerly, shook the outstretched paw, and replied, "Nice to meet you too, Brownie. Sorry but I've never been this close to a bear before."

"I know. I guess we can be intimidating because we're big, but unless humans aggravate us, we really could care less about bothering you. My goal is to make all the sweets I can for everyone to enjoy here in NoHoSap."

"We're looking forward to enjoying those right now. Eliza has quite the sweet tooth and I know I'm hungry." The drool dripped faster from Bebop's mouth as he stared at the bakery racks.

"Go ahead, help yourselves to whatever you want," Brownie instructed with a laugh. "As you can see, there will be more to follow since we're all hard at work. I'll join you once I get these cookies in the oven."

"You don't have to tell me twice. Thanks, Brownie. I look forward to trying those cookies when they're done." Eliza raced Bebop toward the racks.

NoHoSap residents helped themselves to the bakery items on the racks. A ferret blocked Bebop and Eliza before they could join the other hungry partakers. "Grab a plate from over there." The ferret motioned to a stack of plates. "Put what you want on it, then you can eat it at a table over there." The ferret motioned in the other direction. "Please don't eat off the racks," added the ferret with an attitude.

Taken aback, and in a hurry to eat before the other animals snagged the best treats, Bebop asked Eliza to fill a plate for him. She took one, jostled with the other animals around the racks, and loaded it with the items Bebop wanted. Returning with a second plate, she filled it with her selections, and they sat at a table.

"That's a new procedure, although I have to say it used to get messy when everyone stood around the racks eating things right there. We also had fights when two or more creatures went for the same thing at the same time, whether they were reaching with their mouths, hands, or paws."

"I can imagine." Eliza bit into a doughnut. "Yum, this is delicious!" Bebop didn't say anything as he wolfed down the treats on his plate.

They polished off all their selections in short order. Eliza sat back, needing a break before going back for more. Bebop agreed. As they waited for the first round to digest, Brownie ambled over and sat with them.

"Did you eat yet?" she asked since both plates were clean.

"Oh yes, we finished our first plates and are waiting for it to settle before going back for more. Everything was absolutely scrumptious! I'm afraid I won't be able to eat all I want to try."

"Don't worry, you're welcome to come back any morning. We have a bunch of staples we make every day. The rest changes depending on what we feel like making and the ingredients that are in season."

"Will you have any brownies today?"

"Yes, Captain, I knew you'd be looking for those. We made a few batches, will wrap some up and you can take them on your trip."

"Brownie's brownies are the best. That's why we call her Brownie."

"Oh, it's not because she's...."

"No, it's not because she's a brown bear. In fact, since us canines can't eat chocolate, her brownies aren't even brown because they don't have any chocolate in them. They're the best blond brownies ever."

"I wondered about the chocolate thing. Can't wait to try the brownies, Brownie. How did you get into baking?"

"I lived near a large bakery in Russia. The smells from that place drew me just about every night to raid the dumpster where they'd throw out the old baked goods. I wanted to see what the fresh stuff tasted like and made a habit of breaking in during the wee hours of the morning to make treats with their bakery equipment. They wondered where their supplies were going and why things were a mess when they arrived back in the mornings, so they set up traps, and caught me one time when I wasn't being careful. Fortunately, they didn't kill me but instead sent me to a local zoo. A bird from the free world visited almost every day and told us about an entrance to another part of NoHoSap close to the zoo. Some of the other prisoners and I escaped and made it to NoHoSap. I set up the bakery and here we are."

"That's an inspiring story."

"I can't imagine what we'd do without the bakery here."

"You'd eat even more plain nuts, berries, and other fruits, that's what," joked Brownie. "I just fancied it up to give you more fun and variety."

"All this talk of sweets has made me hungry again. I'm ready for another plate and I bet you are too, Bebop. Brownie, can I get you anything?"

Before Brownie could answer, Bebop laughed. "She'll get all she wants once the baking is done. That's part of the reason the baked goods are usually gone by the afternoon–Brownie eats them."

"I'd like to say that isn't fair, Bebop, but you're right," retorted Brownie self-consciously. "I generally do eat what's left by the time we've cleaned everything up. What can I say, a girl needs her nourishment."

"I didn't mean it negatively but was just telling it like it is."

"I can relate to having a big appetite and that's why I'm going up for a second plate. Bebop, I'll fill yours a second time too."

"I'll go over with you. I want to see what's left and what's new. Brownie, thank you for visiting with us. I know you need to get back to work and we don't want to keep you any longer."

"Yes, I should get back. The cookies will be on the rack soon. I'll send the brownies over once they're cooled and wrapped. Good luck on the next project."

"Brownie, many thanks for these delicious treats! I'm looking forward to the brownies and visiting the bakery again. Sweets are my favorite kind of food."

"Don't let Chef Cecil hear you say that," berated Brownie in jest. "I'm touched you enjoyed our offerings. Be safe."

Eliza and Bebop headed back to the racks to fill up their plates again, then savored every mouthful until they were too full to eat anymore. Bebop shook off the food stupor. "We need to get moving. Jazzy's going to wonder where we are." He jumped up and walked away from the table. Before he made it far, a heron holding a bag in his mouth walked into his path. Eliza took it and the bird said Brownie didn't want them to leave without it.

"Thanks, Ron. Can't believe I almost forgot the brownies." The bird bowed its head, turned, and ran off to retrieve its next delivery.

As Eliza and Bebop left, Brownie looked up from the mixing bowl in which the next morsels were being made, and Eliza thanked her again. Bebop hastened the pace once they were back in the hallway, leaving Eliza to jog after him.

CHAPTER 36

FLYING

They continued at a fast clip after leaving the bakery. "Bebop, I don't think you should be running this soon after eating." Not wanting to get bloat for real after having faked his death from that cause, he let up on his pace, but Eliza still had to walk as fast as she could to keep up.

They took the elevator to the surface and found Jazzy waiting on a large boulder. The trailer used for the tree plantings sat next to it and held a large, clear water tank. When Jazzy saw Bebop and Eliza she jumped into the tank and called Stets. He trotted over and stood in front of the trailer. A small monkey and squirrel appeared out of the foliage overhead and hooked Stets into the harness on the trailer. Bebop told Eliza to hop on Stets and the group left. They went in a different direction than to the tunnel. The new route had a wider path riddled with trees and rocks but Stets wove around them expertly.

"Where are we going?" Eliza had never been this way before.

"It's a different entrance we use for larger loads that won't fit through the tunnel," advised Stets. "We only use it when we have to. We'll end up close to a parking area on the outskirts of the cemetery, which is convenient if we need transportation."

Bebop asked, "Stets, is Thiha there? We shouldn't go out to the lot until he's there."

"Mission Command told us he's there waiting."

"Good. That way we can load right into the truck and be on our way, hopefully before anyone sees us."

Eliza wondered who Thiha was, but figured she'd find out soon enough. She preferred being in control of her schedule and found it difficult not to know all the plans and players ahead of time. She had to let those feelings go in favor of allowing Bebop to run the mission as he saw fit.

"Duck your head, Eliza," shouted Stets. Eliza complied and they immediately went under a tree branch that would have hit her in the face if she hesitated in lowering her head.

"Thanks for the warning, Stets, but next time please give me a little more advance notice."

"Sorry, I don't often have anyone on my back and don't think about that until the last minute. At least I remembered before it was too late."

"That's true. Any other spots I should be prepared for?"

"No, we're just about there. They'll have to open the gate. Bebop will let them know."

Bebop barked three times—his loud threatening bark. The group entered a thicker part of the woods, shading the sun amidst the trees. A wall of pine boughs parted in front of them. Eliza looked to see what moved the wall and saw huge salamanders hanging on ropes on each side. A second wall followed the first and parted just in time as the group moved through. To Eliza's surprise, there was yet a third wall of boughs that opened too, offering triple protection to keep this entrance secure from unwanted visitors. As they passed the last wall Eliza peered sideways and spotted another large salamander hanging from one of the ropes that drew the boughs back. It waved, smiled, and yelled, "Good luck!"

They exited into a small dirt parking area. Eliza recognized it as the lot at a far corner of the cemetery, in an older, infrequently visited section. A medium-sized delivery type truck sat in the lot. When the group came into view a short brown-haired man jumped out with a big grin.

"Hello, Jazzy, Captain, and Stets," greeted the man. "And you must be Eliza."

"Hello, Thiha." Bebop greeted the man. "Eliza, meet Thiha, our trustworthy and courageous pilot."

Eliza jumped off Stets. "So nice to meet you, Thiha." They shook hands.

"Good to see you again, Thiha," shouted Jazzy from the tank. Eliza noticed the tank now held only half the water it did before they left. Apparently much sloshed out on the trip from NoHoSap.

"Let's get Jazzy in the truck and head to the airport," said Thiha. Stets walked the trailer behind the truck. Thiha pulled a remote control from his pocket and used it to maneuver a lift out from under the truck and placed it under the tank. He raised the lift to position the tank at the same level as the back of the truck. Next, he climbed into the truck, released an electric forklift fastened to the side, and used the forklift to maneuver the tank into the truck.

With Jazzy and the tank safely in the truck, Stets said goodbye and disappeared into the forest with the trailer. Thiha closed the back door of the truck and motioned for Bebop and Eliza to hop into the cab. "To the airport," he announced when he took his seat behind the wheel.

"How was your flight in, Thiha?" asked Bebop.

"Not bad, Captain. Hit turbulence along the way but that front should be out of here by now for smooth flying to the Keys."

"Where did you come from, Thiha?"

"Do you mean today or in general?"

"Sorry, I meant today, but I'm interested to hear in general too."

"I flew in from Washington D.C. this morning. Not too long of a flight. My home country is Myanmar. I was a pilot in the military there and escaped about three years ago."

"I'm glad you made it out. I can't even imagine what you went through. Do you miss it, though?"

"I miss Myanmar every day but don't miss being in the military at all. It's very painful to think about what's going on there and that I was part of it."

"I'm sorry. I didn't mean to bring up bad memories. Hopefully, you're enjoying it in the US."

"Overall, it was a good move to come here, although there are challenges and many new things to learn. At least I had my piloting skills and had no trouble finding work in my field. I now fly cargo planes for a living. My company lets me use one of the planes they recently took out of service because they bought a new fleet, and I'm able to help my NoHoSap friends with that."

"It's our gain to have found Thiha."

Thiha laughed. "I thought I was going crazy when my cat started talking to me."

"They did that to you too? I feared for my mental health when they first contacted me."

"Yeah, I guess my cat had a connection to someone in NoHoSap Mission Command and when she heard they needed someone with flying experience, she let them know about me. I've always loved animals and felt I was in tune with the natural world but had no idea about anything like NoHoSap. My parents would have understood it better since they're more connected to the environment than I am. They're farmers and come from a long line of people who depended directly on nature to live."

"NoHoSap is an awe-inspiring place. I'm honored to be working on Mission Command's climate change mission. I didn't know what I should be doing to fight climate change. I think that's the way a lot of people feel."

"I agree. In my country, there seems to be a disconnect between older and younger folks about living in harmony with the environment. The older generation understands how our actions impact our world, but the younger generation is focused on surviving and not saving the planet."

"It's promising you two are more engaged in the fight than you were before joining us. Now we have to figure out how to get the rest of you humans on board."

"That's the challenge, but we'll get there. That's why we're the Change Agents."

"What are the Change Agents?" asked Thiha.

Bebop gave his take. "That's the name for those of us addressing the climate crisis. For some reason you humans seem to enjoy banding together around a cause that has a name."

"You bet we do. It makes us feel like we're part of something bigger, which motivates us to take action."

"The Change Agents. I like it," said Thiha with a smile.

Jazzy chimed in through the window at the back of the cab, "If the Change Agents moniker helps the humans get charged up, let them run with it, Bebop."

"That's fine, but they should be focusing on the projects at hand and not be distracted by names and gimmicks. We're not a group of superheroes."

"Depends on how you define superhero," suggested Eliza. "A seal and dog that talk and direct missions to get things done—seems pretty super and heroic to me."

"Thanks, but that's enough. We need to get down to business." Bebop remained unimpressed.

"We're here," announced Thiha. Eliza looked out and realized they were on a runway at the edge of the cargo part of the airport. The passenger terminal that Eliza always used when taking a flight glinted in the sun at a distance, across countless commercial runways. It made sense they wouldn't take a passenger flight or airline plane on a trip with the animals.

"Jazzy, we'll have you in a full tank soon." Thiha parked the truck next to a cargo plane and jumped out. Eliza heard a splash and, when she looked through the window at the back of the cab, saw Jazzy out of the tank, waiting for Thiha to open the door.

Bebop and Eliza joined Thiha behind the truck. He opened the door, raised the lift, and Jazzy rode it down to the ground. As she did,

Thiha hit a button on the side of the plane and a ramp came out. Jazzy waddled up the ramp into the plane's cargo hold. Thiha, Bebop, and Eliza joined her. The large cargo area stood empty except for a large water tank smack dab in the center, for weight distribution purposes. A ramp led to the top of the tank, which Jazzy navigated and then slid into the water. She surfaced and exclaimed, "Now that's more like it. Thank you, Thiha, for filling this with cold saltwater."

"I thought it best since you'll be in such warm water in the Keys."

"I'll enjoy every moment in this coolness." She dove under and all could see her through the glass tank wall, twirling as she swam around.

Thiha led Bebop and Eliza to the cockpit and they each took a seat. Eliza buckled herself and then Bebop in. The airport's control tower sounded over the radio and Thiha taxied down the runway. When they received the go-ahead, he stepped on it and the plane ascended into the sky. Eliza looked back to check on Jazzy. She surfaced briefly for the take-off, but dipped back under once they reached altitude.

Eliza couldn't wait any longer to hear details about the project. "What's the plan when we arrive?"

"I was just going to fill you in. After we land, Thiha will bring us by truck to a remote beach. Another of our human friends, Rosaline, will be there with a boat and she'll take us to the project site. Our team will be waiting there with fragments from our coral farm. Then it's into the water for reef restoration and pictures. Once the day's work is done, we'll spend a couple nights on the boat and do the same thing tomorrow and Sunday morning before heading back."

"Must be a big boat. Will we have time to stop at the coral farm?"

"It is a big boat and yes, we'll visit the farm tomorrow morning."

"Thiha, you're all set to pick us up at the beach Sunday and fly us back, right?"

"Yes, sir. I have another flight tomorrow, but the weather's supposed to be clear and there shouldn't be any delays."

"Good. Let's enjoy the rest of the flight before a busy couple of days."

"Yes, relax everyone. We'll be there soon," Thiha advised.

CHAPTER 37

SEABOUND

The passengers dozed off, only to be awoken by Thiha as he descended to the airport. He landed the plane smoothly, disembarked once the plane stopped, and re-appeared with a truck. They reversed everything they'd done at the beginning of their journey and were on the road shortly after landing. Eliza hadn't been to the ocean in a while and enjoyed taking in the scenery. As they came closer to the beach, the trees thinned, and sand became the dominant landscape.

They parked in a small sand area and Eliza heard the ocean surf when she exited the truck. Taking a deep breath of the sea air, Eliza closed her eyes, listened to the shorebirds, and smiled. Bebop held his nose in the air, nostrils twitching back and forth, also smelling the marine scents. Eliza wanted to ask if he remembered the first time, she took him to the beach but didn't want to embarrass him. Nonetheless, she reminisced how he'd run and run in the sand and chased the waves as they approached and receded from the edge of the beach. After she threw a piece of driftwood into the water, he ran to retrieve it and a wave blindsided him. It knocked him over and tussled him up the beach, then back again. Eliza's heart stopped as the surf dragged Bebop toward the ocean, but he fought back against the wave, stood and ran out. He never went close to the water after that other than the swimming hole at the cemetery. No wonder she'd been concerned when he jumped into the stream to save Ringloo and Junior.

Jazzy shuffled down the ramp from the tank, rode the lift to the ground, and galumphed into the sand. "Let's get to the water. I know the surf will be warm, but this sand is super hot. I miss New England temperatures already."

Eliza suddenly recalled that during her first trip with Bebop to the beach on Cape Cod, she saw a seal in the water just offshore from where she and Bebop walked. The seal followed them along the beach, diving under and popping its head up as though watching them. "Jazzy, when I took Bebop to the ocean the first time, a seal seemed to watch and follow us from the water. You mentioned you used to see us there. Was that you, by any chance?"

"Yep, that was me. It looked like you watched me back."

"I did. I'd never seen a seal in the wild before. Bebop, do you remember seeing her?"

"I think I saw her a few times but was more interested in smelling things that washed up on the beach than looking out at the water."

Jazzy chuckled. "I still laugh whenever I think of that wave bowling you over, Bebop."

To Eliza's surprise, he didn't seem to be upset by Jazzy bringing that up. Instead, he smiled as though remembering it fondly, but rapidly snapped back to the present. "We should get moving. Rosaline is probably waiting for us."

Thiha slid the ramp back into the truck and asked if they wanted him to accompany them to the beach. Bebop advised they'd be fine and thanked Thiha. Bidding them adieu, Thiha said he'd see them back there Sunday. The trio headed down a sand path through the beachgrass and dunes. A warm, gentle breeze rustled the grass and blew gently against their faces. At the end of the path, the beach opened up and ran for miles in each direction. Waves crashed onto the shore with repeated roars.

"You're here!" yelled a voice from down the beach. Eliza saw a young woman with wild hair running toward them. When she made it to the trio, she asked in a Caribbean accent, "How was your trip?"

"Uneventful," replied Jazzy matter-of-factly. "Rosaline, meet Bebop and Eliza."

"Pleased to meet you." They greeted Rosaline almost in unison, while Bebop held out his paw and Eliza held out her hand.

"The pleasure's mine. It's nice to meet you both in person after hearing about you from Jazzy." Rosaline shook the outstretched paw and hand. "The boat's over there." She pointed to a small rubber boat on the beach.

"I'm going for a swim first." Jazzy made a beeline toward the water.

Bebop, Rosaline, and Eliza walked to the boat and Rosaline invited them to get in before she pulled it into the water. Bebop obliged to avoid getting wet. Eliza declined and instead threw her bag and sneakers in and lifted the rope handle on the side of the boat opposite Rosaline. With two people it moved easily over the sand and into the water. When her feet hit the water, the warmth surprised Eliza, reminding her of bathwater.

"Wow, this water is much warmer than I thought it'd be."

"Yes, we had a hot, sunny summer that heated it right up," observed Rosaline. "Usually it's somewhat cooler by now, but in the past few years it has gotten warmer during the summer and takes longer to cool down in the fall. Yet another symptom of the climate crisis we're battling."

"The symptoms are everywhere," Bebop added. "At least humans are noticing them more than they used to. Now we need to get more people to do something to address it."

"You're preaching to the choir, Bebop, but we're doing what we can to spread the word," said Rosaline. "OK, it's deep enough for me to start the motor now. Eliza, jump in." Rosaline lifted herself onto the edge of the boat and gracefully swung her legs over. Eliza watched and tried to do the same but kept either losing her grip or not swinging her legs high enough. Too proud to accept any help from Rosaline, she eventually managed a clumsy landing in the boat.

"Where's Jazzy?"

"She's probably already at the research vessel." Rosaline motioned further out over the water. Eliza followed her gesture and saw a large boat with a cabin and a narrow metal walkway jutting over the water in the front. They headed straight toward it.

"That's the Starfish, my research boat," Rosaline announced proudly. "I'm using it for my doctoral research and am happy to also be able to use it to help your crew."

They pulled up at the back of the Starfish, which had a wooden platform affixed near the motor not far above the water. An open door above the platform allowed easy access inside without having to navigate over the back of the boat.

"Hop aboard," instructed Rosaline. Eliza climbed from the rubber boat onto the platform, opened the door, and stepped into the boat. She turned to help Bebop do the same. Not thrilled to be out on the water, he did his best to hide it. He made it into the boat without incident, much to his relief. Rosaline jumped from one boat to the other. Holding a rope attached to the rubber boat, she walked to the side of the Starfish and lifted the dinghy into the research boat, then tied it down along the side to keep it from flying out. As she finished, they heard a splash and Jazzy jumped onto the platform, then scuttled into the boat.

"Felt good to stretch out and swim after the trip, but I don't like how warm the water is. Even coming out further it didn't cool off much."

"We were just talking about that because Eliza also noticed how warm it is."

"No wonder the reefs are bleaching with these temperatures. Our restoration efforts can only do so much if the water conditions continue to decline."

"Speaking of restoration, let's get moving and start today's work."

"Ay Ay, Captain. Brace yourself." Rosaline asked Eliza to close the door above the platform. She didn't want to take any chances that Bebop could fall out. With the door closed, Rosaline turned the boat's key and the engine rumbled on. She punched it up to speed gradually while the front of the boat lifted up out of the water and leveled off, staying out of the chop of the waves and making for a smoother ride. Bebop sat down nervously.

Eliza surveyed the boat. All were gathered in the rear in a rectangular area surrounded by thick, porcelain-colored fiberglass sides about three feet high. Rosaline stood comfortably at the wheel in a podium like protrusion from the floor of the boat. The front half of the vessel contained a cabin with windows, offering a place to get out of the weather. Narrow walkways ran along each side of the cabin to the front of the boat, which had a small open area that led to the "gangway" hanging over the water, surrounded by metal rails.

"The restoration site isn't far away," yelled Rosaline over the noise of the motor, wind, and water that splashed against the boat. "We're headed over toward the Key you can see in the distance thataway." Rosaline pointed ahead and Eliza barely saw what she assumed was an island.

Eliza stood next to Bebop, who looked scared to death. He closed his eyes and turned his head when pelted with splashes of water that blew over the sides of the boat as it cut through the waves. "It'll be fine Bebop, you won't even have to go in the water. We'll do all that. You're very brave to be out here."

"I really thought about not coming but didn't want to look like a coward. How can I expect the members of my team to do something if I'm not willing to be there and support them?"

"Spoken like a true leader," commented Jazzy. "We knew what we were doing when we put you in charge of the climate change mission." Eliza couldn't help but be proud of Bebop's bravery and leadership.

The group traveled the rest of the way in silence, soaking in the sun and sea air.

CHAPTER 38

UNDERWATER WONDERS

"This should be it," announced Rosaline as she put the boat into neutral. Eliza wondered how she knew where they were, since she didn't see any markers.

"Jazzy, this is the place, right?" inquired Rosaline. "We're at the coordinates you provided."

"I'll check," replied Jazzy as she moved toward the platform, Rosaline opened the gate, Jazzy jumped into the water, and then disappeared. She resurfaced a few minutes later and confirmed they were at the right spot. "Come on in with that camera, Eliza. Our team is down there with the fragments. You'll see a few octopuses–Cephalay, Cephalee, Cephaloo, and Cephali–and a bunch of crabs–Fiddle, Faddle, Fuddle, Pitter, Patter, Putter, and Potter. They work fast and I told them to wait to start until you get down there."

Eliza took her shirt and shorts off to reveal her bathing suit, donned the snorkel gear, took the camera, and went to the platform. "Wait, I just remembered I brought some fins for you," informed Rosaline, as she opened a compartment along the side of the boat. She pulled out a pair of fins and handed them to Eliza, who put them on and stood awkwardly to get the feel of having them on her feet.

Just as she readied herself to jump in, Jazzy said, "Oh, and don't be alarmed if you see sharks circling. They're protecting the site from curious onlookers. We didn't want anyone snooping around before we arrived." Eliza hesitated. "Don't worry, they won't hurt you. They're working on the mission too."

Eliza waved to Rosaline and Bebop, jumped in, and dove underwater. She saw the sharks and choked back a wave of terror as the theme music from 'Jaws' played in her mind. Surfacing, she swam to get the feel of the fins, which propelled her much more effectively than her feet.

Looking underwater, a bleached reef sprawled out below. Far from the vibrant, healthy reef she saw in NoHoSap, the magnitude of damage struck Eliza. This reef also lacked the activity that took place in and around the vital reef. She wondered what happened to all the other life that depended on reefs when they died, as this coral had. Reminding herself to be optimistic, she hoped the restoration would be a success and the reef would be a hotbed of action again.

She dove deeper and discovered a frenzy of activity as crabs and octopuses affixed live coral fragments to the reef. Eliza snapped pictures and videos of the intricate work being done by the diligent team members, capturing their dexterity as they tenderly tied the live coral fragments onto the bleached structure. The fragments came from a cage and Jazzy monitored the supply chain from there. Full of pieces when Eliza first arrived, the team worked speedily, and the receptacle emptied in no time. Once all the fragments were affixed, Jazzy brought the empty vessel over to the workers. The crabs held onto the frame, the octopuses took the cage, and swam away. All waved as they left while the octopuses took turns carrying the cargo and its passengers.

Eliza followed Jazzy back to the surface, thankful for the fins on her feet, allowing her to keep up somewhat better. They popped their heads out of the water and Eliza realized they were further from the boat than she imagined. When she'd gone up for air while they were working, she didn't check her location. Jazzy invited Eliza to hold onto a flipper for the trek back. Eliza almost declined but decided to let Jazzy pull her to avoid losing steam on the swim back. Arriving back at the boat, Bebop immediately made sure they were OK and asked how it went.

"Very well," advised Jazzy. "The team moved right along and that part of the reef looks much better now. They'll keep monitoring it, checking the fixation points, making sure conditions are conducive to continued growth, and spreading the word to bring reef inhabitants back and create the ecosystem needed for success."

"I'm looking forward to checking the pictures and videos and getting those posted right away." Eliza climbed onto the platform and into the boat, with Jazzy following.

"Let's go in the cabin to view the footage," suggested Rosaline. "It's usually easier to see it there without the sun's glare. Also, that's where the hardware for the satellite connection is located and it can be easier to get a signal."

Everyone followed Rosaline indoors. Surprisingly spacious, monitors and other research equipment filled the cabin.

"What are you researching for your doctorate?" Eliza asked Rosaline.

"It's very relevant to this project. I'm studying the resiliency of restored reefs to varying climate change stressors. Since the reef system is very complex, the research covers not only the restored coral but also the algae and other life, plant and animal, that live in or near the reef. I track the time it takes for the reef to fully regenerate and support the ecosystem, as well as how higher water temperature, increased sunlight exposure, higher acidity and other variables affect algae die-off and coral bleaching throughout the restoration period. With many variables, it's difficult to isolate impacts, but I'm working through that with the goal to figure out how we can improve the success of restoration in the face of the warming climate. As we discussed earlier, it's great to affix new coral, but if it just dies with the next season of warm weather, it wasn't a **productive exercise.**"

Bebop, Jazzy, and Eliza stared at Rosaline, not wanting to admit they didn't understand much of what she said. Eliza spoke up, "Very complicated, but true about not wasting efforts if the coral doesn't survive. No sense spending time and effort on something that won't make a longer-term difference."

"Exactly. I'm not the only person trying to figure this out. A bunch of us are working on different aspects of it to come up with a comprehensive plan."

"That's exciting. How did you get involved in this line of work?"

"I'm from Jamaica and have spent all my life in and near the ocean. As I grew up, we all noticed the reefs degenerating. At the same time, storms became more intense and wrought havoc on the reefs and fisheries, not to mention our communities. We were in a downward spiral, and it's continued that way. There's no time to recover from one natural catastrophe before the next hits. I've been mesmerized by reefs from the first time I saw one while swimming as a young kid. When I saw them dying, I wanted to do what I could to bring them back and keep them healthy. I won a scholarship to attend college in Florida and have been blessed to continue receiving educational and research support to the doctoral level where I am now."

Jazzy added, "A sea turtle who used to see Rosaline in the ocean and at the reefs alerted us about her. He knew we wanted to partner with humans and thought she'd be a good connection."

"I talked with my reef friends while studying them in tanks in the lab and also when I brought samples in from the ocean for my research. To my total surprise, one day this sea turtle talked back to me! I thought I was losing it–figured I must be hallucinating because I hadn't had enough sleep or had been in the sun too long," Rosaline chuckled.

"Join the club." Eliza laughed. "Seems we humans all had similar reactions when we were first contacted."

"We didn't know how else to do it." Bebop defended their actions. "We have the ability to talk. Why not make contact directly that way. We didn't want to leave any room for you to attribute the communication to anything other than us."

"Well, it sure worked. The turtle told me very little about the mission and the next time I saw him he had a waterproof smartphone. I talked with Jazzy over the phone, who I didn't know was a seal, and she filled me in on the project. From that moment on I was hooked and have been providing support whenever I can."

"Thrilled to have you onboard," said Jazzy.

"I second that," Bebop added.

"Glad to meet another Change Agent," Eliza said enthusiastically.

Bebop shook his head while Jazzy smiled slightly.

"What?"

"We've named ourselves the Change Agents because we're agents fighting climate change. Bebop thinks it's silly but we humans who are involved in the mission think it's fun and cool to have a handle."

"Nice, I like that. The Change Agents." Rosaline said with pride.

"Let's take a look at the pictures."

"So impatient, Bebop. Here they are." Eliza held the camera in front of everyone to show them the shots, but Rosaline found a cord in a drawer and offered to plug the camera into a computer monitor. Eliza brought the footage up for everyone to view. They followed the same process they did in NoHoSap by first identifying the pictures to be deleted. Once those were out of the way, they focused on the rest and ultimately chose what should be posted. All agreed Eliza captured the restoration perfectly.

"The personalities of the crabs and octopuses even come out. It looks like they're posing," observed Jazzy.

"I noticed that too. They seemed to do it more as time wore on. I think they liked the idea of being on film."

"What a difference in the coral once the fragments were affixed."

"Yes, they looked much better with the new fragments. I'll send these to Lee for posting right away?"

"Yes, let's get them out there." Bebop agreed.

Eliza went to work transferring the footage. While she did, Bebop announced, "I'm hungry. When do we eat?"

Rosaline answered, "I brought the food you instructed and will set it up on the table here."

"I'll get us some fresh sea delicacies." Jazzy waddled out of the cabin and dove from the platform into the water.

"Thanks for mentioning that Bebop," Eliza said. "I'd been busy and hadn't thought about eating, but we did miss lunch. Here are the brownies from NoHoSap. I hope they're still in one piece." She pulled the bag Ron gave them from her backpack and placed it on the table, crumpled and compacted from the trip.

Rosaline removed containers from cupboards and the refrigerator and put them on the table. "Here are the salads and bread you wanted, Bebop. Hopefully, you'll like them."

"I'm sure I will. Thanks, Rosaline."

Eliza finished sending the pictures and videos and came over to the table to relax. She, Bebop, and Rosaline then sat there looking at the food and getting hungrier while they waited for Jazzy.

"What do you think she's getting?" Eliza pondered.

"Well, she can't get any meat because of our NoHoSap pact. I don't know what she may bring back."

"There's a lot of edible seaweed down there. She's very limited if she can't bring back any shellfish or fish."

Jazzy's head popped up near the platform and she jumped onto it. Covered in kelp and other seaweed, she announced, "Hope you're hungry."

"Jazzy, you made quite the trip to gather this variety of plants." Rosaline commended.

"Only the best for the team."

Rosaline gathered everything in a large bowl and brought it to the table. "Eliza, do you want any of this cooked? I usually put it in some broth to soften it up."

"That sounds good to me." She'd never eaten seaweed, looked at the raw stuff with suspicion, and hoped cooking would make it more palatable.

Once the broth heated and the seaweed cooked, all gathered at the table and chowed down. The food didn't last long and there wasn't much conversation, since all focused on eating.

When they finished, Eliza said with disappointment, "I don't even think I have room for brownies."

"No worries, those will make a nice breakfast." Bebop looked at the brownie bag longingly.

"Yum, good idea."

Rosaline showed Eliza and Bebop to their sleeping quarters below deck. Jazzy opted to stay on the deck near the platform and ocean. All bid each other good night.

Not tired enough to sleep, Eliza caught up on texts and emails. As she did, an idea dawned on her. Since doing the story at the cemetery, she tried to think of other ways to combine her job with the climate change mission. Now it hit her. She could be the station's climate change correspondent. In that role, she'd cover stories about climate change, ranging from how it occurs, to its impacts, to how to reduce carbon emissions. She wanted to run it by Bebop, but he appeared to be asleep. She called him in a hushed tone, increasing the volume until he woke up.

"Bebop, I have an idea and need to see what you think about it. I don't want to do anything without your approval."

"Alright, what is it?" Bebop's eyes were half-open from being woken.

"What do you think about me trying to become the station's climate change expert? I could cover stories related to climate change, and that would give me a platform to also cover what we're doing on the mission when the time is right."

Bebop closed his eyes and Eliza thought he'd fallen back asleep. She waited before repeating her inquiry. "Bebop, what do you think?" Nothing broke the silence other than the waves lapping against the side of the boat.

"Bebop?"

His eyes popped wide open. "I think that's a perfect idea! Maybe if you combine your work on our mission with your job you won't feel as torn trying to keep up with both independently."

Eliza smiled, jumped up, and hugged him. "Thank you, Bebop! That's the way I saw it and I was hoping you would too."

"Yes, I think that'll work well." As he spoke, he put his head down and went back to sleep. Eliza calmed her excitement and continued checking messages on her phone until she dozed off.

CHAPTER 39

THE FARM

"Rise and shine." Eliza opened her eyes to see sunlight streaming in from one of the windows to the deck. Rosaline, who gave the wake-up greeting, stood in the doorway. Eliza sat up, stretched, and saw Bebop asleep on the far side of the below-deck quarters.

"Good morning. How long did I sleep?"

"Not too long. It's 7 a.m. and Jazzy said you should get up if we're going to keep the schedule today."

Jazzy stuck her head in the doorway next to Rosaline'. "Hurry up if you want any of those brownies."

"That's right. I need to get moving. I don't want to miss out on those." Bebop roused when he heard the word 'brownies.' "You're up."

"Can't miss breakfast. I heard something about brownies and that got me going."

The group gathered around the table. Eliza pulled the brownies out of the bag, placed them on a plate, and all ripped into them like they hadn't eaten for days. After devouring the delicious treats, they sat back to let it settle. All were pleased Brownie sent a bag along for them to enjoy and that Eliza and Bebop hadn't eaten them on the trip from NoHoSap.

Eliza asked whether she should take pictures of the coral farm. Bebop looked over at Jazzy, who knew the potential downsides much better than he did. "Not right now. The farm is a fixed location with workers on a consistent basis. We shouldn't take any chances that someone could find it based on pictures you take. It's too big a risk."

"Makes sense."

"Speaking of that, if you haven't already, turn off location services on your phone. I'm doing it for the boat's radar now." Rosaline fiddled with the boat's dashboard, then started the engine, drowning out the calming sound of waves lapping against the side.

"Off to the coral nursery." Rosaline punched the throttle and they were off. Bebop hunkered down near the door to the cabin, having discovered there was less movement in this central spot and water didn't reach him when it sprayed over the side. The rest of the crew stood in the back area, taking in the ocean sights and enjoying the sea breeze and splashes of saltwater from the boat cutting through the waves.

The sun shone brightly, with hardly a cloud in the bright blue sky. Eliza didn't travel to these climes often but thought it seemed warm for the time of year. She wanted to ask Rosaline about it, but the sounds of the engine, waves, and breeze made it difficult to have a conversation without yelling.

When the boat slowed and it quieted somewhat, Eliza mentioned the heat to Rosaline, who confirmed the pattern continued the record warm weather all this year, then elaborated. "While many focus on the warmer air temperatures, the increased amount of sun heats up the water too. Warmer water obviously negatively impacts the plants and animals that live in it. Also, warmer oceans fuel hurricanes and more severe storms, which have devastating effects on people and structures on land as well as on ecosystems in the ocean."

Jazzy commented, "In addition to being a researcher and doctoral candidate, Rosaline is a teacher and can't pass up an opportunity to educate those around her."

"I don't mind the lesson. It's nice to see such passion for a topic."

"I could go on and on, but since we're at our destination, that'll do it for now." Rosaline put the throttle in neutral and the boat glided to a stop, rolling with the sea waves.

Jazzy jumped into the water as soon as the propeller stopped. "Come on in. You'll like it, Eliza, the water's warm. Rosaline, you're coming too, aren't you?"

Rosaline hesitated and looked at Bebop. "I didn't want to leave Bebop alone up here, especially since the boat would be adrift because I don't want to drop anchor and risk destroying any coral on the bottom."

Bebop saw the disappointment on their faces. "I'll be fine. You won't be gone that long and what could really happen to me or the boat in that amount of time?" He tried to sound convincing, even though nervous about being on the ocean by himself.

"Rosaline, looks like you're going with us." Eliza donned her snorkeling gear. Rosaline didn't hesitate, pulled her snorkel equipment out of a hatch toward the stern of the boat, put it on expertly, and jumped in before Eliza made it to the platform.

"Don't let me hold you up." Surprised her dive mates left her behind, Eliza looked at Bebop. "You're sure you'll be alright?"

"Yes, go ahead. It'll give me a chance to take in the scenery." Bebop tried to persuade himself he didn't mind being left alone.

"See you in a bit." Eliza jumped in and swam after Jazzy and Rosaline, who hadn't bothered to wait by the boat for her. Eliza reached them to find Jazzy diving and twirling underwater while Rosaline lay belly down on the surface, her masked face in the water surveying the sights below.

Jazzy explained to Eliza, "When we get down there, you'll see coral fragments of all sizes hanging on strings. They're grouped according to the time they were affixed. You'll see new ones just starting as well as pieces ready to be attached to reefs. Our workers are gathering the fragments we'll use in our project today, allowing you to see how they're selected. More workers will likely be around the smaller pieces because those need more care. They clean and rid the fragments of bacteria and other organisms that could smother or otherwise destroy them. There should also be workers bringing new fragments to the nursery in the hopes they'll grow."

"That's my favorite part," said Rosaline. "I love seeing our workers and other creatures bringing broken coral to us that is then used for restoration."

"Where do they get the fragments?"

"It varies. There's a big influx after storms because the stronger currents break coral off the reefs and can carry them for miles. Our crews search for these and bring them here to grow rather than die. A fair number come from areas where people run into them with boats. Our lookouts notify us when that happens, we send a crew, and put the word out. That way anyone in the area who can carry coral will hopefully bring the fragments to the nursery. Also, you'd be surprised by the amount of coral that creatures bring in on their own if they find pieces that have been dislodged. Just last week a grouper brought in a turtle shell full of pieces she collected. There's huge interest in restoring our reefs since many depend on them for habitat and food."

"I can't wait to see it."

"Let's go." Jazzy plunged underwater, Rosaline followed, and Eliza clumsily brought up the rear.

Arriving at the coral farm, the scene astounded and enthralled Eliza. The sun shone brightly through the water, illuminating every-thing in a calming tone. Structures like roof antennas with strings hanging off the vertical arms were lined up row after row. Corals of differing shapes and colors hung from the strings as though adorning sparse underwater holiday trees. The strings and corals swayed gently back and forth to the rhythm of the sea current.

As Jazzy described, the coral sizes increased from one end of the nursery to the next. Rosaline led them to the far end of the farm, with the largest corals. Octopuses and crabs cut pieces from the strings and deposited them in the cage from yesterday's restoration. A fully restored reef lay past the end of the nursery, encouraging the fragments hanging near it to create similar living reefs of their own once they graduated from the farm.

Captivated by the brilliancy and life of the healthy reef, Eliza watched fish of all shapes, sizes, and radiant colors swim among the coral. Similarly, a myriad of crabs and other crawling creatures milled on the seafloor at the bottom of the reef. Rosaline swam over to Eliza and pointed to a large stone crab chasing a bright blue fish away, and a smaller crab carrying what appeared to be a barnacle.

They swam back to the part of the nursery with the smaller fragments and watched octopuses affixing new pieces that just arrived. Some waved their tentacles at Eliza, recognizing her from yesterday's project. Jazzy motioned with her flipper that the time had come to leave. Eliza tore herself away from the calming underwater tableau.

Lifting their heads out of the water, they spotted the boat floating further away than they expected. Worried about Bebop, Eliza noticed him standing in the stern, looking down at the water anxiously. Since he likely wouldn't be able to see or hear her, she swam toward the boat instead of yelling for him. Stopping to catch her breath, Eliza saw Jazzy surface next to the boat. She startled Bebop, as she intended, and he jumped back, then hastily gathered his composure, acting as though he hadn't been fazed. Eliza laughed and swam the rest of the way to the boat. Rosaline made it back just after Jazzy. Eliza eventually joined them.

"Bebop, how'd you make out?"

"No problems. It's very peaceful here. I talked with some seagulls and terns and then found a shady spot while waiting for you to get back. I think I'm getting used to the waves constantly moving the boat under my feet. How's everything at the nursery?"

"All's in good shape. Coral's coming along nicely and we're receiving a steady stream of new stock. I hadn't checked it in a while. Thank you, Bebop, for hanging out here by yourself and allowing me to take a dive."

"You're welcome, Rosaline. Eliza, what did you think?"

"Magnificent. I'd seen pictures of coral farms before, but there's nothing like seeing the real thing. Rosaline, what was up with those crabs you pointed out?"

"They're our bouncers. They get rid of the undesirables for coral growth–certain fish, various worms, barnacles, mussels, sponges, and other organisms that can harm coral."

"Cool. They did a commendable job warding off that fish and carrying the barnacle away."

"It's a full-time job, but they keep the fragments safe."

"Where did you get those trees the strings hang from?"

"Almost all the materials we use were discarded by humans and ended up in the ocean. Some are coral trees that may have been dislodged from other nurseries, but our team cobbled most of them together from things they've found. At least we've put them to good use."

"You sure have."

"Hang on, we're heading to the project site. It's not far." Rosaline sent the boat off to a brisk start, the occupants bracing themselves.

CHAPTER 40

Restoring and Storming

The group didn't travel far before Rosaline stopped the boat again. "We're here. I'll stay topside with Bebop."

Not one to wait for a swim, Jazzy jumped in. Eliza took the camera, bid Bebop and Rosaline adieu, and hopped in too.

This project was a bit different from yesterday's because the reef contained bleached and healthy areas, as well as restored areas in between. Jazzy led Eliza to the part of the reef being restored for today's project. When they arrived, the crabs from yesterday waved, danced, and bowed to Eliza. They clearly enjoyed getting attention. Eliza readied the camera, and they went to work, adding flourishes to their movements that Eliza hadn't seen the day before. Unlike the crabs, the octopuses were more intent on attaching the fragments than putting on a show. The work moved along seamlessly while Eliza snapped pictures.

Eliza saw sharks circling in the distance, making her heart beat faster. She avoided doing anything to attract their attention, even though Jazzy said they wouldn't harm her. Eliza swam to the healthy part of the reef, rolled the video, and slowly swam back to the work-site, documenting the huge differences between the healthy reef, the freshly restored reef, and the bleached reef. When she made it back to the workers, they were almost finished attaching fragments.

After the team affixed the last piece of coral, Eliza heard high-pitched noises in the water. She looked over at the crabs and they appeared to be singing. Jazzy swam over, saw the look of disbelief on Eliza's face, then smiled to acknowledge the crabs were, in fact, serenading her. The octopuses came over too and each floated one tentacle out toward Eliza to say goodbye and thank her for her work. She extended her hand in appreciation, allowing the tentacles to touch it. They tickled and stuck to her skin before the octopuses pulled them back. Humbled by being accepted in their underwater world, she waved as her new friends scurried and swam away.

Eliza followed Jazzy back to the boat. Bebop welcomed them with relief. The group went into the cabin to view the footage Eliza captured from today's work. Many of the shots were similar to those taken yesterday, but Rosaline commented the crabs were more animated. All enjoyed the pictures showing the contrasts among the healthy, bleached, and restored reef. Eliza sent the selected pictures and videos off to Lee to post.

"I'll check the postings and reactions from what we did yesterday. Should I pull those up on the computer screen to allow all of us to see?"

"Absolutely." Rosaline connected the phone to the computer. Eliza went through the posting sites and all were heartened to see a significant number of likes. Lee's initial postings were designed to get people talking about the right things. For example, she said that if animals are doing what they can to thwart global warming, humans should too. This resulted in some productive discussion as well as the usual comments asking how animals did these things, could the pictures be doctored, etc. For the most part, all on the team were happy with the progress.

Jazzy excused herself to go diving in search of food for dinner. Rosaline checked the radar and weather forecast for the following day. They planned to do another restoration in the morning before the crew headed back to NoHoSap.

"I'm a bit concerned about the forecast for tomorrow. A cold front's supposed to move through and bring rain and wind for tomorrow. If that pans out, we may want to cancel tomorrow's work."

"What's the timing on the front arriving?" Bebop wanted to complete the work but had no interest in being at sea in a storm.

"Currently showing mid to late morning, but that can change in an instant."

"We'll have to keep an eye on it. Let's see what Jazzy thinks. You and she have the most experience with the weather around the oceans."

Bebop no sooner mentioned her name than Jazzy jumped onto the platform, again covered with kelp and other seaweed. She dragged herself into the cabin and dropped it on the floor. Rosaline rinsed it off, cooked some in a pot, and the team came together for dinner.

"Jazzy, Rosaline checked the weather for tomorrow and a front is moving in. It's supposed to storm mid to late morning based on the current forecast. Do you think we should cancel the project tomorrow?"

"I sensed changes coming when I was just out there. If the wind and currents pick up, we won't be able to do the work even if we wanted to. While we're all here, though, it would be nice if we could do one last project in the morning. I'd rather not call it yet because it may turn out to be fine. Let's wait and see how things are tomorrow."

"Fair enough. Rosaline, please keep an eye on the radar and let us know if you see any changes for better or worse. Regardless, let's plan to get an early start in the morning with the goal to be out of here with our work done before the storm hits."

"Ay ay, Captain."

All were tired from the day at sea and fell asleep shortly after dinner. A strong wind woke them as the sun rose. The gust shook the boat and sent its bell clanging. Rosaline ran to the dashboard, turned the radio on, and checked the radar while the rest of the team scrambled above deck. The waves raged, two to three times the size they'd been the prior days, rocking the boat haphazardly.

"The front came in much faster than they showed overnight. Looks like the rain isn't far behind and the gusts are supposed to get stronger." Rosaline spoke loudly above the wind and waves.

"We should head to shore," Jazzy announced. Bebop agreed, trying to keep his balance as he stood in the swaying boat.

"On our way." Rosaline pulled up the anchor and turned the engine on. She tried to keep the boat moving with the waves rather than crashing into them, but as the wind blew stronger and the waves grew larger and came from all directions, it became more difficult. The rain arrived, pummeling the boat's occupants with heavy drops. Eliza felt sick while the boat rocked and pitched, the bell clamoring constantly as the waves and wind buffeted the boat every which way.

Bebop tried to keep his balance in the stern while jostled from the undulating boat and pelted by rain. Rosaline shouted, "Bebop, sit or lay down and you won't be moved around as much by the waves."

"What?" Bebop couldn't hear her and moved closer. As he did, a wave hit the boat, pitching it sideways violently and sending water over the side. Bebop lost his footing, fell on his back, and slid on the water-soaked deck toward the rear. His legs flailed wildly, and his eyes widened in terror as he glided toward the opening above the platform. Rosaline yelled, "Shut the gate!" Eliza screamed, "Bebop!" and lunged after him, falling on the slippery deck.

Jazzy catapulted herself over the wet deck toward the opening. Bebop's speed as he slid toward the gap didn't allow her adequate time to maneuver the gate closed, and instead, she body blocked him to keep him in the boat. As he ran into her, Jazzy shouted, "Cut the motor!" She knew the force of the hit would push her into the water and didn't want to risk being cut by the propeller.

The collision thrust Jazzy overboard. As she crashed into the surf, she looked back to see whether her efforts slowed Bebop enough that he didn't fall in too. His hindquarters dangled in the angry water as his front legs held onto the platform for dear life. Eliza and Rosaline rushed to his aid, snagged him under the shoulders, and pulled him back in. While they did, Jazzy's head slipped beneath the water.

"Bebop, I thought I might lose you again!" Eliza hugged the soaked and shaking Bebop, reminding her of the not-too-long ago rescue in the stream after Ringloo and Junior fell in.

"You two should go into the cabin and out of this weather." Rosaline shut the gate above the platform. Another wave washed over the side of the boat as it rocked.

"No, we need to get Jazzy back. She saved me and I need to know she's OK." All watched the agitated sea, looking for Jazzy.

"I'm sure she's fine. The ocean is her element and she's been in many storms before. She'll be back soon. I'll keep the motor off to enable her to get back to the platform without needing to dodge the propeller in these waves."

"Rosaline's right. Jazzy can handle this and will be back before we know it."

Bebop looked out at the sea, the top of his head furrowed with worry. Eliza and Rosaline couldn't rid their minds of the image of Jazzy, awkwardly hitting the water sideways and looking back at them before sinking below the surface. Not the typical way a seal entered the water, they hoped she was alright and not hurt or disoriented enough that she couldn't find her way back to the boat. The more time passed without a sign of her the more they feared the worst.

HOPING

The wind and rain eventually lessened and the sky brightened, but no sign of Jazzy.

"What am I going to tell the Alliance members if we don't return with Jazzy?" Bebop sat and searched the ocean forlornly.

"Don't think that way, Bebop," consoled Rosaline. "We don't know she's not coming back. It seems like we've waited an eternity, but it really hasn't been that long."

"If you say so. Let's give it a little longer before we head back in." The rain continued falling lightly and the boat rocked to gentler waves, but Jazzy didn't appear. Bebop stood up, told Rosaline to head back to shore, and walked into the cabin with his head and tail down. Eliza followed him.

When inside, Eliza pulled a towel from her bag and dried Bebop off while he stood, looking dejected. When she finished, he lay down and put his head on his front paws with a sigh.

"We don't know if anything bad happened to her, Bebop. It's probably very difficult to find the boat in these rough seas."

"It only happened because she tried to save me. I should have stayed inside when I couldn't keep my footing. Better yet, I shouldn't have come on this trip in the first place, but I wanted to be a part of it to support the team."

"Don't second guess yourself. Who knew a wave was going to come over the side of the boat, knock you over and send you flying? I should have shut the gate near the platform last night, then we wouldn't have had an issue. I'm not writing Jazzy off yet."

"I hope you're right, and that Jazzy isn't gone."

"I'm extremely grateful she saved you, Bebop. I don't want to lose you again, and we have a lot to accomplish together on the mission." Eliza sat next to Bebop on the floor and petted him to try to make him feel better.

"If it weren't for her, or for you saving me from the stream for that matter, I wouldn't be here now. I owe you both my life."

"And I owe you mine. You don't know how much you've brought to me, Bebop. The joy of our times together when you lived with me, the purpose you've given me since making me part of the mission. Thank you."

"I'm glad we can spend time together again. And I'm sorry for leaving you when I did."

Eliza hugged him, finally forgiving him for the pain he caused when he died, or she thought he died–relieved to no longer harbor the feelings of hurt and betrayal.

Rosaline shouted, "We're just about there." Bebop and Eliza came out of the cabin and saw the beach in front of them.

"Eliza, please untie the rubber boat. I'll drop anchor here and we can go to shore."

Eliza obliged, Rosaline set the anchor, and Eliza and Rosaline lifted the rubber boat out of its secure spot and into the water. Rosaline lowered herself in, followed by Eliza with her bag. Bebop stood nervously on deck, not wanting to step foot into the inflatable dinghy as it floated and moved atop the waves.

Eliza covered for him. "Good thinking, Bebop, we wouldn't want your toenails to puncture the boat when you jump in. Rosaline and I can lift you over. Eliza climbed back onto the Starfish, and, with some difficulty, the two humans lifted Bebop safely into the rubber boat. He immediately lay down in the center.

"Smart, you remembered what I said about lowering your center of gravity." Rosaline started the motor and they headed toward the beach. The wind and rain had stopped and the sun peeked between the clouds, revealing the silver lining at the edges.

Eliza saw someone on the beach. "There's Thiha. Hey, is that...?" Rosaline touched Eliza's arm and shook her head 'no' indicating Eliza shouldn't finish her sentence. They both looked down at Bebop, who couldn't see the beach over the sides of the dinghy, then smiled at each other.

When they reached shallow water Rosaline turned the motor off and raised it up. She and Eliza stepped out of the boat and into the water, then dragged the boat onto the beach. Bebop stood up and jumped out, not able to get on land fast enough. A greeting of "What took you so long?" rang out.

"Jazzy! You're alright!" Jazzy lay on the beach next to Thiha. Bebop ran over to make sure she wasn't hurt.

"What did you expect, that some rough water would do me in? I thought you knew me better than that."

"We waited and waited, but you didn't come back. I didn't want to think the worst but couldn't help worrying. Thank you for saving my life!"

"You would have done the same for me. I'm glad I could help. I was a little discombobulated after hitting the water. When I got my bearings, the water was very rough, and I couldn't find the boat. I figured I might as well meet you back here."

"Thank goodness you're OK," Rosaline said. "We told him not to fret, but I have to say I got a bit concerned myself."

"I did too," admitted Eliza.

"Good morning," broke in Thiha.

"Sorry, Thiha, good morning," Eliza said. "Thiha, meet Rosaline. Rosaline, this is Thiha." The pair greeted each other. "We had some scary moments out there today when the front moved through. Jazzy kept Bebop from sliding into the ocean but she fell into the water awkwardly in the process and we were worried about her."

"Jazzy told me and said you'd be pleasantly surprised to see her here. Luckily, I flew in before the storm and wasn't impacted in the air."

"Good thing, if flying a plane is like maneuvering a boat, it would have been a challenge in that weather. I'm glad it cleared up but too bad we weren't able to get today's project done."

"The nursery crew will take care of that later this afternoon. We won't have footage of it, but we have a lot of good shots from the other projects."

"You sure do. I've been following it on my phone," said Thiha. "I especially liked the shots with the octopuses working. It's mesmerizing watching all those tentacles coordinating to tie the coral on."

"I'm going for a swim before I have to get in the travel tank." Jazzy took off toward the water.

"I'll get the truck ready for her." Thiha turned and walked back to the truck. Bebop followed him, eager to put distance between himself and the water.

"Thanks for everything, Rosaline. I enjoyed working with you."

"Likewise."

Eliza reached into a pocket in her bag, took something out and gave it to Rosaline. Rosaline looked at it and joyfully exclaimed, "A Change Agent pin!"

"You're a Change Agent and need a pin."

"Thank you! This is so cool. I'll wear it proudly."

"Take care, Rosaline, and all the best to you with your doctorate work." Eliza walked toward the truck and Rosaline pushed the rubber boat into the water to bring her back to the Starfish.

CHAPTER 42

RETURN TRIP

Jazzy finished her swim and caught up with the others at the truck. Thiha had everything prepared and she hopped into the tank. Bebop already waited in the truck, ready to go. Eliza climbed in and they reversed the way they came just a few short days ago.

In what seemed like a blink of an eye, they landed back at the airport near NoHoSap. Eliza exited the plane and waited to help get Jazzy out. Thiha mentioned that rather than Jazzy disembarking here, he'd instead take her to the coast, near her home. Eliza went back into the plane to say goodbye and saw Jazzy and Bebop talking. When they finished Eliza thanked Jazzy for not only teaching her how to snorkel like a pro and take underwater pictures, but also leading the projects this past weekend, and, most importantly, saving Bebop.

"I'm delighted to help with the mission and am grateful I could keep Bebop from falling into the ocean. Thank you for bringing the word to humans, helping us on this mission, and being such a good friend to Bebop. He won't say it but he really missed you after he had to leave you and appreciates your support now."

"I was angry at him for faking his death, but now understand why he did it and am fortunate to have him back in my life."

They said farewell and Eliza left the plane. Jacob had arrived on the runway and talked with Thiha while Bebop waited in the van. Eliza joined them and asked Jacob if he brought what she messaged Lee about. He confirmed he did, and Eliza asked that he give it to Thiha.

As Jacob placed an object in Thiha's hand Eliza said, "Thiha, this is for you."

He opened his hand and smiled at the pin he'd been given. "Change Agent. Thank you!"

"Thanks to Jacob for getting more pins. I gave mine to Rosaline and we want to be sure we all have them."

"Lee got your text and we coordinated to be sure I'd have pins for the pickup today."

"Very nice, I'm proud to wear it." Thiha put it on his shirt.

Eliza thanked Thiha for all his work, then she and Jacob walked to the van, where they found Bebop sound asleep after the stress of the day.

"Let's not wake him until we're back at NoHoSap. He deserves to sleep after the weekend he had. I don't think he slept well on the boat and was on alert the full trip, anyway. Not to mention what happened today when he was almost swept out to sea, poor guy."

"He was almost swept out to sea? What happened?"

Eliza described it all to Jacob. "I don't think he's going to want to go near water for quite a while."

"I don't blame him. Geez, we're very lucky it ended up OK. Speaking of storms and ending up OK. Ringloo's out of critical care and can move around on her own. She, Junior, and the kits are going to live in Mission Command for a while."

"That's excellent!"

"Definitely. Oh, and Lee's at Mission Command this afternoon. Do you want to see her? She's been hard at work with posts and comments. I took a look at the posts from your work this weekend and they're pretty awesome. You captured very cool footage."

"Thanks. Yes, I'd like to catch up with Lee. I also need to comment on posts before I get any further behind. The one good thing about wrapping up early in Florida because of the weather is we're back here earlier and can get more accomplished on this end."

Bebop remained sound asleep when they arrived at the cemetery parking lot. Eliza roused him to get out of the van and make the short trek to NoHoSap. He revived himself enough by the time they descended to Mission Command that others wouldn't necessarily know how exhausted he was. After leaving the elevator, he said he needed a nap, thanked Eliza for all she did over the weekend and gave her a high five. He walked away, remembered he wanted to tell Eliza something, and turned back. "Let's take a couple days off and meet back here Wednesday after your workday. In the meantime, be thinking about ways to implement the second sub-mission."

"Sounds good, and will do. See you Wednesday." Bebop stumbled off in a sleepwalking trance.

Jacob and Eliza walked to the media room. They arrived to find Lee sitting with her back to them and a wall of video monitors in front of her.

"Nice job with the postings, Lee."

Lee turned, smiled, and replied, "Thanks, Eliza. Excellent work with the footage for the posts. We're picking up speed. There's been an uptick in followers and comments. Seems that people are less suspicious of human involvement or doctoring of pictures with sea creatures. Some have come right out and said they believe these pictures more than the tree planting ones. I guess they feel it's less likely the crabs and octopuses were trained than the animals who planted trees."

"That's good news. Your posts include just the right amount of narrative presented in a balanced non-controversial way. If you don't mind, I'll sign on over here and try to get caught up on everything. It's been hard to review it all while on the project. Oh, and thank you for the extra pins. We should all keep a couple on hand to give to others working on the mission."

"I don't mind at all and you're welcome."

"Thiha really appreciated the pin. I'll leave you two to do the tech work. Let me know if you need anything." Jacob turned and left.

Eliza worked on the social media comments until falling asleep as she sat in front of the monitor. Lee told her to go home and get some sleep. Too tired to argue, Eliza signed off and grabbed her bags to leave. Lee appeared to be going strong, but Eliza encouraged her to also take a break to avoid burning out. Lee said she would, all the while fixated on the monitors as her right hand flew typing responses and reactions. Eliza shook her head and smiled as she left, happy to see Lee fully engaged in helping with the mission.

When Eliza made it home, the tiredness caught up with her again. She wanted to crash onto her bed for a good sleep, but instead went through the mail, did her weekly chores, made dinner, and checked work emails. As usual, by the time she turned in, she didn't have nearly as many hours to sleep as she wanted, but tomorrow would be another day to catch up on rest.

CHAPTER 43

BACK AT THE OFFICE

Eliza wanted to stomp on the alarm clock when it rudely woke her the following morning. She hit the snooze button and buried her head under the covers, desperate for even a few more minutes of sleep. The alarm rang five minutes later, and Eliza called it names as she silenced it, forcing herself to stay on her feet rather than lay down again. She woke enough for her sensibility to kick in, realizing it would be much better, in the long run, to get up. It would be a busy day at the station, particularly because she had to catch up from having Friday off. After hurrying to wash up and get dressed, she took an apple from the fruit bowl on her way out the door.

"Good choice," lauded Noli from Eliza's shoulder, startling Eliza. "Healthy, local produce—you can't go wrong with that."

"Thanks, Noli, and good morning to you, too. One of these days I won't be surprised by your greetings."

"Just keeping you on your toes. Looks like you had a productive weekend."

"Sure did. It's good to be back, though." Feeling guilty, Eliza decided to take the car to get to the station faster. She drove off with Noli sitting contentedly on the dashboard.

While she drove, Eliza thought about Bebop's comment on ways to implement the second submission. An idea burst into her mind. "Hey Noli, do you think you'd be able to communicate with humans if, unlike me, they couldn't understand or hear what you were saying?"

"Depends on what I was trying to tell them and whether they were paying attention to and thinking about what I was doing. I communicated quite well with you without talking when I kept crawling on the window in your office to let you know I wanted to go outside."

"That's true."

"People swat at me, try to step on me, or open the window to get me out of their car all the time. There has to be a way to turn those reactions into something productive."

"Good point, Noli. That's what we need to figure out." Eliza's voice trailed off as she pondered how the NoHoSap team could engage humans.

Eliza remained deep in thought while she parked, absentmindedly lifted her bag, and walked into her office. Noli settled on the windowsill to enjoy the morning sun while Eliza went to work on the computer. She no sooner focused on the story she needed to complete when an email from Ira appeared announcing a national journalism organization nominated Zeke for a prestigious journalism award. She went to his office to congratulate him.

Stopping at his door, Eliza didn't bother to say good morning or otherwise let Zeke know she was there. "Way to go! That's quite the honor to receive an Excellence Award nomination."

Engrossed in his work, he jolted to attention when he heard her voice. Seeing her in the door, he relaxed and smiled self-consciously. "I'm wrapped up in this piece and didn't hear you. Thanks, Eliza. I wasn't expecting anything like that at this stage in my career, but it's nice to know I've been noticed."

"For sure! I've heard the nomination process for that one is pretty rigorous. It's quite an accomplishment to be nominated."

"Yeah, it'll be nice to add that to my qualifications. How was the long weekend? Nice tan by the way."

Eliza didn't realize she tanned enough for anyone to see she'd been in the sun. This time, though, she prepared ahead to have a response since she figured he'd say something about her vacation.

"It was very nice. I ended up going to Florida. I have a friend there who's doing doctoral research and we went snorkeling."

"Wow, a spur of the moment trip. Nice to see you're branching out."

"Figured I'm too young to be stuck in my relatively narrow comfort zone. I would have contacted you for a walk if I'd been here." She didn't want Zeke to think she blew him off or had no interest in his offer to walk with her.

"Not a problem. I'm glad you took time off and even got away." Though he acted nonchalant, his mind celebrated that she'd been gone and hadn't ignored his walk invitation, as he initially assumed. "There's plenty more time to go for a walk with you and Bop. I've followed the links to your posts about the trees in the cemetery. There now are posts showing sea animals restoring reefs, taking action similar to what the animals were supposedly doing at the cemetery."

"I saw those posts too and wondered if there's a connection." She surprised herself with the ease at which she now lied, not liking the personality trait, but also not yet comfortable telling Zeke the truth.

"It's very interesting and coincidental with all of these activities being posted. I don't know what to make of it, to be honest with you. Wouldn't that be something if you'd seen part of the action while you snorkeled in Florida?"

Eliza hadn't expected or been prepared for this comment. She couldn't tell if Zeke thought she may be tied to it somehow and fished for information, or if the idea never crossed his mind. She tried not to look guilty, a difficult task for her usually honest self. "That would have been something to see. I did visit a couple of reefs, both ones that had been bleached and others that were healthy. The difference is striking."

"I can imagine. There were pictures of that too and they were sobering."

"Whoever does it, I hope we can restore the reefs. Anyway, I better get back to work. Congratulations again on the nomination!" She scurried away from the door, not wanting to be rude, but knowing the longer she talked with Zeke the greater the likelihood she'd tell him about the mission. Spilling the beans had to be avoided at all costs, especially since she hadn't cleared it with Bebop. Chuckling to herself, the irony struck her once again at how her former pet now controlled her actions.

Back in her office, she hunkered down on her story for that evening's news. By the end of the day, the fatigue from the busy weekend caught up with her. She went for a short walk after arriving home, had a fast dinner, caught up on the mail and bills, and went to bed early, for once.

CHAPTER 44

PITCHING

E liza expected Tuesday's workday to fly. Not only did she still have to catch up from being away, but she also planned to pitch the climate correspondent idea to Ira. She'd pitched stories to him before, including the one from the cemetery, but the correspondent idea involved a bigger commitment from the station, making her nervous.

When she arrived at work, she sought Zeke's guidance. Stopping at his office door, she cleared her throat to announce herself. "Good morning."

He looked up and laughed. "That's better. Thanks for not startling me again. Good morning."

"I wanted to run something by you that I'm nervous about." Zeke perked up as he listened intently. "I think the station should have a climate correspondent to cover the ins and outs of the climate crisis and let people know what they can do to fight it, and I want to fill that role."

He raised his eyebrows and tilted his head while considering the idea. Eliza watched him and waited impatiently for his reaction. "That's actually a great idea. Climate change is such a timely and important topic and deserves regular attention. Go for it!"

"I'm trying not to be insulted that you're surprised I actually came up with a worthy idea."

"No, I didn't mean that at all. It came out the wrong way."

"Don't dig a deeper hole. It's fine, I'm nervous about making the pitch to Ira and it's putting me on edge."

"Look at it this way, the worst result would be Ira saying 'no.' Even if that happened, you'd continue what you've been doing, and nothing would be lost. And I'm sure Ira would give you credit for coming up with the idea and bringing it to him."

"Yeah, that puts it in perspective. Thanks, Zeke."

"I have to admit, I'm always nervous before playing a jazz gig. I worry about messing something up, particularly on my solos. But then I think the worst that could happen if I made a mistake would be people may think I can't play and may not hire me for any more gigs. That wouldn't be much of a loss for some of the places I play." They both snickered in agreement, knowing he played in a fair number of dives.

"Honestly, unless you screwed up the melody to a standard tune, probably no one other than you, and maybe the other band members would even know it. That's one of the nice things about jazz, it's improvisational. You could always say you meant to do something because you were being innovative."

"Good point. Thanks, Eliza."

"Thanks for the pep talk. Here I go."

"Good luck."

Eliza marched to Ira's office while her confidence was up. It didn't take long for her to appear back in Zeke's office.

He looked up, surprised to see her so soon. "That was fast."

"Yes, it was." Eliza sounded dejected.

"Well, at least you tried."

"That I did." She sighed. "And he liked the idea! I'm the new climate correspondent!"

"Congratulations!" Zeke stood and gave her a high five–the way they often celebrated successes.

"Turns out he'd already been thinking we should do something on the topic but hadn't come up with a way to approach it. My idea provided the missing piece and he approved it right away."

"Alright! See, there wasn't anything to worry about."

Eliza turned to leave and heard Zeke comment. "Change Agent, nice." Eliza spun around, alarmed, wondering why he'd call her a Change Agent. "Your pin, it's a nice pin." He pointed toward the lapel on Eliza's suit jacket. She looked down and remembered she'd put her pin there earlier this morning to boost her confidence about the pitch to Ira.

"Oh, thanks. I forgot that it was there." She breathed in relief that he didn't find insider information about her Change Agent role.

"What does it mean? Change agent for what? You're not in some secret change agent society, are you?"

"What? No, it's nothing like that." Her mind raced, thinking about how to answer his questions. Tempted to spill the full truth, she decided now wasn't the time, and wove a yarn somewhat near the truth. "I'm in a social media group focused on climate change and one of our members recently had these pins made. I thought it also fit with the climate correspondent thing I wanted to pitch."

"Yeah, that it does. Nice pin in any event, and since now you're the climate correspondent, you can wear it in that role."

"Good point. I guess I can." Eliza thought wearing the pin could be a nice way to mobilize people around a cause, the Change Agents cause. Things were coalescing in ways she hadn't anticipated, encouraging her. She couldn't wait to tell Bebop.

"Congrats again, Eliza. You're going to be a great climate correspondent."

"Thanks, Zeke. And thank you for encouraging me to talk with Ira. Without that, I'd probably still be sitting in my office worrying about it."

"I'm glad I could help. Let me know what else I can do. I wouldn't mind being a Change Agent too."

"OK, will do."

Walking back to her office, she marveled at how the climate correspondent and Change Agents pin and moniker evolved in such a short time this morning. She saw exciting things ahead for the Change Agents and chuckled to herself that Zeke expressed interest in being one. Pondering how much longer she should keep up the charade and not let him know about her work with Bebop, the NoHoSap crew, and the rest of the Change Agents, she imagined how he may react if he knew the complete story.

CHAPTER 45

RED ALERT

The following day began as usual, with the alarm ringing too early for Eliza's taste. She forced herself not to hit the snooze button and instead got up and went through the usual morning routine, including rushing out the door to get to work.

As she drove to the station, she continued thinking about a topic that had been on her mind since yesterday–what story should she cover first as the climate correspondent? When Ira approved her request for the position, he suggested she do a piece soon to enable the station to publicly launch the climate correspondent role. They both agreed it should be an attention-grabbing story. Eliza contemplated options to fit the bill.

After settling in her office, she continued researching a story for the evening news about a proposal to broaden the types of containers covered by redemption laws. By early afternoon she'd completed the research, written the piece, and finished the wrap-up when Noli landed on top of her computer monitor.

"Eliza, I have an urgent message from Bebop. He needs you in NoHoSap as soon as possible. He's mobilizing the full climate change team on a crisis that must be addressed immediately."

"What? What's going on?"

"Here, I'll let him tell you." Noli placed her tiny headset on Eliza's desk and flipped a switch to turn the speaker on.

Bebop's voice blasted out. "Eliza?" Eliza jumped at the volume and hurried to shut her office door and avoid anyone hearing the conversation. Returning to her desk, she motioned for Noli to turn the volume down.

"Eliza?"

"Yes, Bebop, I'm here. Noli has you on speaker and I can hear you."

"We have an emergency. Mosa alerted us to a fire deep in the Amazon rainforest. We don't believe humans are aware of it yet, but no doubt they will be very soon. We haven't mobilized on prior fires there, but she thought now that we have more humans helping us, we may be able to help. She hopes if we're involved, we'll be able to limit the destruction." Dumbfounded, Eliza thought about the enormity of this task.

"The Alliance convened an emergency meeting at Mosa's request, and they want us to do what we can. We can't afford to lose more of our forests since they're vital carbon sinks that remove carbon from the air. As fire frequency has increased, we've developed fire-fighting techniques in NoHoSap and are prepared to go after this blaze. Thiha's flying in to bring a contingent to the rainforest tonight. We're gathering our resources now and will be ready to leave when he gets here. Eliza, we need you to be part of this."

"Wow!" Otherwise speechless, Eliza gathered herself and tried to think rationally about how she could accomplish what Bebop asked. She wanted to go with the NoHoSap team but first needed to explain her sudden departure to Ira. Realizing she couldn't say 'no' without putting her commitment to the climate mission in question, she resolved to figure it out one way or another. "OK, Bebop, I'm on board. I'll be there as soon as I can. I need to excuse myself from work, go home and pack some things, and then Noli and I will meet you in NoHoSap."

"Very good. See you soon." Noli turned the speaker switch off and put the headset back on her tiny angular head.

Eliza's mind raced as she paced across the floor, thinking about what to say to Ira. "*Think, Eliza. I was just off from work Friday and now need more time to go to the Amazon and fight a forest fire. I don't know how long I'll be gone, and humans don't even know about the fire yet. There must be some way to make this a climate correspondent project. Think."* She kept pacing until the idea came to her, then hustled to Ira's office before losing her nerve.

"Ira, can I run something by you?"

"Sure, Eliza. Did you come up with a story to launch the climate correspondent role?"

"Yes actually, I did. It's a big one."

"Good, that's what we wanted."

"Right, I think it'll be an attention-grabber." She hesitated, then dove right in. "I received a tip that there's a fire brewing in the Amazon and I'd like to cover it. The national news outlets generally do that sort of thing, but I thought we could get in front with our new climate focus."

Ira stared at her in disbelief, unprepared for a request of this magnitude.

Eliza anticipated he may react that way and took advantage of the silence to continue. "I know it's a huge request, but I think folks in our community would appreciate our having local coverage there. They already associate me with the cemetery story and know of my storm rescue of Maria and Sophie. If we're going to cover climate change, you can't get a much bigger story than a rainforest fire."

Ira's expression changed from puzzled bewilderment to budding interest. "How much would this cost the station and how long would you be gone?"

"Good news–the cost will be minimal. I have a connection who has a plane, is going there anyway, and hooked me up with a place to stay. I'd only need long distance and internet service on my phone, and I'll cover any food and other incidental transportation. I'd leave today and don't know how long I'd be gone–depends on how the fire does or, preferably, doesn't, progress."

"The cost makes it an easier sell. You'll finish the story for tonight before you go?"

"Yes, sir."

"I can't afford to send a cameraperson with you. You'd be on your own to take pictures, videos, and self-tape. You'd also be responsible for sending the footage back here so we can air it."

"Understood."

Ira considered the request and announced his decision. "You talked me into it. I hope this pans out. If not, it could be the end of the climate correspondent and you'll be back to covering legal/environmental material."

"Thank you! Yes, I realize the future of the climate correspondent role is riding on this assignment. You won't regret it. I'll make the station proud." Not generally one to brag or be over-confident, Eliza hoped she didn't end up eating those words.

She hurried out of Ira's office and back to her desk to put the final touches on the story for that night. After sending it to the evening producer, she packed everything up and ran out of her office with Noli on her shoulder. Preferring to go out the back exit because fewer people would see her leaving the station during work hours, she realized as she opened the door that she should tell Zeke about the big project. She turned and hurried to his office, telling Noli to hide in her pocket until they left the building.

Zeke looked up when Eliza stopped at his door. "Was that you running in the hall? Where are you going in such a rush?"

"Yes, I'm the culprit. I'm headed to the Amazon tonight for my first story as the climate correspondent."

"You're what?" Zeke's mouth dropped open.

"I got a tip about a wildfire in the rainforest and received approval to cover it."

"Woo hoo, that's big news! Congratulations! I'm shocked you got approval."

"I am too. It helped that it won't cost the station much since I already have a way to get there and a place to stay. Ira must have figured he didn't have much to lose."

"How are you getting there and where are you staying? I didn't know you had contacts in South America."

"Contacts through the Change Agents group. I'm taking a cargo plane and staying with locals–nothing fancy." Eliza surprised herself by the way the half-truths rolled off her tongue. "Time to get going, pack, and head to the airport."

"Good luck! I look forward to seeing the coverage. If you need anything from here or I can help in any way, let me know."

"Definitely will! See you when I'm back." She turned, ran to her car, then sped home, all the while planning what she'd pack for the Amazon.

CHAPTER 46

INNOVATIONS

By the time Eliza packed and left her house, the afternoon traffic rush delayed her arrival at the cemetery. She ran to the mausoleum door, carrying a couple of bags of travel gear. Monty greeted her and warned of the uproar in Mission Command while everyone prepared for the Amazon firefighting project. The tumult became evident when they reached the elevator, finding a flurry of activity as creatures removed boxes and other objects from the elevator and loaded them onto trailers. The scene became exponentially more chaotic when the elevator door opened to Mission Command. Animals ran here and there carrying various items while birds swooped overhead, doing the same.

"The Captain asked that we meet him in the lab."

"That's a place I haven't seen yet." They headed in a new direction and walked past a rock wall into a vast, high-ceilinged space. Lights on the walls as well as hanging from the ceiling, made it one of the brightest Eliza had seen in Mission Command. Lab benches filled the open area and lined the walls. Diverse creatures worked at and on the benches and a cacophony of voices filled the air.

"There he is." Monty took off toward the right. Eliza saw Bebop deep in conversation with a giant tortoise.

"Captain, Eliza's here." Monty broke into the conversation. The tortoise turned and looked up at Eliza, then said hello.

"Eliza, meet Alda." Bebop gave a proper introduction.

"Very nice to meet you, Alda."

"Alda's one of our science wizards and heads up the innovation team. She's developed firefighting tools we'll use in the rainforest. They've been tested here, and we were just talking about how to use them on a much larger scale."

Monty interjected, "I'm going back to keep tabs on the truck loading with Thiha and Jacob. Hopefully we can fit what we need into the truck and van."

"Good idea, Monty. Make sure things are packed as efficiently as possible. We need to maximize the space we have."

"Roger that, Captain."

"OK, Alda, explain again how we use the armor."

"It's very important to keep the substance wet for as long as possible. Apply it immediately before it's needed. When that time comes, the animal can be submerged in it, which gives the best protection, or it can be sprayed on or applied to the necessary areas. For example, with our feathered friends who need certain feathers on their wings unimpeded, the armor would be applied to everything except those parts. It should also be put inside their mouths to allow them to catch sparks without being burned."

"Wait, what?" Eliza blurted out. "You have something that prevents burning?"

"For a time, yes," answered Alda. "It's a gelatinous substance made from flax seeds, deep sea thermal vent bacteria, aloe, and water. The mixture impedes fire and heat, but with prolonged exposure, the substance dries out and the creatures become vulnerable. Here's a sample of it."

Alda held up a half walnut shell filled with clear, gooey gel. She instructed Eliza to put her hand out and, when she did, Alda dumped the gel into it. The gel cooled her hand where it touched.

"Spread it out a bit and wait." Eliza did and the gel soon dried into a thin, flexible layer on her hand. Eliza clenched her fist and moved her hand around, even tried to shake the substance off and it wouldn't budge.

"Cool. How long does it protect against fire?"

"Our tests indicate it can last as long as two hours without direct exposure to flames and up to forty-five minutes in the line of fire."

"This armor allows us to have creatures working in fire zones to build fireproof barriers, dig ditches, catch flying sparks, put out coals the fire has left behind, and more!" Bebop couldn't hide his excitement.

"We've also designed this mask material to make it easier to breathe in smoke." Alda motioned to what looked like a pile of green fabric on the ground nearby. Eliza picked up a piece to find a soft, thin, supple material that felt and looked like a leaf but could be folded without breaking.

"What is this? Seems to be a leaf, but it's soft and pliable."

"It is a leaf, but we've processed it to make it porous enough to breathe through. Each leaf is chewed by multitudes of ants or poked by stingers of countless wasps and bees (except honeybees, we don't want their stingers to stay in the leaf and the bees to die in this process). As a result, each piece has millions of tiny holes to enable creatures to breathe when the leaf is over its mouth or nose. The stinging and biting process softens the leaf to make it not only porous enough to breathe through but also supple enough to be folded and scrunched. We tested all kinds of other options, ranging from wasp nest paper to bird nests to tightly knit spider webs, but this worked the best."

"Amazing!"

"I don't know what we'd do without Alda and the rest of the inventors on her team. Alda, you're a lifesaver. Keep producing the armor and masks. We're bringing most of our stock with us now and will need the supply replenished. Who knows how soon we'll need it again."

"On it, Captain. Good luck in the Amazon. We'll all be pulling for you."

Eliza said goodbye to Alda as Bebop turned to leave. On the way out, they passed all types of creatures at the lab tables working on countless experiments. Many involved electronics that Eliza assumed were discarded by humans. At other stations, it appeared the natural capabilities of various beings were tested.

Bebop read her mind. "In addition to using items humans have thrown out or "recycled," we study the special adaptations of the natural world and figure out how we can use them on a broader scale. The armor and mask materials are two examples of that. We prefer not to rely on human technology and to instead take advantage of what nature has already given us. That said, to the extent we can use what humans feel is trash, we benefit from their technology and lessen the chances one of our own will be hurt or killed by the items people discard."

"It's all fascinating to me. I thought I was in tune with the environment and nature, but I never thought any being other than humans could build and accomplish the things I now see other creatures are doing. I'm embarrassed to have been so egotistical."

"Don't apologize. There's a reason we don't make our capabilities known to humans. We don't want you to know. There's no reason for you to unless we're facing the potential destruction of our world, as we are now, and we need your help."

CHAPTER 47

SUPPLY AND COMMAND

Bebop and Eliza left the lab and walked to the trail leading to the back exit from NoHoSap, near the cemetery parking lot. The path teemed with animals, birds, and reptiles carrying objects or pulling trailers full of equipment, including computers, radios, pulleys, ropes, mask material, barrels of water and armor, spray guns, and more. After waiting for a gap in the travelers, Eliza and Bebop fell in line with the caravan on the trail, passing through the wide-open pine bough curtains manned by the salamanders.

They reached the parking lot, where Thiha loaded materials into his truck and Jacob did the same with his van. Never far from Jacob's side, Oji tried to help, but appeared to be in the way more than anything. Both vehicles neared the capacity of how much they could hold.

Bebop motioned for Monty. "Monty, go back and tell them not to send any more out right now. We have to see if we can even fit what's already here into the vehicles." Monty flew off.

"Team, first priority is to load the armor and spray guns, then the masks. If we have room once those are packed, we'll follow with the rest." The animals pulling the trailers with the noted materials came forward and the items were loaded. Soon both vehicles were packed full, even though plenty more waited to be loaded.

"That's it. We're done. Thank you, everyone! You all came out on short notice to get us packed up and out of here quickly. We'll be in touch remotely and I know you'll do what you can from here to continue helping with this mission." The creatures gave various well wishes before taking the trail back to NoHoSap.

"To the airport." Bebop and Eliza rode with Jacob and Oji in the van.

"I'm sorry I can't go with you, Bebop. They won't let me out of work at the last minute."

"I could probably get out of school, but my parents and Jacob said I better not even think about it."

"Not a problem, you two. You can keep an eye on things here. Thanks for helping us move everything into the vehicles. We still have our work cut out to get it on the plane."

"We'll do all we can."

Eliza thought about the logistics of posting footage from the upcoming adventure. "I'll send pictures and videos to Lee and she can post as she did during the reef restoration. Jacob, please be sure she's not working on the posts 24/7. She needs to sleep and eat. I know she gets wrapped up in taking care of our social media presence, but we can't have her exhausting herself. I'm afraid she will unless you get her to take a break."

"I know what you mean and have the same concern myself. I'll make sure she unplugs."

"I'll distract her from the screens and get her to do something with me," offered Oji. "I can be very annoying when I want to be."

"You don't say." Jacob rolled his eyes.

Before Oji could retort, the vehicles pulled up next to Thiha's plane and all jumped out to move everything to the cargo hold. When Jacob and Thiha opened the back doors of the respective vehicles and revealed the packed contents, Eliza wished they had all the help for the unloading as there'd been for the loading. As she stood thinking about where to start, something flew by her ear. She looked but didn't see anything, then felt it fly by the other side of her head. Swatting at the air, she heard a voice, "Careful, you almost hit me." A bat alighted on top of the van door.

"Sonar, what a nice surprise to have an Alliance member here! I'm sorry, I didn't know that was you."

"I don't try to, but tend to startle people because I'm very quiet." He surveyed the van's contents. "I'm not finding anything I can carry to the plane."

"Sonar, with your view from the top, you're the perfect one to direct us on loading the plane. Take a survey of what we have and then direct us to pack it in the spot that makes the most sense in the cargo hold."

"Good idea, Bebop. Our goal in loading is to keep the heaviest stuff toward the middle of the plane." Thiha wanted to be sure he ended up with a plane balanced to fly more efficiently. They went to work unloading the vehicles and placing the items on the tarmac, enabling the heavier ones to be loaded into the plane first.

Eliza peered inside the plane, surprised to see the tank that transported Jazzy still in the middle, half full of water. She asked Thiha if they could empty the tank and move it to make room for more from the trucks. Before she could finish her question, she heard a rhythmic swooshing that sounded somewhat familiar. Looking in the direction of the sound, she realized it came from an oversized alligator with boxes tied to his back, ambling up the ramp to the cargo hold.

"Make way, coming through," announced the jumbo-sized reptile.

"Chompers! We really rate to have two Alliance members here with us."

"We like to get involved when we can, and I thought I could be of assistance with this trip."

Thiha removed the boxes from Chompers' back and stowed them in the cargo hold. "Thanks for moving that stuff. Feel free to get in the tank whenever you'd like."

"I think I have at least another few trips in me." Chompers turned and headed out of the cargo hold and down the ramp.

The group loaded everything onto the plane and secured it with tie-downs. They bid Jacob and Oji farewell and Chompers settled into the tank. As Thiha reached for the button to shut the cargo hold door, a large white bird swooped into the cargo area.

"Schnee, I thought you may not make the plane."

"Not a chance, Bebop. I was a little delayed, but no way was I going to miss you. Good to see you again, Eliza."

"Good to see you again too, Schnee. What a treat to be working with three Alliance members on this project."

"You mean four Alliance members. Mosa's already on-site and we'll meet her there."

"That's right, thanks for reminding me, Bebop."

Thiha sat in the pilot seat in the cockpit and Eliza and Bebop strapped themselves into seats behind him. Thiha soon had the plane in the air and cruising south. Eliza asked how long the trip would take and he said it should be eleven to twelve hours, which included a stop in Puerto Rico to refuel. She asked if he'd need a break to sleep when they stopped. Thiha appreciated the concern but advised he trained for such long shifts, flew them regularly and would be fine.

Bebop took advantage of the flight time to fill the team in on the plan when they arrived. "Mosa already has crews mobilized fighting the fire. It started on the outskirts of an illegally lumbered area. One of the first areas hit by loggers in this part of the forest, access isn't ideal, at least not for humans. There are few villages in that area and the lumber cutters left a while ago, so no humans were involved in the fight when we last heard from Mosa. That's sure to change once humans discover the blaze. We'll land as close to the fire as we safely can and Mosa will have a team there to unload everything. Mosa's crews are focused on clearing areas, building barriers to stop the fire from advancing, and putting out embers in the already burned areas, preventing the flames from flaring again. Chompers, you'll help with the water supply. Sonar and Schnee, you'll mobilize a contingent to catch sparks and beat the fire back. Eliza, you'll capture all this on film as you've been doing for the tree planting and reef restoration. Thiha, you'll catch up on sleep when we arrive and then be available as needed. Any questions?"

Sonar asked, "Is Mosa gathering flying creatures for Schnee's and my work?"

"Yes, all the teams will be ready when we arrive. Once we unload, we'll douse them and Mosa's crews with armor, affix breathing masks and get to work. While you're all out in the field, I'll be sure we have armor and masks ready to reapply as needed. Chompers, we'll need a water supply for the armor in addition to the water you'll be directing for firefighting."

"Got it, Captain. We'll take care of your water first and then work on redirecting other water bodies to stop the fire."

"Sounds like we're going to war."

"We are, Eliza, we're going to battle against the fire. Once humans join in fighting the blaze, you'll have to tell them what we're doing so we can work together and not against each other."

"You want me to acknowledge that I know what the creatures are doing? Should I say I'm working with you?"

"You don't need to say you're working with us. Just show them what you've observed and how those activities fight the fire. All they need to know is you've been researching these, and other actions and the only logical conclusion is we're doing our own thing to fight climate change, including this fire. Eventually we're going to have to come clean and reveal our partnership with humans, but the longer we can avoid doing that the better."

"Got it."

"We'll need all our energy once we arrive. There won't be much time to sleep because we have a lot to do. Hard as it may be, try to get some rest on this flight."

"Thiha, you're sure you'll be alright if we're all asleep?"

"Definitely. When I transport cargo, it's just me in here and it doesn't faze me. I'm well caught up on sleep and also have a nice supply of caffeine. We'll be in Puerto Rico before you know it and that break will be all I need to get revived."

All except Thiha nestled in and a quiet calm settled over the plane. When they arrived in Puerto Rico, Thiha kept the door to the cargo hold shut and the occupants undisturbed. Bebop and Eliza awoke and exited from the front of the plane for fresh air. Being the middle of the night, all lay still at the airfield. Thiha stretched and jogged in circles to get his blood flowing while the airfield attendant refueled the plane. Bebop and Eliza went for a short walk under the clear night sky, a light tropical breeze brushing their half-asleep faces. With the plane fully fueled, Thiha ushered the sleepwalkers back into the cockpit and strapped himself into the pilot's seat. He taxied down the runway, lifted the plane into the sky, and began the last leg of the journey. The rest of the team slept soundly in the back.

CHAPTER 48

PREPARATION

The sun streamed through the cockpit windows when Thiha roused the team. "Sleepy heads, we're almost there. Look what we're up against."

Sonar awoke first, flew to the cockpit, and looked down. "Oh my. We have our work cut out for us."

Bebop and Eliza looked out the windows next to their seats and saw enormous plumes of grey and black smoke billowing upward. "Whoa, you aren't kidding, we have work to do."

All watched the smoke rise from the vast landscape, transfixed by the extent of the smoke and, therefore, the fire. The green forest glimmered in the far distance, well beyond the burning areas. Stunned at the immense area under fire, the team members silently questioned how they'd be able to have any impact.

Bebop sensed and addressed their doubts. "Remember, one step at a time. It may look like a huge undertaking from here, but if we break it down into manageable pieces, it's not as intimidating."

"I can't see anything from back here," Chompers said from the tank, "but I can smell it. Based on the strength of the smoke odor, the fire must be massive."

The other team members each breathed in deeply, all now smelling the fire in addition to seeing it.

"Time to get down to it." Thiha began the descent.

As the plane lowered, the scene below grew more vivid. Towering flames reached into the sky. Mammoth trees blew in the breeze, their green branches waving for help before being engulfed by the fire. The smoke smell in the plane intensified. Eliza couldn't help but cry as she watched such a vital habitat being destroyed. She imagined hearing the living creatures as well as the trees yelling in terror before perishing in the flames. Glancing at the team members gathered in the cockpit, she saw all were similarly impacted by seeing the annihilation. Schnee averted her teary eyes, Bebop stared in utter disbelief, Thiha focused on the instrument panel, and Sonar flew into the cargo hold to avoid seeing the devastation.

Bebop addressed the somber group. "I didn't account for the emotional toll seeing the blaze from this vantage point would have. I'm thankful Mosa and her team haven't seen the extent of the fire. Please don't say anything to them. As big as this fire may appear, we have to believe we can make a difference in battling it. That's why we're here. Think of it this way, every life saved is a victory."

"The field where we're landing is below," Thiha announced. "Prepare for a bumpy landing and make sure you're secure. Chompers, apologies in advance if you lose water from the tank."

Bebop, Schnee, Sonar, and Eliza scrambled for the restraints. Eliza strapped Bebop, Sonar, and Schnee in, then threw ropes to Chompers that were affixed to all sides of the plane. He gripped the ropes between his huge teeth to minimize the extent to which he'd slosh around in the tank. Eliza belted herself in right before the plane pitched back and forth, up and down.

"Brace yourselves, coming in for a landing!" The plane's wheels hit and Thiha immediately pressed the brakes as hard as he could and pulled levers back to engage the reverse thrust.

After an extremely rough ride on the landing area, the plane stopped, and its occupants breathed sighs of relief. Eliza unstrapped Bebop, Schnee, and Sonar and looked back in the cargo hold to check on Chompers. He appeared shaken as he stood in the tank. Most of the water spilled out during landing and now streamed across the cargo hold floor.

Thiha opened the cockpit door and a wave of hot, humid, smoky air blasted in. He then opened the door to the cargo hold, allowing the tropical, soot-laden air to engulf the team. Sunshine filtered by smoke greeted them as they exited the plane. Chompers climbed out of the tank and shuffled down the ramp to join his flight mates.

"Welcome to the Amazon," greeted a voice from behind. The group turned to see Mosa. She looked exhausted, but very relieved to see them. "I wish your visit was under better circumstances."

"As do we, Mosa, but we're glad to be here to put all our forces to work against this foe."

"We need all the help we can get. We have a crew to help unload the plane." Mosa turned and roared. An array of monkeys, lizards, what looked like giant guinea pigs, and birds appeared around the newcomers.

"Do you want to set everything up here?" Mosa asked Bebop. "This is the area from which the trees were harvested and the fire's currently running in the opposite direction. Hopefully, this will remain a safe spot."

"Looks good to me."

Mosa turned to her Amazon team. "Crew, this is Captain Bebop. He's commanding the climate mission and will give the orders. His team members are Eliza, Chompers, Thiha, Sonar, and Schnee." Each waved or smiled in acknowledgment after being introduced.

Bebop took the floor. "Thank you for the introductions, Mosa, and thanks to all of you for being here to help. Each and every one of you is a valued member of our team in this fight and we appreciate your assistance." He looked into the cargo hold and continued. "We have a lot to unload. Let's get to it. Things in similar containers should be dropped in the same general spot."

Everyone went to work, turning the area into a whirlwind of activity. With the plane unloaded, the unpacked items in the field formed an encampment of sorts.

"Great work! Mosa, where should Sonar, Schnee, and Chompers meet their teams?"

"Chompers' crew is gathering at the river, which flows on the far edge of this field, over that way." Mosa pointed to a far-off spot.

"Thanks, Mosa. We'll first get a water supply coming over here and then work on getting water where we need it to stop the fire."

"Chompers, your team includes armadillos and capybaras. They'll dig a ditch to divert water in this direction." The giant guinea pigs from the moving crew scurried over when Mosa mentioned capybaras. The largest capybara told Chompers there were more near the water, all ready to dig once they determined the exact ditch location.

"I like that preparation. Let's get going." Chompers and the capybaras headed off toward the river.

Mosa then informed, "Sonar and Schnee, due to the size of your crews, we're sending them to you in waves, the first of which should be here soon."

As if on cue, the sound of fluttering filled the air. A cloud-like object approached over the horizon. The sound grew louder while the cloud grew bigger. As it came closer, all realized the cloud consisted of thousands of flying birds, butterflies, and other insects of every shape and size. They created their own wind by flapping their wings. The sky over the field filled with the flyers, which landed on every surface available–the ground, plane and equipment.

"Phenomenal!" Sonar exclaimed. "And this is just the first wave?"

"Yes. They'll keep coming until we have everyone."

"Astounding! Now I know why you needed both Sonar and me to work with all these flying friends," said Schnee.

"Well done, Mosa, well done." Bebop became more optimistic after seeing the assistance Mosa assembled.

Sonar asked if such a large contingent would be able to hear him giving instructions. Thiha scrambled to connect some wires to the plane and came back with a radio mouthpiece from the cockpit, which he placed in front of Sonar after testing to make sure it worked.

Addressing the crowd over the makeshift microphone, Sonar's voice rang out. "Greetings, all. Thank you for coming out to help fight the fire. Our air assault has two purposes. One is to catch flying sparks and prevent them from spreading the fire to new areas. The second is to beat the flames back with our self-created wind and stop the blaze from advancing. If your mouths aren't large enough to catch sparks, that's fine and we'll happily use your wings to create wind."

Stepping aside, Sonar yielded the mouthpiece to Schnee. "You'll need protective gear to help keep you safe. We have fire retardant gel, which we call armor, for your bodies and inside your mouths. We'll apply that here. It's effective for a limited time. As a result, you'll have to be aware of how long since the last application and be sure you return for another coat before you risk injury. The armor is flame retardant, not fireproof, meaning it won't protect you if you fly through the fire." Squawks, buzzes, and other calls of acknowledgment rang out from the throng. "For the spark duty, you'll catch sparks in your mouths and squash the fire piece by piece. For the wind part of our role, we'll give orders for everyone to line up in front of the fire and, when we send the signal, flap your wings in unison against the flames."

Sonar added, "Remember, you're the first wave of our flyers. We'll have many more working with us from the air. Let's get that armor on. Our vats of gel are here. Please come by in an orderly fashion and we'll apply it one by one."

Mosa recruited monkeys and kinkajous to assist with armor application, a process supervised by Bebop and Eliza. They gently sprayed the gel on most creatures, painted it by hand on the more delicate bodies, and swabbed it inside the mouths that were large enough to catch sparks. Thiha watched to get a feel for the process before excusing himself to go to sleep.

The armoring process went surprisingly fast for the number of flyers. With the first wave almost done, Mosa summoned the next, Sonar and Schnee explained their assignment, and they were armored. This continued for wave after wave of flying creatures.

Bebop estimated they armored millions of flyers. By the time all waves were protected, they were almost out of armor. Eliza voiced concern and Bebop pointed to numerous containers piled up in another area, noting they contained the dry ingredients for the armor. He said they needed water and could then make another batch for the next round of applications. Speaking of water, he surveyed the field to check for Chompers' and the ditchdiggers' progress bringing water to the encampment area. As he did, Mosa came over.

"Mosa, any sign of human help yet?"

"The few locals are continuing to do what they can. Their resources are very limited, though. I'm told they sent word out about the fire and we should see a larger human presence at some point, but I don't know when."

As they pondered the next move, a capybara sidled up next to Bebop and announced, "The ditch is dug, Sir. It's over there." The group discovered a neatly dug trench not far away.

"Here comes the water," the capybara announced before emitting a high whirring noise, answered by similar sounds further away. They heard gushing water and the dry ditch became a flowing stream. Bebop instructed the armor appliers to collect the water and add to the gel ingredients, allowing them to stock back up on armor.

CHAPTER 49

RECONNAISSANCE

Mosa suggested that Eliza follow her to check Chompers' progress with his team and they'd then go to the front lines. Bebop gave Eliza a huge backpack full of masks for themselves and the front-line fighters.

Mosa led Eliza toward the river in the direction Chompers headed when he left. When they made it to the water, though, he was nowhere to be found. Mosa surmised the crew must have moved toward the fire. She disappeared under a large tropical plant hanging over the river. "Eliza, what are you waiting for?"

"Oh, sorry, I didn't know you wanted me to follow you." Eliza ventured after Mosa and found her with her mouth clamped on the end of a large, hollow tree that looked like a boat. As she wrestled it out from under the plant Eliza picked up a side and they placed the boat in the river. Mosa told Eliza to get in, hopped in herself, then roared twice in succession.

They sat in the boat as it crept downstream with the current. Thrown off by the slow pace when they should be hurrying, Eliza searched for paddles or another way to propel the boat. Mosa said, "We'll be moving faster soon enough."

A noise in the water near Eliza startled her. Looking in the direction of the sound, she saw what appeared to be two dolphins, one light pink and the other grey. "Dolphins in the Amazon?"

"Of course, two species live here." Mosa chuckled at Eliza's ignorance. "We have one of each to help us today." The two dolphins jumped out of the water in a synchronized fashion.

Meet Otob and Kooshee. They'll take us to Chompers." The dolphins took hold of vines hanging off the bow of the boat and pulled it down the river, much faster than Eliza would ever have been able to paddle.

As they moved along the water, the air warmed and the smoke thickened. Eliza pulled two masks from the backpack, putting one on Mosa and another on herself. The material filtered the smoke out very well, making it much easier to breathe. Eliza heard the fire crackling, nervous to be that close to it.

The dolphins slowed at a fork in the river and followed the right branch after Mosa signaled. As the boat rounded a bend, Chompers' voice filled the air while he shouted directions. Mosa told Eliza to ready her camera. The boat completed the turn and the scene stunned Eliza. Chompers stood next to what appeared to be a dam of Amazon River creatures—caiman, anaconda, otters, turtles, manatees, and more dolphins, to name a few. They redirected the flow of the whole river toward the fire.

"Never in my life…." Once the initial shock wore off, she snapped pictures, trying to capture it all for humans to see. The dolphins maneuvered the boat to enable her to see the complete dam. The creatures comprising the structure were intricately interwoven, blocking as much water as possible. Chompers continuously gave directions to change position if any creatures looked to be tiring, as well as to shout out general encouragement.

"Hope you brought your underwater camera too. Jump in and look underneath."

Fortunately, Eliza had the waterproof camera, along with her snorkel and face mask. She unpacked them, replaced the breathing mask with the snorkel mask, and lowered herself into the water.

Eliza never imagined a sight more unbelievable than the top of the dam, but underwater left her speechless. Huge trees and rocks stacked on the river floor rose up a few feet. Above that base, creatures with no need to surface for air formed the dam. Thousands of piranhas glinted brilliantly as the sun hit their sides. Huge eels were intertwined throughout the mix along with a myriad of other fish, including what looked like large catfish. All were packed tightly together to block and reroute the water, moving in sync to keep the water flowing through their gills or other breathing apparatus.

When Eliza first saw them, a wave of terror hit her since she'd been conditioned from horror movies to fear most of these creatures. She choked back that reaction, though, and moved closer to take pictures. She captured every angle she could think of, surfaced near the boat, and told Mosa she couldn't believe the underwater part of the living dam. Back in the boat, Eliza relaxed, grateful to have made it out of the water in one piece.

Mosa instructed the dolphins to bring the boat to shore. They swam as close as they could, pushed the bow of the boat onto the bank, then took their places in the dam. Mosa and Eliza climbed out and congratulated Chompers on a job very well done. Eliza offered him a mask, but he declined. "Save it for those on the front-line."

"We have crews along the rerouted river to direct the water as needed," informed Chompers. "We're creating a water barrier inland to keep the fire from advancing. Mosa, thank you for arranging for these creatures to be here. It's tiring work and critical to have replacements coming at intervals to give everyone a rest."

"Every creature accepted the call to fight this fire. They're thankful to be able to do something about it instead of falling victim to it. I'm glad we mobilized for this."

"I am too. It's empowering to have a hand in our destiny instead of relying on humans to fix their messes, which we know doesn't happen often enough." Remembering Eliza stood there, Chompers added, "Present company excluded."

"It's fine. I don't take offense. I know where you're coming from when you say things like that."

"Ready to head to the front lines?" Mosa asked Eliza.

"Ready as I'll ever be." Eliza put her breathing mask back on and the pair trudged into the jungle.

Mosa steered clear of overgrowth as much as possible to make the passage easier for Eliza. What with being wet from swimming and the tropical air being warmed by the sun and fire, Eliza found the heat and humidity almost unbearable. The beauty all around helped take her mind off the temperature. She'd never seen the color green as brilliant or varied as in the rainforest. Daggers of sun shone through the blowing canopy, putting moving spotlights on the vegetation below. Towering trees with hanging vines created a magical scene, in which all sounds were muted by the heavy air and abundant plant life. Nearby branches came alive with frogs and insects Eliza previously saw only on nature shows.

Further ahead and no longer hearing Eliza, Mosa called to her. Not hearing a reply, she backtracked to find Eliza standing, captivated by the rainforest.

"I know, it's a gorgeous place, but we need to keep going if we want to save it from being burned."

Shaking her head to break the trance, Eliza followed Mosa once again. As they walked toward the even warmer air of the fire and stench of fresh smoke, numerous animals, birds, reptiles, spiders, and other insects passed them going the other way, rushing to leave home before the fire overtook it. Feeling the urgency, Mosa sped up the pace.

Eliza heard crackling and objects crashing down coming from ahead. Mosa turned and they broke out of the forest and into a clearing. They were at the edge of the river and in another hub of activity. A throng of capybaras and huge armadillos busily dug along the banks, surprising even Mosa. "They did it. They rerouted the whole river to bring it here. This was dry land earlier this morning."

"Really?" Flabbergasted at this revelation, Eliza brought the camera out. She walked along the new water body snapping photos and videos. Hearing chatter to her side, she turned away from the river to find hordes of monkeys, tapirs, snakes, kinkajous, jaguars, and lizards clearing dead wood out of the forest and building walls from stones found on the forest floor.

"They're building a barrier and taking fuel away from the fire." Mosa followed Eliza to the other area of activity, clearly proud of the crew's work.

"I've never seen this many different kinds of monkeys." Eliza watched as howler, spider, tamarin, capuchin, and squirrel monkeys, among many others she didn't recognize, worked together. "I don't even know what many of these creatures are."

"The Amazon is a place of never-ending surprises and secrets. I doubt many of these beings have ever seen a human. Don't be surprised if they stop and stare at or smell you to figure out what you are."

"Thanks for the warning. I'll get masks for them."

"No need. I'll tell them to take a break and get some water along with masks." Mosa roared and the creatures filed by on their way to the masks and water. As Mosa predicted, many stared at and sniffed Eliza, while others took a wide berth around her and watched her suspiciously.

CHAPTER 50

SKILL SETS

As the creatures went back to work, Eliza did too, documenting all the activity to avert the fire. Deciding to do a report for the station, she wiped the sweat from her face and attempted to calm her unruly hair. She turned the self-video on, introduced herself as the station's new climate correspondent, and explained the unexpected opportunity to cover a fire in the Amazon rainforest for the station's inaugural climate story. Launching into the substance of the piece, she described the miraculous activities she discovered, then panned to the workers behind her and explained what they were doing to stop the fire. She then moved the camera over to the rerouted river and described its origin. Acknowledging these sights were hard to fathom, and she'd have trouble believing them too if she weren't seeing them with her own eyes, she assured the viewers all was real and not staged or concocted. She promised continuous coverage allowing the viewers to experience these discoveries with her.

After editing, including adding pictures of the living dam, she sent the story off to the station, hoping they'd air it and wouldn't think she'd gone off the deep end. She also messaged Lee to tell her to look for the story and then post comments.

Moving to another vantage point to take more shots, Eliza heard rumbling overhead. The noise grew louder. Mosa came over and both looked at the sky. A fast-moving cloud advanced, but it waved and turned, unlike a typical cloud. Remembering the sound, Eliza shouted, "the flyers!" The cloud moved toward the flames shooting from the forest. When it maneuvered close to the fire, it changed from a cloud to a barrage of missiles darting out and back, while flyers caught and extinguished sparks. A breeze blew the flames forward and the missiles went back into formation, the thunder became a roar, and the flyers beat their wings in unison, chasing the flames back to where they came and beyond.

Enthralled by the spectacle, Eliza remembered to roll video, hoping the footage would do justice to the display. The effort ended before the armor lost its effectiveness. The cloud then reformed and flew away. A lone bird flew out of the cloud and came toward them.

Schnee landed near Mosa, out of breath. "We have quite the flying team. I can't believe the numbers. What did you think?"

"Magnificent!" lauded Eliza.

"Agreed, but Schnee, do you think your efforts are controlling the fire?"

"Honestly, it's hard to say because this is a big blaze. I tell the team that we're definitely not helping the fire, and anything and everything we do must have at least some positive impact to thwart it." She looked at the surrounding activity. "Nice work here. By the way, it looks like humans are joining the fight. From the air, we could see them mobilizing not far from here on the northern edge of the fire. Stay safe, you two." Schnee flew away to catch up with the flyers.

Mosa turned to Eliza. "Our crews will keep moving along this perimeter and hopefully the fire won't spread beyond it. Now that the humans are here, let's go see what they're doing." Before leaving, Mosa told the crews to keep up the great work. She also reminded them to take breaks for water, sustenance, and rest, to maintain their energy to keep fighting.

CHAPTER 51

INTRODUCTIONS

Their travels to meet up with the humans wound Mosa and Eliza through verdant rainforest littered with rock outcroppings. Mosa commented on the abnormal quiet. The birds, amphibians, and insects that made for a constant hum had left to either fight the fire or flee to safer areas.

As they drew closer to the fire, the smoke stench burned their nostrils, even through the masks, and helicopters pulsed overhead. They heard crackling flames and falling trees, compelling them to pick up the pace. Voices yelled, indicating the proximity of the humans.

The pair continued walking until fire crews appeared in a clearing ahead. Mosa told Eliza to keep going and she'd hang back, out of sight. As Eliza approached the people, she realized she had no idea what to say to them. How would she explain why and how she got there? Concerned the fire crew would think it odd that she just appeared out of the forest and had been covering this story since before they arrived, she decided to be vague and say she received a tip from someone who knew the area. Taking a deep breath, she entered the clearing and walked toward the humans.

People rushed here and there around her, preparing to fight the fire. She wandered through the area trying to stay out of the way. The firefighters shouted to each other while preparing their equipment as the fire advanced toward them. Intent on their work and facing away from Eliza, they didn't see her initially. Eventually, one of the crew toward the rear noticed her and came over, eyeing her quizzically.

"This is a dangerous area. What are you doing here?" he asked loudly. Other crew members gathered around him.

"I'm a reporter and am covering the fire." No one said anything and she continued nervously. "We're glad you're here to fight this blaze."

"As you can see, we have a lot to do so better get back to work. Be careful out here." The crew members turned to their jobs.

Eliza didn't want to lose their attention. "I discovered some intriguing sights that suggest the rainforest inhabitants are working to fight the fire too."

"Yeah, we talked with some local villagers, and they said they tried to put out the flames and built berms around their village."

Not surprised they assumed she meant humans when she referenced rainforest inhabitants, she clarified. "I meant different rainforest inhabitants, not people but animals, birds, and snakes, to name a few. I have camera footage showing their amazing firefighting techniques." The fire crew chuckled skeptically while she reached for her camera. As she did, a thunderous sound approached from the sky. Eliza smiled. The timing couldn't have been more perfect. The humans looked up, searching for the source of the noise.

"You can see it for yourselves." Eliza watched the sky with a knowing glint in her eye.

The light above faded as though a cloud blew in front of the sun, the flyers appeared overhead, and the sound morphed into a near deafening din of wings flapping. The flyers gathered in the air and faced the flames flaring out of the forest. A shower of random missives shot out of the cloud as the flyers darted back and forth catching and extinguishing sparks.

The humans couldn't believe the sight. One asked, "Are those birds? What are they doing?"

Another commented, "Looks like they're catching sparks blowing in the wind to keep the fire from spreading."

Astonished, the firefighters stood and watched the activity. As though the spark catching didn't amaze them enough, the flyers went back into formation, flapped their wings in unison and blew the flames back until they no longer sprang above the trees. Their job complete, they flew away in the direction from which they came. Flying low as they left, Schnee saluted Eliza, who grinned and waved back.

Shocked, the humans turned toward Eliza, not knowing what to say. "See what I mean? I was as surprised as you the first time I saw it. Not only that, but the creatures have also diverted a river, dug ditches, and cleaned out fire lines to keep the fire from advancing. They're working toward you from that direction." She motioned toward the right edge of the fire.

"I never would have believed it if I hadn't seen it myself," said the person who appeared to be the leader of the team. The rest of the firefighters agreed. "Looks like we're coming to this party a little late. We'll add what we can to beat this fire and are very pleasantly surprised to hear there's already a head start on what we would have tried to do."

"The animals don't have any way to douse the flames. They're trying to contain the fire but can't put it out."

"That's one of our focus areas. Our helicopters will drop water and fire retardant on the blaze in strategic spots. We're also working on a fire line over there where crews are digging a ditch. Be careful out here." The leader yelled for the crew to resume their work.

Unsure whether to go back to Mosa or continue forward to talk with more humans, Eliza looked toward the forest and saw Mosa motioning her to come back. She sidled away, no one noticing her departure as they were engrossed in their firefighting duties.

Eliza joined Mosa in the forest, "The communications seemed to go well, Eliza. What did they say about the flyers?"

"They were in total shock and didn't know what to say. Schnee timed that one perfectly. Nothing helps people believe something better than seeing it."

"She has a knack for getting things done exactly when needed. Maybe it has something to do with her internal migratory clock. Let's get back to the plane. On the way, I'll show you what we're doing in the areas that have already burned."

Mosa led Eliza through the forest's dense growth to an area charred and smoking as far as the eye could see. Burnt trees and vines littered the ground. Eliza choked back tears, pained not only because the fire ruined such a beautiful, lush landscape and killed its inhabitants, but also because it devastated a place that played such a critical role in absorbing carbon.

Not knowing how hot the ground remained, she hesitated to walk on it. Mosa told her she'd be fine as long as she stayed away from smoking spots. The ground crunched beneath Eliza's feet as she walked. Hearing sounds from more than just her feet, she stopped and noticed huge snakes slithering over the coals, joined by lizards and a multitude of small rodents walking or scampering everywhere. Suppressing her initial repulsion and desire to run away from the snakes especially, she instead watched what all were doing. To Eliza's bewilderment, they searched for coals that still hid fire inside and, when they found them, crushed them either with their bodies or nearby rocks.

"Astonishing! I'll never cease to be amazed by the ingenuity of the natural world."

"Humans aren't the only beings who can control their surroundings."

"That's very clear. How arrogant of us to think we have such a leg up on everyone." Eliza took more pictures, excited to show the gamut of fire-fighting techniques the creatures used.

When Eliza finished, Mosa said they weren't far from the plane, and strode away across the charred landscape. A field appeared ahead, and they arrived back at the makeshift home base in short order, just in time to see the setting sun.

CHAPTER 52

RESPITE

The encampment buzzed with activity as Mosa and Eliza approached. After having caught up on rest, Thiha helped armor the flyers. They arrived nonstop for new applications before going back to the front lines. Additionally, monkeys loaded lowland pacas and deer with containers of armor to bring to scorched areas for the ground crews to protect themselves while putting out embers. Bebop supervised the workers, telling some to take breaks and revive themselves while instructing others to return to work after having rested. He joined Mosa and Eliza.

"How goes the fight?"

"As well as can be, Captain. This is a monumental fire, but we're attacking it from all angles to increase the likelihood of success. Chompers' team is rerouting the river, building fire stops, and removing easy fuel from the forest. The flyers are intercepting sparks and beating the fire back and our ground teams are busy surveying burnt areas and squashing fire remnants."

"It's absolutely incredible to see what everyone is doing, Bebop. I have footage of it all."

"I'm happy to hear of all the activity and that Eliza's capturing it. One thing we're not doing is putting the fire out. Instead, we're focused on keeping it from advancing. We don't have the capacity to dump water on it, which we knew we lacked."

"Humans have arrived on the northern edge and should cover that. We visited them after Schnee alerted us they were here, and Eliza talked with them."

"No worries, Bebop. The humans said they'll start water dumps." "I'm glad they're here and will implement additional techniques to kill the fire. Let's keep our crews moving forward in all respects. Ideally they'll connect with the humans soon."

"The humans saw a wave of flyers so now know some of what we're doing, Captain."

"Generally, I'd want to be cautious about humans seeing our activities, but the gravity of this fire and the fact that we're all out here fighting it leads me to view it as a turning point. Eliza and her news station are posting our activities for people to see. If the information's out there, there's no need to hide it from the humans who are here working as we are. It's good they saw the flyers and know some of our capabilities. We need to combine forces and take the fire on together."

"I did a story from the front lines that should hit the news shortly if it hasn't already."

"Excellent."

"I don't know about you, but I need a rest, water, and food. Bebop and Eliza, do you need a break?"

"Food and water would be great," Eliza acknowledged.

"No, I'm fine." Bebop resisted.

Thiha came over. "I hope you two can get this guy to stop working for a few minutes. He's been after all of us to make sure we get breaks, but he hasn't stopped since he arrived. I'm afraid he'll keel over if he keeps this up."

"That does it. You're coming with us, Bebop." He begrudgingly complied and followed Mosa and Eliza to a cooler spot under one of the plane's wings. They all sat wearily.

Mosa signaled to a kinkajou, who enlisted the aid of a couple spider monkeys. The animals brought a delectable array of fresh fruits to the resting group—bananas, pineapples, papayas, coconuts, mangoes, avocadoes, figs, and other delicacies. Bebop and Eliza praised it as the freshest, most flavorful fruit they ever tasted. Mosa said it made all the difference when the fruit ripened on the plants in the sun instead of being picked before fully developing and then ripening in dark storage areas.

As they rested and enjoyed the smorgasbord, a group of tapirs arrived carrying sloths on their backs. Mosa rushed to their aid, with Bebop and Eliza not far behind. "You found them!" exclaimed Mosa.

One of the tapirs replied, "Yes, thanks to the monkeys. The sloths were way up in the treetops and refused to move away from the fire. Our monkeys devised a vine pully system and lowered the sloths down from the trees. Even if our sloth friends had moved, it would have taken hours for them to reach the ground, and we didn't have that long to wait. We barely got them out as it is. The fire engulfed their trees as we left."

Mosa said, "We didn't want the sloths to be lost to the fire since we knew they weren't nearly fast enough to get out of the forest. I sent teams of tapirs and monkeys to pull as many as possible from the trees." She turned to the tapir. "Are the other teams close behind?"

"They should be. The fire's moving swiftly and we're going back for more sloths. It's time-consuming to find and get them down, but we'll work on it until the fire prevents us. We'll leave these guys with you." The tapirs tilted sideways, and the sloths slid off their backs and onto the ground, sullen after being disturbed from their homes much less transported here and deposited in such a way.

Mosa reassured them. "Very sorry to move you, but there's a fire burning the forest and we needed to get you out before the flames devoured you."

Grateful to have been rescued, the sloths winked in understanding and smiles gradually crept across their faces. Mosa motioned for them to take some food and otherwise make themselves comfortable. The sloths moved leisurely toward a pile of leaves the kinkajou deposited near the fruit.

CHAPTER 53

ATTENTION

Tired after a hard days' work, Mosa, Bebop, Eliza and Thiha continued resting after welcoming the sloths. Eliza checked her phone to see how her story had been received. When she tapped the screen, it came alive with countless notifications of likes and comments on her posts. New alerts came in constantly. The ringer had been off while out in the field and when she turned it back on, the pings rang incessantly. Elated, she held the phone up, beamed from ear to ear, and informed the team they weren't going to believe it. Her footage of the dam, flyers, diggers, and clearers appeared to be going viral! Additionally, the national news outlets picked up her story via her station's reports, giving more credence to and interest in her videos.

"Excellent! Congratulations and great work, Eliza." Bebop gave her an enthusiastic high five. "Mosa, when do you think the rerouted river and our diggers will connect with the humans?"

"Should be tomorrow early afternoon."

"Good, not much longer. Eliza, you should be there to take pictures and cover that from the inside. There may be other reporters there by then, but they won't be prepared for what will happen. You'll beat them to the punch."

"Eliza and I will leave in the morning to be sure we're there when the diverted river connects with the area where the humans are working."

"We'll continue our work from here for as long as we have supplies. We estimate we have enough armor for most of tomorrow but won't have much left after that."

"Should I travel back to NoHoSap for more armor ingredients?" offered Thiha.

"Hopefully the fire will be under control before we run out, Thiha. If not, we'll have to decide whether it makes sense for you to make that trip. I'd like to avoid it if we can."

"Let me know. I don't mind making a run for supplies."

The group polished off more delectable fruits and found comfortable places to sleep. Rather than laying down, Eliza wandered around the encampment taking pictures while checking the barrage of notifications from her story, humbled and honored to be receiving such attention. Although most comments were positive, some posts discredited her work, saying the footage must be fabricated and slamming the station for airing the story. Heartened, she saw that Zeke replied to each and every negative comment and defended her, the footage, and the station. She appreciated his support and messaged to let him know, then posted more pictures on the station's site, and sent others to Lee for broader distribution.

She stumbled on the sloths, uncharacteristically cuddled together seeking solace while their homes burned. Waves of night flyers, consisting mainly of bats, came and went under Sonar's direction. Hoping to catch footage of their work, Eliza snapped pictures and videos, but the lack of lighting compromised the picture quality.

CHAPTER 54

FIREFIGHT

The sun rose on another tropical day of firefighting. Day flyers swooped in for armor applications. Schnee took over running flyer shifts, allowing Sonar time to rest. Birds and butterflies flitted in the sunshine while waiting for armor. Eliza marveled at the sheer numbers of flying creatures as well as the myriad and brilliancy of their colors. Toucans made her laugh, harpy eagles intimidated her, and the variety of macaws and parrots struck her. Blue morpho butterflies and butterflies with transparent wings left her in awe. She took pictures but the camera didn't do justice to the beauty before her. *There's no substitute for being here*, she mused to herself.

Eliza, Mosa, Bebop, and Thiha ate fruit together before Mosa and Eliza headed back to the front lines. Taking the fastest route, they traipsed over the burnt area they covered yesterday and found the stowed boat. Mosa pushed off from the bank and called for Kooshee and Otob, who whisked them downriver to the living dam.

"Chompers, how's it going?"

"We're tiring, Mosa, but holding up as well as we can by taking regular breaks. Fortunately, we have enough creatures to allow everyone to rotate out of the dam and get some rest.

"That's a very good thing. Humans have arrived along the northern perimeter and are digging their own ditch. We plan to connect our river diversion with their ditch later today.

"Alright! We'll be prepared for curious onlookers, especially those who want to follow the rerouted river to see our living dam."

Mosa thanked Chompers and everyone else for their hard work and assured them they were making a big difference in the fight. She and Eliza then continued along the rerouted river, guided by Kooshee and Otob. The sun rose higher in the sky, baking everything under it that the fire hadn't already burnt. Eliza's eyes teared as the boat glided by the charred remains of the forest on one side of the river, which had been vibrant only yesterday.

Post-fire crews busily extinguished glowing and smoking embers. Eliza recorded a story on this part of the firefighting effort, since she hadn't covered that in yesterday's piece. Holding the camera up to catch a broader view, she described how the rainforest creatures worked to ensure fires didn't reignite in spots that already burned. She then showed the charred areas and zoomed in on the activity to put out any lingering flames. A few edits and she sent the story to the station, also alerting Lee and sending her some footage.

The fire barriers created by the diverted river, cleared areas, and rock walls successfully prevented the fire from jumping to the other side of the water. Fire still raged in the forest just back from the water, though, as smoke billowed and flames shot from the canopy ahead to the right.

Otob and Kooshee slowed as the channel became too shallow for them to swim. The diggers worked busily in front of the boat to create a new riverbed for the water to follow, while the clearers continued removing dead wood and building stone walls along the new riverbank. Mosa and Eliza climbed out of the boat, lifted it from the water, and thanked the dolphins before they turned and swam back to the dam.

A capybara advised they sent a scout ahead and humans weren't far away.

"That's exactly the news I hoped to hear. Eliza, go let the humans know they're about to connect to the work of the rainforest creatures."

Eliza left and, when she heard people shouting instructions, haphazardly appeared out of the forest near where they worked. Surprised at this unexpected visitor, the firefighters stared at her with both annoyance and confusion. Hoping to see at least one of the people she talked with yesterday to avoid explaining herself again, none were in sight. She walked past the fire crews, saying hello and telling them to keep up the good work.

Eventually she saw the leader of the crew who witnessed the flyers and walked toward him. He greeted her first. "Welcome back. You said you're a reporter, right?"

"Yes, sure am."

"I thought so, a couple other reporters arrived late yesterday. I mentioned you and they tried to find you."

A voice shouted from a distance. "Hey, are you the reporter?" Eliza turned to see a clean-cut man and well-dressed woman walking toward her at a fast clip.

"Yes, that's me," she yelled.

The pair made it over to her, each out of breath and sweating from the tropical heat mixed with the added warmth of the fire. Eliza immediately recognized them as well-known reporters on competing national news shows. Introductions followed and Eliza acknowledged that their reputations preceded them.

The man said, "We saw the coverage on your station after it made national headlines."

Eliza subdued her excitement at having been out in front of the seasoned journalists on the story.

"That footage was unbelievable," the woman noted.

Not sure from the tone of her voice whether she complimented or questioned the validity of the footage, Eliza tried not to sound defensive, "Yes, what I've seen here is nothing short of incredible. The creatures seem to be fighting the fire themselves, protecting their habitat and the planet."

"Our stations told us we better get down here, so we didn't miss out on any coverage, but you beat us to it nonetheless."

"Maybe you can show us where the animal activity is occurring," suggested the man.

Although suspicious they may try to squeeze her out of a story, Eliza preferred to believe the reporters wanted to work together, but tempered her answer, nonetheless. "Be happy to. Did the firefighters tell you about the flyers yesterday?"

"Flyers, what are those? They didn't say anything," the woman said.

The man indicated he hadn't heard about them either, then it dawned on him, "Wait, are those the birds that were in your story?"

"Yes, that's them. And there were bats doing the same thing last night. Seems the creatures here are very serious about stopping the fire." Eliza turned to the crew leader. "Speaking of that, remember yesterday I mentioned the animals diverted a river and were digging ditches and doing other things to contain the fire?" He signaled affirmatively. "Well, they're almost here, ready to connect to your work."

"What?" exclaimed the reporters in unison.

The crew leader didn't seem as startled at this news. "Really? After yesterday nothing would surprise me. Where is this connection supposed to occur?"

"Follow me." Eliza led him back to where she emerged from the jungle.

Noises of digging and brush clearing filled the air. The group didn't wait long before a group of capybaras and armadillos, heads down and digging feverishly, crashed through the brush, with the water of the river not far behind. Groups of other creatures followed—monkeys, tapirs, kinkajous, jaguars, and lizards—clearing a wide path and stacking up rocks to make walls alongside the water. Eliza laughed while shooting pictures and videos. The humans stared in utter shock and disbelief at the scene before them.

Eliza resisted the urge to yell, 'Surprise!' not wanting it to come across the wrong way. Shaking off their incredulity, the reporters summoned their camera crews and told them to start rolling.

The crew leader motioned for the rest of his team to come over. Seeing the work of their animal kingdom counterparts, they all cheered. Startled by the noise, the rainforest creatures stopped working. Eliza indicated they need not worry, and the animal crews danced and cavorted around making their own happy sounds.

As the cacophony continued, Eliza heard a rumble. A wave of flyers arrived! The humans looked up at the sky bewildered. Flyers darted back and forth catching sparks flying from the flames, then went into formation and beat the flames away. Shortly after the fire began backing down, a gust of wind blew the flyers toward the blaze. The onlookers on the ground watched in alarm. Breaking formation, the flyers flew every which way, trying to escape the fire, some colliding with each other and falling to the earth, dazed.

Realizing wind meant the fire could easily blow out of control, the crews hustled back to their firefighting jobs. Humans and nature's beings worked side by side against the fire enemy, exactly what the Alliance wanted to accomplish with the climate mission. Eliza ruminated that perhaps the mission could be successful after all.

As the wind grew stronger, the situation looked dire. Flyers flew haphazardly above, thrown off by the random gusts of wind. The fire advanced faster than the fighters could hold it off. Soon it would jump the cleared area and the diverted river, spelling disaster for not only the forest but also the people and creatures who'd just been celebrating.

Eliza considered whether they should keep fighting or start evacuating. As she weighed the pros and cons of each, something hit her in the head. She swiped it away absent-mindedly, then something hit her back, then her arm, then her face. Looking up, she realized she'd been hit by rain! Big, heavy drops of tropical rain!

Everyone became aware at once and immediately stopped what they were doing to look at the sky and let the water hit their faces. As rain pelted the flyers, they landed around the people and animals, the water washing the armor and soot off their vibrant wings.

The wind brought sheets of rain that hit the flames, sheet after sheet until the blaze backed down. It continued pouring but no one minded and instead all danced in jubilation. Humans and nature's beasts transitioned seamlessly from fighting alongside each other to celebrating with one another. Even the reporters joined in. Eliza laughed when the male reporter threw his jacket to the side and the female reporter kicked her shoes off and danced in the rain. Eliza filmed the festivities.

The rain fell long and hard enough for the fire to be extinguished once and for all, leaving only smoldering whisps–the inferno's dying breaths. The diverted river no longer flowed, the living dam having been dismantled, giving the creatures who comprised it a well-deserved break.

The crew leader came over to Eliza, told her he never imagined anything like this could happen, and apologized for doubting her when she first told them what the animals were doing. The reporters stopped by too and echoed his thoughts. Eliza thanked them and wished them well. She watched the humans and animals congratulating each other in their own ways–hugs, licks, fist bumps, high fives. It warmed her heart, and she took pictures to show Bebop and her new international audience.

All soon realized they had to go back to their own worlds and departed in their separate directions. Eliza hoped this would be the beginning of working together on the larger climate fight. As everything wound down, Eliza prepared a story showing the demise of the fire and the collective happiness that followed, then sent it to the station. She and Mosa trekked back to the plane to share the success with the team.

CHAPTER 55

OBSERVATIONS

On the way back to the plane, Mosa and Eliza traveled over mostly burnt landscape–the easiest route to maneuver but the most difficult to behold. Although she'd just celebrated victory over the fire, it saddened Eliza to see such a large area of rainforest lost. A catastrophe for not only the plants and animals that perished, but also for the planet in losing such a vital carbon-absorbing resource.

They arrived at the encampment to find rainforest crews loading the unused equipment and supplies into the plane. The sloths had been returned to the forest to find new homes, and Thiha dozed to stock up on sleep since he'd fly them back soon.

Bebop looked tired but relieved to welcome them back. "Well done, team!"

"You would have loved to see it, Bebop. Humans and our rainforest team working side by side against the fire. It gives me hope for the future."

"The scene touched even me," admitted Mosa, generally not one for sentimentality.

Sonar chimed in, "Just when we thought all may be lost as the wind blew us toward the flames, the rain rescued us. We could hear the humans and our teams cheering us on from the ground and I have to say it really inspired me."

"I'd never heard encouragement like that before," Schnee said. "I'm glad you decided to join us on that day flight, Sonar, and were able to experience it too."

"We'll take this victory, but after all our efforts, the rain is what saved the day." All were silent after Bebop's blunt analysis, questioning whether their work made any difference whatsoever.

Eliza tried to lighten the mood. "We made significant progress and if it hadn't been for the wind, that fire would have been contained by our efforts. By holding the fire back as long as we did, we kept it to a size the rain could extinguish. I refuse to think nothing we did made a difference and the rain would have killed the fire regardless. Plus, the connection we made with humans is invaluable."

"I'm with you," said Chompers. "We did a good thing coming down here."

"Wait, I didn't mean to be a downer or take away from anything we did. Great work everyone! The bottom line is the fire is out and that's what we came here to accomplish. Let's enjoy a farewell meal and then rest up before we head back to NoHoSap."

The group savored the Amazon's delicacies, saving some for Thiha to enjoy on the return flight. They then found comfortable spots in the plane and hunkered down to sleep until Thiha awoke and they'd begin the trip back. Although Mosa wanted to stay and help with the recovery efforts, she decided to go with them to NoHoSap because Canlup called a meeting of the Alliance after hearing the firefighting success.

Thiha woke up in the wee hours of the morning and checked that his passengers were secure before taking off. The engine noise roused everyone but the exhaustion from the intense firefighting kept most of them asleep, Eliza being the exception. She reviewed emails and voluminous social media posts even though she had no wifi access in the air. Her messages and comments would send when they landed, and she might as well prepare them while she had time.

She read Zeke's reply to her message thanking him for his support. He said she scooped the national news reporters on the story and he and everyone at the station were very proud of her. Ira already lamented whether they'd be able to keep her on the local news in light of the broader exposure she now enjoyed. Zeke mentioned people asked where she received the information about the fire early on, but he reminded them that she's not required to reveal her source and rightly kept that information confidential. Eliza thanked him for the updates. She also sent a message to Ira thanking him for the opportunity to cover the rainforest fire.

Eliza then checked the social media coverage. Every post garnered millions of views and shares, leaving her blown away and overwhelmed by the reaction. Lee did a superb job linking to the posts on the station's website and adding the additional footage Eliza sent her. There were the usual comments questioning the validity of the photos, but the clear majority of chatter said they saw the stories on the news, and it didn't appear the scenes were fabricated in any way. She reviewed as many posts as possible before dozing off and joining the other team members in sleep.

CHAPTER 56

FAREWELLS

"We're back," Thiha announced. No one in the plane stirred. "Time to wake up." He spoke louder as he unbuckled and walked into the cargo area. Bebop jumped up ready for action, with the rest of the team also rousing from their slumber.

The cargo door opened to Jacob and Oji standing there, all smiles. "Welcome back!"

"What a fantastic job fighting the fire!" lauded Jacob.

Oji added, "I got to see the pictures and videos when I sat with Lee and they were awesome! Now I know what I want to be when I grow up–a reporter like Eliza!"

Never having thought of herself as a role model, Eliza laughed inwardly since she felt she still needed to figure things out herself. "Just be sure to follow your heart, Oji."

"Thanks for the welcome and kind words, you two. At least we don't have as much to unload from the plane as we did on the way out, although I don't know if it'll all fit in the van."

"No worries, Bebop, we have the truck too," Thiha said.

Pleased to be back in cooler climes, Eliza breathed in the crisp air. The team went to work moving everything out of the plane and into the van and truck, then piled into the vehicles themselves and were back at the cemetery parking lot in no time. Already in the evening and with no people around, the crew from NoHoSap came out imme-diately when the vehicles arrived and unloaded the contents. Everyone then made the short trek to NoHoSap.

They arrived to shouts and cheers. All greeted the team and con-gratulated them on a job well done. Bebop appeared uneasy with the accolades while Mosa, Chompers, Sonar, and Schnee took it in stride. As they walked through the crowd, Chef Cecil jumped in front. He invited them to a party to celebrate their success in putting out the fire and said he and Brownie made food and sweets for the gathering. Bebop said they couldn't pass that up and would see all at the party.

The crew took the elevator down to Mission Command and were surprised to see it almost empty when the door opened. "This doesn't happen very often," observed Bebop.

"I don't think I've ever seen this place when it hasn't been hustling and bustling," agreed Mosa.

Chompers added, "Looks like they all enjoy a party. Can't say I blame them."

While the group walked through the main concourse, Can-lup appeared from one of the hallways around the perimeter and trotted over. "Congratulations on the successful mission. Job well done!" Everyone thanked her and Sonar asked when the Alliance would meet.

"We'll meet in the morning. That way everyone may attend the party tonight." Turning toward Bebop and Eliza, her face grew seri-ous. "Bebop and Eliza, you're needed in the medical unit."

"Is it Ringloo?" They assumed she may have taken a turn for the worse.

Canlup looked down, shook her head no, and said only, "Hurry."

Bebop ran to the medical unit with Eliza not far behind. Red met them at the entrance and told them to catch their breath and calm down before she took them back.

"What's going on?"

Red put her hand gently on Bebop's shoulder and responded with sad, soulful eyes. "It's Harold the Wise. He's been here since yesterday and isn't doing well. He wants to see you."

Bebop stepped back in disbelief. "What?"

"Harold's been very sick for some time, Bebop, but he instructed us not to tell you, or anyone else. He didn't want to distract you from the mission or be worried about him as he approached the end."

Bebop looked distraught, unable to comprehend Red's revelation. Eliza put her arm around him. "The end? He's dying? How can that be? I just saw him. He seemed fine. Take us to him. I need to see him."

"Bebop, I know this is a shock, but Harold's been suffering for a long time. He's ready for his pain to be gone and to pass from this life. He waited for you because he didn't want to leave without seeing you. You're understandably upset, but before we go back, take a moment to process this, so you can be there for Harold at this moment."

Bebop stepped away, trying to fathom Harold being on his death-bed. Red motioned for Eliza to join her out of Bebop's earshot. "Harold the Wise is an albatross, one of the founding members of the Alliance, and the one who pushed for us to start the climate mission with humans. He selected and trained Bebop to run the mission. He's Bebop's mentor, and like a father to him."

"Oh no."

"Bebop will need your support, even though he won't say it. I'm glad you're here with him now." Red walked over to Bebop, who'd composed himself somewhat, trying to hold it together for Harold. "He'll be very happy to see you, Bebop." She gave him an encouraging look.

Red led them to a room formed from an outcropping of rock with a view to the sky. The bright night glowed full of stars and a shining crescent of the moon. Mellow fungi lights on the walls gave the room a warm radiance. Harold the Wise lay motionless in a huge nest next to the window opening. Machines beeped all around him, hooked to tubes in his beak and wings. Bebop's eyes widened and his gait slowed when he saw Harold, disturbed at how frail he appeared.

Red said in a hushed voice, "There's no need to add to Harold's discomfort with these machines." She instructed the medical team of mice to undo the tubes and turn the equipment off. They removed the intrusions calmly and gently so as not to disturb Harold. He lay still, his eyes closed, his breathing labored. The mice disappeared quietly after completing their tasks.

Red put her long arms around Bebop and Eliza and nudged them toward the nest, then departed silently. Harold's eyes fluttered open when he felt them by his side. He smiled slightly, relieved, then spread his wings and tried to sit up, but fell back, too feeble.

Bebop placed his paw on Harold's outstretched wing, noticeably upset seeing him in this condition. "Don't get up, just stay comfortable."

Harold closed his eyes, gathered his strength, and spoke haltingly, in a quiet, raspy voice between labored breaths. "You made it, Bebop. And Eliza's here too."

"Of course, we're here, Harold." Bebop caressed Harold's wing tenderly, then realized he hadn't introduced Eliza. "Eliza, meet Harold the Wise. He's guided me and been my rock almost my entire life."

"I'm humbled to meet you, Harold the Wise."

Harold struggled to talk. "Congratulations on the rainforest mission. I followed all the coverage and reports. Bebop, I'm very proud of you."

Struggling not to get emotional, Bebop diverted his eyes from his hero. It pained him to see Harold's cloudy eyes staring blankly, sunken cheeks, dull feathers, and sagging frame. "I tried to follow all the advice you've given me over the years, Harold. We're fortunate the rain came along when it did and put the fire out."

"Bebop, stop it. Don't do that to yourself and your team," Harold spoke firmly but with effort. "Your work gave the rain a fighting chance to extinguish the blaze. Never minimize the hard work and efforts of you and your team." Harold summoned his strength. "If you don't take credit for what you deserve, your team will feel they'll never live up to your expectations and their motivation will suffer. Praise them for the good work they do, even if other factors may have helped achieve the goal."

"Always the teacher. I've lost count of the lessons you've taught me."

"You've learned well, Bebop, and it gives me great contentment that you'll continue doing great things after I'm gone." Harold's voice weakened.

"Don't say that! You have more ahead of you! You just need some rest. You'll be back flying once you get your strength back."

"Bebop, I'm at the end and am ready." Harold closed his eyes serenely.

"No, no, you can't be at the end! You just don't feel well right now. Fight, Harold, fight! Don't give up!"

Harold took a long breath and dug deep for the energy to continue. "My life has been long and full and I'm thankful I helped get some things accomplished, especially our climate change mission with the humans. Keep moving forward in that fight no matter how daunting it appears."

Bebop refused to believe the clear evidence that Harold would soon be gone. "Please don't leave me, Harold. I need you!"

Eliza cried, suddenly reminded of the conversation she had with her father before he passed. Her heart went out to Bebop as she saw him struggling with the same sentiments she had with her dad as he took his last breath before her. Haunted by regret for not letting her father know how much he meant to her, she whispered, "Bebop, tell him how you feel. He needs to know. For your own peace of mind, don't hold back."

Bebop's eyes softened. "I won't know what to do without you, Harold. You give me so much strength from your counsel and undying support. I love you. I should have told you many times before, but I love you."

"Bebop." Harold gently stretched his wing toward Bebop. "I love you too. You're my son. The greatest gift this life has given me is the opportunity to pass the best of me on to you, and to see you shining brighter than I ever could." Harold's voice quieted and slowed. Bebop bent forward to hear him. "Remember, I have total faith in you.... You have all the tools you need.... You get to write the story now.... The future will be what you make it."

Bebop held Harold's wing with both paws, tears running down his face, searching for the right words. "Thank you, Harold. Thank you for everything. I'll miss you always." He stared into Harold's face, hoping against hope to see the life flow back in.

"No need to miss me.... I'll always be there.... Look to the sky... to see me flying... and watching... and gliding... and cheering… you… on."

Bebop gripped Harold's wing, hanging his head and whimpering in sadness. Eliza hugged Bebop.

Harold looked knowingly into Bebop's eyes, conveying he was at peace as he let go. Tranquility descended, the cool night breeze moved an obscuring cloud away from the moon, and the silhouette of a large bird flew gracefully toward the brilliant moon crescent. Bebop cried aloud, suddenly alone and adrift.

Eliza hugged Bebop tightly, knowing nothing could take away the pain of losing someone so dear. As they mourned, the clear night sky shone through the window and the melancholy hoot of an owl echoed in the air.

CHAPTER 57

CELEBRATIONS

While mourning together in silence, Eliza heard movement down the hallway and Bebop looked up. Red and Canlup entered the room slowly, followed by the rest of the Alliance members. They knew from Bebop's and Eliza's faces that Harold the Wise had passed. Gathering around his nest, they bowed their heads for their lost leader and friend. Each paid their respects to the great bird, then exited the room in quiet reflection.

The group stopped in the area outside the medical unit, lamenting the death of Harold the Wise. The party outside Mission Command presented a sad irony. "It's hard to celebrate after Harold's death," Bebop spoke in a monotone.

"That it is," replied Canlup.

Red acknowledged, "I'm glad you were able to see him at the end."

"I'm going to miss Harold." Tusko reminisced. "He and I were partners in crime for a long time. Eliza, you should know it was Harold's brainchild to work with humans in our climate mission. The Alliance talked—argued actually—for years about whether and how to involve humans. We watched your footage from the rainforest together and he said it convinced him we did the right thing to work with humans, and that you're the right person for the role. He thought you and Bebop would lead us to a new day of partnerships and successes in the climate fight. He also told me to spread the word that we can't give up, for the only way to save ourselves and the world is to be successful in this mission."

"He focused on the mission until the end."

"He knew it was the most important thing we had to do. It's our loss that he passed, but he's in a better place now. He led a life to be celebrated."

"That's it, Tusko," Canlup announced. "We'll celebrate Harold at tonight's gathering. We'll celebrate him and our success in the Amazon. He would be pleased with that."

The heavyhearted group shuffled back to the elevator and up to the party. When they arrived, the field and air overhead were crowded with partygoers. Music blared in the distance. In a festive mood, NoHoSap beings celebrated the success of the firefight and new partnership with humans. Canlup and the others weaved through the throng to a large boulder. Video monitors hanging above the boulder showed the celebration extended beyond this part of NoHoSap. One monitor connected to the crew at the coral nursery and another to a crowd of Amazon creatures.

Canlup climbed atop the boulder and let out a loud howl, catching everyone's attention. "Thank you all for coming out to celebrate the stupendous results in our Amazon firefight. Our team, from both here and in the rainforest, natural beings, and humans, worked valiantly and tirelessly in this victory. We thank them for setting the example and giving us hope for a successful partnership with humans to beat the climate crisis." The crowd cheered and whooped loudly. Canlup howled again to quiet them down.

"The fire is only the latest of our accomplishments in the venture with humans. I also want to thank everyone involved in the tree plantings and reef restorations, our nursery and coral crews, diggers, plant waterers, coral fragment affixers, kitchen and bakery crews, tech experts, human partners, and all our workers who got the projects done. Thank you all!" Wild cheering followed. Canlup commanded their attention with another howl.

"We have many reasons to celebrate today, but one is tinged with sadness." The revelers looked at each other wondering what Canlup meant. "It is with great sorrow that I let you know our dear friend and leader, Harold the Wise, passed on not long ago."

The onlookers exclaimed their sad surprise and the mood turned solemn. Many put their faces down or shook their heads in sadness.

"Harold's life should be celebrated. It's fitting we're gathered here now, already cheering about the successes on the mission. He played an instrumental role in starting the mission and supported it to the moment he left us. He'll be with us in spirit, and we celebrate him now. May you fly in peace, Harold the Wise." Canlup smiled and looked at the night sky, then put her head down, leading the crowd in a moment of silence for the dear departed Harold.

A loud blaring noise shattered the quiet, jolting everyone to attention. Tusko stood with his trunk in the air, trumpeting proudly. He then saluted, "To Harold the Wise!" and trumpeted again.

Canlup joined in, "To Harold the Wise!" and howled. Mosa saluted and roared, then came Chompers with a salute and bellow, then Bebop with a salute and two barks. Soon the crowd rang with salutes to Harold via a myriad of noises and calls. The mood turned to celebration again, for both Harold and the successes of the mission.

Eliza convinced Bebop to accompany her to the food stations, where they found Chef Cecil happily dishing out his delicacies to a long line of hungry creatures. He enjoyed letting everyone know what the offerings were and explaining how they were made. After passing through the line and getting their food, Eliza saw Lee and Midnight. She waved and walked toward them, but Bebop didn't follow, advising he preferred to be alone and would catch up with her later. Eliza said she understood and continued over to Lee.

"Lee, great job on social media! You always know what to post and say to keep the conversation going in the right direction."

"It's much easier when I have great content like the pictures and videos you sent. Those scenes were awe inspiring! Must have been something to see in real life."

"Yes, I couldn't believe my eyes most of the time. Just when I thought I'd seen it all, something even more wonderful would occur. I never imagined the story and footage would go viral. It doesn't get better than that."

"Or so you thought. The attention we've received up to now is beyond our wildest dreams, but it just got even more incredible. Our posts are now being tracked by social media influencers and not only the climate change folks but also animal science and social action circles. A few well-known celebrities have also viewed, commented, and shared it."

"Lee, that's excellent! Marvelous work and congratulations! We're getting our message to the mainstream—just what we wanted. We'll be driving change before we know it!" They gave each other an enthusiastic fist bump.

Jacob and Oji approached. "Well-deserved celebration you two. Congratulations!" High fives and fist bumps were shared all around. "Us humans are definitely in the minority."

"I'm pretty well used to it now, but it was odd at first," admitted Eliza.

"It struck me the first few times I came, not all that long ago now that I think of it. I enjoy being one of the only humans."

"Thanks for making me a Change Agent, even though I'm young and can't help you much yet," Oji observed, fiddling with her Change Agent pin.

"What do you mean? Change Agents in training are Change Agents just the same."

"I have a lot of friends who'd love to be Change Agents and wear the pins. They already do a lot to help the planet against climate change."

"Very encouraging, Oji. We can never have too many Change Agents. We'll have to start mobilizing their help." Eliza looked toward the sweets bar. "Anyone want dessert?" The others were too full from Chef Cecil's spread, leaving Eliza to venture over to the baked goods by herself.

The sweet treats were set out on a number of ledges near a bonfire that lit the area and kept everyone warm. Already picked over by the hungry multitude, Brownie kept a watchful eye on the display and restocked to the extent she had anything left.

"Brownie, you've been busy."

"We baked everything this afternoon, doing double duty to be sure we had treats for tonight. Can't have a party without sweets."

"I totally agree."

Chattering and yips sounded from behind Brownie, then a voice said firmly 'calm down!'

Brownie snickered. "I think they had too much sugar because they've been wrestling and playing nonstop."

"Who are you talking about?" Junior and Looloo rolled out from the bushes behind Brownie. Jacee ran out after them and Ringloo appeared soon after, walking cautiously but resolutely.

"Ringloo, good to see you! How are you feeling?"

"A little sore and uneven on my feet, but joyful to be alive, much less out and about."

Jacee came over and hugged Eliza's leg. "Alive thanks to Eliza." Junior and Looloo continued playing and bumped into Ringloo, almost knocking her off her feet before running away. "Careful!" scolded Jacee.

Ringloo laughed and reiterated, "Just happy to be alive," then followed Jacee as he chased after the kits.

Eliza filled a plate with desserts and left to find Bebop. She discovered him sitting alone near the edge of the party, staring into space. Settling next to him, she offered him treats. He ate one and declined the rest.

"I'm very sorry about Harold."

"Thank you. At least he didn't seem to suffer. I know he'd been around a while, but never thought he'd leave us this soon. If only there were more time with him."

"We never know how long we have. Your unexpected death taught me that."

"I know. I'm grateful to have known and learned from him." Bebop shook his head, trying to shake the sadness and numbness away. "I'm sorry, Eliza, for faking my death. I had no idea how it felt to lose someone close to you, until now. I'm very sorry to have put you through that."

"You can't understand the pain until you've experienced it. I know why you did it, Bebop, and accept your apology. Let's make the most of our time together now."

"One positive thing that's come of this is that I'm even more motivated to make the climate mission successful, to honor Harold's memory."

"I'm with you, Bebop. We have a lot to do, but little by little we'll get there."

"Yes, we will. Speaking of that, let's take a couple of days off before we start the next project. I need to process Harold's death, and time to rest will be good for all of us."

"Good idea. Want me to keep you company a little longer tonight?"

"No, I'll be OK. It's a lot to get my head around and will take some time."

"I understand. You know how to find me if you need anything." Eliza paused before leaving. "Bebop, great work on the Amazon fire-fighting project and the whole climate mission. I'm proud of you."

"Thank you, Eliza. That means a lot, especially now."

Eliza hugged Bebop, headed for the tunnel, and exited NoHoSap.

CHAPTER 58

NEW BEGINNINGS

When the alarm rang the following morning, Eliza uncharacteristically woke right up, ready for the day. She hadn't been this excited to get to work in quite some time. The Amazon firefighting success, positive reactions to her news stories, and connections formed between humans and the animals left her energized and motivated. She now truly believed she could make a positive difference as a Change Agent, inspiring people to pay attention to and do something about climate change.

"You're wide awake and alert this morning." Even Noli's greeting didn't startle Eliza as it often did.

"I know! Maybe I turned over a new leaf."

"It'll be nice for you to get a couple days off from the mission and catch up on sleep. You've been going relentlessly for too long now."

"Thanks for the concern, Noli. We'll take it as it comes. Time to get moving to the station. Look at that, right on time too. No need to run to the bus stop this morning."

Leon and the regulars on the bus asked questions about her trip for the entire ride, having seen her on the news. When Eliza made it to the station and walked to her office, everyone congratulated her on the rainforest stories. She'd no sooner signed on to her computer than Zeke popped in.

"There she is—the reporter of the day! Way to go with that coverage! It must have been quite the trip."

Eliza blushed. "Mornin', Zeke. What a whirlwind! I'm happy to be back, though."

"The footage of the animals' work is phenomenal. I might have been skeptical, but after what I saw at the cemetery with the tree planting and what you showed going on in the Amazon, I'm a firm believer the animal kingdom is doing its own thing to fight climate change. Who would have thought?"

"I hope the camera did it justice."

"Definitely did, and your coverage really put it in perspective. I loved the way you reported the story, then panned over to show the proof. The shots clearly weren't set up the way some people argued."

"Good, I'm glad it came across well."

"For sure. You captured the excitement in the last story about the fire being put out. I stood up and cheered along with you."

"That's what I strive for, to engage the viewer."

"We all envied you when the story made the national, then international, news. None of the other stations had any information on the fire yet and had only our coverage to show. You scooped the entire world!"

"I'm still overwhelmed by that. Thanks again, Zeke, for all the support and comments on negative posts. I really appreciate it."

"My pleasure."

Ira stuck his head in the door. "Eliza, super work! We couldn't have asked for a better way to launch the new climate correspondent series, or for anyone more suited to the role. I had my doubts about approving the trip, but it turned out to be the absolute best thing I could have done."

"Thank you, sir. I didn't want to let you down."

"I'm hearing from not only owners of smaller, local stations like ours, but also national news outlets congratulating us on getting the story first. They're trying to find out how we beat them and everyone else to it. Thank you, Eliza, for bringing this opportunity to the station. Keep up the good work. The climate correspondent is here to stay."

"Great! It's going to be difficult to top the fire coverage, but I'll keep the climate stories coming."

"Looking forward to it." Ira turned and left.

Zeke chuckled. "You're his favorite reporter now. He'll probably do whatever you want to be sure you stay with the station. You should ask him for a raise."

"Very funny. I'm not that bold and don't have any other opportunities right now anyway."

"You just got back but I'm sure you'll be hearing about other potential jobs. Wait and see."

"Right, will do. I'm just thankful the coverage received positive attention, the fire is out, and I'm back home."

"I am too. You'll have to fill me in on your adventures and what the Amazon is like. I first need to get back to the story I'm working on for tonight's news, though."

After he left, Eliza settled into her desk chair to tackle the accumulated mail. The lack of sleep caught up with her by mid-afternoon and she decided to go for a power walk to energize herself. As she kicked her dress shoes off to don sneakers, Zeke stopped by, saying Ira needed to see them in the conference room. Dress shoes back on, she followed Zeke.

Eliza entered the room and it exploded with, "Surprise" from her co-workers, followed by Zeke honking a party horn in her ear. She jumped back and held her hand to her chest from the unexpected reception, then laughed. A 'Congratulations' banner hung across the front of the room. Underneath the banner, a long table held a big sign lauding 'First Scoop Honors' with an ice cream sundae bar next to it. Ira invited Eliza to get the first sundae and everyone celebrated Eliza's and the station's success with an ice cream social.

As the gathering disbanded, Eliza found Zeke. "I needed an energy boost and that sundae sure did hit the spot."

"I'm going back for another one. It's only going to melt, and you can never have too much ice cream."

"I'm with you. By the way, I have a feeling you may have had something to do with this party. It has you written all over it."

"No, I didn't even know about it." He smirked.

"You're not a very good liar. I see that grin on your face while you try to act innocent. Thank you, though. It means a lot to be recognized like this. And I love the scooped theme."

"Glad you enjoyed it. I expect you to remember this when I accomplish something big."

"So noted."

"Now that you're back, I'd still like to get out there and walk with you and Bop. I also want to explore becoming a Change Agent."

"That'd be fun to walk and for you to be a Change Agent." She still couldn't picture him working with the animals but appreciated his interest. "Once I get caught up from being away, we'll set up a walk. Enjoy your next sundae."

Eliza returned to her office, invigorated for the next part of the climate change mission and hopeful the Change Agents could drive humans to action in the climate fight. She looked at Bebop's picture on her shelf. This time, though, instead of getting teary-eyed and hearing him question her career choices, she smiled and heard him say, "Keep listening to your heart and our whispers in the wind. We're going to accomplish great things together."

THE END...

ABOUT THE AUTHOR

Sarah E. Lewis is the author of The Change Agents: Whispers in the Wind. She developed a love for animals and the environment while growing up near Albany, New York, where her imagination was fueled by spending time in nature. Educated at Middlebury College (B.A., Environmental Studies), the Syracuse University College of Law (J.D.), and the State University of New York College of Environmental Science and Forestry (M.S., environmental science) she entered private law practice.

As an environmental lawyer she protected land for agriculture and conservation. Following the death of her beloved canine, Bebop, she wanted to honor his memory by writing a story about him and, at the same time, inspire people to save the Earth. After practicing law for over twenty-five years, she followed her passion and became an author while continuing to practice law. Her active imagination kicked in and the Change Agents were created.

Sarah enjoys being outdoors and can be found at some point during every day exploring natural areas on foot or skis with her energetic dogs, Bop and Jazz. They never cease to bring a smile to her face, even if the fun is peppered with moments of exasperation because one or both has eaten or rolled in something nasty. Striving to be a good environmental citizen, Sarah acknowledges she's a work in progress but will keep improving and invites others to join her in that journey.

During the course of writing the book and as an outgrowth from it, Sarah formed a Change Agents group on Facebook and launched a Change Agents website. The goal of each is to spread positive messages about what we like in the world and don't want impacted by climate change and give tips on what we can do to slow the warming. Sarah encourages everyone to be a Change Agent by doing what's comfortable for each of us to fight climate change. She believes that each and all of us can make a difference in the climate crisis, we just need to start and keep going.

TOGETHER WE CAN DO THIS!

https://www.facebook.com/SLBauthor
www.facebook.com/groups/ChangeAgentsGroup
www.climatechangeagents.com

Enjoy this book?

We invite you to leave a review on
Amazon and Goodreads!